IRINA

IRINA

A NOVEL BY

PHILIP WARREN

ISBN: 978-1-7367794-1-5 (Paperback)
ISBN: 978-1-7367794-2-2 (E-Book)

Library of Congress Control Number: 2021905268

Any references to historical events, real people, or real places are used fictitiously.

Cover design by Evocative
Interior design by Stewart Williams
Copyedit by Brooks Becker

Printed by Kindle Direct Publishing in the United States of America

First printing edition 2021
The PineLands Company, Publisher
New Wilmington, Pennsylvania

www.philipwarrenwriter.com

*Irina's story is dedicated to the millions
down through the centuries
whose lives were taken
because of hate, greed, and bigotry.
May they rest in
God's eternal peace.*

AUTHOR'S NOTE

The Polish Language

While the names of characters and common Polish words are rendered carefully, their sounds, even if spoken only in your mind, may be unfamiliar. For your ease, I have provided below phonetic assistance for names and words, alphabetically. There is a presumption that many French words and phrases used are more generally understood. In Polish, as in French, always roll the "r's."

Irina Kwasnieska—*Yee-ryn-ah Quaz-nyez-skah*
Ambrozy Rudzenski (Father)—*Om-bro-zhy Roo-dzen-ski*
Antony Tirasewicz (Bishop)—*Ahn-toe-knee Tier-as-sheh-vitch*
Bardzo Dobrze—*Bard-Zaw Daub-Zheh*—Very good!
Bela Kinizsi (Sir)—*Bay-lah-Che-kneeze-si*
Berek Joselewicz—*Bay-wrek Yo-zel-eh-vitch*
Boleslaw III (King)—*Bo-yes-whaw*
Deena Sklowdowska—*Deenah Skwaw-doff-ska*
Dzjadzja—Gia-Gia—Grandfather
Dobrze—*Daub-zheh*—Good!
Duzo zdrowia—*Dew-zhaw zdraw-vee-yah!*—Good health to you!
Djenkuje—*Jenk-coo-yeah*—Thank you
Franciszek Montowski—*Frawn-cis-shek Mawn-toff-ski*
Gniezno—*Knee-yez-no*
Ignacz and Maria Kwasniewski—*Igg-knots & Mah-ree-yah
    Quaz-nyez-skah*
Jan Brezchwa (Count)—*Yan Bresh-vah*
Janos Tomori (Captain)—*Yahn-ose-Tah-mor-ee*
Janus and Eva Joselewicz—*Yan-oose & Ava Yo-zel-eh-vitch*

Janusz Krawcyk—*Yan-oosh Kraff-chick*

Jerzy Andrezski—*Yare-zhy On-dresh-ski*

Kazimierz Wielki (King)—*Kahz-ee-mersh Vee-al-key*—Casimir III the Great

Krosno Odrienskie—*Krozno Odr-jhan-ski-eh*—Krosno on the Oder

Matka—*Maht-kah*—Mother

Martinus Madrosh (Father)—*Mahr-teen-us Mah-drosh*

Nie—*Nyeh*—Is it not so?

Ojciec—*Oy-chech*—Father

Ostrow Tumski—*Awstrow Tomb-ski*

Pan—*Pahn*—Mr.

Panie—*Pah-knee*—Mrs.

Pawel Tokasz—*Pa-vel Talk-osh*

Poznan—*Pauz-nahn*

Prosze—*Praw-sheh*—Please

Shimanski (Father)—*Sheh-mein-ski*

Srodka—*Shrawd-kah*

Szczecin (*Shetchin*) and Wroclaw (*Vraw-cwav*)

Szlachta—*Schwack-tah*—nobility

Tak—*Tahk*—Yes

Teofil—*Tay-oh-feel*

Tomasz Wodowicz—*Toe-mah-sh Voe-dah-vitch*

Ulica Zydowska—*ou-leetz-ah Zhih-doff-skah*—Jewish Street

The Warta River—*Var-tah*

Wesolych Swiat Bozego Narodzenia—Ves-o-ick Schviunt Baw-zheh-gaw Nah-raw-dzen-yah—Happy Christmas

Wielko Polska—*Vee-yel-ko Pole-skah*—Greater Poland

Wigilia—*Vee-lee-yah*—The Vigil (before Christmas)

Woda—*Vaw-dah*—Water

Wojciec—*Voy-chech*

Wozna—*Vawz-nah*

Zuzanna Kwasniewska/Tokasz—Zuzzie—*Dzu-dzahn-ah Quaz-nyez-skah/Talk-osh*—Dzu-dzee

Zygmunt Sokorski (Duke)—*Zig-moont So-kor-ski*

In traditional Polish, a female is usually addressed with an "a" at the end of her name whether she is married or single. Irina Kwasniewski may be her given name, but referring to her as Kwasniewska will get her attention and informs other listeners that you are addressing her and not a male member of her family.

CHAPTER I

1378

POZNAN, POLAND

With each step deeper into *ulica Zydowska*—Jewish Street—fear crept beside her. What Irina had already seen in the city tore at her hopes, and she shivered in the damp gloom.

Firelight painted the slippery cobbles with dancing yellows and oranges as she eased her fingers along the slick courtyard wall. The splintered planks of the Joselewicz gate lay in the street like discarded kindling. Her heavy felt boots, sodden from the long walk into the city, slowed her steps as smoky air filled her throat. She opened her lips to cry out, but no sound came.

Peering through the gate's wreckage, she could see that a blaze, having caught wood and straw, had begun to climb over the feet of those tied together. Over the crackle of flames came the gasps of familiar voices, voices she had come to love. Her eyes went from the flames to the people she knew, who struggled not to scream away the pain. Neither did they plead, so certain was their fate. She only hoped they knew to breathe in the heavy smoke, the only way to hasten their end. This was a sad bit of life's lore she'd once learned from old Joselewicz. *Did you remember what you told me?* She heard their final rasps rise with sparks into the chilled night air, and except for one, their heads lolled into their eternal sleep.

Irina shuddered, sobbing. *Moj Boze—My God—how could you let this be?* Amidst the inferno, she sought a glance from the one remaining awake to the pain, the one she loved more than any other. When their eyes met, she used her hands to give her Berek Joselewicz the only message he could take with him.

The stench of burning flesh—his flesh—made her turn away from what she could never have imagined to be the gate to hell. She retched into the gutter.

1410
GIVERNY, FRANCE

Irina awoke, trembling, and sat up in the great carved bed, her gown drenched in the nightsweat that had become her companion of late. Whether this was caused by the disease she knew was slowly consuming her or by visions of the long dead troubling the night wanderings of her mind, she did not know. What she did know was the one moment she had just lived again was but a small part of her story. *Why can I not forget?*

She didn't recall Velka walking with her from the salon to her bed chamber, but they must have done so right after the rain stopped. *Why does this night seem so much like the other?* Somehow, her treasured servant and companion had managed to get her into bed, and for that and so much else, she had learned gratitude to the one Almighty God who had protected her for nearly fifty years.

To be sure, the woman she saw in the nearby looking glass was not the girl who had journeyed to France from Poznan more than thirty years before. Hair that had once been auburn now hung long, gray, and unbraided, lank strings against her neck. Her body shook with the pain that racked her. She was sure the belly that had once grown a new life now grew something that would end her own. That she would not live to see Giverny's next spring flowers, she felt sure.

Throwing off the coverlet, she attempted to rise, grabbing at the bed's headboard. She gasped, laboring to breathe the early dawn's chilled air. Steadying herself, she glimpsed the swaying grasses just catching the sun's earliest radiance. Ordinarily their dance in the shifting breezes seemed magical, but this morning, the sight out her window made her dizzy and she fell to the floor, knocking aside the candle table.

She cried out but knew Velka was fast asleep in the next room. Catching sight of her treasured blue cape, she pulled it over herself once more and murmured to the God she knew was listening. "How could I have lived so long? How could I have done all the things I have done, yet not the one thing I must?"

No answers came. She did not expect them. Irina had begun to hope she would once more see the only child she had borne, that there existed some mystical balance scale allowing her the necessary time. Yet discomfort jostled the morning as she lay curled into a blue sphere, waiting for her shivers to melt into the sun's first rays.

As to God, that he existed at all had been difficult to accept in her early years, given what she had seen happen in His name. *What did I know of God? What I knew was what the priest told us. The Mass was in Latin—not Polish! What did God know of me? Did He care for us?*

She wondered if her once deep doubts remained as a mark against her in the ledgers of heaven, even though she had long come to believe there was an Almighty watching, waiting.

In the mist of semi-consciousness, she could hear Velka's voice. Despite the old servant's cooing words, Irina knew that her life was seeping away, that whatever was consuming her would not go away with the turning of many more seasons.

Velka helped her mistress to the privy room—Irina refused to use a chamber pot—and to her morning ablutions. In a shallow tub of tepid water, Irina shook with cold once more as she sponged herself carefully, completely. Cleanliness had always been her habit, even as a mere peasant, a servant girl.

Fresh once more, Irina prodded herself to dress for the day's routine, but could not find the will. She was not hungry and had little strength. She was exhausted from the wrenching scenes in her night journey. Never before had she felt this way. "Velka," she began in her easy French, her voice a whimper, "put me back in my bed. Perhaps I will mend by the noon hour."

"Yes, My Lady. I will bring you hot tea." Velka spoke Polish to her, their most fluent tongue, even after decades away from their homeland.

After a while, Velka returned and waited for Irina to finish the steaming cup, as if the simple gesture of taking it might also carry away her cares with the porcelain. She plumped up her mistress's pillows and bade her rest. "You will be well soon. You must give yourself time."

Irina did not believe the faithful Velka but surrendered to the comforting softness of the large down pillows. She let her mind drift to places in her heart by which she had paused many times before, and let each memory unwind as if from a spool of thread. She knew that for many of the events she thought she remembered, she herself could not have been present. She had come to rely on others for many of the missing pieces, and surmised still more, but prayed only that the one Omniscient Being would find a certain justice in assuring the rest of her story be told. It was one of pain, love, and cruelty, all too common in her time, but it was also her story of triumph in a brutal world ruled by men.

The throbbing pain in her stomach returned. To Him, she made her plea once more. *If it is soon that I come home to You, Great God of all, will you not let me see my son again?*

She forced a smile, remembering young Berek, tall for his seventeen years. Black curls framed brilliant blue eyes and a smile to melt December's river ice. As the sun-bathed breeze whispered forgotten things, she allowed herself to remember more of what had happened that day so many years before, to Berek, and to her.

1378

POZNAN, POLAND

The ancient path to Poznan was hours long, and each step became its own vow to leave the Kwasniewski family farm and never return. Hot tears stung Irina's eyes in acceptance of the truth. Her family had tossed her from their lives like the contents of a chamber pot. There would come a day, she promised herself, when the hurt would sink so deep in the well of her memory, she would forget she had ever lived in the village of St. Michael. By nightfall, she would be in the embrace of her beloved Berek and the rest of the Joselewicz family, and a new life would begin for her. Of that, she felt certain.

Newly green hillocks awash in wildflowers greeted her along the wagon track. Usually two muddy ruts after a rain, today the tracks were two deep scratches in the rich, dark earth every farmer desired in his fields. Even so, her felt boots, though nicely padded, yielded to every stone as she wended her way in the waning afternoon sun.

Many were the times she'd walked this same path with her mother to Srodka, the market village nestled on the hill lying just above the great city of Poznan. As country women, they wore kirtles of wool in winter and undyed linen in summer, along with colorful babushkas designed to catch a man's eye. Few had a change of clothes, so what began as new and bright soon became grimy with farm dirt and cooking grease. Yet they were protected from the weather and warmed at night, and that's all that mattered. They often went barefoot in good weather, saving their thick felt boots for colder months.

Of luxuries such as hose, boots, and clean clothing, Irina had only dreamt while living on the farm, but since working in the city for the Joselewiczes, she'd become accustomed to urban ways. Now, thanks to her mistress, *Panie* Eva Joselewicz, she wore nicely made felt boots all year long. How her life had changed, and because it had changed for the better, her walks between Poznan and St. Michael were usually spent in easy reverie. Today, it was different—in so many ways.

Thoughts of the family into which she was born would not leave her. Ignacz Kwasniewski had been her ideal of a man and father, and for the first thirteen years of her life, she leaned toward his every word. She loved his stories about the past, about Poland, and about their ancestors, savoring them as other children savored sweet treats.

"Our people had means once," Ignacz said as part of his ritual dispensation of family lore around the supper table. "Long ago," he would say, "the Kwasniewskis were people of wealth, even minor nobility. Now, we have nothing except each other." At that, Ignacz would hug her and her siblings so tight they could not stop giggling.

What had been scribed in everyone's memory, he told them, were images of pillage and slaughter wrought by hordes from the east. "They roamed everywhere, leaving no village elder alive. Overnight, our clan was reduced to farming just to eat." Tears hung in the corners of his eyes.

Even so, Ignacz cherished his world as it existed. A few miles from the road to distant Gniezno in the east, and to Poznan in the west, St. Michael was a quiet place. He laughed out loud every time he spoke of it. "There is no inn to serve food and ale and nothing to see, just a collection of peasants all working hard for our next meal, and the landlord's next ten meals! Everyone knows each other in St. Michael—hah!—most of us are relatives. We barter amongst ourselves, sing and drink at our weddings—if we can find anyone to marry—and cry together at our funerals. Someday, perhaps, it will be different. One of you," he would say, pointing to each of his children in turn, "will find a pot of gold and make us rich again." Then he would laugh again, and Irina would fall asleep dreaming of a sweeter life.

She had heard her father's words over and over but never realized how important his dreams were to him. From the time she was little, Irina knew she was her father's favorite, that he had special hopes for her, and she did nothing to discourage him. "Tell us more," she would always say.

"It was in the reign of Casimir the Great that Irina was born," he would remind the family. "Poland was a great state, respected amongst nations, but now, Louis is king and he is no Pole. Times aren't so good." Looking directly at Irina, he went on, "You are the oldest, Irina, and our family has many children, as it should be, but it is becoming more difficult to feed all of us."

Her mother, Maria, a plump and energetic woman, smiled from ear to ear when her husband told his stories, exaggerated or not. Often, she told Irina not to let her father spoil her so, that she wouldn't be a child for long, and would soon have to help the family. Irina thought that what had happened to her in Poznan was exactly what her father had hoped. She would later learn how wrong she was.

Along the cartpath, shadows lengthened, and Irina stumbled when her foot found the ground's hollow of an empty rabbit's nest. The sun was beginning its long slide toward evening, and she needed to hurry. As she trudged on, letting the sweet mix with the bitter, she realized with the speed of a lightning bolt why a household of once abundant love had come undone.

. . .

Father Martinus Madrosh knelt to recite his daily prayers, a regimen of meditation he cherished, when a rap on his oaken door startled him.

"Father Madrosh," Squire Jan Brezchwa called in a loud whisper.

"Yes?" the older man replied, and the duke's aide entered, his young features tense in the soft light.

"You must come quickly, Father. There is a messenger from Gniezno."

"Usually four days from here, *nie*—is it not?" His long, dark robes hung on him as he rose, suggesting size to spare.

As if the squire could not tell whether the older man was asking a question, or simply reminding himself of the distance, he said, "He made the ride in less than two, Father. He is said to bear grave news, and that is why Duke Zygmunt summons you."

Madrosh did not move quickly. He was considered old by his peers, many of whose lives ended before the beginning of their fourth decade. As he neared his fifth, the priest's hair and beard were already grey, and his prominent nose guarded a face wrinkled with the cares of others. The older man trailed behind young Brezchwa, who fairly loped ahead with his long legs under a solid frame. Madrosh could barely remember when the color of his own hair as a youth was much like the rich brown that crowned Brezchwa's handsome head. He lifted his robes a bit so that his aching legs could move a little faster along the already ancient and uneven stone passageways of Sokorski Castle.

In the duke's chamber, they waited while the bedraggled messenger devoured bread, cheese, and ale in the kitchens below, lest he collapse, his news with him. Duke Zygmunt sat, anxious like a father waiting to hear if he'd had a son, his left hand working the large ring on his right.

Candles planted atop their silver sticks awaited duty. Soot graced the walls, just as grime blotted the tapestries around them. Until then, Poznan—once the capital of *Wielko Polska*—Greater Poland—had enjoyed a quiet spring day. Night was advancing and the men grew impatient, their faces creased with concern.

"This would not be the time, I suppose, to speak of Father Rudzenski," Madrosh wondered aloud.

"Who did you say?" The duke's response was perfunctory, distracted.

"Father Ambrozy Rudenzski, the pastor at the Church of the Heart of Jesus."

"What about him, Madrosh?" Impatience laced his words.

"The priest has been missing for several days now. He is not to be found and there are rumors aplenty, My Lord."

"Yes," the duke nodded absently, but knowingly. "Of him," he said, looking directly at Madrosh, as if the priest should know more, "we will speak more, no doubt. It is a disgrace."

"A disgrace, My Lord?"

"Look not to me for an answer, Madrosh. Look to your bishop."

They were interrupted by a servant who lit several candles, giving light to shadow. At nearly the same time, Squire Brezchwa appeared with a man bent over with the weight of heavy tidings, if not the fatigue of two long days on horseback. Bowing low, the rider said he had come at the behest of Bishop Gromek of Gniezno.

"The bishop?" The duke's prominent eyebrows arched in surprise. He stood, towering over the rider. "Not from the Duke of Gniezno himself?"

"The duke no longer lives, your excellency. He was on campaign further to the east when plague struck. They say the Mortality took him in a single night and day."

Duke Zygmunt reacted as if struck full in the chest.

Madrosh spoke. "So it is the deadliest of plagues, not the variety that takes its time to kill a man."

"If only it were true, Father," the messenger responded. He lowered his eyes. "The kind of plague you speak of, the Black Death, has struck as well. We know that many of us will die—whether it will take a day or a week to claim us will be the only mystery. The bishop wanted you to know, so that you can prepare."

"Prepare? Prepare how?" the duke boomed, frustration edging his words. His brown hair, once a shade of ginger, shone in the warm candleglow. Once again, he nagged the amber-embedded gold ring on his right hand, the weight of it wearing against the skin, as though the symbol of office sought residence elsewhere.

Shrugging his shoulders, the messenger scratched out with a broken voice, "Pray?" His answer was feeble, though all present professed a belief in an almighty and every-present God.

The duke scoffed. Madrosh shot him a look of careful reproach, then looked at the news bearer.

"You have kept this to yourself?"

"Why, F-father," he began, stumbling into silence.

"I see," said the priest. "That means word has already left the castle!" Madrosh rose and took a step toward the miscreant.

The nameless messenger stepped backward, then saw he was not to be struck. Attempting to redeem himself, he went on in earnest, "Some say the Jews are to blame."

"Bah!" It was Madrosh's turn to be scornful. "Such is the babble of ignorance," he said in a voice louder than intended.

The duke, however, leaned forward. "The Jews, you say?"

Madrosh again glared at his worldly master, surprised at the encouragement he gave the oaf from Gniezno.

"That is what everyone says," he repeated, warming to his message, his eyes shifting from duke to priest, from priest to duke, not knowing who might strike him. "They say Jews poison our wells and that's how the plague comes. They say Jews murder our children and drink their blood."

Remembering his vows, Madrosh kept his arms to his sides. He knew that violence would change neither the man's heart nor his mind. "That is plain nonsense, and your bishop would not have wanted you to come so far carrying such garbage."

"Yes, Father. I am only repeating what I hear from others," he said, managing to be humble and defiant all at once.

The duke said, finally, "You have said enough. I gather we have little time, then."

"The plague is on its way, your excellency, and many have already gone to meet the Almighty. Whence it will come, I cannot say." The nameless rider bowed deeply as he and the squire were dismissed.

"Shall I see that Bishop Tirasewicz is informed, Your Grace?"

"In good time, Madrosh. In good time." He paused, then added, "but he will be of little help, I'm afraid." He cast his gaze into the middle distance, as if something there had greater claim on his attention.

. . .

On the cartpath, Irina kept between the ruts to avoid the puddles streaking the way ahead. Each footfall deepened her brooding. *How could my family do this to me? It was they who sent me to live with the Joselewiczes!* Until today, she had not fully perceived that her father's dreams of a new day, of prosperity and comfort, had somehow centered on her. Turning her gaze back toward St. Michael, toward the family farm, she nested in the grass that was already attracting the dew, and with her arms wrapped around her knees, she put her head down, remembering.

Irina knew she had been both a joy and a burden to her parents. Their delight in her childhood had turned to worry as Irina became just another belly to fill when there was very little with which to fill it. She and her four brothers and two sisters lived a quiet and happy life, barely aware of a peasant farmer's realities.

For Irina, everything changed near the end of her twelfth year. More was expected of her as she went along to help her mother sell vegetables and bread from their stall in Srodka, but the few pennies earned were never enough. One day, an answer to family prayers appeared in the person of *Panie*—Mrs.—Eva Joselewicza, patroness of a well-off merchant family. Occasionally, she chatted with Maria Kwasniewska about ordinary things. "A sheepdog, is it?" she said that day, nodding toward the black, brown, and white pile of fur guarding the stall.

Maria shrugged and laughed at the same time. "It is the village's dog, *Panie,* but it follows Irina everywhere. We cannot get rid of it." The women laughed as Yip barked a greeting, his tail wagging furiously.

On one such occasion, *Panie* Joselewicza turned her attention to Irina, remarking to Maria on how well the girl followed her mother's instruction, and how pretty and bright she was. The very next week, *Panie* Joselewicza asked Maria if young Irina might be trained to work at their large house in Poznan, on the far side of the Warta River.

At first, Maria was taken aback by the offer. Girls often went to work in the houses of the wealthy, but the Joselewiczes were Jews, and people said so many awful things about the Jews. She spoke carefully so as not to offend a purchaser. "*Panie* Joselewicza, she is my eldest daughter, and what would we do without her?" There ensued a delicate conversation about how many mouths the Kwasniewskis had to feed, and how the Joselewicz family would treat a girl in their service. After a further few weeks of talk between the women and between Maria and Ignacz, the arrangement was made.

All the while, Irina listened, bewildered. *Am I a bunch of carrots to be bargained?*

"What a wonderful opportunity it is for us," Ignacz exclaimed at the supper table one evening. "Irina," he said, "your service in the city will allow you to earn money for our family and, in time, earn the attentions of a young craftsman there!" He chuckled in anticipation. "Perhaps a carpenter or an ironmonger. A young man with a good trade will lead you to a prosperous life, little one."

Life's intrusion into the family idyll was something not unexpected, but a shock nonetheless. Irina's voice caught in her throat as she pleaded, "But *Ojciec*—Father—will you not miss your little Irina?"

"Of course, my dearest daughter," he answered, in a matter-of-fact, final way, "but we must all do what we can for the family. It is an answer to our prayers—and you are the oldest girl."

Irina remained silent, as was expected of her. *I am but a girl, someone to serve men and have their babies. What I will not miss is waiting on everyone's needs without so much as a "djenkuje"—thank you.*

"The Joselewicza woman will be a good mistress for you, Irina," Maria added. "She will be firm, I am sure, but unlike some Jews I have heard about, she will not mistreat you."

Irina sat still, biting her lip. *I will miss home because it's home, but there's much I will not miss. They would never sell away one of my brothers!*

"You will be coming home often—with coins for us," Ignacz made sure to note, "and in a short time, you will not be homesick for St. Michael," he said, trying to lighten her mood.

When October came, just after harvest time, Irina turned thirteen, and her life changed. Maria and Irina walked to Srodka for one of the last market days on the Fareway, and then to the Joselewicz house. The sheepdog, Yip, was not far behind. There were tears, but Maria spoke only about her rule of life. "Sadness never mends a broken heart, my little one. Never waste time on sadness."

They stood at the massive wooden gates, iron straps holding them to a dressed stone wall that surrounded the large two-story house busy with animals, servants, and noise. They could hear the chickens clucking in the courtyard mingling with voices of those talking over the conversations of the animals. Irina wiped the tears from her eyes, forced a smile for her mother, and entered a new life. Yip made his choice and scampered in, close by her side.

As prosperous merchants, the Joselewiczes had foodstuffs aplenty for their daily table, and Irina was made to feel welcome. They had two children—Berek, the eldest, and Esther, whom they called Esterka—and while Berek was a few years older than Irina, Esther was her own age. "You will not have much time to spend with our children, Irina. You will have too much to do," the mistress cautioned her, and Irina immediately understood the difference between them.

Much was expected of her, and the mistress spent many morning hours schooling her in the rules and behaviors by which she must live. Irina ate and slept in the undercroft with the other servants and animals, but at mealtimes, she served the family upstairs. *Panie* Joselewicza directed her how and when to serve food and drink, and to sit by the door to the stairs, waiting and listening, so that she might anticipate their needs. It was a routine that gave her much. Watching how women of wealth comported themselves was a fascinating glimpse into a world unknown to the village of St. Michael.

Yip inserted himself into the household with ease. "Why did I never think to have a good dog like this Yip?" *Pan*—Mr.—Janus Joselewicz demanded of no one and everyone one evening after dinner. He patted his belly and laughed as he bent down to give the dog a neck scratch. "You have a good companion, Irina," he said, turning from the table and peering at his servant, waiting in her usual place. "Yip is a member of the family, just like you!"

Two years passed. Irina enjoyed her work and learned a great deal from listening to *Pan* Joselewicz converse with traveling merchants and tradesmen. The household staff adopted her, and on occasion, she escorted her mistress to shops near the family home, but never did *Panie* Joselewicza take her to Srodka to see her mother. "I do not want your mother to see you as a servant, Irina. It would not do," she once said. *Panie* Joselewicz lived up to the terms of her agreement, and Irina returned home every six weeks or so for a Sunday visit. Often, cured meat, little sacks of spices and other things from the trade routes—gifts from the mistress herself—accompanied her on the walk to St. Michael. Ignacz and Maria were proud of their beautiful daughter and the pouch of silver pennies she brought for them.

Then came this particular Sunday, and after the midday meal with her family, a torrent of anger washed away everything that had bound them as family. Betrayed by those who should have loved her most, Irina clung to one hope in her life, one place she could go.

Damp from the dew, Irina stood up, remembering her mother's words about sadness. As she strode in the twilight toward what she believed would be a new life in Poznan, she caressed her belly every little while without a conscious thought of doing so. Imagining herself as part of another family brought on a smile. Yet what her father had said dampened what joy she carried.

. . .

Candlelight threw long shadows against the mottled stone lining Duke Zygmunt's chamber. "Do you think there is any truth to the man's report, Madrosh?" Zygmunt remained at his council table, his expression glum, his square jaw resting on his fist. His sandy hair and his brown eyes were washed of color, the shine of life having lost its luster, as if the cruelties of earlier years had come to rest there.

"The plague, you mean? No reason to doubt it, Sire." Madrosh's voice was muted, serious.

The duke looked up. "Not that, Madrosh. The poisoned wells. Drinking the blood of children."

"My Lord," Madrosh responded, surprise filling his words, "there is no truth whatsoever to any of those lies." After a moment, he added, "Even so, the messenger was letting us know what many are thinking."

The duke nodded, eyeing the counselor warily. A true man of God was he, but definitely a stranger to the realities of life around them. God may be in his heaven, but he did not spend time in the streets of Poznan, the duke noted, and about God's rules, he had his doubts.

"About the Jews, I hold no warm feelings," he said, not looking at his companion. "I deal with them because they are the best at business matters, but I will not be in their company if it can be avoided. As to what our messenger said, I often wonder if there may be some truth to his words."

"I understand, Sire, yet it is your duty to support the teachings of the church. You may remember the pope himself denounced such notions many years ago."

"Perhaps, Madrosh," he conceded, playing with the ring on his finger. "Like most, I am not a lettered man, and that is why the church and its priests are so valuable. You and all of your brothers of the cloth are wise and learned. We depend upon you to advise and guide us." Annoyance lacing his words, he added, "So, how is it, then, that I would remember or know much of anything said by a pope so far away, so long ago?"

Madrosh bowed, smiling. "I am sure Bishop Tirasewicz could have assigned almost anyone to you, Sire, and you would have been better pleased."

The duke had asked himself more than once why had the bishop assigned this man to him. Probably to rid himself of a righteous man, he supposed. Knowing Tirasewicz's personal predilections, that must have been his reason. Yet he shared none of those thoughts with his advisor. "Your humility is appreciated, Madrosh, but you will have to help my failing memory.

Why are they so many? And are you truly certain they are not somehow to blame for the plague?" The gold on his finger gleamed in its new rotations.

"The Polish kings and princes of old made this happen, Sire. You know this. After the Mongols slaughtered much of our wealthier population, King Boleslaw began inviting the Jews to settle here because they had the skills and learning we needed to regain our greatness. Their descendants now make our land their home."

The duke nodded. "Well and good, my dear fellow, but few Poles know or care much for history. Even fewer of our countrymen know our borders—or care much about the Jews."

"True enough, Sire, but that is not their fault—or the Jews'. Poles know their king—and their duke—but borders change every generation or so, and very few of our people ever live to see grandchildren, much less watch them grow to maturity. What they care about is raising and feeding their children, one season at a time. That is why, Sire, your leadership is so important. You are *Szlachta*—our nobility!"

Duke Zygmunt eyed his adviser, wordlessly bidding his counselor go on.

"Many Poles have nothing to do with Jews in their daily lives," Madrosh said, "and so they know nothing about them except what they hear in church or in Srodka on the Fareway—just like the pitiable rider this very night."

Madrosh paused. "Again, my lord, these are new times. You must set an example."

"You say so, Madrosh, yet I fail to understand why I have somehow become responsible for the plague and the Jews!"

...

For Irina, her countryside—lands she could pretend belonged to her— had always been beautiful, the flowers reminding her of the Easter season just past. The sweet smell of lilies in the church; the blest basket of ham, sausage, bread, butter, and eggs on Holy Saturday; and the commemoration of Christ's rising the next morning all summed up a season of new life and new hope.

During the holy days that year, Irina had suspected that she, too, was carrying new life, news she could not keep hidden for much longer. She was keen to give to her mother and father—if she had not lost the baby by the time the trees were fully leafed. The balmy days of May, blissful for everyone else, were anxious for Irina. Her mood had become somber, as she realized that a time of new life might not be one of joy alone.

Further along on the cartpath to Poznan, Irina forced herself not to shed another tear for her family. *What was it my matka—mother—said about sadness?*

Despite her resolution to wipe it from her mind, she could not. What had happened only a few hours before all came back. Every word.

It was on the fourth day of her visit when anger shattered a Sunday's peace. At her place around the rough, wooden trestle table, near the fireplace where the day's soup simmered in its pot, she soaked the last crusts of bread in her barley broth steeped with carrots and onions. The other children had been shooed away, and she sat, quietly, finishing her meal.

"What is the matter, my daughter?" Maria had asked as she tidied up their meager hut. Ignacz rested on the only chair, holding his gaze on the pair.

Irina inhaled deeply, and after a long moment, said, "I am with child."

Ignacz lurched forward, the chair's wood creaking at the strain, and glanced at Maria simultaneously. Irina could see his breath quicken as he waited for more words, words to tell him of a young man with a good trade who might help better all their lives. "And who is the father?" he demanded, cutting to the core of his paternal interest.

Irina swallowed hard. "It is Berek Joselewicz," she said, and lifted her head with a wan but hopeful smile.

In one quick motion, Ignacz rose, and from what seemed his giant's height, bellowed, "You ignorant girl!" He slapped her across the face, jolting her like a crack of lightning. Irina had never felt his hand before. She fell sideward off the bench, but quickly reclaimed her balance.

In that one flash of her father's anger, something changed in her. Standing, she took an equal place in the room and glared at the man she had once adored. Her father froze. For just a moment, she wished Yip were there, lying on the hearth. The herder would have taken a bite from his hand, but Yip was at his new home, watching out for his new family, the Joselewiczes. *Why did I leave him in Poznan?*

Then Ignacz said calmly, but with certainty, "The Joselewiczes are like all other Jews, and they will not take you back. Do you not understand, daughter, that a business relationship with a Jew is one thing." It was not a question. It was Ignacz's fact. "Mingling of blood is quite another, as even peasants know! That boy Berek used you for his pleasure, and when he knows what he has done to you, he will deny you!"

"You are wrong, *Ojciec.*" Defiance underlined her rising voice. "Berek loves me and would never desert me."

"You poor fool," Maria said, her voice flat, resigned. "You will have to stay here in hiding and leave the baby in the woods for the boars when it is born. We do not want it and we would not want anyone in our village to know you bedded with a Jew. How could we keep our heads up at Mass?"

"I will never give my child to the animals," Irina stated without emotion. She felt the sting of another slap, this one by her mother's hand. Returning the blow with a look of hurt, but not fear, Irina saw the regret on her mother's face.

Ignacz issued his command. "You either do as we say or leave us now—forever. No Jew bastard will live in this house." Tears glistened in her father's eyes, and her mother turned away. A stillness enveloped the room.

"There is no choice for me, then." She spoke the words softly, with finality. She reached for her sole personal possession, a large, blue woolen blanket that protected her from rain and warmed her on cold nights. After lacing her felted boots, she looked up at them, hoping. Seeing their hard faces, she uttered not a word, and without looking back, walked through the farmhouse door into the afternoon sun. Despite the day's pleasing warmth, a chill descended upon her.

Now, a few hours later, Irina looked ahead and trudged on, only one goal guiding her steps. *I want to be with Berek.*

...

Madrosh could not rest. The duke's words troubled him. His underlings would follow his signal, spoken or not.

As the supper hour neared, he sought the castle's crenellated walkways high above Poznan's rooftops to march away his irritation at the duke's persistence in ignorance. In the sun's fading light, tendrils of smoke drifted upward that seemed to come from other than cookpots. Then he heard the faint railings of townsfolk, and he sensed that word of plague was spreading. An ugly night lay ahead, he thought.

And what did the duke's words about Father Rudzenski mean? The priest had been at several parishes around the city and seemed popular at all of them. Only recently had he been assigned to the convent Church of the Heart of Jesus where he was minister to the nuns and their work amongst the poor. And now, he'd disappeared. To what disgrace was the duke referring? Madrosh pushed the thought out of his mind. He would satisfy his curiosity later, but for now, he gave his full attention to what lay below him.

Madrosh returned to his apartment. Without a thought to seek permission, he summoned a messenger and dispatched him with a handwritten note for Bishop Tirasewicz. The note suggested only that the duke "was concerned for the order of his city, and care should be taken that Christians not be permitted to commit serious, mortal sin."

"Hurry," Madrosh commanded the messenger, "and deliver this note to no other hands." He watched as the bewildered man ran to his task, then turned to find young Brezchwa waiting patiently at the door.

"Squire," he commanded, acknowledging the man, "I am sorry to disturb you at the supper hour, but as you can see and hear for yourself," he said, gesturing to the opening in the castle's outer wall, "there's a bit of devilry about the city."

A thread of smoke snaked into the room. "What would you have me do, Father?"

"You need not bother the duke with this, young Squire. Before our repast is finished, I wish you to leave our company—discreetly, mind you—and go without the walls on my behalf. You may begin your first sleep after you return with a report."

"Do not worry yourself about my sleep, Father. I will make second sleep all the longer."

"Just so, my son. Between first and second sleeps, there will be many who will have no rest this night, and so, you must be my eyes," he said, and paused. "I gather our Tomasz has been dispatched to protect the duke's interests," he said, "but why would the duke's castellan be assigned such a task?" Madrosh stopped himself when he saw the puzzled look on the young man's face. "Are you telling me something, Squire?"

Brezchwa lowered his eyes. "Perhaps I should not speak so, Father, but Tomasz Wodowicz will not bring honor upon our duke by anything he does this night."

"Tell me why you believe so."

"There's a reason why people call him 'Tomasz the Terrible,' Father."

"Ah! I can only hope the duke's orders have been honorable, however." Brezchwa remained silent. "I want you to don attire without the duke's markings. Leave the castle, then walk over to *ulica Zydowska*. See what the townspeople are doing there, but do not involve yourself."

"Why, Father, to Jewish Street in particular? What should I see there?"

"I do not know for certain, Squire Brezchwa, but as you say, what may happen on *ulica Zydowska* may dishonor us all."

The young squire turned to leave, but Madrosh put a hand on his forearm. "A moment more, Squire. What is all this about Father Rudzenski? The poor man is missing, and the duke used the word 'disgrace' when the matter came up."

Brezchwa took his eyes away from Madrosh's own and looked away, seeming to be embarrassed by the question. "Have you not heard, Father? He walked into a pitchfork."

"What!? Wait." Shock struck the old priest.

Squire Brezchwa did not respond, but bowed, and turned to leave the old man's chambers.

...

Irina had never felt so alone. She wished Yip was at her side. Not because she needed a companion. Growing up on a farm and walking to and from Srodka in the early morning with her mother was one thing, but walking alone near nightfall was another. She could be easy prey for robbers—or, worse, wolves. Just one of either kind of predator would be the end of her. She quickened her pace, chastising herself for her reverie.

The brilliant red-orange sunset did nothing to quiet her fear or soften her resolve, and nothing eased the shock of having her father and mother turn on her. It was better, she brooded, to think of the Joselewiczes. *Will they accept me? Will they turn me away, too?* She shivered in the fading light, *but there'll be no more tears from me tonight!*

Irina had been proud to work for the Jewish family, no matter what her parents said from time to time. *They didn't turn away from the silver pennies, did they?*

The estate where the Joselewicz's lived on Jewish Street was the most imposing of several that backed into the hillside gently sloping away from the Warta. It was large and sturdy, and though coveted by many in the city, *ulica Zydowska* was a location shunned by wealthy Gentiles. The stone wall surrounding the two-story abode was high enough to keep out most intruders, but the wooden double gate, wide enough for the largest carts and wagons, was left open in daylight. The elder Joselewicz had always reminded the servants, "I am a merchant! How can I trade with those coming off the river barges if you lock them out?"

In less than thirty years, she had learned, the patriarch made his wealth trading in salt, spicegoods, and anything else Janus Joselewicz thought would sell in the lands where Germans would pay well for what he had to offer.

One day, she learned more than she could ever have expected. Alahum Qurechi and Rudolf Shafer, an unlikely pair, darkened the Joselewicz gateway in the forenoon. They were announced by another servant who'd run up the stairs ahead, and *Pan* Joselewicz was obliged to receive them. He signaled to Irina to prepare some light refreshment but told her to remain in the room.

The household knew to find Berek whenever traders appeared, but he had been sent to the city to deal with Tomasz Wodowicz, Duke Sokorski's castellan, on a matter regarding warehouse rights near the castle. Likewise, Joselewicza was off to the market, but it would not have mattered. She'd made it known she would not deal with Muslims or Teutons if she could help it.

The two traders trundled their way up and into the Joselewicz dining room, which also served as a place in which to do business. Each man was garbed in an array of expensive silks not seen on those below the nobility. One wore a turban with a jewel at the front and the other, a green velvet cap with a ridiculously long feather canted off to the side. Irina could see them eyeing every corner of the room. Janus rose to greet the men and bade them to sit around his table. At once, Irina presented goblets of a hearty red wine and a tray of dates and small round bread loaves, from which the men could pick whatever clump of crust and breadmeat they chose.

Irina returned to her place as the men commenced bargaining in a language she did not completely understand, as it seemed a mash of several tongues. Each man spoke faster than her ears could hear the words. Occasionally, the stream of words revealed some she knew. At first, they went on over the price of spices like cinnamon, galangal, and nutmeg. Then she began to hear more Polish and German words as they commenced bargaining about amber, a much-coveted gem found in the Baltic.

A sort of tree resin, it was translucent, golden, and said to be of another age. Nevertheless, women prized it for their jewelry, and, indeed, Poznan was not far from what the elder Joselewicz knew to be a trading route for the gem. Joselewicz was fervent in his refusal to deal with them for amber, she could tell. She suspected his refusal had more to do with the fact that one of his bargainers was German, and for some reason the Germans thought amber was theirs alone to trade.

The bargaining went on for nearly an hour, at which point she could discern the men bringing their talk to a close when a deal was struck on cinnamon and nutmeg. It was all about the price of things, Irina had come to know from her work there, and once a deal had been struck, there was little else to say.

All at once, the men stood up and nodded curtly to Joselewicz, who walked them to the door at the head of the stairway down to the courtyard. To Irina, he gestured she should follow them to their horses. She knew what to do. She had done it before.

In the courtyard, the men muttered some words in Polish and German, and what she heard startled her. In effect, the Muslim said to the German something about the old Jew not getting the best part of the deal. The German sniggered something about one day getting "a deal he won't like at all." Irina said nothing but stood by, like the invisible servant she needed to be.

Back upstairs, *Pan* Joselewicz lifted his eyebrow as if to ask his question. Irina told him what she thought she'd heard. Joselewicz laughed, pensive. "You see, dear girl, I did not try to cheat them, even though they thought I would." He walked to a window over the courtyard, as if to make certain the traders had gone. "Those men, one a trader from the east and the other a broker from the west…" he paused. "Well, they hate Jews like me, but they need me in the middle, and for now, there's no way around me."

"What's it like to be a Jew, *Pan* Joselewicz?" It was a question she'd wanted to ask a hundred times, but never dared.

The old man looked at her. He sighed. "To be a Jew is to be like a little mouse in a house with many cats."

"But you are not a rodent, sir," she said, indignant.

"Yet, that is what they think of us. To them, we are rodents to be eliminated if possible, but in the meantime, they must deal with us. For our part, it will always be our task to outwit the cats—not to steal from them, but to be smarter than they are. That, my dear girl, is the only way we have always survived."

She thought he'd finished. "*Djenkuje, Pan* Joselewicz." Irina gave a small bow and turned to go about her duties.

"You know, Irina, people like those two are a problem for Jews today, and they will be a problem for us a thousand years from now, *nie?*"

Irina nodded, grateful to be the frequent recipient of whatever wisdom Janus Joselewicz cared to dispense. Occasionally, she wondered why he confided in her so much, but she finally realized the answer was simple: it was her duty to be ever-present and as all servants, a good listener.

Another time, she was surprised when he related how he and his young family had survived the persecutions of 1367. "We bribed our way to safety, Irina. Others were not so fortunate." At first, he seemed embarrassed to admit this, but then he shrugged and added, "Someday, you will understand the things you will do for your family."

The Joselewicz's lived quietly and associated with others of their class and kind, careful not to draw the envy of their powerful Polish hosts. The patriarch often reminded his family and staff, "Do not give anyone reason to hate us!" One day, in fact, he wondered aloud for Irina's ears, "I hope we have not overstepped with this house and our many servants—like you!" She did not know what to say, so said nothing.

Too, Janus and Eva Joselewicz had been careful in raising their two children, Irina observed. Still under twenty years of age, they were old enough to marry, but neither had done so. *Pan* Joselewicz made no secret of his desire to choose their mates with care so that family traditions would live on and be carried with pride. There was still time, he'd often voiced, to make those choices for them. In earlier days, his words had made sense to her.

Now his words disquieted her with each step she took toward Poznan.

Thinking about her few years there, Irina knew herself to have been impressionable and trusting. She found the family to be like many others, even like those in quiet St. Michael. They lived, squabbled, and loved each other fiercely. They were not ashamed of who they were—mice in a cat's world.

After a while in their service, Irina felt like one of them, and although she never lost touch with her native faith, she found nothing unusual or objectionable about the Jewish beliefs held devoutly by the family. *Do they not believe in the same God as we? Were Jesus, Mary, and Joseph not Jews as well?* It was more complicated than that, she knew, but the mysteries of Almighty God did not trouble her. Yet *why would you, moj Boze—my God, let your children hate the Jews?* The Joselewiczes were good to others and to her. *What more could I ask?*

Berek was another matter. At first, she discouraged Berek's familiarity, and for some while, he paid little attention to her. A few months after her fifteenth birthday, he renewed his interest, and more often than not, Irina felt herself redden whenever he spoke to her. She sensed his interest was not casual. "Know your place, young master, as I know mine," she once said playfully, careful not to offend her mistress's handsome son. Over time, like water wearing away a riverbank, her caution slid away with his smiles and the constant twinkle in his clear blue eyes. One day, Berek kissed her. She pushed him away.

Flushed, she did not know how to deal with the feelings stirring inside her. For months, she kept Berek at a distance. Yet she trembled when she heard his voice, and flushed when she felt his glance. She wondered if others noticed how unsteady she became when he was near.

In time, Berek's words captured her, and the distance between them evaporated. "Your beauty is like the passage of a day. Your eyes reflect the sky on a clear morning, your auburn hair makes the sun shine brighter at noon, and your skin sparkles in the sun's setting."

"Keep away, Berek," she had said. "Your words melt butterfat, and I could not stand the heat." Thinking about her words later, she wished she had not said them.

The day came when, once again, Berek kissed her. One kiss led to another and she did not refuse him. One touch led to another and she did not push him away. One afternoon of quiet passion led to many more. They felt no guilt or shame.

At first, they had been like pups tumbling in a flour sack, but after a time, their love for each other seemed only natural, and hers for Berek grew to a passion she could barely contain. Cherished were her days in the Joselewicz household. Emotional intensity guided her every sense, awakened her curiosity, and allowed her mind to take in everything offered to her. Berek and Irina vowed their love, and when they spoke of it, they willed their youthful hearts into believing all would be well with the elder Kwasniewskis and Joselewiczes.

So caught up was she in the pleasant daydream on her way toward the city, Irina didn't immediately notice the wisps of an early-evening breeze that carried a scent neither pleasant nor expected. It came from a place she could not see, where the sun made its daily farewell, from the direction of Poznan.

She was not far from Srodka, the market town where her mother had bargained her away, and on such a spring evening, she should have been sensing an earthy scent as new sprouts pushed up the dirt and felt air for the first time. She was not. Whatever it was, the smell became an unwelcome companion.

. . .

"Sire," Madrosh began, noting the duke had not moved from where he'd been sitting earlier, "surely, you are aware that parts of the city are afire, that the people have broken your peace. Have you commanded your men to restore order?" Duke Zygmunt shifted in his chair, the fire in the hearth casting its light on the gold threads surrounding the embroidered Sokorski shield on his surcoat.

"Who are you, good priest, to make demands upon my steward-ship of Poznan?" The duke began giving his amber ring new rotations.

"I make no demands whatsoever, Sire." Madrosh stood a little distance from the fireplace inasmuch as his long, black woolen robes kept him well warmed. "It will not be good for the people to think you do not care about them, and if your men attack the Jews, your people might wonder if your men would turn on them, someday."

"Madrosh, I do not care what they think. What is more, you should counsel your own bishop before you presume to advise me in such matters."

"I beg the duke's pardon if I have overstepped, but Bishop Tirasewicz is bound by the dictates of Rome in the matter of the Jews and he will, no doubt, conduct himself accordingly."

Duke Zygmunt snorted with disdain.

"Do I misunderstand something, Sire?"

"Your bishop has no love for the Jews, Madrosh, and I doubt if he will remember what Rome requires of him."

"Hmm!" Then he said, "When I saw the disturbance beginning, I sent a messenger to the bishop beseeching his action as a shepherd of the church."

"Hah! You might be surprised at what action he might take, my dear counselor! Indeed, how is it so wise a man as you does not know his own bishop?" Again, his focus was in the middle distance, as if an answer lay beyond the present. Without turning toward his priest, he asked, "But in truth, what would you have me do?"

"Sire," he continued, assuming the role of mentor as well as counselor, "you are the Duke of Poznan. Of the eight thousand souls surrounding your castle, many are Jews. They have been welcomed amongst us for over a century now, and you are well aware of their prominence in our merchant class."

"I do not care for your lecturing tone, Madrosh, and you have yet to tell me why I, as Duke of Poznan, should do anything for the Jews!"

"You see, Sire, the people, all of them, want someone to give them guidance when it matters. When *Kazimierz*—Casimir—died and left his kingdom to Louis of Hungary, you know how that was viewed by the nobility. It left all of us wondering if we had a country, or if anyone cared about our nation. In the same way, the poor, the landless, and, yes, the Jews have been mere gamepieces in our sordid squabbles."

"And so?"

"When the plague comes, Sire—if it is not already here—there will be many deaths, chaos, stealing, and godlessness. We know not how or why the Great Mortality pays us such deadly visits, but surely, it is not the fault of the Jews, or anyone else."

Duke Zygmunt's eyes and brows rose a notch, as if he were still doubting Madrosh's arguments.

"The Jews would never do what that messenger accused them of— they have so much more to lose than others," Madrosh continued.

"And what is more," Madrosh said, feeling the strength of his argument, "the Jews die from the plague, just as we do."

Grudgingly, Duke Zygmunt nodded in agreement. "You speak sensible words, Madrosh, yet I find them such a distasteful people. So, what must I do?"

"You must issue clear orders to your men, especially Tomasz, your castellan, and his fool, the one they call Big Franciszek."

"Take care with your words, priest. I do not know why you speak so of them particularly. They are loyal to me, and they would do only what they think I would do."

"With my deepest respect, Sire," Madrosh hastened to add, bowing as he spoke, "is it possible these men and others may have concluded you do not believe in Jewish liberties, that you harbor views, such as...?" Without completing the sentence, he jerked his head back and to the side, a reference to the messenger from Gniezno.

"It is not for you to remonstrate with me. I will do what I think best, as I am sure my men will."

A verbal slap is far less a sting, Madrosh thought, *than the knowledge I have failed in my pastoral duty to my duke.* In one sweeping motion, Madrosh bowed once again, more deeply this time, and attempted a humble demeanor, unusual though such a posture was for him. What came as a greater shock was what master said next.

"None of that will matter, my good man. We are leaving tomorrow—or soon thereafter." The ring on his finger found its rest. The amber glint held steady in the candlelight.

Stunned, Madrosh awaited his master's words.

"This very day, not four hours before the rider from Gniezno arrived with his news, another messenger came to us from the west. It seems that the King of France, Charles V, has invited all the nobility between the Portuguese and the Russians, and between the English and the Italians, to convene in Paris before the year is out."

Dumbstruck, Madrosh could blurt only a feeble rejoinder. "Sire, such a trip requires weeks of preparation, and in any event, I must remain here with the people."

"We will consider the Great Mortality a bothersome visitor, but not for us." As quickly as the duke's affable composure had departed, it returned with his own reminder of a convenient reason to leave the plague behind him. "You will accompany me to Paris, Madrosh. I could not manage this journey successfully without you, though I would prefer you find softer ways to proffer your advice."

Madrosh chose not to respond, but to listen.

"You may not have noticed, dear man, but ever since the first messenger gladdened my day, I ordered preparations begun. Now we will complete them in greater haste and decamp before we ourselves are overcome by the reaper."

"And your subjects here, Sire?" The priest could not hide the beseeching tone behind his words. The candlelight played on the wall, as smoky threads breezed in from without, animating the shadows into ghostly images.

"There are plenty of priests and nuns to care for them in their last hours, Madrosh. There is nothing I can do to stop what must be God's will." Then he added, "As for the Jews, there is little I can do." Duke Zygmunt paused. "In any case, Tomasz Wodowicz will see to them."

...

At the crest above Srodka, Irina passed a rock outcropping, just before the cartpath dipped the last mile or so toward the Warta. The more she walked, the more doubt about Berek's love shrouded her. *What if my father spoke the truth?* She brooded. *If Berek will not have me, walking into the swift waters of the Warta would be sure and final.*

Then, she doubted her own self-pity. *If self-murder is a sin, wouldn't it be a greater evil to take the life of my child?* There were some, she had heard, who knew of potions strong enough to take the life of an unborn child, but she did not know such people. What God thought about such things, she did not know, but killing her child made no sense to her, and she resolved not to do so, no matter what her parents had demanded. *It will be different for us!*

While she did not want her child to be the lure for marriage, she could not change that now. Guilt swept in. *Did I let him touch me for my father's dream of a pot of gold?* As fast as the thought came, she banished it, and yet no one would make her marry a Jew. Likewise, she suspected, few Jews would want to marry a poor, landless girl born of the church. *I will leave that choice to Berek, but I know what it will be.*

Her mother's dictum sat in the forefront of her mind. *Waste no time on sadness.* Hurrying now as the setting sun cast long shadows of gloom, she took the first few steps down the Srodka Fareway, now empty of its stalls and market-day bustle.

A cool breeze stirring in the air, she threw her blue woolen square over her shoulders. All at once, the smell she had for a moment forgotten swept up the Fareway, bringing with it a gust of smoky air and bits of cinder. She gagged, grasping her belly. Leaning on the nearest post, the scene before her came into focus. It was not the warming glow of a setting sun that she saw.

Across the river, fires roared just beyond Sokorski Castle. They lit up the evening, a yellow-orange halo growing brighter over the city. Squinting in the stinging smoke, she tried to make out more of what lay before her. Then, as if the hand of the devil himself clenched her heart, she saw that many of the flames leapt from the part of the city where the Joselewicz family lived—on Jewish Street.

. . .

The black-robed man, taller than his visitor by a head and a half, tore the wax-sealed paper from the mud-spattered underling in front of him. As he did so, his gold, ruby-encrusted pectoral cross swung on the gold chain around his neck. "What is this you bring me, messenger? It is late!"

"It is not for me to say, Your Grace." The man's eyes roamed the marbled entrance way of the fabled mansion where Bishop Antony Tirasewicz ruled the See of Poznan.

"What are you looking at? Things you might steal?"

"No, Your G-grace," he stammered. "Duke Zygmunt would not be happy with me if I committed an offense against someone such as you."

"Just so. Wait while I read this." His coal-black eyes narrowed as they flanked the pointed, hawk-like nose. Paper? Paper was expensive, and as such, used carefully. He had heard this convenience was readily available in Italy and France, but it most definitely was not in *Wielko Polska*—Greater Poland.

His thin lips stretched into a barely visible line as he considered the contents of the message. Then he looked down at his visitor. "No one at the castle need be concerned." He made the nameless man repeat his words, then dismissed him.

"Josef, saddle my horse," he yelled to his man when the messenger had departed.

. . .

At the castle gate, the man walked under the portcullis, abreast of the guard standing with his face to the city. Wearing a brown tunic with black hose above his leather boots, he startled the guard. "Ho, man!"

The guard challenged him and reached for his sword, but relaxed when the stranger threw back his hood and stepped into the torch-light. "Why, Squire Brezchwa, I did not recognize you! Why are you not in the duke's colors?"

Breschwa chuckled to further put the guard at ease. "I am set with an errand for Father Madrosh, and I wanted you to see me so that I may return to the castle without incident."

"No need to worry, Squire, though I must report all comings and goings to Castellan Wodowicz."

"You should feel free to do so."

"That I will, when he returns."

"Is he out of the castle, then?" Brezchwa asked, to confirm what he knew. "So many others are hurrying here and there, as if to pack for a journey."

"Yes, Squire. The castellan and a few men are out to ensure order. Have you not noticed what is going on not a few streets over? It looks like the Jews are getting what's coming to them."

Surprised at the man's remark, Brezchwa started to put the man in his place, but saw it would be pointless. "I saw from up above, but I will not be out long."

"Be out with care, Squire, no matter what errand the good Father sends you on this night."

As Squire Brezchwa started without the castle walls to protect him, the guard called out, "And best not be long, good Squire. The gates will close if the trouble worsens or whenever Tomasz Wodowicz himself returns."

. . .

Irina held her belly and began to trot her way down Srodka's Fareway, looking neither left nor right until she stopped to catch her breath at the foot of the Mary and Josef, the arched stone bridge spanning the Warta and leading to the island in the center of Poznan. Firelight splashed the wet stones of the bridge.

Crossing over, she made her way to the quay at the end of the shipping canal just below the castle rising high in front of her, its imposing cut stone deep in shadow of the advancing night. People streamed back toward the bridge scurrying toward Srodka, slowing her progress.

The scene along the canal was one she had seen many times, but never at nightfall, and never in the midst of so much turmoil. Along the fortress's eastern wall ran a wharf laid by the masons with rough-cut blocks of limestone. Thick poles sunk deep in the canal bottom allowed boats and barges of various sizes to tie up and disgorge their goods.

The fortress itself served as one wall of a seemingly endless parade of wooden structures, simple warehouses stacked with every imaginable tradegood. *Pan* Joselewicz stored his merchandise in many of the sheds, convenient were they as staging points for goods moving into the city or moving them west via land routes.

Activity continued along the frontage, but not much. Men unloaded sacks and bales from boats pulling at their ropes, as if in a hurry to be on another journey. Irina could see them struggle with the day's final burdens, but she knew they would stay the night there protecting their masters' wares.

What she further noticed was the horde of rats scurrying across the tie-lines, their presence unremarkable because they and their human hosts shared the same spaces, day and night, sometimes scrambling for the same bits of food. The four-footed passengers easily traversed the short distance on the ropes, chirping amongst themselves as they scrambled across the gravel in search of food and nesting.

Irina was headed to where the castle wall turned away from the river, cutting across the island known as *Ostrow Tumski*. Some of the rats made their way into the city ahead of her. Two squares further west lay another bridge crossing the Warta's main course, and a short walk further would take her to *ulica Zydowska,* where the Joselewicz's lived, where smoke and noise filled the air.

Weary, hungry, and fearful, Irina paused before stepping past the castle gate. Two cart-widths across, the gateway was empty. A guard stood there, dumbly staring at the human stream hastening toward the bridges and away from the noise and chaos, their varied shapes creating distorted shadows from the firelight nearby. Irina paused. *Fear must have many friends.*

To one of them, she called out, "Why are you leaving?"

A voice shouted back, "Plague—again. It's the filthy Jews!"

"Plague?" she wailed in the din.

Cried another, "People will be dying of it! Leave now if you want to live." The words seemed rote, the tone, terrifying.

Talk of plague was enough to make men say and do things—horrible things. St. Michael's isolation spared her such fears. For a moment, she thought of her family who had that very day disowned her. *At least they will be safe in St. Michael.* She could barely remember the last outbreak, yet knew it would be better for her—and her child—if she turned and left with the others.

She touched her belly and knew she had no choice. She had to go on. As she made her way along the wall and into the city's narrow streets, her felt boots, already damp from the dew along the cartpath, began to slide when they did not otherwise stick in the mud and animal droppings streaking the stony streets.

The noise and the heat of the fires, along with the clatter of cart-wheels and the hooves of horses assaulted her senses as she reached the head of *ulica Zydowska.*

She could see people being dragged from their houses and beaten.

There was a lifeless body not ten yards ahead, sprawled in the street. *Is it a woman?* Blood was everywhere. Someone attempted to heave the corpse out of the way, like one might deal with the carcass of a dog or a pony. The Joselewicz house was just beyond the curve in the street, where she could not see.

Irina turned and ran back the way she came, and as she rounded the corner, she collided with a man there. He was standing still, watching. "Oh!" Jan Brezchwa put his hands on her shoulders to keep her from falling.

"I am so sorry, *Pan.*"

"This is not a night to be running in the city, alone. You should be with family." He tried to look into her eyes, and in the flickering light of the nearby fires, he saw only the face of a frightened girl. "Is there some way I can help you?"

"No, *Pan.* You are right. I should be with family." She pulled free and ran back into Jewish Street.

. . .

The man astride the black horse was himself garbed in black, from his hooded cape down to his gleaming leather boots. From the far end of *ulica Zydowska,* he guided his mount around the rubble, human and other, but did not concern himself when the horse stepped upon the soft carcasses clinging to the cobbles. Which or what did not matter to him.

Ahead, thirty or so yards from the walled house of Joselewicz, men fought with swords and implements of all kinds. A sheepdog ran through the melee, growling, biting, and barking.

The horseman did not wish to become entangled in the frenzied bloodletting; that would not do. He reined his horse and waited. "Plague," he whispered to himself. "How convenient."

In the midst of the mayhem, he saw the man he was expecting, a man also on horseback who wore the colors of a nobleman. Approaching near, the man said, "Yes, Bishop?"

"Tomasz Wodowicz, see to it that what you do is in the best interests of the people of Poznan. There must be no misunderstanding."

Fevered sweat dripped from Wodowicz as he dipped his head in submission, "Yes, your Eminence."

Turning the black stallion away from the chaos, Bishop Tirasewicz slowly made his way back to his palace, his inspection completed, the objective accomplished. His thin lips curled to a rare smile.

CHAPTER II

1378

Standing as still as a church statue, Irina tried to take it all in, slowly comprehending that the noise and anger of the people on *ulica Zydowska*—tradesmen, craftsmen, and common laborers—centered on the Joselewicz house. Her house. The wooden gates having been smashed open, the rioters surged upon the unprepared family defenders, dispensing whatever violence they could. She kept to her place in the alleyway, and in the torchlight, saw several men on horseback, men with swords, men with authority and purpose.

Irina steadied herself, one foot in a puddle of urine tossed from a chamber pot up above. She ignored the smell's assault to concentrate on what she could see ahead. She knew fear had stolen the joy of her news, and gone was her courage. Her desire to be with her new family, urgent hours ago, now vanished with the threat to her and her unborn child.

People were attacking with a ferocity she had never seen. They screamed, grunted, swung whatever tools, clubs, and implements they had. After a few moments, she identified some of the other Joselewicz servants, people with whom she worked every day. There was Malmus, who worked with the animals in the undercroft. There was Josefina, a large woman who dressed the slaughtered animals for meals and feasts. There was Stanislaus, the stable boy, and one or two others. Some were Jews, some were not. It did not seem to matter. The people of the town bludgeoned them all in fevered vengeance.

She was able to pick out one of the men when the firelight caught the metal of his sword. It was her beloved Berek shouting encouragement to the household members in their pathetic defense of the family and townhouse. At his side, spitting and biting, was Yip, ever protective of his new master. Irina supposed Janus, Eva, and Esther to be inside, already in their hiding place, along with their treasures.

Maybe courage fails only when you think about it. "Berek! Berek!" she shouted. Irina doubted he could hear her, but she wanted him to know she was there. She wanted him to know their news. She wanted him to fight all the harder so they could be together, happy in the knowledge of a new world they would give their child.

Irina watched her beloved, her lover, her knight fight with courage, his sword glinting in the light, his long dark hair lustrous from the heat of combat. He refused to succumb, even with so many of his pitiful army already felled by axes and clubs.

Just then, she saw what appeared to be a man wearing a stonemason's apron strike Berek's shoulder with a hammer. He screamed in pain as he was shoved to the ground to collect the killing blow.

Yip leapt upon the stonemason, biting him on the neck. A big man with yellow hair threw the dog off and kicked him hard in the ribs. Yip could only yelp as he flew against the wall. Irina took a step toward her man but dared not take another.

Then she saw something she had never expected. One of the men leading the carnage of *ulica Zydowska* was from Duke Zygmunt's household. She had seen him dealing with Janus Joselewicz many times, always arranging matters for the castle. It was the man common people called Tomasz the Terrible. Now she knew why. *But why would the duke's man be doing this?*

Thick in body and face, Tomasz never smiled. Instead, he was given to a smirk that revealed the odd, useless short tooth at the front of his mouth. She remembered his heavy brows were often hidden by matted hair the color of a donkey's hide, and his eyes were like dark coals, cold and soulless.

Tomasz wedged his horse between Berek and his attacker, and for a moment, it seemed as if Tomasz would rescue him. "Don't kill this one—we want him!"

One furtive step at a time, Irina crept up the street and placed herself in an opening between the houses across from the Joselewicz gate. From there, she could look directly into the courtyard where men were stacking wood in two circles.

Berek and the few servants, wounded but still alive, were dragged into the courtyard and made to stand in the center of one of the circles. Their captors then tied their upper arms firmly behind them, one person to another. A heavy silence fell. Irina gasped, her mouth dry in terror.

Tomasz focused his attention on Teofil, the elderly footman, bent with pain and caking blood. He dragged him toward the stairway leading to the second story, where the living quarters were, and all but ran up the stone steps with his elderly baggage. Teofil could not keep his balance, and it angered his captor. The man who had always had a reassuring smile for Irina and for the young people who visited had no composure left to him. There were only the whimperings of an old man loyal to a generous master, preparing to meet the Master of all.

Teofil stumbled again and again, but Tomasz's only reaction was to curse him as a tool of the Jews, a fool who would pay the price for service to the hated ones. Yanking an arm away from the old man's body, Tomasz gave no mercy.

From what Irina could see, Tomasz had taken the old man into the family's rooms where they remained for several minutes. Irina heard shouting, then cringed as an agonized cry filled the air—Teofil's cry. In the courtyard, the others cheered. Reappearing, the barely conscious Teofil grasped his wrist to stanch the blood from the stump where his hand had been.

Right behind them, two of Tomasz's underlings pulled the elder Joselewiczes and their beautiful daughter—Little Esterka to Teofil—down the stairs and into the courtyard. Leaving the household with his men, Tomasz the Terrible climbed back on his horse and, eyeing his prisoners with disgust, spat out the words Irina knew she would hear in nightmares for the rest of her life: "Burn them! Burn them all."

Into the second circle, just a few paces away from the first, his henchmen tied them all together, back-to-back, Mother Eva to Esther and Janus, the hands of one clasping the hands of the others. Teofil, now oblivious to the world, they threw into the circle at their feet.

Janus Joselewicz begged, "Let our son die tied to us. *Prosze*—please!"

Tomasz glared at the elder Joselewicz, as a man might consider an animal. "'*Prosze*,' says the old Jew. Hah! There's more gold than the few pieces you gave me, you filthy bastard. You can see your son in hell!"

To one of his men, he said, as if buying a loaf of bread, "Don't burn the house—someone else will enjoy it."

In quiet, tearful whispers, Janus, Eva, and Esther expressed their love for each other, and called out their love to Berek. Then, they quieted, and bowed their heads.

With glee, the men set torches to wood and straw, but in the damp night, it took a minute for the fire to find its way. Eager townspeople stood around the circles, the growing flames illuminating their eyes, aroused with delight, and their faces, etched with hate.

Yanking the reins of his horse, Tomasz turned the animal and cantered from the courtyard. With him and another armed horseman were two others on foot pulling a small cart filled to overflowing with rugs, silver pieces, cutlery, wood carvings, and other treasure found in the house.

When she was sure they weren't coming back, Irina crept across the street toward the opening in the wall where once-firm wooden gates had kept out nighttime intruders. Now the gates lay in a death of their own. Leaning in shadow against the damp stone, she peered intently at the scene before her as the air thickened. After an agony of long seconds, Berek's eyes met hers through the smoke and flames. Neither cried out.

They held each other's gaze, but for only a moment. Irina wanted to tell him of her love. She wanted to tell him of her news, their news. Thinking quickly, she spread the fingers of each hand, and placed them, splayed, on her belly, as if she were carrying a small melon. With her hands in place, she looked into Berek's eyes and amidst her own tears, gave him a smile of love, of fulfillment, of secret, shared treasure. When he lowered his eyes to her belly, she saw his sudden recognition. Clenched in pain, he did his best to give her a smile in return.

The pyres creaked in fury. At first, the onlookers taunted and cursed their captives. Then they, too grew silent as the shapes within the circles seemed to shrink away before them.

Irina could not watch as her Berek disappeared quietly in the white-hot air. The stench of human flesh, crackling and roasting, assaulted her nostrils. She turned to the darkened street outside the courtyard wall, gagged and then retched, wrenching her insides. In dumb-struck fear, she could not speak. Her heart beat so fast and so hard, she could not catch air to breathe.

She had come to be with Berek, with the only other people who loved her. Janus, the good, gracious father. Eva, her new, most gentle mother. Esther, who reminded her of her own littlest sister, Zuzanna. And now they were gone in smoke rising to the heavens on a starless, cruel night.

Where are you, O God of us all?! Why? She knew the answer. Her parents had taught her. They were Jews.

In the gutter, vomit dripping from her mouth, she spat her vow. "This will never happen to me or my child."

...

Shaken, Irina retreated into the darkness several cart lengths away from the Joselewicz gate. There, she crouched down in the gutter, the day's vegetable peelings and other refuse her bed. Pulling her blue woolen cloak around her, she slid even further into the night shadows.

In her mind, she put aside what she had just seen for fear she wouldn't be able to control herself. She thought of St. Michael, where, unless trading caravans stopped on the main road nearby, visitors and news were rare. There, it was natural to put Berek out of her mind, to let him remain beyond the edge of the village, where, as always, it was as if time was never-ending and as if nothing existed outside of it.

That Berek and his family were Jews had, somehow, never mattered to her. In her circle of life, nearly all Poles knew little or nothing about the Jews except what they heard in church or on market day. What they had heard all their lives, they did not like much. Jews were thought to be greedy and distrustful, an alien race to be despised—at least, that's what they heard from pulpit to parent, from father to family.

They knew not why their beloved *Kazmierz Wielki*—Casimir the Great—wanted the reviled ones in their midst, and in so many ways, it seemed, the common people were powerless to change the lives they had to live. Unknowingly, Irina realized, Poznan was the real world she had been fated to join. For ordinary people, she knew, ignorance was a way of life. While they might know their king, the noble who owned their lands could change every generation,

To Irina, there was nothing unusual about her and Berek, except that she was a Catholic and he, a Jew. Everyone knew how things were. With a studied blindness, the church readily absolved young men, boys really, who bedded with girls their age before marriage. If no pregnancy occurred, the couple chose their marrying time when the boy was released from his family responsibilities and found a trade. If a child was expected, the boy and girl hastily wed with the approval of family and church. They produced as many children as nature permitted them, because so often, many did not survive more than a few years. This cycle, Irina had come to understand, repeated itself unendingly.

Irina was not one of the lucky young lovers of her age, her pregnancy being an almost immediate consequence of their physical love. Yet she felt lucky that her lover was young Berek Joselewicz. She knew he would want to marry her. His family was wealthy, indeed, with a large house in Poznan, and many doors to open for anyone tied to them by blood or water. Or so she had hoped—until the evening of the Lord's Day, when God himself seemed to be somewhere other than on Jewish Street.

It began to drizzle. Unfazed, she clutched the cloak tightly about her and stared into the darkness.

Her greatest fear had centered on what her parents foretold, that despite her hopes and dreams, Berek would spurn her as peasant garbage. That notion had so played itself in her mind, that she found herself wondering how she would deal with the total rejection. How she would raise a child disowned by its father. She had thought that would be the worst consequence, but the cruel and violent death of Berek and his family was beyond anything she could have imagined.

For what seemed like hours, she sat, soaking in the steady, light rain, letting her emotions run in all directions. One minute her spirits floated above the pillage around her, lifted as they were by Berek's love for her. Overwhelmingly, however, she felt herself slipping into a vast chasm of loss, into a place where the future did not seem to matter after all.

With a sudden growl of thunder, a lightning bolt reached from the black sky to strike the gates of another estate just up the street. Its crash sent sparks and wood splinters in all directions. For Irina, the shock was enough to shake her dark reveries. She repeated her vow to the heavens: "This will never happen to me or my child!"

Then came a deep, steady rumble from the sky, the likes of which shook the stone wall against which she cowered. It was as if God had been there all along and was just now sounding his displeasure with the people he made. *Will You come to my side?*

Irina let the rain strike her face as she regained a sense of her surroundings. She forced herself to think of the future, of the human seed within her that she must safeguard and nurture, now more than ever.

In the blackness, crouched in the puddling water, she drew her knees tight under her chin. The rain fell heavily, blotting out what little light had remained from the fires. She heard nothing but the rain. No other being moved about at this end of *ulica Zydowska* now. The killers had left with the downpour—on to other victims or, spent of their vicious energy, to bed with their nightmares.

Irina knew she could not stay where she was, but in truth, she had no idea where to go. The Joselewicz family was gone. Her heart hurt as if a sword had cut it in two when she began to grasp the finality of that fact. In all likelihood, she reasoned, all or nearly all the Jews with whom she'd become acquainted in Poznan through the Joselewiczes were now dead or running into the darkness. In her work as a family servant, she knew almost no one in the city who was not a Jew. Except for a few others just like her, who had similarly come from somewhere else in the city or the countryside, there was no one. The butcher, the poulterer, the greensman, the bakers, they were all Jews, and now dead or gone. She was alone.

Quietly, she struggled upright, ready to move further away from the horror just inside the courtyard. *I must not stay here.* She stopped herself. *Or could I?*

. . .

His grace, Antony Tirasewicz, Bishop of Poznan, was a tall, spare man who enjoyed the pleasures of his position. One of them was not rising at dawn when cocks crowed throughout the city. It was just as well when he'd been up late the night before.

With candlelight dancing on the ledger books, the bishop sat in his study, staring into the warming fire not far from his feet. Leaning on his elbows, his index fingers touching at the point of his chin, he rocked back and forth using his fingers as a fulcrum. It was the kind of respite he particularly enjoyed—reflecting upon his good fortune.

He had missed first sleep and now mused patiently awaiting his regular time for second sleep. Old habits were hard to break. Like most people around him, he went to bed at nightfall so as not to waste candles. Yet no one, not even the farmers, could sleep the whole night through. So, somewhere around the tenth or eleventh hour after noon, one could see and hear light and movement all over the city. People talked, visited neighbors, and, he laughed to himself, procreated the next family member for them and Holy Mother Church. In his case, he worked on his account books until sometime after midnight, when he and the rest of the world, it seemed, slept until their rising. He rarely saw a dawn. Sunrise was for his staff to enjoy.

Appointed by Pope Gregory XI at Avignon in 1372, sponsored by a Cardinal and a noble, Tirasewicz had reigned over his See with aplomb and comfort. The nobleman to whom he owed fealty was Zygmunt Sokorski, Duke of Poznan, and were it not for the duke's power and means, the bishop's existence would have been meager. Considering his benefactor more fully, he perceived the duke to be neither a smart nor thoughtful man, but honored him, in his presence, at least. Surely, the duke knew Jews had nothing to do with the plague. Had the man but a silver penny's worth of cleverness in him, he would never permit an ogre like Tomasz to be his face in the city, and neither would he let the man be thought to act on the duke's beliefs—as he saw him do tonight. No, it was just not done. Yet, the bishop thought, just as the duke was useful to him in one way, Tomasz was useful to him in others.

Another point of pride for his grace was that Poznan had once been the Capital of *Wielko Polska*—Greater Poland—and that very fact endowed him with a palace worthy of a church prince. In Poland's largest royal city, the bishop was pleased to preside over its cathedral, Saints Peter and Paul, a Romanesque structure in existence for nearly three hundred years and where Poland's first rulers were entombed.

Casimir the Great—*Kazimierz Wielki*—had once reigned in the city, but he had one great flaw. He loved the Jews too much! Indeed, the people called him "the King of the Serfs and the Jews." His tolerance for the accursed tribe had been infamous and long-standing, and, for certain, Jews had been a welcomed people in Poland for more than a hundred years. In Poznan, the large Jewish community even had its own synagogue. Allowing them to have their own place of worship was too much, the bishop fumed on a regular basis.

Casimir was eight years dead now, and without sons, the country was ruled from afar by Louis of Hungary. And so Tirasewicz no longer had to pretend fealty for a sovereign living in the shadow of the cathedral. Love for the Jews was where the bishop and his pope also parted company. If there were as many Jews in Italy as in Poland, the pope would see things differently, he felt sure.

At some point in his mental meanderings, he wondered if people knew how much gold it took to maintain the palace and the church, not to mention his manner of living. He wondered, too, what certain people might think if they knew how much gold he had borrowed from Poznan's wealthy Jews, especially Janus Joselewicz.

As he thought further of Tomasz Wodowicz's work that evening, he put his concerns aside. Now no one would ever know about his indebtedness to the Jew. The bishop knew himself, however, and his love for the finer things life offered would not be put aside so easily. From whom would he borrow with Joselewicz gone? Monies would have to be secured, one way or another.

He retrieved a quill full of ink and began to scratch figures on the church ledgers when a tap at the door disrupted his ponderings. Before he could look up, Father Taddeus Shimanski rushed in, fairly trotting into the circle of candlelight over the table behind which Tirasewicz conducted his monetary labors.

"Bishop Tirasewicz," the priest said, breathless as he stood above the man whose quill was poised over paper as if it were cutlery over a plate of roasted meat. "There is a messenger outside. He comes from Duke Zygmunt."

"Another message? From the duke himself? At this time of night? What on God's earth is so important that I be so rudely disturbed just before second sleep?" Another of the storm's thunderclaps punctuated his words.

Father Shimanski took a step back. "Your Grace, I ask your forgiveness, but the man said it was urgent."

"Nothing urgent happens when I am, uh, praying, my young priest!"

"Yes, Your Grace. The man seems anxious to speak directly to you. May I bring him in?"

"If you must."

In a moment, one of the duke's men entered, his boots trailing a track of mud on the polished, stone floors. The bishop looked at the puddles of mud, annoyed. "This is the second time this night I have had to endure the mud of the city on my polished floors! Josef," he shouted toward another room, "come in here and clean up the filth as soon as this person leaves."

"Your Grace," the man bowed deeply and went on, not waiting for the bishop's acknowledgement, "Duke Zygmunt begs to inform you that a messenger from the west commands the duke's presence in Paris, and someone from the church may be expected to accompany him."

"May?!? For what reason must I uproot myself to Paris? Such a journey will require a year's time before I return—and will cost a great deal." He stopped when he realized he was attempting to reason with a messenger. "And when shall this journey commence, my good man?"

44

"Tomorrow, at dawn, Your Grace."

"Has the duke taken leave of his senses? It takes many days to prepare for an absence of such duration!" Again he remembered to whom he was speaking. The bishop pursed his lips, then turned to Father Shimanski, appealing for an answer.

The priest hastened to speak. "I believe there's more, Your Grace."

"How much more can there be?" he growled.

The messenger cleared his throat. "There was also a rider from Gniezno. From Bishop Gromek there."

"Yes? Why did Bishop Gromek not send the man directly to me?"

The messenger moved the phlegm around his tongue, apparently enjoying the suspense he brought to the situation.

"Speak, man!"

"The Duke of Gniezno is dead, sir. From plague." He paused, allowing the facts of the catastrophe to sink in. "And that is why, Your Grace, all of you must leave Poznan at the earliest moment. The plague has come."

Tirasewicz blanched. "The plague. Yes, I was already aware of its coming from, well, never mind," he said, forgetting yet a third time he was speaking to an underling. "You may go. Tell your master I will prepare as quickly as I am able—and if you can, take your mud with you!" Turning to Shimanski, he said, "You will not sleep this night, Father! You know what to do. The duke will be impatient, but I suspect all the hurry will not hasten our departure."

The bishop turned again to his account books. Head in his hands, he wondered how he would pay for several months of travel to Paris, living there, and then returning. He must find an excuse.

When he thought about his good fortune—his newly-sound financial condition and an escape from the plague—he could not stop himself from saying aloud, "Thanks be to God!" Hypocrisy went only so far, he admitted. He knew who and what he was. His prayers were empty, his religious gestures meaningless. In rare moments when he let truth enter his heart, he always decided it was easier to enjoy the trappings of his life.

As he prepared for bed, he heard further rumbling outside the wall opening. The wind rose, flickering the candles, and heavy rain began to pelt the palace. He tied the woven matting across the opening, but the wind yanked it free. *Why must I endure such a miserable night?* It was one more reason he did not relish such an early rising after so busy and stimulating an evening.

Laying his head on the silk-covered goosedown pillow, he sighed. "Plague of any kind is frightening. Ministering to the sick and dying will be for others." He sank into the black night.

. . .

Duke Zygmunt slept fitfully, his dreams disturbed by twin demons of greed and hate. He

knew Madrosh, the good man of God, was right in all that he counseled about duty to his

people. Yet, in his heart of hearts, the duke did not consider the Jews his people. Yes, Casimir and Boleslaw before him had sought the Jews' talents, and through their royal eyes, the Polish kings had done their best to nurture their kingdom. *But why so many of them? And why can't they be more like us?*

Warmed by the woolen coverlet, Zygmunt tossed in his feather bed, his head and heart protesting what his king and his pope had told him. People—even people at his station—were jealous of the Jews and their many skills, especially their diligence in making money they would then lend back to the Gentiles at high rates of interest. In truth, jealousy most often matured into resentment, and when an excuse presented itself, it was oh, so satisfying to let the Jews be blamed.

Sometime around midnight, as he lay trying to justify himself, the castle walls shook with a shriek of thunder and a howling wind. In a moment, the billowing leather draping his window sent a candle flying. After watching the window covering flap and snap at the wind's whim, Zygmunt made a vain attempt to tie it shut. First sleep had been fitful. Second sleep would be nonexistent, he feared.

Looking heavenward, the duke prayed for the storm's retreat, but to no avail. Puddles formed on the wooden plank floors, soaking the expensive carpets laid to warm his feet. An insistent rap on the door took his attention away from the storm's fury.

Squire Brezchwa entered and waited for the duke's acknowledgement. Sitting on the end of his bed, his whole attention on the noise outside, the duke finally looked directly at him, and Brezchwa spoke. "Sire, the storm has soaked everything in all the wagons being readied for the journey. What shall we do?"

"Where is the castellan?" he asked flatly.

"I beg your pardon, Sire. Tomasz and his men returned to the castle not long ago, but," he added, clearing this throat with meaning, "I suspect they are in no condition to continue the work."

"They are drunk, you mean."

"Yes, Sire."

"They will no doubt want to forget what they have done this night."

Brezchwa agreed once more, then repeated his question.

"Have those who are sober drag all our goods under roof and begin the drying process over hot coals in the chambers below. Tell them all to take care nothing catches fire," he said, with the dejection of one whose plans have gone terribly awry. He paused, then went on. "Tell them to make all speed with the drying so that we may depart come Tuesday's dawn."

"Yes, Sire."

"Oh, and Squire, send word to the bishop of the delay." Bemusement edged his words. "The last thing I want is to annoy the man of God." He gave his squire a wry smile.

. . .

Irina took a few careful steps to avoid slipping or, worse, finding her footing on someone who had recently been alive. *Not even the thunderclaps can wake them this night!* As much as she knew the sight would sting her eyes, she forced herself to lean through the gate opening.

Only a sleeping guard remained, oblivious in his stupor to the storm's ravages around him. It was Tomasz the Terrible's henchman, the oaf they called Big Franciszek—a truly bad joke of a name because the -*zek* ending suggested the opposite of big. Behind his back people said "Big," referred to his size, -*zek* to his power of reason. He had wedged himself in a niche just inside the undercroft near the stairway to the second story, and near the twin circles of embers, smoldering now in two lonely, sodden mounds.

As Irina crept across the courtyard, illuminated by lightning every few moments, she kept her eyes on the snoring Franciszek, and away from the small mounds of bones and ash. Were the guard to awaken, she had no idea what she would do.

Of one thing she felt certain. *I will sleep where no one else will sleep this night.* She slipped silently up the wooden stairs, where, even in the dark, she was familiar with the spaces. As she reached the third step, with eight more to go, the snoring hulk stirred. Perhaps his body sensed the presence of another.

Irina stopped. She waited, barely breathing, until Franciszek fell to his snoring once again. Slowly, she crept up the stairs and reached the doorway. Once more, Franciszek stirred. She summoned hope that the man would have fitful sleeps for the rest of eternity. *How could he ever close his eyes in easy slumber?*

From the top of the steps, she could see that he was awake, but groggy as he moved his head from side to side trying to comprehend where he was and what was happening around him. His actions became like those of a shopworker who had just remembered he'd forgotten to bolt the door for the night. With surprising speed and agility, he moved around the spent pyres. Not giving them a second look, he walked quickly to the smashed wooden gate, and with a struggle, managed to create a barrier of sorts. Though the rain had slowed to a drizzle, Franciszek found every puddle as he hurried back to a dry haystack in the undercroft.

Within a few minutes, Irina could hear the big man snorting a song of deep sleep. She waited a bit longer just to be sure, then found her way through the house to the room that had been Berek's. Thinking about him made her think of Yip, but he was nowhere to be found. She thought the worst, adding him to the long list of those who had departed her life in a single day.

She dropped onto the straw-filled bed sack and let her emotions take hold, crying softly for all she had lost. Then, after only a few moments, she stopped. Waste no time on sadness, her mother had said. She had to think things through, but carefully. Yet she was so exhausted that all she wanted to do was lay her head down for a few hours before the dawn's light.

Warmed with one of Berek's sleeping woolens, Irina soon found herself deep in another world of fear and flight, uncertainty and cruelty. Her mind wandered in the dark caverns of unconsciousness and let her discover old and new pathways as the night slipped by. She saw herself, Berek, and an infant, happy on a country farm, or in a village shop, or at his parents' house—anywhere. The ever-faithful Yip was there to protect them. Then she saw herself horribly alone, and her child, stillborn.

Well before first light, she awoke, her fists clenching the soft wool that warmed her through the damp and cool spring night. Her eyes opened wide as she remembered first one thing, then another.

It seemed unlikely that Tomasz and his men had found all the Joselewicz valuables. Indeed, from what she remembered seeing the night before, there had to be much left. Quietly, she rose and let her eyes adjust to the shadowed objects surrounding her. She left the room and moved to the large space in the middle of the house, on each side of which were several sleeping rooms for the Joselewicz family and Teofil, their faithful retainer.

In the large room that served as a dining area, a place to meet and entertain guests and business visitors, Irina looked quickly to see what might remain. The large cabinets and storage boxes had been ransacked, chairs and benches upended. There was a large puddle of drying blood on the floorboards where, no doubt, Teofil had suffered some of his last pains on earth. She gagged when she spied a severed hand lying in the midst of the scarlet pond. It was odd to think that Teofil's hand was the only real substance left of him. At once, she put it out of her mind, focusing instead on the absence of cutlery, eating platters, small weapons, candlesticks, and the like. All were all gone.

She noticed, with relief, neither of the two large cabinets had been pulled away from the walls where they stood. She went to the one on the far side of the room, swung open the door, and easily stepped inside.

Facing the back of the large box, she pushed on the top left corner of the backboard. It did not give. Then she knocked softly. No response. She knocked again. Still no answer. She finally leaned against the wood and in a hoarse, firm whisper, said, "It's Irina. Open up." Still nothing. She repeated her whispered message and added, "I'm alone. It is safe! Open up."

With the smallest of sounds, the wood creaked and the back of the cabinet swung like a door into the wall itself. When the day's first light washed across the hiding space, there stood a trembling, speechless Velka, the kitchen girl. *How did she stay hidden there?*

Irina put an index finger to her mouth signing silence. Gently, Irina put her hands on Velka's shoulders and led her out into the room. Then she reached back in the space, just large enough for the kitchen girl and one other—or for Esther and her mother if they could have gotten there in time—and felt around in the crevice above where Velka's head had been. Falling into her hand was the small leather pouch she hoped would be filled with many of the same silver pennies the Joselewiczes used to pay her. She was wrong.

Along with silver, there were a great many solid gold coins. She had come to know about this place one day a few weeks earlier when she had been bringing in a platter of food for mealtime. There was Berek's mother, Eva, doing something very odd in the cabinet.

Surprised, *Panie* Eva looked around to make certain no one else heard her, then explained that this was a second hiding place for the family. She said no Jew believed in only one safe place since tortured servants were often compelled to reveal its whereabouts. Many Jewish families, Eva had said, learned to have second and third hiding places. She swore Irina to secrecy, begging her not to tell anyone what she knew, not Janus or Esther or Berek. Irina had kept her promise. *How did Velka come to know of it?*

While the light in the room grew, Irina led Velka to a small window opening looking out over the courtyard. What remained of the storm was a steady drip of rainwater finding its lowest puddling point. There was no other sound except for a cock crowing here and there and a barn animal or two wailing to be milked or led outside. Many masters would no longer come for them.

Soon, Irina heard what she had expected. Big Franciszek awoke with the sun and the calling of the roosters. She could hear his stream as he relieved himself against an undercroft wall, and then saw him walk outside and stretch himself in the sunlight. Briefly, he looked at the two circles of ashes as if he had no idea why they were there. As he came a bit more to his senses, he shuffled toward the gate, moved a few boards, and left.

Irina could hear him clomping up *ulica Zydowska*. She waited.

Turning to Velka, a girl of about eleven years, Irina asked, "Are you all right?"

"What happened? Where is everyone? I could not sleep with all the terrible noise."

"Dead." It hurt just to say the word. "Dead, all dead. Burned in the courtyard." Little Velka shrunk in horror and began to cry.

"We must act quickly, Velka, and you must do exactly as I say. Speak little. One thing we have to do will be very unpleasant and you will help me do it without a word or a tear. Do you understand me?"

"Yes," she said in a faint voice. Short and sturdy, Velka had been orphaned shortly after birth when her entire family had been felled by an earlier outbreak of plague. Poznan was where cultures and wares blended in a great stewpot of simple barter, high trade, and disease.

Irina had often observed that Velka was a hardworking, if simple girl. She had been cared for by the Joselewiczes from the time they found her in a dirty rag outside their gate years before. No one knew if her family had been Jewish, and the Joselewicz family did not seem to care one way or the other. Velka repaid their kindnesses with loyalty and devotion. Orphaned once again, Velka would now be in her charge. *Can she be loyal to me?*

"First," Irina said, still keeping her voice low, "we must find the best clothes here that will fit us. We will take just a few things."

"And then? Where will we go?" Velka asked plaintively, her demeanor willing but uncertain.

"I don't know yet, but we can't stay in this house, and we don't want to stay where someone might remember us as working for Jews."

Tears washed Velka's face. "I understand, but I don't want to leave them."

Quietly, firmly, Irina said, "They are no longer here to leave. Come." At the window opening once again, she pointed to the piles of black and gray ashes in the courtyard. "There they are," she said, trying to be final, but not cruel.

Velka stared for a long moment, her tears drying with the hard reality before her. "We must go then," she agreed, her eyes wide with fright.

The two gathered new belongings, remaking themselves as young women of prosperity, a mistress and her servant. They hurried downstairs, where Irina scanned the undercroft looking for a tool of some kind.

"Come," she said to the curious Velka when she found a hay rake.

"What are you going to do?

"I'll show you, and if I hesitate or start to cry, I give you permission to slap me hard. We have only a few minutes before the murderers return. Come."

. . .

As the sun rose over the castle courtyard's lake of mud, Tomasz shook himself into consciousness. His small room wasn't much, but it was better than the rude barn in which he'd been born. It was far better than the rat-infested piles of straw his men called home. At age twenty-two, he'd come a long way, and far he would go! He smiled to himself. Taking in the morning air, he coughed and spat, but a feeling of deep satisfaction enveloped him, along with the desire to relieve himself, then fill his belly with whatever the vermin had not already infested.

He smiled, taking pleasure in the knowledge so many in the town had joined him and his crew in burning and looting the Jews' properties. It must have been the right thing to do, he reasoned. He supposed some had assumed that if the duke's castellan was leading the rampage, he must be acting under the duke's authority. He chortled to himself, spilling ale down the front of his tunic. "Let them think what they will!"

Fully awake, he mentally recounted the houses and people they had plundered and burned. He knew there was no truth in the lies spread about the Jews, but they were an easy target, and the plague was a perfect excuse to filch their goods.

But something wasn't right, he concluded. As he rumbled around in the courtyard, he couldn't put his finger on what troubled him. Something was out of place. Something did not fit.

Surveying the activity around him, Tomasz splashed through one puddle after another, scolding underlings already hard at work. He supposed the storm had been more severe than he had thought, but then, he'd been drunk and slept through it all. It was a good thing he had given orders to prepare for the duke's journey. Now all the bustle centered around low fires built to steam and dry the goods still un-packed. He began to think of ways to deflect blame should the duke be displeased about the delay in their departure.

One of the many workers—common peasants required to work for the duke—ran up and gave him his reprieve. "Sire Tomasz, we will be heading out tomorrow morning as it will take us another day to dry and pack the wagons once more."

"Thanks be to God," Tomasz exclaimed loudly, then farted.

A few hours later, after he'd downed his first mug of cold ale, the feeling of something amiss came back to him. What was wrong had not to do with the burning of the Jews—for that, he would make his confession and be forgiven. Everyone who had participated in the night's events would do the same, and if there was any guilt at all, he grinned, it would be washed away with a priest's absolution.

No, what bothered him had to do with the goods and trea-sure—there wasn't enough of it. He'd made a mistake. Pillaging the craftsmen first had been profitable, indeed, but they could have wait-ed. For Poznan's jewelers and silversmiths, it would have been harder to hide their wares. His mistake had given Joselewicz time to hide his valuables. As a merchant who lent money to his duke and others in high station, he must have had more—much more. Good thing he left the ox, Franciszek, there to keep watch. Too much to drink and too much to guard made the marauders careless and allowed the old Jew to somehow deceive them.

He should have gone there first, just after the hungry messenger from Gniezno filled his mouth and emptied his knowledge in the castle's kitchen. It would have been the perfect surprise for old Joselewicz! Over his shoulder, he could hear the sound of Big Franciszek's voice.

"Franciszek, you oaf!" Tomasz's own voice cut through the clamor of the morning. "What in God's name are you doing here?"

Stopped in mid-breath, Big Franciszek tried focusing his eyes toward the sound of the voice he knew so well. It was a demand he did not expect. "Why, Sire, I'm here to get my breakfast," he answered factually but submissively, though Tomasz had never been knighted.

"I can see that, idiot! Who is back at the Joselewicz house?"

"No one, Sire," he responded, groveling. "I pulled the gate closed as far as it would go, and after I've eaten, I intend to go back there to await your orders." He nodded his head in such a way as to suggest his was a most sensible approach.

The scowl on Tomasz's face remained unchanged when he barked, "You were not to leave there, fool! Someone could get in and steal what we missed."

At this, Big Franciszek showed his complete confusion. "But Sire," he reasoned, "didn't we get everything last night? What could be left?"

"We could not have gotten everything. There must be more. Get back there now," he commanded. "I'll be along shortly." When the underling made no immediate move, Tomasz screamed, "Now, you fool! Run!"

. . .

Irina and Velka crept down to the courtyard, at which point Irina paused, making sure she knew to which pile of ashes she must go. She moved toward the one on her right. With the wooden rake in hand, she reached into the middle and began to pull back and forth through the blackened rubble. Bits of clothing, bone, and ash moved in a sopping mush. There were three skulls.

Velka took a step backward, almost tripping. "*Moj Boze*, Irina! What are you doing?"

"I think I have it." That the blackened skulls belonged to people she cared for she put completely out of her mind, detaching them from anything in her memory. In the other circle were the remains of her Berek. Those she would let rest. *I love you, my dear one, but I will not follow you. This is now about our survival—and nothing else.*

"Did you say something?" Velka demanded in a hoarse whisper.

Irina pulled toward her a blackened, shapeless mass the size of a very large apple.

"Why do you want that mess?" Velka protested.

"You'll see. You'll see," she whispered.

Irina had not told Velka the whereabouts of the last hiding place Eva had revealed to her, a place where *Panie* Eva had confided there was a somewhat larger bag of coins. She kept this treasure at the end of a leather thong tied to her waist and left to nest below her ample mid-section. Because Eva was a large woman who wore billowy skirting, the bag could hang there, near the other treasure Janus said she possessed—where no one would ever notice it. Eva had chuckled as she said "the other treasure." Eva's simple bravery amazed her.

The melded mass, cooled by the drenching rains, weighed more than it appeared. Using a rag, Irina rubbed a small part of the lump in her hands, and the unmistakable gleam of gold and silver met the morning sun. Then she placed it in a velvet pouch she could fasten to her wrist. She saw Velka purse her lips as her eyes grew large. Before she could react, Irina commanded, "Say nothing. We must go now. They will be coming back soon."

As they hurried back inside, Irina heard a whimper. They listened. Then, another. She turned, looking in every direction seeking someone alive. There was no one. Then another cry. Irina walked through to the far end of the undercroft, and there lay Yip, whose tail wagged furiously when he saw her. She knelt and stroked the dog's head and back. He tried to raise himself and finally did so, with great difficulty.

When Irina tried to hug him, he recoiled in pain. "Yip, I am so sorry. I saw the man who kicked you, and someday he will pay. Lie down, boy, and let yourself heal." Yip was having none of it. "Well, alright, you can come, but you're too big to carry." She kissed his head and rose.

"Come, Velka, let us wash. Then we must hurry."

"Wash?"

"Yes," Irina commanded in an urgent whisper. "We will not carry the streaks of filth on our hands and faces that servants wear."

"Even our betters do not wash, Irina! Why shall we?"

Irina faced her companion directly and spoke sternly. "We wash, Velka, to leave behind the dirt and ash of what happened here, and because I insist on it."

...

By dawn, the village of St. Michael was awash in mud and downed branches. Roof thatch from the two-stall shed that Ignacz, Maria, and the children called their family home had gone into the wind, which left their few belongings open to the night's downpour.

Not that any of them had much more than was on their backs, Ignacz knew well, but what they had was precious to them. To him, more precious was each member of his family, even a daughter with child. What had happened the day before was something he regretted more than anything. He did not like the Jews, but he loved his Irina. He made up his mind, and though he'd not said a word about it, he was impatient to act.

Maria was busy salvaging their meager goods and preparing something hot and edible for them to start the day, when Ignacz came in the rough opening serving as a doorway and made his announcement. "As soon as we eat and tend to the animals, we will leave for Poznan."

Maria was dumbfounded. "Leave for Poznan? For what reason, Ignacz? There is so much to do here after the storm."

"All of it can wait. We will leave the older boys to repair the roof and watch out for the animals, but the rest of us will find our daughter."

Maria scoffed. "You, my husband, are a greater fool than our Irina."

"Not a fool, Maria, but a father. Yes, what she did was wrong, but we cannot abandon her. She is young and alone."

"If she is right, all the Jews will be looking out for her."

"We'll see if that is true." He looked around at the wide-eyed little ones. "Be quick now. If we get to Srodka by mid-afternoon, everyone gets a scone!"

Maria exhaled her new reality. She must obey her husband. "We can trade a few things for goods not to be found in St. Michael," Maria finally agreed. She looked up from the firepit and into the heavens above her. "I hope we will not regret it."

After giving instructions to Edouard and Peter, Ignacz and Maria gathered their four smaller children and headed down the rutted track that served as a road. They sang songs, said prayers, and talked as the sun rose.

Reaching the junction of the path from St. Michael and the main road from Gniezno, they felt lucky to join up with a small caravan, also bound for Poznan. The family walked with the traveling merchants and listened with awe to the stories of a man who traveled with mules, horses, and carts, all of them laden with goods from Gniezno and points east.

"I have traveled all over," *Pan* Jerzy Andrezski told the children, who listened with eager ears to the tallest man they had ever seen. "And I can tell you stories that would make your hair curl." He proceeded to go on about hunting cougars on the steppes of Russia, and warned them to watch out for Poland's wolves. "They love to eat little children," he laughed. The time went quickly, and shortly after midday, they reached the crest of the hill overlooking Srodka and the Poznan valley beyond.

The Fareway's aromas invited all to sample the delicious roasted meats and warm cakes to satisfy their mid-day hunger, and the entire party stopped to rest. After chatting with the caravan's drivers for a bit, the Kwasniewskis found the chattering crowd spoke of little else but the Jew burnings the night before and the ferocious storm that signaled an end to the violence. Many said the plague was only a rumor and, in any event, would never come to them because the Jews were gone or dead.

The nasty talk seemed harsh and cruel, and hearing the words of self-satisfied hatred from others gave Ignacz pause to wonder if he hadn't spoken similar words to someone he loved. Yet he didn't want any of these people to know his daughter worked for Jews. A hundred things went through his mind, and he rued the day he let Eva Joselewicz take Irina away. Looking skyward, he noticed the sun had just begun its daily march toward the west. Their respite at an end, he climbed to his feet and gazed over the crowd and down the Fareway's long descent to the bridge crossing the Warta. Despite the talk he had heard, Poznan looked as it always did. It must not have been as bad as what they were saying.

On the crowded Fareway, Maria tried to keep her brood together but had trouble counting heads as they pushed through the throng. Partway down the hill, she called out to Ignacz. "Zuzanna is not with us."

"She does that often," Ignacz said with both love and annoyance. "Let's stop and look for her."

"Yes, husband," she said. She wanted to say more but felt suddenly dizzy and faint and, despite the warmth of the day, chilled.

Ignacz himself also began perspiring profusely, and gasped to Maria, "My head. It's like someone drove a hot iron into it. Did we eat some bad food?'

"I don't know, Ignacz. Did you hear me say I cannot see Zuzanna?"

"Yes, I heard you," he replied, irritation mingling with distraction.

"One of our children is missing," Maria repeated, "and I cannot find her. We have to stop."

"Yes," he said, struggling to focus, in spite of the creeping nausea commanding his attention. "You take Marta and Josef. Stephan, you come with me," he directed, grasping the hand of the four-year-old. "When the church bell chimes the next quarter hour, we meet at the bottom of the hill. Call her name as you go. She will hear us."

. . .

Little Zuzanna did not hear anyone call her name. The quarter hour before, she had become attracted to the stall selling sweet scones. She had stopped to look, drawn closer by the smells of sugar, butter, and flour combined to form the crumbles atop the little cakes being sold.

Without a word, she had sat down on a stump next to the stall. Nearby, a man was playing some sort of musical instrument and singing a song she did not understand. She was enthralled by the music and the happy noises of the crowd. Others joined in with him, sang a few words, and laughed heartily. Zuzanna spoke to no one and no one spoke to her, lost as she was in the sweet sounds and smells around her.

CHAPTER III

1378

Irina had been fortunate, and knew it. Silently grateful for the examples of appropriate dress and manners *Panie* Eva had set for her, Irina had been able to make quick decisions about what clothes she and Velka would wear and how they should appear to others.

For herself, she wore colors of wealth and nobility she could never have dared as a servant. Laws and customs required class to be readily discerned by anyone, and such thresholds were never crossed. *Panie* Eva had had no velvets amongst her garments, and certainly she would never have worn scarlet in any material—or purple silk, for that matter, since it was reserved for the highest royalty. Instead, Irina's choice became a dark-blue cotehardie over a dyed tan linen kirtle, and on her feet were well-made leather pattens over white hose. For persons of her stature, of course, cordwainers used tawed, not tanned, leather, which made her footgear stylish but not well suited for rough surfaces.

For Velka's role, Irina chose drab browns and greens for her tunic and skirting, along with a simple hooded cape. As a servant, Velka would not have been permitted hose to wear within her black felt boots. Irina scrutinized Velka's appearance carefully, and she made her "servant" do the same for her.

Thus transformed, Irina Kwasniewska and Velka hastily left the Joselewicz compound. A few steps up *ulica Zydowska*, the rustle of her gown spoke to her good fortune in having served in *Panie* Eva's household. Alone in an unforgiving world with no mother to help her sort things out, she called upon her memories of *Panie* Eva at social events to dictate what behaviors were appropriate for men and women when the Joselewiczes entertained well-heeled merchants. It was all she had.

Yip insisted on accompanying them and struggled to walk alongside, the pain undeterring to the brave little sheepdog, especially when a few moments later, Big Franciszek hove into view. Bumbling toward them, with worry crowding his face, the sheepdog bared his teeth, took an aggressive step, and commenced a long, low growl.

Velka whispered fiercely to Yip, and Irina put her arm on Velka's to steady them both as Franciszek came closer. The giant of a man looked neither happy nor fed as he hastened along Jewish Street, and in passing, he took no notice of them.

Irina breathed in relief, and turned her mental energies to what she would say if anyone challenged them. *Who are we? Why are we here? Do we have escorts? No guard for women alone? Why is a well-dressed lady traveling on foot with her servant?* Irina knew she had to have answers and began to puzzle them out.

The meandering, narrow, gritty streets of Poznan, still puddled from the rains, required the young women to use their wits in choosing every turn. Although both of them worked in the city, they, like most servants, had little reason to wander far from where they slept and ate, and so did not know the streets well. She thought they were headed back toward the island and the castle, but within a few minutes, she had no idea where they were. In vain, she tried to find the twin spires of the cathedral. They kept walking, so as not to appear lost in a city of strangers. On constant patrol, Yip kept the curious at bay.

In the early morning light, people were already at their day's labors while smoky fires cooked porridges or steeped hot coals the smithy would use to shoe horses and shape metals. The bakers, the tanners, the weavers, and the coopers were all at work. The smells of food, raw materials, the unbathed, and by-products of a city without sewers filled their nostrils. Irina caught bits of words as they walked, but she heard little of the previous night's rampages. It was as if they had never occurred. Plague and murder had not yet claimed the morning talk, it seemed.

Within an hour, they passed the shop of Laskowski the cobbler for the second time and Irina knew they had a problem. As they walked by, she saw the man look up from the leather last he was shaping, and when their eyes met, she realized he knew he'd seen the two of them earlier.

Irina panicked. Immediately, she understood he would wonder about two well-dressed women wandering through a craftsmen's alley twice in the same hour. At best, he might ignore them, but at worst, he would cause them undue and unwanted attention. As she reached for Velka's arm, her companion wasn't at her side, but was several feet away, her gaze apparently fastened only on the piles of dung in her path.

Tension arose in her voice. "Velka!" she commanded, her tone that of a mistress toward a servant. When the girl finally looked up, she said, "Come here, foolish girl! You have taken us the wrong way!"

Dumbfounded, Velka stopped and looked at Irina, her face wrinkled in puzzlement.

In a much softer voice, Irina said, "Never mind, girl. Come with me." Out of the cobbler's sight, she put her arm around Velka's shaking shoulders and said, "I am so sorry, sweet soul. We were almost found out, I think, and I said the first thing that came into my mind."

Velka's soft brown hair fell over her dampened eyes as she looked up at Irina's warm smile. "What is amiss, then?"

"I must be honest with you, Velka. I think we are lost. The alleys are so narrow, it's hard to see the sky to find the morning's sun. We will have to walk a bit further away until I can see our way forward."

"But who will you ask? Where are we going? Aren't you hungry yet?"

Irina stopped and faced her companion. "I don't know, Velka. We will have to find a square or a fountain, and then some food." She inhaled and let out her breath, waiting for other passersby to give her a bit of space. "Last night I had no faith that God exists, but now I have no choice but to seek His help."

Velka held back her tears, regaining her composure only when Irina once again put her arm around her. "Come. We will find our way."

After another round of aimless wandering with Yip as their

protector, they came upon a small square.

"Ah, we need to turn ourselves this way."

"How do you know that?"

"See the sun?" Irina pointed upward. Then she turned. "See over there? You can just make out a church spire. It is there where we want to go." She had no idea where their steps would take them. It wasn't to the cathedral that had two spires. The church they could see had only one.

Velka broke into a bright smile.

One thing Irina knew for certain was she and Velka could go nowhere near Jewish Street ever again. They could not appeal for help at the castle, and they could not make their way toward St. Michael. *We shall go in the one direction that takes us away from yesterday.*

Here and there, they saw the devastation wrought by mobs burning out their neighbors, encouraged, surely, by a few sips of ale. "It's easy to see where some of the Jewish merchants had their shops," Irina said. "The only good fortune to have visited here came with the heavy rains that kept the fires from sweeping the city. These fools almost let their hate burn them all out."

She kept her eyes on the distant spire as they gathered the stares of many. *Is it because of the colors we wear?* Where the working men and women were garbed in browns, grays, and dull greens, Irina's top was dark blue and trimmed in rabbit fur, while Velka's dress, though simple, was well made. Only Yip's presence, ever wary and unfriendly to all, gave them some assurance of safety.

As the pair walked along, they talked in low voices about the horrors they'd been through overnight, but Irina decided her companion need not be burdened with her losses. To Irina, none of it seemed possible, yet it had happened. It was a lesson, she knew, for her heart and head never to forget. *Life is short. Do not hesitate—and there is no time for sadness.*

After a long silence, Velka said, "When we reach the spire, then what?"

"I do not know. What I do know is we had to leave Jewish Street— and what we saw there."

"Are you scared, Irina?"

"Last night, I was scared out of my wits." When she said this, she stopped, turned around, and faced her "servant." "What I learned, Velka," her voice steely in resolve, "was that being scared did not help me and it did not save the Joselewiczes. So, no, today I am not scared. Today, we take charge of our own lives. Understand?"

"I think so, but I'm not like you, Irina."

"Then will you trust me—no matter what?" Even as she said the words, Irina knew she had to hide the fear she felt.

"Yes, Irina."

"Then try to remember. I am now Lady Irina Kwasniewska, and you are my servant." She looked down at Yip. "And you're to take care of both of us," she said to the dog, and scratched his neck. Yip's tail signaled ready acceptance of his duty.

"I understand, My Lady," Velka said, crying softly, and showing every bit of her age.

At that, Irina continued their procession. Irina had chosen her words carefully. She had almost said being scared had not saved "my Berek." Velka did not know about their love. She did not know about the baby she was carrying.

"Why did it have to happen?" whispered Velka.

"I heard people say the plague is amongst us."

"Have you seen anyone with plague?"

"No. Not so far. Listen to what the people are saying. It makes no sense to me. But plague is plague, and people blame the Jews. We must take care."

As the morning wore on, they began to hear muttered rumblings of pestilence, passed from person to person, from wharf to wayfare. It was said the disease came from Srodka, and that the Jews had been caught poisoning wells.

Leaning toward the ear of her servant, Irina whispered, "They know what they've heard from the person next to them." What the elder Joselewicz said was true: news was always tainted by ignorance, and good sense seldom overruled rumor. She noticed, too, that such news was passed on with both glee and terror. Glee, because it gave them something important to say, and terror, because they knew the plague might come for them. Irina made sure she and Velka kept moving.

"Why do these people hate our Jews? The Joselewiczes—all the people we know—would never harm anyone," Velka said.

"I know," Irina said. "These people know that, too, but hate needs no reason."

"Why hate the Jews?"

She is so innocent. "Envy breeds hate, dear one. What's more is that for some reason people always fear those who are different, and for those who they fear and come to hate? God help them."

Not long after she had assured Velka no plague was to be seen, they spotted three people bent over, retching in the muddy alleyways that passed for thoroughfares. Other people out and about noticed them as well and stepped well clear of the ill ones. Irina, too, had vomited that morning, but she knew it was the sickness her mother had had each time she was with child. She knew it would soon pass, but she did not want anyone to see her. She had told Velka she did not feel well, and not to worry. *Velka wants to trust me, and I must never let her down.*

The evening before, when Irina had been so fixated on her reason to hurry back to the city, she had not fully considered the possibility that she could be one of the many who would soon sicken and die. *The strangers warned me, didn't they!*

She reminded Velka—and herself—that seeing people sick in the street was not all that unusual. Sickness of one kind or another—often from rotten food—was ever-present. The young women did not pause to observe those who were obviously ill, yet well enough to step outside for whatever bodily discharge overcame them. Stench fouled the morning air, and in a natural reaction, the pair kept their mouths and noses covered.

As they walked, Irina noticed something else. Without much noise or notice, the merchant and middle classes were already throwing large sacks of belongings into carts. "They will depart the city for any refuge their coin pouches might buy them," Irina said to her companion.

"I see. And they make no farewells to anyone outside their household," whispered Velka.

"Ah, but look. A few servants will leave with them, and the rest will have to look after themselves. No escape for them!" Irina saw Velka quickly cast her eyes downward. Sensing another thought might cross Velka's mind. She added, "Never to worry. I would never leave you."

Velka looked up, beaming.

"And the poor," Irina continued. "They, too, are terrified, but they cannot ready themselves to leave. They have no possessions, and they have nowhere to go. I heard *Pan* Joselewicz say that the underclasses were the first to face life's demons. At the table one time, he told the family there was no point in trying to outrun a terror, only to meet up with it down the road." Irina hoped their talking might make them appear less afraid to some who might take advantage of them. "Even so, we are not waiting here for our fate."

Not long after their scare by the curious cobbler, they were moving slowly amongst the hustling mass of people when a tall, nearly tooth-less man barred their way. In a loud voice, he said to Irina, looking her up and down, "What are the likes of you two doing here amongst the poor? Why aren't you leaving the city along with your rich folk?"

Irina wrapped her hand around the thick silk strings of her pouch, ready to swing her ball of precious metals at the man's head if need be.

"It does not concern you why we are here. Now, step out of the way," Irina demanded.

Brave with morning ale, no doubt, the lout did not give way. "Let's see what you might be carrying in your little bag," he said, reaching out to take from Irina the means for their survival. Before his hand could reach his prize, however, Yip leapt from the ground, pain and all, and clamped his jaws on the man's wrist. The would-be robber yelped in pain and tried to shake off the dog, reaching at the same time for a knife with his free hand.

At once, Velka stepped forward, knocked his knife hand aside and kicked him solidly in the groin. Next, she grabbed Yip's collar and tugged him away while their assailant doubled over. Without so much as a look around to the growing crowd, Velka extended her hand and said, "My Lady?" a sign to her mistress they could proceed.

Wide-eyed and astonished, Irina grasped Velka's arm and the two of them walked on, equally impressed murmurings from the crowd filling the air behind them.

The incident reminded her of what the elder Joselewicz said one day after a Gentile tradesman had left. "Do you know in what way a man is like a wolf?" He turned his head to look at her and raised his eyebrow in expectation of a good answer, but when Irina remained silent, he said, "In *every* way! Watch out, Irina—the wolves are everywhere." *How well he knew!* She then recalled her father warning her about wolves, too. Only he was talking about being alone on a pathway. "They come from nowhere," he had said. "Usually in packs of two or three—all the easier to bring down their prey." The more she thought about it, the more she realized how lucky she had been not to have encountered a predator on her walk from St. Michael to Poznan. She shivered. *Was it luck? Or was someone watching over me?*

As they walked on, Irina couldn't help but admire the tiny Velka, a mere girl who didn't let her size defeat her. Irina made up her mind that in a world filled with the kind of wolves old Joselewicz and her father cautioned her about, they would learn to fear. *Whether someone is watching me or not, I will be sure to watch out for myself. No oaf will get the better of me, no matter how much shade he makes!*

By late morning, they were near the city's newer parts when Velka muttered something about not having eaten anything that day. Despite all the smells of stews and soups, of breads and pastries, they dared not stop.

Finally, they'd reached the great spire. It stood atop the Church of the Heart of Jesus, they learned, and its stone finger pointed to where the noonday sun would soon take its position. Irina looked first at the church, then at Velka.

"We'll go in for a bit."

"Why? It's a church. Aren't you hungry?" she demanded yet again.

"I'm starved, but we need a bit of rest. This is a good place for rest and gratitude."

"What have you to be grateful for? We've lost everything! Our family in the city, the place where we slept and ate," she protested, fighting another round of tears.

Irina smiled at her young companion. Though not many years

separated them, the difference seemed vast. Velka could think only about what lay immediately ahead. Irina, on the other hand, knew more than their empty stomachs mattered this morning.

"Just two hours ago, we were lost, and now, we are found. That is enough reason to visit this place." Truly conflicted, her inner feelings conveyed another emotion, she knew. *I cannot forget last night and a God not very almighty.* Yet habit was habit, and for some reason, she was still standing, and in front of His own house. *Where else do we have to go?*

They climbed the steps, seven in all, to reach the great front doors, each three times as high as the people who walked through them.

"Yip! Stay here." The sheepdog wagged its tail a few times and rested on its haunches where the sun warmed the stone and, no doubt, the poor dog's hurts. As they entered, they heard a choir singing a hymn to Mary, the Mother of God. The nuns' voices rang in great beauty throughout the stone cavern. Irina hoped the priest would not see them—she would not have much to say to him. On Sundays, she was allowed to attend Mass at the cathedral, the church closest to the Joselewicz compound, but, she thought, the priest there was no man of God. He was a man of the altar wine, and died from it. *I have no reason to trust a priest right now.*

Rapt in their attention to the beautiful words of the song, the pair found a place for themselves and knelt on the stone floor. The deep blue of Irina's gown caught the light gilded by the single stained-glass window high above them.

"So, you have come to speak to Jesus's heart?"

The strange voice startled her. "Y-yes. Y-yes, Sister," Irina responded as she looked up at the woman in white and black above her. "In truth, there is much to say."

"Indeed. It is good to see those who honor the Almighty with their presence," the nun replied. She was dressed mostly in heavy woolens but wore a starched, white wimple that surrounded her face and draped over her shoulders. "I am Sister Mary Elisabeth, Mother Superior of our convent here."

"Oh. This is a convent?" She did not offer their names.

"Yes, we are the Dominican Sisters, in service to this parish, and to the poor of Poznan. Is there something we can do for you?" These words were relayed with the utmost kindness, a tenderness so different from what they'd experienced the past day and night.

Velka had never known her parents, and Irina had just lost her own to anger and fear. Her eyes became teary and Velka could hardly suppress her tears when hearing the older nun extend her heart to them.

"We do not wish to impose," said Irina, quickly recovering, and remembering their roles as mistress and servant, "but we have been travelling through your city the entire morning, and have not found a safe place to take bread." She took a deep breath. "I am so sorry, Sister. I am Irina Kwasnieska and this is Velka, my attendant."

Irina watched the older nun carefully. She wasn't sure the woman believed her. Sister Elisabeth seemed to be making up her mind about something as she took in their mud-spattered clothing. Finally, she nodded to herself and said, "Come, my children. We will feed you. I want to hear all about you and your travels." She smiled broadly. "And your other companion may join us," she said with a wide smile, nodding toward the shaggy dog that had followed them inside and crept quietly out of the shadows.

...

Tomasz refused to be seen running anywhere but to his duke's command. Even so, he propelled himself at a quickstep to the Joselewicz house, his furtive, dark eyes glancing in every direction as he went along. Once there, he stepped across the courtyard, giving the smoldering piles of char nary a regret. He took to the stairs, three at a time. At the top, Big Franciszek stood guard, just inside the doorway.

"Did you look around?" Tomasz demanded.

"No, Sire, I thought I should wait for you."

"You shouldn't think, Franciszek, but it's good you waited. I wanted to see if things were as I left them." He paused, rubbing his temple. "Not that I remember all that clearly." Tomasz stood in the center of the room and inventoried what he saw. He walked into each sleeping room and back into the main room.

"Someone has been here. The Jew girl's clothes are gone and some of the mother's things are missing as well. It makes no sense! You're sure no one was here?!"

"I'm sure, Sire. I was awake until very late," he lied.

Something about one of the large cabinets caught Tomasz's eye. Stepping through the pool of blood, now nearly dry, Tomasz kicked aside the hand pointing its guilty finger at him, and stood staring. As he swung its doors wide, full daylight filled the interior, and he saw it.

"God's curses! Look at this—a secret door. Someone was here!" He ran his hands all around on the inside of the cavity. "This must be where the real treasure was hidden. Those filthy Jews! We should have done a bit of work on them—we let them off too easy!"

"Yes, Sire," Franciszek agreed, then looked away and muttered something about the bonfires—"but not an easy death, to be sure."

Tomasz glowered at his underling. He would repay the insolence later. "Someone must have stayed hidden here all the time you were awake," he said with biting sarcasm.

"Yes, Sire," he said again, this time in submission.

"We'll have to find whoever it was. Are any of the servants left alive?"

"I don't know, Sire. Who can I ask?" Franciszek laughed, and said, foolishly, "We killed all the Jews and their people."

Tomasz swung an open hand hard across the side of Franciszek's head. The big man did not move fast enough.

Returning his gaze to the cabinet, Tomasz said, "The space behind the secret door is too small for a large man. It was for the mother and daughter. One way or another, we'll get them. Nobody gets away from me and takes what is mine. I'll find out who it is if it's the last thing I do."

A clatter of boots running up the stairs broke their talk. It was one of the duke's house guards.

"Hurry, Sire Tomasz, the duke wants you back at the castle immediately. You must supervise the packing. The duke insists on leaving first thing in the morning."

"Why so fast?"

"Plague. It's already spreading in the city!"

. . .

Jerzy Andrezski saw the Kwasniewskis shamble down the Fareway as one large family and thought them good people. He had wished them well as they parted from the caravan, and he went on to haggle over goods he might take on a return trip. He'd agreed to meet the caravan master on the castle wharf to take charge of his goods and property, so he had at least an hour to himself.

As he sauntered from shop to stall to shed, surveying the wares of the leatherers, trinket makers, and ironmongers, he sought the bread and pastry stalls for a bit of sweet sustenance. Then he would be off to the city, hoping to meet some of the traders there with a view to a profitable arrangement, something that had thus far eluded him.

At one of the pastry stalls, where a good-sized crowd had gathered, he spied the littlest girl belonging to the Kwasniewskis, and assumed the mother or father were nearby. Smiling, he remembered she and the other children had been enthralled by his stories of derring-do amongst the Cossacks.

Further down the hill, he stopped at a less crowded place and leaned against a tent pole until the girl working there spoke to him. Finally, she said, "Sir, are you alright?"

Surprised by the question, he said, "Of course. Why do you ask?"

"You look so pale, sir, and your eyes are shining."

"It's nothing. I've had a long journey, and now I need something to eat and drink."

She waited on him, and he sat nearby under a shade tree to enjoy the modest repast. Aloud, but to no one, he said, "Phew! I didn't think it was so warm today."

A bit unsteadily, he rose and took himself to the bottom of the Fareway, where he saw the Kwasniewskis napping against the retaining wall. He decided not to disturb them, feeling as he did, and thought only to find lodgings in Poznan for the night.

Across the bridge and onto the island they called *Ostrow Tumski*, he dragged himself further into the ancient city of narrow streets, strong smells, and wary people. The longer he remained on his feet, the more he felt sickness overtake him. He decided to see the caravan master on the morrow. His mind seemed a bit fuzzy as he studied his surroundings, but he had long ago learned that if sick in a strange city, the best thing to do was find a big church with a convent. The nuns were always good for a bit of care, and he strained to make one foot go in front of the other.

...

Maria, Marta, and Josef made it to the bridge just as a church bell clanged the quarter hour. Feverish, Maria could see her little ones were not well. "Bad food," Maria muttered, refusing to let any other thought command her thinking.

Within a few minutes, Ignacz stumbled into view. Maria could see people stepping aside as he wobbled like a midday drunkard. Little Stephan complained of being cold while Ignacz shed streams of sweat onto his tunic.

"It must have been moldy bread we ate up the hill," Maria continued to insist, her look revealing altogether different emotions. "Or they used rancid lard."

"No Zuzzie," Ignacz said, then repeated it. "No Zuzzie!" He put his head in his hands as he leaned against the cold stone wall. Sweating profusely, all he could do was give her a glance of compassion.

Maria cried. "In one day, we have lost two daughters! Our oldest and youngest, gone!" Maria knew in her soul she was too weak to climb back up the Fareway. At first, she tried to tell herself not to worry, that someone would take care of her Zuzanna. Then she forced herself to her feet.

"Wait here!" she stated with all her strength. "I will look once more. You rest with the children."

Ignacz's eyes rolled in his head. Too exhausted to argue, he slumped down next to the stone parapet, spying as he did so clusters of flowers caressing the river's edge. They were drowning in black ash. He wanted only to close his eyes.

"Ignacz!" Maria commanded. "You must stay awake—you must watch the little ones."

Hours passed, it seemed, or maybe mere seconds. Maria returned, eyes reddened, despite her otherwise frigid reserve. She bent low to Ignacz, grasped his shoulders, and said resignedly, "Let's get across the bridge. We can talk to the gatekeeper at the castle about Irina and Zuzanna. Maybe someone can point for us where the Joselewiczes live."

Together, the five of them walked, swayed, stumbled their way over the Warta. When at last they made it to the gate, the guard there spied them with both distrust and fear.

"Here, now! Don't come closer." Others nearby heard the guard and surveyed the Kwasniewskis warily. "You're sick! Don't you know there's plague about?"

"Plague!" exclaimed Maria, bewildered. But as she looked at Ignacz and the children, she suddenly knew what she had earlier shut from her mind. "Of course not! It's the rotten bread those pigs in Srodka sold us. All of us ate some. We'll never again buy another thing there!"

. . .

"Tell me about your journey," Sister Elisabeth inquired of her two young guests as the sun shone brightly over the high church roof and into the adjoining convent's courtyard. New shade granted by the sun's afternoon shadows felt cool and refreshing. The nun was more than a little curious about the girls in front of her. They were well-dressed young women of apparent means, but things did not seem right to her practiced eye.

"We have been walking through the city, but lost for a time, I'm afraid." Irina said the words but seemed uncertain about them.

"Oh? Where are you coming from?"

"Near Gniezno." Irina hesitated, apparently unwilling to say more. She lowered her eyes, her face flushed.

The nun saw signs she had often seen before. "What's the matter, my child? Why don't you tell me?"

Irina took a deep breath. She took two more bites of bread and cheese, apparently considering her words. Velka sat stone-like behind her mistress. She seemed scared, but of what, the old nun could not fathom.

After taking a sip of wine, Irina began to speak. "My husband, Berek, and I, along with our attendant," she began, "left Gniezno a week ago, sent west by his family with an armed escort so that we'd be safe from the plague." She glanced at Velka.

"Why just you three? Why not the rest of the family?" Sister Elisabeth inquired gently.

"I am with child, and the family insisted we leave quickly. They said they would follow. There was talk of plague everywhere. Coming from the east," she added.

Mother Superior listened quietly, reserving judgment.

"I'm in my third month, I think, Sister Elisabeth." Irina dared not look at Velka.

"I see. And where is your husband and the rest of your party?" At once, Mother Superior realized she was asking too much. She said, "I'm sorry for so many questions, but you have aroused my curiosity."

"My Berek is dead," Irina stated matter-of-factly. "We were travelling in a small group when we were attacked by highwaymen. Berek defended us as best he could, as did the two soldiers with us, but he was killed along with one of the men." She held her eyes closed for a moment.

"And what happened to the other guard? You didn't want to turn back?" Sister Elisabeth waited for the tears that did not come.

"Our escort knew the family's plan and refused to disobey orders, but he was afraid. He brought us to the castle in Poznan, but left us before dawn. What happened here in the city must have frightened him. Then our horses disappeared. Perhaps he felt his duty was done."

"You didn't think to stay at the castle, then? Duke Zygmunt would have sheltered you."

At this, Irina hesitated. "We did stay there, Sister" she lied again, "but without an introduction to the duke. The castellan was gone, and there seemed to be a good deal of commotion with everyone hurrying to load carts and pack horses. Then the storm came and the turmoil became even greater. One of the duke's housemen put us in a room and saw to our needs."

"And this morning?"

"The household did not seem to have time to deal with strangers."

"You weren't taken to the duke?"

"No, Sister. I decided our best course was to leave, and we did so just after dawn, when we discovered our guard had run off."

The nun nodded and smiled, having been offered an incredible tale. Two well-dressed women with a guard—if one existed—could not have been ignored. "If I may ask, Irina, you seemed to be thanking God. For what are you grateful?" She knew it was an odd but understandable question.

"At least the soldier brought us this far. We have our lives and coin, and so far, the Great Mortality has not touched us! And Mother Superior," she said, bowing her head forward in respect, "we were led to this haven, to you."

Sister Elisabeth smiled with pleasure. She was sure that most of what she heard was only a distant cousin to the truth, but she could not discern where truth and falsehood failed to meet. The young mistress seemed very unsure of herself. "Please excuse me. The church is unusually busy this afternoon. Our pastor is not," she said, pausing to collect the best words, "here to direct us. I shall return shortly." Rising to leave, she turned and said, "Please rest. When I come back, we shall talk about what we should do with you."

. . .

As the afternoon wore on, the perfect Poznan sky had gone to heavy, ash-gray clouds hanging low over the Warta River valley. Jerzy Andrezski had already shed his cloak, as it seemed too much for him to carry. He was short of breath, and by the time he found a shady place at the fountain in the great square fronting the Heart of Jesus, he could hardly stand.

He watched the church's giant bronze doors, surprised to see the number of men, women, and children entering there in the middle of the day. The nuns greeted them all, he was pleased to see, and it took him several moments to realize why so many were seeking the church's sanctuary. Was it a place of miracles?

From his years of experience and travel, Jerzy knew what was happening to them—and to him. People called it the Black Death because for many, skin would turn a black or a deep blue. A few days later, large swellings would appear, often on the neck, and there would be fever, chills, and uncontrolled vomiting. Jerzy had seen children abandon parents and parents abandon children in the hope of avoiding their fate. Otherwise, the stricken lay in suffering for a week before God's mercy came to them.

For some reason, he had learned in the east, some would die within a day, practically overnight. It was another kind of plague—what they called the Great Mortality—because those who died quickly never developed the ugly, visible marks on their bodies, but death was death. For either visitor, the doctors had no known potion or poultice. Lucky ones were not touched by the plague, and no one knew why, but of those who were, nearly all died. *Will one of these grim take me?*

Resigned to his end, he stood and decided that if he was to die, doing so in the very bosom of God's house made sense to him. The hereafter must be better than this, he thought, though belief in an Almighty was something about which he was far from certain. At the top step, he waited for still others to gain entrance. "I am a merchant from the caravan," he said in a bare whisper to the nuns who greeted him. They did not seem to mind grasping his arm and helping him along. His voice was weak, his skin wet with fever. "Will you take me in?"

Sisters Elisabeth and Eugenia welcomed the large man of middle age, garbed in wealth but carrying death. "Yes, this is a place for those in need of rest," the older nun said caringly.

He forced his misty eyes full open and spoke his mind, with words that seemed not his own. "I will not die," he droned, "because you will save me."

"Just what is the name of this man I must save?" asked Mother Superior with bemused concern, but tenderness underneath. She seemed surprised he had found their door.

"It is Jerzy Andrezski who will serve you, Mother."

Sister Elisabeth smiled as if she would not know him long, as if he would soon serve their one Master in another world. As with all the others admitted, she became busy making the merchant comfortable.

· · ·

As the day rushed to its end with smoke and clouds crowding the sunset, Ignacz knew his family needed rest. They were bone weary and very sick, but their search for a place to lay their heads proved futile. Everywhere, people wanted nothing to do with them. No one knew anything about anyone named Irina, and no one would speak about the Jews. Most puzzling, people denied any knowledge of the Joselewiczes. Irina was gone, and Zuzanna seemed hopelessly lost.

At last, they found a cow barn a few lanes back from a main thoroughfare, itself near the great market square. Without troubling to find the owner, they entered and Maria collapsed into the hay, too tired to cry out.

"*Matka*," Ignacz said, uttering one word in such a way as to speak whole paragraphs to a woman he'd loved his entire life. As he knelt beside her, it took all of his strength just to speak the two sounds of that one endearment.

"Ignacz, we are dying. The caravan. The caravan brought us the plague. And we didn't find Irina. Poor Irina! Zuzanna! The children, where are they?"

Ignacz thought first about their sons at the farm. The plague would not find them there, he hoped. He saw through bleary eyes Marta and Josef, with blue eyes and the beautiful yellow hair of sunshine and innocence, and little Stephan, with big, soft, brown eyes like those of a small deer. They were snuggled against their mother. "They're here with us, Maria. Who can know about Zuzzie?"

Maria forced back her tears, having no time for sadness, after all. With strength leaving her, she sighed. "Perhaps she will be the lucky one."

· · ·

Several minutes had elapsed before Sister Elisabeth returned to Irina, appearing weary and worried. She sat heavily, and after a deep breath, brought her attention to the young women with a soft smile. "And so, Lady Irina Kwasniewska, what shall we do for you?"

Irina brightened when she heard herself addressed with respect. After some moments, she found her words. "Truthfully, Mother Superior, I am not sure what to do now, but we should trouble you no longer, and should be on our way." She paused. "I am not without means, however," she said hastily, but in a manner that might have mimicked one of the Joselewicz clan, "and I am willing to offer support to your convent in gratitude for whatever assistance you may provide."

Sister Elisabeth seemed to be appraising her. Finally, she spoke. "If you have been travelling for several days or a week, it is possible you have not touched the plague—unlike so many others," she said, tilting her head toward the front of the church." She paused, obviously pondering something.

The door to the meeting room opened, and an older, determined nun walked directly to her superior, bent low, and whispered a few words. Irina could not make them out, but sensed the intensity of the message. The older nun bowed slightly and left.

"It seems," their benefactress proceeded quietly, "that God has made your decision for you." Before Irina could ask, she continued. "Sister Rose informs me that Duke Zygmunt and his people are about to leave the city, if they haven't left already. Apparently, those were the duke's preparations you saw and heard at the castle. As it happens, Bishop Tirasewicz is himself readying some members of his palace and desires that some of the sisters join him. Perhaps tomorrow morning. Because you are in a position to recompense the bishop, you and your servant may be welcome on this journey. I will find out. Thus, you will be provided safe travel."

"Oh, Sister, I am most grateful, but will you not be going?" Irina's voice broke.

"No, my young lady, I am not. I, along with most of the sisters, will remain to care for those who need it. There will be much to do. Two sisters, I think, shall accompany you and Velka. You should prepare yourselves immediately."

"But the bishop is going?"

The Mother Superior cast her gaze to the stone floor, and when she looked back at Irina, her face was like stone. "I'm sure the bishop has left many good men to hear last confessions. Go now."

"Thank you, Mother!" Tears cornered in the young woman's eyes. *How much more emotion can I bear?* They had learned enough to know that of those who remained, few would survive. Irina reached into her precious pouch and pulled out a gold coin. "You will need this."

The Mother Superior's eyes, too, were moist. She embraced each young woman, saying, "Bless you. Go now to the very back of our convent—you will need your night's rest, and you," she said, looking directly at Irina, "have still another life to care for."

• • •

In his position as civil leader and master of the city and its environs, Duke Zygmunt made it his business to know everything of importance before anyone else in his retinue. Before his baker, before his bishop.

In one day, two messages had arrived that changed everything. An invitation to Paris and a warning about plague gave him two reasons not to dawdle. Whether rumors about the Jews were true mattered little to him, although he found the accusations somehow satisfying. Whatever Tomasz had done was done. What could he do about it? One thing he could do, he concluded with a smile, was to ensure every last trinket Tomasz and others had taken would be considered a tax on their misbehavior. If the Jews were dead or gone, well, so be it. The castle coffers could always bear filling.

"And what a fine piece of chance that this wealth should come when so many need to travel to Paris—at my expense," he ruminated aloud. He chuckled. His only concern throughout the evening was the pious attitude of his counselor, a man who held the high moral ground and was not so easily mollified. "Poor priest, he just does not know how the world works."

The plague, alas, was real, and could not be wished aside. There had hardly been a year since mid-century when the dread disease had not struck somewhere in the vastness of the kingdoms surrounding his own, stealing the lives of thousands. Wherever the pestilence chanced to light, it was like a deranged bird in random flight dropping the seeds of its evil fruit. It had been some years since one variety or another had inflicted itself upon Zygmunt Sokorski's domain, but he decided to elude its grasp, if at all possible.

The duke and his entourage of nearly forty fortunate souls, family, servants, and soldiers decamped from Poznan in record time. Had the storm not appeared Sunday evening, he might have left the city by Tuesday morning, but the storm's severity made his schedule for him.

Interestingly, he thought to himself, smiling, the threat of plague had somehow made the drying process go faster, and with hard work, all was ready on Wednesday morning. Preparing for a journey to so distant a place as Paris would have been tedious at another time, but having to do so in the spring made everything easier. They were travelling light, he knew, but fortunately, many royal houses along the way would give them comfort and replenishment.

To no one would he ever admit his abject fear of an end from plague. Before battle, he had been scared, but when men faced each other with swords, he could defend himself. Plague permitted no defense, knew no class, and rarely left survivors. That fact he well knew. He needed no excuse to leave the city in advance of the Great Mortality, but an invitation from the Holy Roman Emperor made haste even more desirable—and convenient.

Two hours before the day managed its end, he and the favored few departed. It was not customary for an entourage to depart so close to nightfall, only to set camp some few miles distant, but the duke knew that to wait even a few hours endangered them all. Moreover, he guessed it could be most difficult to leave the city by next light once news of plague maddened the lower classes—and laborers within the castle—beyond even his control. He wondered if Bishop Tirasewicz would take his leave of the city in time. He wondered, too, if their departure would even make a difference in their living or dying.

. . .

Irina and Velka, along with Sisters Margaret and Marta, their bundles of clothing, and Rosta, a serving man, all awaited the bishop's blessedly delayed assemblage. As the minutes passed, Irina studied Sister Marta. She was immediately drawn to the young nun, if for no other reason than she had the same name as one of her little sisters. It made her wonder about her family, if they missed her, and if they truly despised what she had done. In her mind's eye, she could see little Zuzanna winking at her and smiling broadly.

When, at last, the bishop's wagons rumbled into view, a high tension prevailed, but it was not Mother Superior who came to greet him. It was Sister Rose who bowed in homage to His Grace, Antony Tirasewicz.

"Excellency. Mother Superior is indisposed and begs your pardon for not greeting you. She and several of the sisters are making their way through the city to secure provisions and prepare for what's to come." Her look suggested Mother Superior would never beg his pardon, but the old nun kept to her best manners.

"No offense taken," Bishop Tirasewicz responded, not offering his ring to be kissed. It was as if he wanted no contact, even from atop his coal black stallion. In his high, thin voice, devoid of emotion, he inquired, "Are these the ones Mother Superior wishes me to take under my protection?"

"Yes, Bishop." There was no respect, only obedience. "Lady Irina Kwasniewska and her serving girl will be with you, as well as Sisters Margaret and Marta. Rosta will take care of their baggage."

The cleric shot his piercing gaze in the nun's direction, and looking down at her over his hawk-like nose, he parted his thin lips to form his words with a superior tone. "I hope Mother Superior knows what an expense I must bear to take these strangers."

"She does, Bishop." In so saying, Sister Rose cast a glance in Irina's direction.

"Excellency," Irina said in a quiet voice, bowing deeply, "we are prepared to support ourselves and these others of the convent in gratitude for your own generosity." Irina carried off her imitation of nobility with grace. The bishop smiled in return, especially when offered a small pouch, clearly of some weight. He looked askance at the dog by the woman's side, but she carried gold, and he didn't seem to mind touching it.

"Welcome, my children," he said with a broad, forced smile. "Let's be off. We are half a day behind Duke Zygmunt and we must join him in two days' time if we are to have his protection in the days ahead."

. . .

"Should we be taking this child?" the young novice asked her Mother Superior, as they and two workingmen made their way back toward church and its sanctuary.

Mother Superior did not respond. She and her two young assistants sought whatever foodstuffs they could buy and carry, not for themselves, but for the few who would survive the plague. Too, they would sweep the streets of those visibly ill. In the case of the pretty little girl, she could not fend for herself. Now they were laden with food, ale, several stricken adults, and a small child.

Mother Superior knew from prior visits of the dreaded disease that time was not a friend to them. Of the two kinds of plague, the more aggressive variety allowed its prey no chance to say goodbye, no consolation of a priest's blessing. Sadly, the dying somehow shared the disease with nearly everyone who spent even the briefest time with them. Whatever the circumstance, the nun knew, in the end, there was nothing to do for any of them except make their last hours of some comfort. Everyone was at risk, but aloud, to no one in particular, she said, "What else is to be done?"

"You said something, Mother?"

It was too early to determine what kind of plague had come to them this beautiful May. Everyone knew that the springs and summers had been wetter the past few years, and the winters, harshly cold. With the damp days and nights, people seemed more prone to illness, and the plague spread like a flooding stream after a torrential rain.

In the meantime, the nuns had already collected six or seven people who were clearly ill, but could walk. She tied them, one to another, with a heavy string, so that they would stay together and follow her to the convent courtyard, where, she knew, most would see their last bit of sunshine. In hours, there would be many more, and the nuns would go out again like the fishermen on the river casting their nets.

"Yes, in answer to your question, Sister," she finally said to the trembling novice, barely sixteen years of age. Each time the plague struck, the Dominicans performed their mercies, and a number of them would die. Mother Superior herself had thus far eluded the grim reaper, but she wondered how many in her charge would be alive by the end of May. "Yes," she repeated, "this one seems to have no one to care for her, and if her people are able, they will know where to come to find a lost child."

Then, leaning down and giving the child a big smile, she asked, "What is your name, little one?"

The little girl did not respond to the question but asked one of her own as the lady in black reached for her hand. "Do you know where my mama and papa are? Did they leave me?"

"Of course not, little one. They will come to the church to find you."

The child smiled brightly, happy to be in someone's care, anyone's care.

At the church, the young novice took the little girl to the kitchen where Sister Rose, the cook—and the only nun older than Sister Elisabeth—could keep an eye on her.

Sister Rose bent low and with a broad smile that spread wrinkles all over her face, looked at the child closely. The little one in front of her did not seem to be from the city, judging by the homespun, simple clothing, ragged from wear and giving off wisps of a barnyard. The child's soft, light-brown curls, tinged with auburn, topped a serious and pretty face.

"And did you tell the other sister your name, little one?"

The girl did not respond at first, but said, at last, "They call me Zuzzie."

"Child," she said, "it is as if you just left here. You could be Lady Irina's little sister!"

CHAPTER IV

1378

Stanislaus the potter profited little from his time in Srodka. The usual run of business wasn't there, and indeed, as he scratched his beard and pulled a nit from its depths, people seemed to be moving faster all day long and few wanted to buy.

Mutterings about the Jews and the Great Mortality were aplenty, but he knew from years chatting with caravanners one had nothing to do with the other. It did little good to tell people that, however. It was the only truth they knew, after all. And when they were in a growl about something, they bought little from the stalls.

He hadn't wanted to stay the night in Srodka, but all the craziness in the city meant it would not have been safe to make his way back to his small household in Poznan. He'd had a miserable sleep, but this morning, he trudged his way down the Fareway, laden with straw-packed sacks of bowls, cups, and simple pitchers.

At the far side of the Mary & Josef, he took a good look around him. The arrival of eastern caravans usually heralded excitement, cele-bratory noise, and quenched thirsts. Today the voices around him told a different story, however. Sounds of the night before were burdened with the fear of being on the wrong side of the mob. The evidence of spent wrath was everywhere. Overturned carts, a dead horse here and there, a number of burnt houses, and not a few untended bodies, already beginning to bloat, created obstacles in his path. Flies flour-ished, but not on him.

With his precious goods in hand, Stanislaus danced over the

wasted goods and lives and hurried on his way. Already, there was a stench clinging to the air. From loosed bowels and decaying flesh, the air seemed thick with more death.

As he pondered this, he began to perspire and seemed unduly weary from his short journey, one he'd made hundreds of times. His soiled tunic became damp with sweat, and the wooden rack of goods on his back grew heavy. Perhaps it was a good thing the shop wouldn't be busy this day, though a few extra pennies for food wouldn't hurt.

Once back at Poznan, he first checked to see if anything had been filched, a frequent occurrence with no one around to attend things. His wife and three children had died of fever some years before, and now he was alone. Next, he went around back to the barn and stood at the entrance, his form casting a long shadow across the hay-strewn mud floor. He swore again as he saw shapes sleeping there. Then he noticed that flies had gathered on them and that none of them slapped away at the rats scampering over their legs.

Stepping closer, he kicked at the legs of the man. Stiff, he was. They were dead, all of them. Apparently, a mother and father with three little ones. Dead. But of what? There wasn't a mark on them. They just seemed at peace, as if in deep slumber after a long day's work.

What killed them? It couldn't be plague, he reasoned. None of the five had the telltale buboes or festering blisters he had seen years before. Stanislaus decided not to take chances. Why would this family die all together, all at once, and in his barn? It was puzzling, to be sure. They weren't there yesterday morning, he knew, and it was an aggravation he didn't need.

He hurried to find a cart so they could be taken away, quietly. With some effort, he hoisted the bodies onto the cart's wooden bed. He felt badly for the family, but worse for himself. He couldn't stop sweating, and now his head hurt. They weren't his responsibility, but if neighbors knew they died in his barn, they might burn his house—and with him in it.

Slowly, quietly, while many were napping after their midday meal, he pushed the cart, overladen and covered with straw, to a nearby field and dumped the bodies there. On the way back, he thought about things. Whether the Jews did anything to deserve their fate or not, life was bound to be better without them. But without them, he wondered, who would people blame for their bad fortune?

He swatted away the flies that now seemed to follow him as he wandered back to his barn. When he felt his strength begin to drain, as rainwater from a gutter, he thought it was from all the exertion lifting and dumping the dead ones.

· · ·

As Bishop Tirasewicz hurried his entourage to depart the city, their progress was slowed by the poor and sickly who surrounded them begging for food or coin. Orders to his armed outriders were clear. "Ignore them," he commanded. His closed lips were as tight as his purse. "In a few days, they won't have need for money or food." The caravan stopped for no one and no reason.

Heading in the general direction of Silesia, the caravan could have the river carry it, but the river would not take them to the one place Bishop Tirasewicz wanted to be—within the protection of Duke Zygmunt Sokorski. Besides, it seemed to him that plague always followed the rivers, not the woods.

Carts, wagons, and horses served as conveyances for most of the party. The bishop and his priests rode horses while simple carriages—carts with solid wooden wheels—carried Irina, Velka, and the two nuns. Rosta and all the other servants walked. Six armed men, soldiers in truth, accompanied the party. Having a dog along proved a good addition—that little Yip was an attentive watchdog, the bishop noticed, but he proclaimed his hope that "the beast doesn't eat too much."

Because the roads were little more than rock-strewn tracks, it was not the least bit comfortable for any of the sojourners, but the choice had not been his to make. The duke's party, the bishop believed, was just ahead of them. Even before leaving Poznan, the bishop had dispatched Father Shimanski to overtake Squire Brezchwa and suggest to the duke a particular stopping place on his way to Brandenburg. Given the signs of heavy, recent travel along their way, the bishop felt certain he would meet up with his forerunners in relatively short order.

Antony Tirasewicz had no intention of living simply or in rough circumstances. His destination was a safe, and definitely out-of-the-way, place in the large network of monasteries dotting the countryside. There he could command a comfortable space, would not be deprived of food and drink, and, most importantly, would be insulated from a world where plague was a mystery nearly as great as the Trinity.

Of his charges, the bishop cared little, with the possible exception of the interesting young woman who paid well for the privilege of being in his care. Allowing a sheepdog to come along should earn him an early release from purgatory. He snorted. Now, if Duke Zygmunt would deign to take him under his financial protection as well, the bishop thought that would be best of all. He smiled to himself, even as a light rain began to fall, and said to the spring air, "St. Stephen's ought to provide an interesting encounter."

. . .

After days of travel under circumstances most uncomfortable for those unused to the rocky paths through Poland's western woods, palisades of the Monastery of St. Stephen the Martyr came into welcome view. Had the bishop not told them what to expect, Irina and her companions might have seen the large compound of civilized structures as some sort of apparition set to deceive the weary.

Bishop Tirasewicz had let it be known he'd visited the monastery many times and all would feel comfortable in the rustic, yet safe environs of the monks' redoubt. Covering a large expanse of land, the monastery was constructed mostly of timber felled to make room for it, and with stone from the nearby quarry of a sinful, but repentant noble, he told them. It included a cavernous chapel, a dormitory for the seventy-some monks who resided there, and kitchens and barns.

From her position in the lead cart and nearest the bishop, Irina couldn't help but notice the relief on his face when evidence of the duke's presence showed itself around the compound. She also found it interesting that St. Stephen's could provide necessities for the large number of travelers.

The bishop explained, to no one in particular, "This will be a good place to pray for God's mercy on all those left in Poznan." There were grateful "Amens" from the assemblage, and immediately, they dismounted, desirous of food and drink.

As Irina and her companions stepped down from the cart, she came face-to-face with the most imposing man she had ever seen. Suddenly, quietly, there he was, waiting. Her eyes came just to the man's chest and she had to bend her neck backwards to see the top of him. An older man—probably more than four decades, Irina guessed—and already graying—he was dressed in a deep amber robe trimmed with strips of fur the color of dark earth. His hood was a similar mass of heavy cloth and fur covering a head on which most of his brushed hair served to disguise the bottom of his face. As if he'd been allowed only so much foliage, almost nothing was left to warm the top of his head, and so the hood served a most useful purpose for him, given the distinctly chilly spring nights.

Irina was not surprised by the man's garb so much as his size and presence. She stood, waiting, while the other travelers went off in search of comfort. The man seemed to have no other purpose than to greet her.

"Father Martinus Madrosh, My Lady," he pronounced, following his words with a slight bow of the head.

A priest! Irina blushed at the sound of the word "Lady" but decided it was something she could get used to. Contrary to her earlier feelings, she took a liking to the man before her. "Irina Kwasniewska," she said, hesitating as she extended her hand. She had no notion whether a lady would do so to a priest.

As she spoke her name, she felt her lips turn to ice as she spied a pair of faces not many feet behind the giant priest. Tomasz the Terrible, the yellow-haired oaf at his side like a lost dog, walked past them ever so casually, as if a monastery was exactly where one would expect to find two murderers. *Why does God let these evil ones escape their just fate?* Yip showed his teeth but remained resolutely at her side.

"Pleased," the priest responded, giving her hand a gentle kiss. "Is anything amiss, My Lady? You—and your dog—seem suddenly ill at ease."

"No, it's nothing," she said, forcing a bare smile. "It's the long travel, and Yip is careful of strangers."

Madrosh nodded. "Then I must not keep you long, My Lady. Most call me Madrosh, by the way. You may do the same."

"Then, Madrosh, who are you, exactly?" She forced a composure she did not feel.

"I am counselor to Duke Zygmunt Sokorski, representing His Excellency, the Bishop. No doubt, the duke will have me look after you on our journey together. It will be a long one."

"You have the advantage, Madrosh. I am here on the advice of Mother Superior. I know not where we go or why we go there. Yet you knew I was coming? Why would someone so important as yourself be assigned the bother of a young woman, her servant, and two novices?" Irina asked her questions pleasantly but felt answers were in order. It seemed the role of a lady came easily.

Madrosh tipped his head forward slightly, his lips forming a smile of acquiescence and acknowledgement. "Ah, one who asks direct questions. You see, My Lady, I knew you were coming before you left the convent. It is my responsibility to be aware of the unusual before such happenings come to the attention of the duke. Ah," he paused, "you mention a servant. Are there not two?"

"Rosta has been assigned to me, yes, but he serves the nuns as well."

They walked together across the forecourt, past the barn, and into the refectory, the monks' dining hall. Yip followed. There they moved toward a large fire in the middle of the room, the smoke of which wafted upward toward an oculus in the ceiling. They sat and warmed themselves, Yip staying close to his mistress.

"A woman of substance and her servant unexpectedly appearing at the church in prayer was sufficiently unusual for me to be informed. Though I know Mother Superior well, I remain uncertain as to exactly why she chose to send you along."

At this, it was Irina's turn to bow her head, in humility, but not in shame. Looking directly into the soft, gentle brown eyes of the elder giant, she confessed, "I am with child, Madrosh. My husband was killed by highwaymen on the way from Gniezno. It's that simple."

"I see then. Mother Superior wanted to protect the child—and you. She spoke well of you, and did you and your servant a great kindness. In this particular detail, you had the advantage of me, My Lady Irina. So now I understand."

"Understand?"

"Duke Zygmunt will not remain long at St. Stephen's. He will travel west for many weeks and for many hundreds of miles. You may stay here with the bishop and return, eventually, to Poznan. Or you may join us—we journey far westward to the city of Paris in the Kingdom of France."

"F-France," she stammered. "Why would I go to France?" In the Joselewicz house, she'd heard talk of great countries to the west, and France was one of them. Its name was all she knew, but she did not feel she should reveal her ignorance to this man just yet. "This is too much for me to comprehend at this moment." This was, indeed, the only true answer she could provide.

"Mother Superior said you were a worthy person, and now I see why she was so earnest in her request that we welcome you. It is clear to me that you, more than any other traveler, have much to consider." He smiled and left her with that thought.

Irina remained still, thoughtful. She was glad to escape the plague, to be sure, but all the way to France? In her heart of hearts, she reminded herself, she wanted nothing to do with Poznan—she did not want to return to the place where her beloved Berek had been murdered. But to travel with the duke and the very people who killed the father of her child? She had not imagined such a choice would be possible, but as she pondered further, a most satisfying possibility began to present itself. She smiled. *A stay at St. Stephen's could be most satisfying, indeed.*

. . .

At the evening repast the monks had prepared for their illustrious guests, Irina was presented to Duke Zygmunt by the bishop, and while their brief conversation was formal and appropriate, it seemed to Irina the duke took a liking to her. In truth, she found herself charmed by him, difficult and confusing it was to feel a sense of warmth toward a master of murderers. Irina wondered if he knew what his men had done.

They were seated on the rough wooden benches usually occupied by the permanent residents of St. Stephen's, and while the surroundings were rustic, the food was excellent—at least as good as that served in the Joselewicz household. Roasted rabbit, venison, and pig, each in its own sauce made with flour, onions, and the juices of the animal. There were lettuce greens, oat and wheat breads, currant jams, and pastries of various kinds. Irina feasted, smiling to herself when she thought of her baby also enjoying such good food.

Dining quietly and making little conversation with those around her, Irina clenched her teeth to keep from saying the wrong thing to someone at whose mercy she now existed. At their trestle table were the duke; his bishop; the monastery's abbot, Father Kaminski; Madrosh; some of the elder monks; and the two novices. Others of lesser rank were served at other tables farther from the fireplace.

She watched most closely the two men haunting her dreams, Tomasz the Terrible and Big Franciszek. Their actual, physical presence in the closed space of the monks' refectory seemed somehow more threatening than when she spied them in the Joselewicz courtyard. Together, as if joined by evil, the two men were drinking with the others and behaving in the boorish, bullying manner she would have expected. Seeing them freshened the disgust she felt and furthered her resolve.

As the evening wore on, when the diners' wits were sufficiently dulled by ale and wine, Irina signaled to Velka for the two of them, quietly, to step outside the hall. From one of the deep, pocketed folds of her heavy gown, Irina drew several pieces of silver gathered from the various hiding places of the Joselewicz household. Along with the one or two coins, the small cache contained symbols of the Jewish religion.

Giving these to Velka, she whispered her instructions.

• • •

Sister Rose was thoroughly perplexed by the behavior of the beautiful child entrusted to her care. Little Zuzanna, the name she had finally called herself, stayed quietly in the convent kitchen, refusing to play with the few other healthy children. Everything about her was unusual for someone so young.

The elderly nun loved the way she cocked her head with a smile when called to a task. "Zuzanna! Help me mix the flour and water. We must make meat and vegetable pies for those able to eat." Zuzzie made her way to a table top the size of a small room without a sound of protest, and did exactly as told. Sister Rose also marveled how the two cooks, opposites in age and wear, worked together for hours as the convent around them became crowded with living disease, first in the courtyard, and eventually, on the stone floors of the church itself. In the background, new residents churned with cries of the living and whimpers of the dying.

Zuzanna was very young but knew enough to keep away from the afflicted ones now surrounding them. Going near them meant death, Sister Rose had warned her.

"Zuzanna, my child. You must talk to me," Sister Rose said with a great gentleness. "Your mother and father will come for you one day. But for now, they would want you to be safe with us and learn about the God who made you."

"Is God with us here?" she asked, looking up, wide-eyed in innocence, surprising the older woman as her small hands floured the table for baking.

· · ·

Mother Superior knelt at prayer in the convent's small chapel. Hers were prayers of hope, stunned as she was by the human devastation she had seen around the city. Mentally, emotionally, she had always been prepared for plague, one or the other, never both. For the first time in her life, two forms of the dreaded plague had been brought within the walls of the church and its convent. "If ever there was a time to show an abundance of mercy, now would be such a time, dear Lord," she whispered into the still air.

She could deal with those whose sores and pustules around the neck would blacken and seem to strangle the life out of their victims for days—some living as long as a week. They were easy to identify.

The second form was another matter. *How we ready ourselves to care for people who would die in a day?* Most did not know their end was near—they could not say a goodbye, utter a last confession, or live to another sunrise. It was a cruel but quick way to end their misery. She could only do her best, or, she vowed, die trying.

. . .

The next day, after morning prayers in the chapel, the duke and his bishop met privately, with their mutually trusted counselor-priest in attendance.

"At Eastertime, the King of France, Charles V, issued an invitation to men of nobility all over the lands between us to come to Paris and confer on matters of interest to us all," the duke informed his listeners.

The bishop's face showed his surprise. "At Eastertime? This invitation to Paris, my lord—why was it not made known to me earlier?"

The duke thought the man's petulance unflattering. In any event, he was not to be verbally shoved here and there by a rude cleric. Zygmunt chose his words carefully. "Because," he responded with all the patience he could muster, "the invitation arrived in Poznan the same day as the plague, Bishop. I thought my message had conveyed that to you quite clearly. As to the royal invitation, it did not concern you. It concerned me. I wished for you to accompany me, but it appears you are not so disposed." His tone settled any further discussion of territorial interest.

The bishop bowed his head, slightly, in an unusual display of humility. "As you say, My Lord."

The duke knew the bishop's mind. Though not a true churchman by any stretch of the imagination, Tirasewicz spun Rome's line that the church should rule the nobility. *The earth, however, is Caesar's realm, not God's!* "Nonetheless, Your Grace, you and the parties in your company may join me if you wish, and if you can, ah, support the long journey." Duke Sokorski spoke the words he felt he must, but in truth, he had no desire to inflict this priest of gold on a kingdom where men of God might predominate.

"What about Madrosh?" The subject of the question stood to the side, seemingly uninterested in the topic of conversation.

"It would be my wish, if you agree, my dear Bishop, that Madrosh accompany me, representing you if you do not come, but in any case, serving as my trusted counselor on a journey perilous in both the forest and the castle." The duke's square jaw was set.

Bishop Tirasewicz's nod betrayed full understanding—it was not a wish at all. "As you desire. Madrosh shall be your guest, then," the bishop said, sealing the terms of the arrangement, financial and otherwise. "When do you proceed?"

"In four days' time, by which date the monks will supply us with sufficient provisions to help us begin the journey. It appears the plague has thus far not followed us. As to the others with you?"

For the next few minutes, they discussed the priests, nuns, and the young woman travelling alone. Zygmunt settled the matter in plain fashion, the softness of his sandy hair belying his resolve in this and most other matters. "Her family I do not know, but I will look upon the Lady Kwasniewska as I would my own daughter. Returning to Poznan or Gniezno would not be wise for her. I trust you would not object to letting the nuns grace our company and tend to our religious needs, as well as those of the woman with child."

The bishop assented with a dip of his pointed jaw, his lips shut tight. In a moment, he broke his silence. "You are most gracious, My Lord, to host these orphans, as it were." He paused. "Unless you insist, my lord, I will remain behind so that I may tend my flock in Poznan."

Duke Zygmunt smiled, unsurprised by the bishop's words and meaning. He knew full well the bishop was happy to be relieved of his human burden and neither had he any intention of leaving the simple comforts of St. Stephen the Martyr only to martyr himself for the plague nesting in Poznan. "Of course, Bishop. A shepherd must be with his flock." He turned to Madrosh and directed him to inform the others of his plan for them.

"Consider it done, Sire," replied Madrosh with a deep bow.

Then the duke turned back to Bishop Tirasewicz, who was rising to leave. "Just a moment more, Bishop."

"Sire?"

"While you are tending to your flock, see also to your shepherds."

"I fail to see your meaning, Sire."

"My meaning, Bishop, refers to those such as Ambrozy Rudzenski," he said, deliberately not referring to the priest by his title.

"What about him, Sire?"

The duke stood. "You know what I am talking about, Bishop," he said with a bit of a sneer. "He was one of your shepherds and did with boys, as they say!"

Tirasewicz blanched.

"Yes, Bishop. What's more, you knew about Rudzenski. You moved him from parish to parish hoping no one would complain about a priest."

"T-that is w-why, Sire, I moved him to the c-convent church." His stammer was beyond control. "T-there he would have little contact with young boys."

"There are altar boys in every church, are there not?"

"Y-yes, Sire. But the man is m-missing."

"He is not missing. He is dead."

The bishop sat back down.

"He made the mistake of taking a walk in the country, near to the farmhouse where one of his favorites lived." The duke paused to let his listener take in his words. "Unfortunately for him, he met the boy's father clearing manure from the barn."

"Y-yes?"

"And apparently, he walked into the farmer's pitchfork."

"What a terrible accident!"

"Not an accident, to be sure, Bishop."

"Murder a priest?! Then the man must hang!"

"Not at all! No nobleman would hang the father of this altar boy. It is enough the people here on earth know Rudzenski went to hell, Bishop."

"I see." The bishop kept his head down, unused to having other than the upper hand.

The duke leaned across the trestle table toward his bishop, their eyes not far apart. "I charge you to rid your shepherds of any more like Rudzenski, as he is not alone."

"To my k-knowledge, Sire, there are very few like him."

"In my lands, Bishop, there will be none." He paused. "Or they, too, will walk into pitchforks."

"I u-understand, Sire."

As the bishop departed, the duke looked up from his chair at Madrosh, who remained speechless but wide-eyed. "Were my words sufficiently clear, counselor?"

"Clear, Sire. Now I have my answer about the man and find a certain justice in his fate. And you, Sire, have done the right thing."

Sokorski stared at his priest. "Justice has no part in my motive, Madrosh. It is about power. If the people won't support the church, they won't support me, and I don't want them to have a reason to do either."

. . .

Irina spent the following days resting, watching, and thinking. As often as possible, she made it her business to encounter the duke, ingratiate herself, and gain his confidence. Hypocrisy was her friend in this endeavor. Finding herself in a world of men and power, she made up her mind to learn their rules, play by them, and, perhaps, even win by them. Power had purpose, and she had no intention of being crushed by it.

On the day before their departure, just as an afternoon rainstorm darkened the sky, she and Duke Sokorski had another encounter in the long, covered cloister leading from the refectory to the church.

"Walk with me, child," he said, his gait slowed by age and afflictions of battle. Together, they made their way, rain rattling the roof above them. As always, they were followed at a distance by Velka, one of the duke's serving men, and Yip.

"Is there something troubling you, My Lord?" she asked when they found a side chapel nook in which to contemplate. Each lowered themselves to a kneeler and composed their hands in prayer, but it was not words of praise to God that the duke uttered.

"My dear Irina, word has come to me via a certain channel that men in my service behaved disreputably toward the Jews." When he said this, his slate-gray eyes squinting under his bushy brows, his gaze aimed directly into the blue eyes of the young woman in front of him.

Disreputable behavior?! She wanted to scream but could not. *Men in your service murdered the father of my child!* She wanted to grab him by his chest plate and shake decency into him, but she could not. Instead, she returned his stare. "What have you heard, My Lord?" she asked, swallowing the hard knot of fear and victory in her throat, and feigning ignorance.

The duke eyed her with patience. "Your servant," he began carefully, "has let it be known that Tomasz took items of great value from the Jews after he burned them."

His words about burning Jews are so calm, so casual as if he was talking about buying a pastry at a market stall. Irina noted the order of things mentioned being the probable order of value in the heart of the speaker. "Yes," she countered. "Velka and I were making our way through the city when we were shocked to see your man, Tomasz, leading others in beating and looting. Is that what you're asking about?" Irina whispered hoarsely, knowing full well his intended interest lay elsewhere.

"Yes," the duke responded, letting his eyes close for a moment, displaying his patience and condescension all at once. "What they did was, shall we say, outside their responsibilities. I have levied a full tax on such behaviors, which means that Tomasz and his men were required to turn over to me everything taken from the Jews as a penalty for their acts."

What a pretty game! The duke, great in his own eyes, had no interest in horrific murder done in his name, murder so falsely claimed to be for the good of all. His only real interest was in securing for himself the tax on terror he so piously imposed. While she thought through this scheme, real, not suspected, the duke appeared to think she was hesitant to speak.

"Well, My Lady, what have you to say?" This time the question was not dressed with patience.

"My servant girl and I were frightened, My Lord, as we are to this day, because of the violence we saw with our own eyes." *Your violence!* "We came to know what these men can do. We knew not of the tax about which you spoke, My Lord. As we hid in the shadows outside the house of a wealthy Jew, we saw them carry away great piles of coin, plate, and furnishings. We know nothing more, Sire."

The look on the duke's face was one of both satisfaction and disgust. "I see," he said with finality.

Irina made her face show regretful submission. Having Velka make a point of mentioning what she had "seen" to one of the duke's servants allowed all the right things to happen in due course, just as pond waters ripple when a stone is tossed. Her own satisfaction was overtaken by the bitterness of knowing that nothing could ever replace what she had lost. What she was sure of, however, was that men like Sokorski were very predictable in their greed. That was another lesson heard at the Joselewicz table.

As they blessed themselves, stood, and turned to leave, Irina thought she saw a very tall man standing well in shadow.

. . .

The summons puzzled her. It wasn't the bishop or the duke. It was the old priest.

"So, Madrosh," Irina addressed him when she appeared once again in a place where comfort was not her companion. Though she went through the motions of her faith, she had decidedly mixed feelings about a God who permitted unspeakable evil by people He supposedly created in his image. Nevertheless, it was fear of an Almighty that made her want to give thanks when she and Velka entered the Church of the Heart of Jesus, and fear of the same such Presence remained with her. Her further discomfort emanated from the certainty that in such a place, she never felt alone.

Talking with a kindly old priest to ease her journey was one thing. Becoming a devoted companion was another. She called him as he had asked, no title, no other name. "You wished to see me, Madrosh?"

The counselor-priest nodded. "Yes, Irina. Or should I say, 'Lady

Irina."' There was no trace of sarcasm. "I believe you are more than you say and yet not what you say."

"Are you insulting me, Father Madrosh?" she asked, deliberately addressing him now as the priest he was.

"No, my dear, I am showing respect. Perhaps you will tell me some-day, but I believe you carry with you much more than your child." He paused. "Do not fear, Irina. I will not press you and neither will I speak of you to anyone. Yet I know what will soon happen as surely as the sun will rise in the east on the morrow. It will happen because you have made it so, and that is why I respect the young woman who sits with me now."

"You've said much, Madrosh, yet you have said nothing about which I care to comment at present. Someday, I may address what questions you have." She paused. "If and only if you will answer some questions for me."

"A fair bargain," replied the cleric. "I accept."

"Over the past several days, Father, I have seen and heard things—horrible things—that make me wonder if so many people who profess a faith in God actually believe in Him. What God is He?"

The silence seemed to thicken the air.

"Your observation is most profound, my dear, and I suspect it comes because much has harmed your soul. Will you permit me to consider my response when we speak another time?"

. . .

Zuzanna could not help herself. Sister Rose had told her many times to stay in the kitchen to help when needed. She knew, however, that when someone told a child to stay close, it was really because there was something they weren't supposed to see. And that made her curious.

Too, Sister Rose had said God was with her, that God loved her and would protect her. Thus assured, she reasoned that it should be safe to explore. Several times a day, she poked her head around the half-open door into the larger room next to the kitchen so she could see—and lis-ten. It frightened her. There were many pallets of straw on which people lay moaning, even children. On one such pallet close by was an older man, like her father. After a while, she remembered him as the jolly man who told stories to the children as they walked along with all the carts and horses. He was nice to her. Now, she heard him calling out.

"*Woda. Woda*—Water!" he whispered in a low roar, hardly able to form a word. "*Prosze, prosze!*" The light from a window opening streamed in as if pointing to him.

Zuzanna did not know whether he saw her or was just calling out to anyone. She hated to see the nice man in such agony. With a cup of water, she stepped into the light and wordlessly placed it to his lips, letting him sip until he quieted. This she did many times—even when he did not ask. Over the next days, he looked at her and smiled, but she said not a word to him.

. . .

Tension rose amongst all those in the abbey as they gathered in St. Stephen's great room. Otherwise the place where good food could be enjoyed, it was now arranged more like a tribunal. Arrayed behind the large head table were all the men of power, and with the light shining in from behind, they seemed imbued with heavenly approval. Lowest in rank amongst them was the abbot of St. Stephen's, Father Karol Kaminski, there only because he was asked. Next were His Excellency, Bishop Antony Tirasewicz, and Duke Zygmunt Sokorski. Counselor Madrosh stood directly behind the duke. When all had quieted, the bishop spoke on his colleagues' behalf to one of the pathetic prisoners before them.

"Do you know why you are here, Tomasz Wodowicz?"

"I know not, Your Excellency," protested Tomasz the Terrible, now, in this place, not so terrifying, his hands tied with heavy rope. His eyes went from man to man as if searching for a sympathetic glance, but found none.

"You are here accused of crimes against the peace."

"What crimes, Your Excellency?" he responded to the high cleric but looked directly at the duke.

"Despite pronouncements of Holy Mother Church, as uttered by the pope himself, you and your men tortured and burned peaceful citizens of Poznan. It has been determined that Franciszek Montowski

shares responsibility for these crimes." The bishop kept his eyes on the table's gleaming surface.

"They were Jews!" Tomasz cried. "They were responsible for bringing plague, as always. And besides, no one stopped me. Everyone heard the racket and the screaming; everyone saw the fires. No one ordered me to stop." He stared at the bishop.

Bishop Tirasewicz continued to look downward even as he spoke. "What anyone else might have done is not now before this tribunal, Tomasz Wodowicz. We are here to pass judgment. And for the second charge against you, there is the matter of theft from the duke's treasury."

"What did you say? What nonsense!" Tomasz did not trouble himself to address his accuser with respect or title.

"Are you claiming that you paid into the duke's treasury as tax all of the items you took from the Jews?"

"Yes, Your Excellency. Every penny. Every coin."

"Then how is it these silver coins and other religious tokens were found on your person, and on Montowski's person?" At that, the bishop threw open the small pouch at his side, and all saw the glittering silver tumble out to catch a few rays of sunlight and sparkle in the otherwise dim space. The reflected light seemed to add even more value to the goods in front of them.

"I don't know where they came from, Sire," Tomasz protested.

All could see Tomasz the Terrible reduced to pleading with his master. At this point, Duke Zygmunt stood and returned his minion's look with one of his own. He sneered. "You are no better than a boar in the forest, Tomasz! You were seen and the evidence is before us. You and your man, Montowski, dared to bring and conceal your ill-gotten goods right here within my reach!"

"Sire," Tomasz said, abjectly.

"Say nothing. A slug of the earth has no words for me." The duke picked up one of the silver coins and threw it at his once-loyal servant. "You will need this where you're going."

Not comprehending, Tomasz looked inquiringly, beseechingly at his master. "Where, where am I going with this coin, My Lord?"

"For your crimes, Tomasz Wodowicz, I sentence you to a corporal work of mercy."

A look of relief shone itself on the face of the prisoner.

"Tomorrow morning, Tomasz Wodowicz and Franciszek Montowski, you will be escorted back to Poznan by the bishop's men. There you will be assigned the burial of the dead at the Church of the Heart of Jesus. You will perform whatever other tasks the Mother Superior may command."

The bishop blanched at the duke's usurpation of his men's service, but said nothing.

Wodowicz stared at the bishop, as if waiting for him to speak, then turned toward the duke. "Sire, you give me a death sentence!"

"Your fate will be heaven's plan, not mine, Tomasz Wodowicz."

Dumbfounded at the turn of events, Tomasz was, for a moment, speechless. Recovering his voice, he begged, "And the silver coin?"

Give it to Mother Superior in the event of *your* burial. The prayers of the church she will offer without payment, I am certain."

As the duke turned to leave the hall, Madrosh looked across the spectators' faces, and once finding Irina, caught her eye and offered a barely perceptible nod. She did not acknowledge him, but maintained her unflinching look of cold, unforgiving satisfaction.

. . .

As instructed, Velka approached one of the forlorn soldiers waiting near the monastery gate early the next morning. One of two men designated to escort the prisoners back to Poznan, his mood was sour, and Velka felt sorry for him.

"Wojciech," she said with a tone that would command attention, "My Lady wants me to give a message to Tomasz the Terrible. Will you let me speak to him?"

"Why should I?" he demanded, sullen.

"It's important," she said with what kindness she could muster. She knew he might not survive his return to Poznan, and kindness seemed a better coin to offer. He nodded his assent.

Velka walked over to Tomasz, leaned to his ear, and said, "My mistress said when you get back to Poznan, you will know what to do with the dead."

"What's that, silly girl?" he spat.

"Burn them. Burn them all!" Velka repeated the words exactly as she had been instructed. She could see Tomasz focus his attention on something in his memory.

Slowly shifting his gaze to the serving girl, he contorted his face into a look of pure evil, followed by a smile of vengeance yet to come.

At once, Velka knew her lady's instruction had been unwise.

. . .

At mid-morning, Madrosh found Irina sitting in the garden, focused on the young plants pushing through the crust of earth and into the warming, nurturing sun. "I see you're enjoying a bit of quietude."

"You seem to have made an assumption about my going with you, good Father."

"Not an assumption at all. You've shown no interest, by word or action, to go back east—to plague and whatever has caused you so much pain."

"And, I suppose, your reasoning has also helped you form a response to what I said yesterday about the God you believe looks after us all?"

Madrosh smiled. "I am not to be let off the hook, as they say?"

"Let me be direct, Father. All of my life, I grew up with a faith in God, went to Mass every Sunday and Holy Day, but the actions of so many around us make me think few of them can possibly believe in an Almighty, or in an accounting in the hereafter. If they did, how could they commit such acts?"

The priest nodded and for a moment, kept his silence. "There are many answers for you, and the fact that you seek them shows that you care enough to know more."

"Indeed, but what can one learn from the Latin Mass? All I truly know comes from the stories the priests tell us, as if we were children."

Madrosh laughed at this. "And, indeed, you were."

Irina laughed too. "You have me there, Father, but again, why should I believe in a God who seems not to be present amongst us?"

"A-h-h," Madrosh sighed. Irina Kwasniewska's momentary candor told him a great deal. A lady of means would have been taught to understand Latin, and because she would have spent many hours with a priest or nun, she should know much more about the religion into which she was born.

Madrosh sat, thoughtful. Next to him sat a woman neither well-born nor literate, yet in the latter regard, she was not unlike nearly everyone else alive. The parchments inscribed by the monks at this monastery and in other places of its kind were to be read by scholars of the cloth, not scions of the kingdom, and, most assuredly, not its serfs. Like many of the men who chose the priesthood, Madrosh was an exception to the rule of abject illiteracy amongst the populace, from the lowest to the highest.

Bishop Tirasewicz's predecessor saw to it that his young priest would be one of the early graduates of the university at Krakow, founded by Casimir the Great. As such, he was one of but a handful of men who had read the philosophers, had studied with great minds, and had become wise in the worlds of religion, political intrigue, and diplomacy.

In other circumstances, he might have thought his time wasted by being assigned oversight of an illiterate young woman. Yet the woman before him, whatever her heritage, was unusually bright, and instinctively adroit in the ways of palatial politics.

"Is that all you have to say?" She broke his skein of thought.

He cleared his throat and smiled. "My dear Lady, I would not want to insult you by telling you things you must assuredly have been taught already, so you see, I'm not sure where to begin."

Irina began to speak but stopped short. After a moment, she said, "Assume what you want to assume, Madrosh, but tell me about God, if there is one."

"There is one—of that, I am absolutely certain, and he is always present amongst us."

"There's seems little evidence for such a claim, Madrosh. That you'll have to prove—if you can."

"A challenge!" Madrosh smiled again. "You insist on very large demands on this most ill-equipped of God's servants, yet I am not sure what prompts you." His raised eyebrows signaled a question he needed to ask and she needed to answer, but Irina remained silent.

"Let me start by suggesting that if there is a God, one Supreme Being, as it were, he would have to be the essence of perfection, would he not? Flawless in every way. By definition, then, nothing in his creation could equal him because if everything in nature, every living being was perfect, why would he bother, eh? So, if we are all imperfect in some way, what does that truly mean?"

"Interesting words, Father, but all the evil around us makes me wonder if there is a God, why does he not care for us?"

"That's exactly it, don't you see? Do you remember the gospel on Good Friday? Christ tells Peter he will deny his master three times. Peter vows he would never do such a thing, but before the cock crows, he denies he even knows the man from Galilee. Yet, despite his flaws, his deep imperfections, Christ says Peter is the rock upon which he will build his church. Think of it!"

Irina nodded. "But Peter was just being human, afraid of what the Jews might do to him if he acknowledged Christ."

"Exactly. We are all human, we are all flawed, and we all fear something."

"Is that why people go to church and make the sign of the cross, because they are afraid?"

"For some, imperfect beings who differ in wisdom, that is why they show the signs of faith but may have little faith underneath. When that happens, evil lurks."

"Was that true of Father Rudzenski?"

It was a question out of the blue and one Madrosh was shocked the young woman would address so directly. "And what about Father Rudzenski, my dear?"

"The rumors about him—about his disappearance—are many, Madrosh, and none of them give me a reason why I should trust you."

Madrosh nodded. "I think I understand you, Irina, and while I don't know what you may have heard, Father Rudzenski is now dead, having paid for his deeds here on earth. No doubt, he now answers to God Himself."

Irina waited.

"In so many ways, Father Rudzenski's streak of evil furthers the point about how truly flawed we all are, and that Almighty God uses people like him for his own purposes, hard as they are to discern. As for trust, may I suggest you take each person on their own terms and make a judgment about trust yourself." He paused. "But never, never judge me by the acts Father Rudzenski is said to have done." He spoke without anger, but with a direct tone he rarely used. "Never use so fine a rake that you scour away the plants longing to bloom along with the weeds."

"I take your meaning, Madrosh, but you have not proved there is a God. Yet." She paused. "You may have helped me understand something about evil."

Most tenderly, Madrosh said in his softest voice, "You hide your secrets well, My Lady, but what you do not hide well is that these secrets trouble you deeply. Will you not speak of them to me?" He took care to study the young woman, the flutter of her eyes, the quiver of her lips. "Will you tell me?"

"How can I trust you, a stranger? *A priest?* And in the service of the very ones who are part of the evil, perhaps. I am truly alone, Madrosh, and I know not what the future might hold for me or my child."

Madrosh nodded, waiting for more.

"If I tell you some things about myself, will you still be here after the telling? Are you a truly a priest, bound by the confessional?"

"I am. And yes. What you should know is that the Almighty God I believe in loves you now and will love you always." What Madrosh saw on her face was not so much fear but desperation.

"I'm not saying I believe our faith anymore, Father, but I will take you up on your promise." She hesitated, then began, slowly.

"Consider this a confession, then." She took a moment to breathe deeply. "I have been living falsely for some days now."

She proceeded to tell Madrosh about the real Kwasniewski family, her maternity, and what had happened to the Joselewiczes. She explained how she and Velka came by their clothes and monies. She left nothing out. It took only a quarter hour to tell her tale, and when she was finished, she bowed her head, then added, hot tears in her eyes, "but Father Madrosh, I cannot say I am repentant for what I did. So perhaps this is not a good confession. And perhaps you'll want to spend your time elsewhere."

Madrosh reached out his hand and placed it on her head. "I bless you, my child, and declare you innocent before God."

She looked up at him, tears flowing freely. "Innocent, Father?"

"Madrosh," he corrected her with a smile. "I doubt there is anything to forgive, dear Irina. Had Berek lived, it remains to be seen how your marriage would have been legitimated, but it would have occurred, it is possible to conclude. Saying that, and there being no other likely true claimants to the Joselewicz family goods, it would be hard to say you took anything that did not morally belong to you." He could see in her demeanor a lightness, an ebullience he had not yet seen.

"How you carry yourself now is your concern, in the eyes of God," he continued. "As long as you are willing to learn and comport yourself in ways that are to be expected of someone of your new class, no one will treat you any differently." It was subtle, but clear. Madrosh was making an offer.

Irina nodded. "Then I may continue as I am?"

Madrosh nodded in return. "Living falsely is only a sin, perhaps, when it is a matter before God." He paused. "You are not free, however, to impose God's judgment upon others—including Tomasz the Terrible."

"I did not impose judgment, Madrosh. I merely sought justice. Duke Zygmunt passed sentence." She said these words with a trace of smugness in her voice, yet no remaining satisfaction in her soul.

"Shrewdly put, My Lady, but heed well that God may not abide much cleverness of that sort."

I had no idea that the answer to a simple question put to this man would take me partway to eternity! Ah, well, who else can I speak to? Who else will take my questions, my candor? A long journey is ahead, and I may as well take whatever this old man has to give!

"And, Madrosh," she challenged, after a moment, with respectful curiosity, "are my confession and absolution different than those of Tomasz, who kills, confesses, and kills again?"

"In the truest sense, Irina, there is no difference. If a priest absolves Tomasz of his sins, he is so absolved." As she was about to object, Madrosh continued. "People like Tomasz never fully understand the sacrament of confession. When a priest forgives the sins of another, he is doing exactly what Christ himself said could be done by a duly ordained priest of God. If you are repentant, the priest lifts from you the burden of guilt. What no priest can know, however, is what's truly in your heart. And neither can a priest take away the accountability for the sin—that remains between God and the sinner."

"Now I am a bit confused. A man can be forgiven yet not be forgiven?"

"Forgiveness of the sin is but one part of the transaction. Repentance, another. It is the third part that is conveniently forgotten. It is this way, Irina. Suppose a boy steals a pastry from a baker. The baker may run out and catch him, and if the boy is repentant, he will forgive the lad, but depending upon the baker, there must be an accounting for the pastry. The boy or his father must pay for it. In the sacrament of confession, of course, no one can pay for you. But there comes a time for everyone, even unto eternity, when the price of sin must be paid. How the Almighty exacts the price is between Him and the sinner." Madrosh paused, then added, quietly, "It is never death we must fear, Irina, but God's eternal judgment."

"So, Christ did not pay for our sins with his crucifixion?"

"Hah! You think you have trapped me, but the answer to that we will save for another conversation."

For several moments, Irina sat silent.

Madrosh could see she had begun to grasp a difficult concept. "Do you not think, then," he concluded, "that rather than controlling our every action, God wants to see what we do with the life He has given us?"

...

Through the Polish woods they trooped, and as they did so, Wojciech Murawski considered what lay ahead for them. Though he and his partner were on horseback, they couldn't travel faster than the tethered men in front of them could walk. Tomasz Wodowicz and Franciszek Montowski were not easy charges, as both captors and captives knew they were marching to what would likely be the end of their worlds.

Murawski prodded their prisoners to step off at a brisk pace. Encountering no trouble, they would be back in Poznan in something over two days. They needn't be in a hurry, of course. The longer they stayed away from Poznan, the longer they might live.

As they tramped along, Murawski began to wonder if heading to Poznan was the smart thing to do. No one would check on them. He wondered about letting them go, so that they could all find safety. After all, they stole only from Jews, and seemed good enough fellows around the monks' table.

While Murawski warmed to the idea of disobedience, guilt edged his thinking. He shrugged and glanced at his partner, who he guessed had begun thinking the same. Perhaps, he thought, this could work out for all of them.

. . .

Mother Superior and the Sisters in her care made many forays into the city to collect those discarded to disease, especially children left to fend alone. Each time, they noticed more empty houses, more abandoned shops. There was no funeral Mass for them, no blessing by a priest, if, indeed, one could find a priest alive to ease the dead on to eternity. Nearly everyone went to the same final resting place: a burning pyre in a great pit.

By the hundreds, Poznan's citizens left their world in ignominy, in squalor and filth beyond what daily life had ever forced them to endure. The population had been decimated in previous attacks of the plague, Sister Elisabeth knew, and the numberless missing would not soon be replaced.

Several of the sisters contracted the plague and, despite the loving care from their own, all were dead in a day or a week. Defying authority, each was buried with prayer in the churchyard.

One who had not perished was the man who seemed to know he would live to serve them. Amazingly, a man who had come to them some six days before not only remained alive, but had regained his vigor in each of the last two. Jerzy Andrezski, in fact, was delirious at the thought he might actually live another week, another month.

Why he was spared, he didn't understand; many asked if he possessed a magic potion. In one of his more lucid moments, he shared an observation with Mother Superior: the first ones to die of plague seemed to be children and those of smaller build—most women but many men as well. Given the thin existence most common people experienced, few had food enough to achieve a body mass worth notice. Even fewer grew to be a head taller than their peers, as Andrezski had.

"And so, Mother Superior, perhaps it is my size," he laughed, enjoying his good fortune. "In my own life as a wandering merchant, I ate well, unlike most of the poor souls who have spent their last hours here. In fact, I have seen only one other as tall as I am in all of Poznan. Like me, he's a giant but with yellow hair, and I saw him running from the castle the morning I arrived. I'll bet you, Mother Superior, he, too, has survived."

"That would be Franciszek, one of the duke's men." She shook her head. "But not one of God's more pleasant creatures, I am afraid."

"Whatever the reason, I am most grateful."

"Perhaps Almighty God thought to spare you."

"Now that I think about it, I suppose it was His angel."

"His angel?" the nun asked, her tone suggesting Andrezski had wandered back into delirium.

"Each day," he said, "she came on a light beam. Sister, a miracle! The angel just smiled and held the cup to my lips. This is truly a place of God."

"I should surely hope so," she smiled, and walked away, shaking her head in wonder. Jerzy Andrezski and but a handful of others had entered the precincts of her convent carrying the plague and would live to leave. "Could it have been a miracle?" she whispered aloud, then blessed herself with a sign of the cross.

CHAPTER V

1378

In the third week of May, Duke Zygmunt's assemblage rose for a sunrise Mass offered by Abbot Kaminski. Said for the blessings of God upon those who risked all to journey so far from their homeland, it was also intentioned for those who remained behind. As Father Kaminski raised the Host heavenward and spoke the Latin—*Hoc est enim corpus meum*—the sun broke through the misted morning, and as it sliced through the trees, all basked in the glow of what they felt, surely, was God's presence. There were murmurs of awe. It was, perhaps, an auspicious moment, but of the divine, Irina was not so certain.

After the priest's blessing, everyone situated themselves in or on whatever mode of travel they were assigned, then proceeded west and north, deeper into the woods. Irina took a deep breath and felt grateful to be forever rid of Tomasz the Terrible. *Should I be grateful to a God about whose powers I am doubtful?* Happy chatter soon engaged them all. They knew they faced danger, but whatever they encountered, most considered it the adventure of their lives.

In talk here and there around the monastery, Irina heard the duke hoped to reach Paris well before the snows. Everyone knew the importance of that goal. Winters had become brutally cold and long, the worst anyone of age could remember, and no one wanted to be travelling once the season of deep snows and ice came. The length of their journey was part of every conversation, and no one knew just how far was far. True, there had been lore about the great travels of the Crusaders three hundred years earlier, but mostly, neither soldier nor serving man ever ventured far from the place where they lay their heads at night.

Too, there were other uncertainties. No one knew what to expect from strange peoples speaking strange tongues—welcomes or weapons. Irina strove not to let her imagination wander to fear. Of course, there were robbers and wolves, but that was true no matter where one ventured. Seasoned travelers knew their journey would last months, some days traversing but a few miles if they were lucky. There was no high expectation that all would survive such an undertaking, yet for all their unspoken fears, returning to Poznan held little appeal for most. Irina shuddered whenever someone expressed such a wish.

"Velka," she said as they rumbled along, "I am surprised that you, of all the people here, would wish to return to…what?"

"There, My Lady, I knew what I knew. Yes, it was a cruel, dirty, God-forsaken place, but surprises were few." Velka closed her words with a look straight into her mistress's eyes.

Irina returned her gaze, and after a moment, spoke about what she had only confessed to Madrosh. "I owe you much, Velka, and about one thing in particular, I owed you more than a fleeting glance some days back." Again, she paused. "Yes, Berek and I found each other in ways I never expected…or experienced." She gave her young companion a wry, embarrassed smile. "On *that* night, I was coming back to tell him, and then his family."

"But you couldn't." Velka lowered her eyes, remembering.

Irina nodded. "I was at the gate when Tomasz ordered the burnings—in the same words I gave you to tell him. Berek saw me, and when our eyes met, he knew—I know that he knew—what I was there to tell him." She put her hands to her eyes. "That was when I saw him last." There was nothing more to say, but Irina was glad Velka knew, even if it was a "servant" teasing it out of her "mistress." It was clear, too, that she and Velka had settled into their roles, each comfortable with themselves as the young women they were becoming.

Later on that first morning, as Irina noticed what the night's frost had done to wither new growth on the forest floor, Madrosh rode up to the cart in which she and Velka bumped along. He had a young man following like a devoted puppy.

"Squire Jan Brezchwa," he said, tugging at the horse's reins, "on this journey, you will be personal protector for Lady Irina Kwasniewska just as you are to me."

"Yes, Father," Brezchwa responded with a bow of his head to Madrosh and a smile cast in the direction of his new charge. "I will not forget, My Lady."

Irina blushed but merely nodded in return. *Where have I seen this face before?*

As they rode on, Irina turned from the young squire's distraction, and said in a low voice to Madrosh, still alongside their cart, "Why, Father Madrosh, do you address me as 'Lady Kwasniewska' given my confession the other day?" she asked, leaning over to him. "Are you trying to embarrass me?"

"On the contrary, My Lady," he said, and bowed with a conspiratorial smile. "The title continues to legitimize you in this company where you are a stranger. If I may say so, the little fact that I give you such courtesy tells so many others that you are under my protection. And now," he added with a chuckle before he rode off, "you are under the protection of that young man, about the same age as you—Jan Brezchwa."

. . .

Within a day of leaving St. Stephen's, Duke Zygmunt's party reached the western edge of *Wielko Polska,* and there was much for him to consider as they crossed the frontier into Germanic lands. The borders of the various territories were irregular, unmarked, and subject to frequent change. From this point on, everyone they encountered could be friend or foe, and with language always a barrier, much time would be spent discerning the difference.

Many hours in the saddle allowed the duke to think through the politics of the matter without the incessant bother of problems within the walls of Poznan Castle. From the lips of his father, the fear of foreign rulers went back to the tenth century, when Poznan was first invaded by the Duke of Bohemia, and old memories died hard. Often enough, the Germans were no friend to the Poles, but at present, there was peace between them. Otherwise, the Germans would join the others in carving up his homeland, and Zygmunt had come to believe it would always be so. The words of popes might be forgettable, but not the swords of conquerors.

Not many years before his own birth, his city had withstood an attack from King John, whose son became Charles IV, Holy Roman Emperor and, more recently, King of Bohemia. At one point, the king was the *de facto* ruler of Brandenburg, after Otto, successor to Louis II and son-in-law of *Kazimierz Wielki* himself, failed to protect his kingdom. A few years later, Wenceslas, son of the Emperor, was made Margrave of Brandenburg. It was confusing, to be sure, but it was Duke Zygmunt's duty to make sense of it.

If Poznań's plague meant near-certain death, now making a bad political choice would portend a similar end, the duke knew. And so, as he'd said to Madrosh, it made perfect sense for their party to head toward the seat of the most capable military power on their way to Paris.

. . .

The days were long, the travel hard for Duke Zygmunt's party. Whether in the covered cart or on horseback, Irina stayed close to Madrosh and wasted no time in satisfying her hunger for what knowledge the old priest could impart.

"So Madrosh, about God," she queried, as if they'd just been discussing the matter. "You've explained to me there is one Supreme Being, who is a Trinity of beings—the words we say when we make the sign of the cross. You've told me that God's Son came here to offer his life, redeeming us from all our sins, for all those who have ever lived, and all those yet to live. Is this true?"

"Yes, my child. You must remember each of us dies for our sins. If we were perfect, we would never have to die, but because we turned away from God's command in the Garden of Eden—where the church teaches we were made in his image—we are sinners in this life."

"You are confusing me, Madrosh!"

"There are some in the faith, Anselm of Canterbury for one, who say that Christ died as atonement for our sins—payment of a sort. Yet others wonder about a God who would put his own son through such a horrible death just for the sake of satisfaction. Others argue that some in the church used this atonement idea to make men feel guilty for their sins, and urge them on the Crusades to rid themselves of guilt. Another problem with that notion is that some might conclude they may sin again and again with no accounting ever due."

"But not everyone believes as Anselm?"

"No, my child. Others, including a Frenchman, Peter Abelard, expressed the idea that the essence of our faith is about Christ's life on earth, and the resurrection into eternal life—not how he died. They believe that God sent his son to be human, to teach us how to be better children of God. Because Christ became human, death was the natural end, and perhaps his crucifixion had more to do with the causes he championed rather than the need to die a horrible death for us."

"And what is it that you believe, Father Madrosh?"

He looked at her and smiled. "I kneel with St. Augustine, who had doubts about the idea of atonement, when he asked if it was truly necessary to believe that God was so angry with us, he sent his son to be crucified. Was it to appease the Almighty or to keep Him from punishing us?"

"What does it all mean, then?"

"What it means is that Christ's whole life, his very existence, was God's loving gift to us. That he came amongst us—as one of us—is what gives our lives value. If Christ offered his life for our sins, then it was because it was his desire to do so, not because he was required to do so. Can one member of the Trinity require an act by another? Although all of us die for our sins, Christ had to die because he was human and for one other reason: to show us that if we believe in him, we, too, shall rise from the dead and enjoy eternal life. Had Christ not come amongst us, there would only be death, a final end to a life without real meaning. That Christ rose from the dead into eternal life is what he promised for each of us, and what the Almighty wanted for each of us from the beginning—a return to a heavenly Garden of Eden. That is the foundation stone of our faith."

Irina took a deep breath. "This is much to think about."

"Yes, my child, but it is indisputable that Christ died for each of us, and I think you already understand that suffering is not necessary to prove one's love."

For a moment, she lowered head, covering her eyes with her hand. Quickly, she looked back at him. "Yes, Father, on this, we agree." They bumped along the road in silence. "May I ask another question? And we call the Mass the supper of the lamb?"

Madrosh nodded. "You have seen the priest at Mass raise the Host countless times. The bread and wine become the actual body and blood of Christ. It is our way of remembering his sacrifice every time we gather in his name."

"And we must believe that the change really happens?"

"The Holy Roman Church believes so, yes."

"That is difficult to consider. Taking the body and blood...."

"Many of Christ's listeners had stronger reactions than that, according to the Gospel of John. When Christ talks about it, he says he is the bread of life, the living bread come down from heaven, and the bread he gives is his flesh for the whole world."

"Could the gospel be wrong?"

Madrosh shrugged. "I don't believe so. No doubt, Christ saw that some were repulsed by the notion that he would give his flesh to them to eat, and yet he had opportunities to take back those words or soften their interpretation, but he did not. Christ went on, saying, 'Whoever eats my flesh and drinks my blood has eternal life, and I will raise him on the last day. Whoever does so remains in me and I in him.' At the Last Supper, Christ used nearly identical words. Yes, Irina, Christ meant what he said."

She nodded, still uncertain, but followed with another question. "Has the Mass always been said exactly the way we hear it?"

Madrosh nodded, thinking about his words. "We know two important tenets of our faith from the writings of Justin the Martyr going back to within a hundred and fifty years of Christ's time. Even then, when people gathered together to celebrate the Eucharist, there were already the beginnings of the Mass as we have come to know it.

There were readings from the prophets of the Old Testament, from the letters of the Apostles, and prayers of thanksgiving. Interestingly, the Mass as a New Testament sacrifice is similar to the ancient Jewish rituals of prayer and sacrifice. It was where the word 'Amen' appears for the first time."

"I don't mean to distract you, Father, but what does it mean?"

"It is a Hebrew word—a Jewish word—meaning that the person speaking gives his assent to what has been said. Of course, Justin did not write in Hebrew, he wrote in Greek."

"What was the second thing?"

"Justin described in some detail the whole idea of transubstantiation—the changing of the bread and water into the body and blood of Christ. Other writers of that same era described the liturgy and the Eucharist in very similar ways."

"And?"

"You are a curious person, indeed, My Lady Irina. Christians have been attending Mass and saying the Lord's Prayer for over a thousand years now."

Irina took in the enormity of time a thousand years represented. "I don't wish to be disrespectful, Madrosh, but you have told me only what people have done and what they have believed. You have not proven God's existence."

"Curious and persistent, I see," he said with a wry smile. "We have a long journey ahead of us, my dear Lady," he chuckled, "and I won't lose my audience! There are many things to teach you. You are correct, though; the most important of all is God's very existence, and that knowledge will satisfy your soul, indeed!"

"I should tell you, Madrosh, you speak beautiful words, but I remain unconvinced the God you describe would permit the evils I have seen."

· · ·

On their second morning heading east toward Poznan, Wojciech Murawski and the young soldier partnered to him awoke to the unexpected. The night before, they had tied their prisoners securely and settled down in the shelter of low pine branches, walled in only by the darkness of the forest.

"Wojciech!" Tomasz commanded. When the startled soldier opened his eyes, Tomasz waited until terror appeared in their morning gleam, then drove the short sword of the other soldier deep into Murawski's heart. For Murawski, it was a moment of white-hot pain, then eternity.

Tomasz looked over at Big Franciszek, who was holding his hand over the mouth of the dead man's luckless companion, his eyes wide in terror. He never uttered a sound as Franciszek slit his throat.

"Wash away the blood. Take their clothes," ordered Tomasz. "We wear the bishop's colors now, and Poznan will never see us."

. . .

The duke's procession crawled through thick woods and monotonous fields, the sun being its only compass. Although he had learned of a magnetic direction device, none was available to him, and their objective seemed simple enough, the duke thought. Let the sun rise behind the them in the morning, signal them midday by its position overhead, and then lead them toward the horizon as nightfall came again.

The seemingly endless scapes clinging to the flat countryside were punctuated by the occasional village where foodstuffs for horses and for people could be bought or bargained. What Irina noticed most of all was not a shortage of food or goods, but of people. In the Germanic provinces, they learned that earlier attacks of plague had nearly annihilated the population, as thoroughly as if the Mongols had done it themselves.

For the duke, the prices to be paid for bare necessities or services were an unwelcome surprise. Irina knew she'd be asked to make a larger contribution toward her passage, but a new life in a new world for her and her child was worth the price, she had ultimately concluded.

Days passed, then weeks. Frequent and cool spring rains kept their clothes and goods damp, a state only in part relieved by the warmth of a good fire. There was plenty of time for thought and talk, and Irina took many opportunities to test her new friend, the priest. *I have*

*trusted Madrosh with everything, and he gives me his learning, but asks
for nothing? What kind of man is that?*

Always curious to know what was around her, where and how
people fit in the grand scheme of her world, Irina was never at a loss
for questions. It was a pleasure, then, to reach into Madrosh's mental
cupboard for the answers. One afternoon, as the sun dappled them
through the bright-green new leaves of the tall, white birches, she
indulged her curiosity still again. She wanted to know, for example,
where Duke Zygmunt's rank placed him in the royal pecking order.

Irina was not sure she understood how complicated things were
for the powerful, but Madrosh explained that even though Poles had
achieved a great place in the world under Casimir the Great, he had
arranged for his kingdom to pass to his sister, Elizabeth, the Dowager
Queen of Hungary, and Louis, her son, the King of Hungary. As such,
Louis I became the King of Poland, and like all other Polish nobles,
Duke Zygmunt was notoriously passive in support of the Hungarian
ruler. As a result, the poor and the landless, always possessed of an
uncertain future, were "mere gamepieces in sordid feudal squabbles,"
as Madrosh put it.

Their conversation led to the possibility of war.

"For the love of heaven, Madrosh, why would King Louis want to
have another war?"

"It's very simple, Irina. To make war, kings require goods, resources, and, above all, men who will fight for them. The plague has
slaughtered the men of fighting age and the women to bear children in
Hungary as well as our beloved Poland. If there are not enough men, a
king levies taxes on his nobles to hire mercenaries. And without large
numbers of the lowest classes to do the farming, raise the animals,
and perform all mean tasks as part of trade and transportation, and
without the merchants and moneymen to manage affairs, a kingdom
is an empty place. For some, it's about money, but for others, it's always
about land and people."

Days later, still hungry for knowledge and understanding, Irina
sat astride a well-tamed horse, which seemed to provide a better ride
on rougher ground as she began to grow with child. As they clopped

along, Madrosh hummed softly, a hymn, she thought.

"Father," she began, "before we resume our talk of God, tell me about the Jews. I heard Janus Joselewicz say they were protected by the King and his law. Yet they are so reviled by many of our people. Why is this so?"

Madrosh did not answer right away. "It's a complicated history, my dear. Our great king, Boleslaus the Pious, may have unwittingly created the seeds for that hatred when he proclaimed the Statute of Kalisz just over a hundred years ago."

"And this was a bad thing?"

"Bringing in the Jews was not a bad thing. In fact," Madrosh continued, "Jewish culture added much to our own and within a few generations, Poland began to regain its position of power within the Holy Roman Empire.

"Why did it not go well, then?"

Again, Madrosh hesitated. "You see, My Lady, for centuries, there had not been any Jews in our land of which to speak." Madrosh lowered his head. "So many in our religion referred to Jews as killers of Christ for so long, it had become an ingrained belief, I am ashamed to say."

"So, Boleslaw attempted to undo all those centuries of ignorance and hate."

"I could not have said it better, Irina. You understand more quickly than you realize."

"With the Statute in place, why do these horrible injustices still occur?"

"Laws are one thing. Unless they are enforced—everywhere—they are just pretty words on parchment. And the Statute doesn't cover everything. I suspect the Jews are accused of bringing the plague, of drinking the blood of Christians, of poisoning our wells, because the accusers know that to prove any of it is *not* true would be impossible to do."

"Madrosh, do you believe any of it is true?"

"None of it is true, my child."

"Then why?"

"People always need someone to blame for their calamities, do they not? They can't blame God because they're afraid of God. It's much easier to blame people who can't easily defend themselves. And in this case, the Church helped to make the Jews seem like evil itself. Even some words in the gospel strengthen that view. When a group is thus identified, it becomes easy to hate them. And so it matters little whether they are guilty. It's enough for a mob to believe in someone's guilt, true or not, so they quell the blood rising in their chests. Until the next time, that is."

"I see. That doesn't say much about a difference between men and animals. So why has the church not righted this great wrong?"

"It tried, but the effort was far from adequate, it is fair to say." He chuckled derisively."It is nothing to laugh about, but surely, it is an irony of history that when Christianity was a new religion, some thirty years after Christ's death, the city of Rome caught fire and burned for six days and nights. It was nearly destroyed, and the Emperor Nero blamed the Christians, a small, politically powerless group at the time. He literally fed them to the lions. The church, above all others, should understand what the Jews have endured."

Madrosh sighed. "An enlightened leader of a group—even when the group is the church of God, Irina—may proclaim one thing, but its followers may practice another. The difference between what's said from pulpit and what's said over a bowl of soup can be vast. It's an old story."

"Is that really why people do what they do—because they believe in myths?"

"It is very sad to say, my dear Irina, that many people, I believe, merely use the myths to hide the real reasons for what they do to the Jews."

Irina raised her brows inquiringly.

Madrosh said, "Mind you, My Lady, I do not ordinarily discuss such views—with anyone—and certainly not with the duke or his minions."

"With the bishop?"

"Nor with the bishop," Madrosh averred with emphasis. "In my humble opinion, it is little more than jealous greed. Remember that one of the believed talents of the Jews has to do with money, with the art of finance. Many are very skilled in business and many, certainly not all, amass great fortunes and property. Moreover, they lend their monies to princes—of this world and of the Church—and it must gall the borrowers to have to be respectful to those they have been taught to despise.

"So, you can see, can't you, that to have a pretext for stripping the Jews of their wealth—while at the same time shedding themselves of a debt—would have a certain appeal to it. Would it not?"

"Yes. It would—to some! The duke's tax comes to mind. But it is not the churchmen or the nobles who light such deadly bonfires. It's the people themselves, people who have not borrowed money, who have nothing to gain from such behavior."

"You've hit upon the cruel beauty of the scheme, My Lady, and it's been played over and over in times before us. No doubt, it will be played so many times over in the centuries to come. It is this way, Irina, and hear me well. At high levels in the church and at court, popes and princes can say one thing, perhaps even believe what they say, but they profit well when their middlings stir up the poor in the cities and the peasants in the countryside to do their evil work for them. Once this work has begun, it is not easy to put an end to it—at least, not a happy one. The ignorant will believe much that is told to them by their lords, and if it helps to satisfy an ancient bloodlust, all the better!"

I can see that long conversations with Madrosh may be tiring, but he is like the cow that gives so much milk, and I am thirsty!

...

Zuzanna cried mightily. Her sobbing so filled the kitchen air, it nearly drowned out all the usual noises accompanying the cooking of large meals needed at the convent. At some point in Zuzanna's one-person chorus of childhood misery, Sister Rose's concentration was broken, and she became concerned. Zuzanna had been such a happy and grateful child for the weeks she'd been with them; this display demanded Sister Rose's attention.

"My dearest child," she said with utmost kindness. "Why are you crying so? What is troubling you?"

"Why did my family leave me?" It was the first time she had talked about it.

"Did they, Zuzanna? Tell me what happened to you."

"We were up on a hill and I went to listen to all the laughing. Then they were gone."

"Did you look for them?"

"Yes. I called out again and again, but no one came."

"Do you live in Srodka?" asked Sister Rose. She knew the questions had been asked before, but with all the commotion involving the living and the dying, spending time with this lost soul was not the first thing on anyone's mind. Zuzanna spoke little or not at all, and the sisters began to think she was left deliberately—not all that unusual if the extra mouth in a family was female. Or perhaps plague had claimed her parents.

"No. We live on a farm a long walk from here."

"Why were you and your family in Srodka?"

"We were looking for my sister."

"Does she live in Poznan?"

"I don't know. She left our family and we were sad. Her name is Irina. Irina Kwasniewska."

The kettle boiled over, spitting water and sizzling as it hit hot coals. Sister Rose at first ignored Zuzanna's words, busy as she was with the demands for soup and bread. Then it struck her. "Little sister, indeed!" *Yet how can I make sense of this?*

...

Tomasz and Franciszek, now garbed as soldiers in the bishop's service, turned back toward St. Stephen's. They were several days behind the duke's company, Tomasz knew, but he and Franciszek would make faster time, though he needed to think things through before explaining his plan to Franciszek, ever the doubter.

"Tomasz, why are we going back to trouble? Why not go back to Poznan? The bishop may not be coming back for many weeks, and the duke, not for many months, if ever. We could go on as before and no one would know."

Tomasz had to acknowledge the logic of these statements, surprising all the more for coming from Franciszek, a man who rarely thought more than one meal ahead. Yet hate and love always triumph over reason, Tomasz had often heard the duke say. While Tomasz knew nothing of love, he was quite adept at hating those who had more than he. If they were Jews, all the better.

"You might be right, Franciszek, and if you want to go to Poznan, you go! As for me, I will head away from the plague and will settle things with the man who demanded my loyalty, but denied me the same."

"But he's the duke, and who are we?"

"WE," shouted Tomasz, "are the people who did his bidding, Franciszek, and he was duty-bound to take care of us. What's more is that I now know who that bitch is!"

Startled, Franciszek did not understand. "What—who are you talking about?"

"I've been thinking about what that servant girl—Velka—said to me. The woman, the Lady Kwasniewska," he sneered. "She is no more a lady than you, Franciszek. I'm sure I remember her now—she was a serving girl at the Joselewiczes', and I think she was there the night we burned them. She must have been—otherwise, how could the servant know to repeat what I said." As he spoke, his voice became hard and his stare, fixed.

"So, what of it?"

"That's who took the Joselewicz gold, oaf! We have debts to pay. To the bishop, to the duke, and to the peasant girl who calls herself Lady Kwasniewska!"

. . .

In early 1378, King Louis I of Hungary and Poland, then in the thirty-sixth and eighth years of his reigns, respectively, roamed one of his castle's gardens and considered the future of his kingdom. When he ascended the throne of Poland in 1370, he began acquiring lands along the Adriatic, and had been hugely successful on the battlefield. For him, however, it was not enough.

Bundled in furs and heavy clothing against the late snows, he forged a trail with his lined leather boots. His large feet left quite a mark, as would the coming campaign, he thought, smiling to himself. His burgeoning empire needed a water route to the Baltic controlled by Hungary, independent of Poland and its truculent lords. Because he could not rely on Polish nobility, almost none of whom were related to him, spoke the same language, or shared the same culture, he found himself in a situation where his imperial dreams had to be self-sustaining.

Against the advice of his counselors, a taste for expansion of his empire remained in his mouth. Now at the age of fifty-two, he knew those around him considered him elderly. His counselors wished him to focus his energies on the kingship of Naples. Leave the north to the Teutons, they urged.

Not to be dissuaded from northern glory, Louis returned to the warmth of the great hearth fire as a winter storm began to blow, and summoned his most trusted counselor, Duke Vladislaus Jurisic. Jurisic was thoroughly Hungarian, a vassal who would do anything to please his sovereign. Together, they dreamt aloud. If Hungarian conquest proved easier than thought by others, it would be worth sending forth a small but well-armed expeditionary force. It could be reinforced if victory followed victory, they speculated.

Louis and Duke Vladislaus held a secret audience with Sir Bela Kinizsi, a man of distinguished military valor. It was necessary to veil this effort, the king affirmed, because courtiers had relatives everywhere and even in his own household, those with even a trace of Polish or German blood might have trouble guarding their tongues.

"My esteemed Baron," Louis said to Kinizsi, "tomorrow is March 5, my birthday, and in honor of this auspicious occasion, I charge you with a great risk for us, and, perhaps, a great reward."

Sir Bela bowed deeply.

"You will enter into the heart of Silesia, lands now controlled by the Germanic Princes, the Margraves of Breslau, Glogau and Brandenburg.

All three Duchies, just west of Polish territories, lie astride the Oder, and if you can attack and secure the fortress towns in key spots along the river, you will give the Hungarian people a great gift—a way to reach the Baltic!"

Kinizsi, stood, his right hand resting on the jeweled pommel of his court sword. His countenance brightened with each syllable of his king's words. "A water route!"

King Louis continued, "Exactly, Sir Bela! Reaching the Baltic through *Wielko Polska* is of little value to Hungary. It is a water route Hungary seeks!"

Sir Bela's smile remained fixed, as if painted on for posterity.

"If resistance is strong," the king went on, "that will be one thing, and if the Oder is not well-garrisoned, that will be quite another—an opening. We do not desire all their lands, just those pieces we can wrest from them for the lowest possible battle price. Either way, we will learn whether to make this effort now or, perhaps, later. You have two months to secure your troops and prepare a plan of attack when the spring thaw is certain. I know you will make the best of it!"

"Your Majesty," Sir Bela replied, "who would not agree that your birthday is a good day to begin this effort, but is that the only reason, if I may ask?"

For just a moment, Louis stayed silent, thinking. Then, to the surprise of both his trusted men, he laughed out loud. He laughed so heartily his cheeks reddened and he became short of breath. When, eventually, he regained his composure, he said, "Why, Sir Bela, you are a most astute strategist and challenge me in the most diplomatic way." He paused. "Here, I swear you both to the utmost secrecy. This very day, I learned that in one month's time, my dear cousin in Paris will issue invitations all across Europe for men of wealth and power to gather with him. By early May, many of them will make the journey west." He chuckled.

"You both have my apologies, as I have the advantage of a day's consideration of this matter. I have no interest in attending such a costly circus from which I will gain nothing. If our timing is fortunate," he nodded to Kinizsi, "you may find various castles and fortresses along the Oder defenseless. That, my friend, should make your task all the easier."

Sir Bela bowed in admiration. "I will make the most of what one hundred of the best armed men can accomplish, pressing into service others as we move up the countryside. I might suggest, Your Majesty, that at some point in our progress, we will require much greater supplies of men and resources to make our way to the sea."

"Precisely, Sir Bela. The Empire's military wealth is now committed in the south, but if you are successful in taking a few smaller bites from the German apple, we will come with full might to consume it with you, core and all."

"It will be my pleasure, Your Majesty."

. . .

Sister Rose stood in the kitchen's archway and noticed her Mother Superior, most unusually, resting in the small, spare room beyond. Complaining of nausea the evening before, Sister Elisabeth said she needed to be off her feet. Dizzy, she said she was and couldn't seem to stand. Now, in the morning sun stream, she seemed no better.

"Sister Rose," she called in a reedy voice.

Wiping her hands on an apron and taking it off out of respect, Sister Rose moved quickly to her bedside. Despite the possibility of plague she had not hesitated, since she had lived a long life and always depended upon the divine plan for her well-being.

"Yes, Mother."

It was all Sister Elisabeth could do to lift her head. She looked straight into the eyes of her companion in Christ, mouthing the words for water and a cool, wet cloth.

Sister Rose nodded in willing obedience. There was a secret to share, and she had to do it now, or she would never have the opportunity to obtain the advice and guidance on which she had always relied. Returning, she brought cool water and a moist cloth. She held the dying woman's head and let her sip what water she could take. Folding the towel, she laid it across Sister Elisabeth's forehead. The elder nun exhaled and let her head fall back to its rest.

"Mother," Sister Rose began in an urgent whisper, "I will call the priest for you." Both knew such a visit would be for Last Rites, the church's final earthly sacrament.

Able to muster only the faintest of smiles, Sister Elisabeth whispered, "It is too late for that, I think. I'll have to trust in God's mercy." In a last display of her famous humor, she said, "If you have something to say, you needn't worry—your secret will be safe with me."

Sister Rose attempted to match her Mother Superior's smile, but could not. "It's about Zuzanna," she said quickly.

Their words were few. Their time, short.

Sister Elisabeth smiled with knowledge that answered many questions for her. Mother Superior thanked her companion for her life of service, and with great labor, gave the guidance she knew was best. With a wry smile and a look of deep peace, she took a last breath.

. . .

It was near nightfall, a time when birds stopped singing and bats left their roosts, that Tomasz and Franciszek found themselves where they had bivouacked more than a week before. It was the faint sound of Vespers being sung by the monks that guided them. In the gloom, they saw St. Stephen's, its wooden gate caressed only by the dull glow of moonlight.

"Sire," Franciszek said quietly, addressing Tomasz in a deferential manner, though resentment seemed just a word away. "Shall I rap at the gate?"

Tomasz turned his head slowly, not believing that Franciszek would even consider such an idea. He kept his contempt in check, however, because frighteningly dumb though he was, Franciszek was a valuable tool.

"No, Franciszek," he patiently answered. "Do you not see we'd have to explain how we happened to return here? Do you think the lying bastard of a bishop would believe anything we had to say?"

Franciszek looked down at his saddle. "You're right as always, Sire. But why did we come back here?"

"Be grateful, Franciszek, that I am able to think for both of us,"

Tomasz scolded. "The monastery has gardens and pens. We need food, and nighttime is a good time to obtain our provisions—quietly.

. . .

When the days grew longer and warmer, Irina sat on a plank seat in the cart as it rattled along, and Velka napped in the bed of the cart as the afternoon sun shone through the thick trees.

"Madrosh," she called to the priest riding just ahead, "what and where is this Krosno that everyone speaks of?"

"Ah," Madrosh smiled, and steadied his horse. "Some days ago, when you asked me why we traveled in the woods, I thought you would ask me where we were." He laughed aloud. "*Krosno Odrzanskie*— Krosno on the Oder, My Lady, is the next most important visit in our westerly journey. I will not burden you with the labyrinthine politics, but this will be in your interest to remember: It had been under Polish control in the past, as was nearly all the country we have crossed since leaving Poznan. For various reasons, the lands have changed hands several times across the centuries. At present, Krosno is in the Duchy of Glogau. All along our travels you heard people speaking Polish and Germanic tongues. You now understand why." He paused to let her take that in.

"The duke will see the Margrave of Brandenburg, Wenceslas, who has asked to meet at the small castle there. Duke Zygmunt must be very careful in that meeting. At the moment, the Germans may be our allies against the Hungarians. It will not always be so."

Irina laughed and said, "For reasons you suggested earlier?"

"Yes, this is about land, and now, more than ever, about people."

"People?"

"Yes. Remember what I told you? In the Teutonic lands, it's been reported the plague wiped out nearly one half of all men, women, and children over the past forty years. That's why the Hungarians so covet the Polish lands, and why the Poles so hate them. We should be safe at Krosno—the Hungarians have no business here. And for now," he added, "we need the protection of the Germans."

"But do the Germans need us?"

Madrosh gave her a look of distaste. "Hmmh! I should not be so candid with you, my dear. The Teutons have always looked down upon us—they think we are somehow inferior to them."

"Inferior?"

"Yes. Have you not noticed? It seems every group, clan, nation needs someone over whom they feel superior. The Hungarians and the Germans. The Germans and the Poles. The Poles and the Jews. Do you see?

"Yes, I think so. Does Holy Mother Church have a part in this?"

He gave her a sideways glance. "An astute question, and one you should never ask of anyone but me. The answer is not pretty. The church may be married to Christ, but on this earth, it marries itself to temporal powers, and so the bishops to the Teutons support their ambitions while bishops to the Poles support theirs. Christ the shepherd is often nowhere to be seen."

"God permits this?"

"Not God, Irina. Men do."

"Where does all this leave the Jews, then?"

"Just another game piece, and easily expendable, I'm afraid."

"And Krosno?" she asked, returning Madrosh to the present.

"Ah, yes, an important stop, my dear. Our duke and the margrave have much to talk over and both know each other's value in the little wars for lands and people. Moreover, if the duke has been invited to Paris, so has the margrave, for he is a new prince-elector of the Holy Roman Empire."

"And our Duke Zygmunt is ready for word battles with this margrave?"

"You may be assured our duke is well studied, shall we say, in the nuances of our visit here."

Many more questions followed, their discussions of political matters involving family alliances, borders, and ancient hatreds. As the late afternoon shade crept upon them, Irina felt sleepy as the cart rolled in the soft dirt. "I can manage only one more question, Madrosh. Where exactly is this Krosno?"

Just as the words left her lips, the duke's entourage burst out of the woods into a blinding sunlight that danced on a majestic plain matted nearly flat along the eastern edge of the river. In the far distance appeared a castle with its two tall towers.

A broad smile crossed the old priest's face. "Ah, you won't nap now, My Lady. See, there!" He pointed. "There is *Krosno Odrzanskie!*"

CHAPTER VI

1378

Duke Zygmunt's party found a pleasant place to rest on the Oder's banks while soldiers and ferrymen hurried to accommodate their passage across.

Irina remained in the cart, finding herself most comfortable in a semi-reclining position behind one of the seats, and warmed by her blue woolen blanket. Madrosh dismounted and walked to her cart where she could see him at eye level. "I take it we are not able to use the bridge," she said, confirming her own observation.

"No, My Lady, the bridge is too narrow for our carts and cannot take the weight of so many men and horses."

"Of what use is it, then?"

"For us, none at all. It was built as a defensive measure so that large bodies of armed soldiers could not cross into Krosno for an attack. They would have to cross a few at a time, single file. Thus, castle defenders could easily dispatch them."

"So, what is our plan, then?"

Madrosh chuckled. "I counsel the duke on religious and political matters, my dear Lady, but not on ways and means to cross rivers. I understand, however, there is a barge guided by a rope on pulleys. The ferrymen will balance us on the barge and pull us across. It remains uncertain, however, whether we can accomplish the crossing tonight."

Duke Zygmunt rode up and dipped his head with a smile. "My Lady Kwasniewska, our timing this day is unfortunate. It is too late to erect tents, and within the hour it will be too late to cross. I and a few

132

of my men, along with Madrosh, will go ahead and cross the narrow bridge to make ourselves known to the castle warden. You and the other ladies may remain, making yourselves as comfortable as possible, or you can cross on the barge as soon as it can be arranged. In your condition, I leave the choice to you, My Lady."

Irina breathed deeply, trying to adjust her position. "If it's a question of enduring this bed for one more hour or through the night, there is, to me, no choice at all, My Lord. I'll go as soon as can be arranged, thank you."

"Then stay where you are, My Lady, and I will give the orders. We will see you on the other side, where I will see that a good featherbed awaits you."

Irina smiled in thanks, grateful for his solicitous manner. *Would that he had similarly concerned himself with the Joselewicz family!* She turned to Madrosh as Duke Zygmunt rode away. "We have a few minutes, then?"

"Yes, Irina, and then all will be well. Before I am called to go ahead with the duke, let me offer a suggestion." As he spoke, a breeze came up, cool and refreshing.

"Yes?"

"There lies Krosno Castle," he said, pointing across the river, "and what occurs there may be of immense interest to you."

"In what way?" Irina pulled her blanket closer to her.

"You were an astute judge of the interactions at St. Stephen's." He smiled, conspiratorially. "See who talks to whom and how they do so."

"Madrosh, I do not wish to be disrespectful, but the one interchange I will not miss is the one when you at last prove the existence of God."

"May I remind the lady it has been she who on several occasions has changed the subject or, like a rabbit, gone in many gardens in search of a carrot. Your thirst for knowledge is admirable, if not organized." Madrosh laughed out loud.

"So I am an object of laughter to you," she asked in mock hurt.

"No, My Lady. It is only the situation in which we find ourselves. Here I am, never having had to answer such a question before dukes and princes. Yet you, my dear, never fail to ask bigger and wiser questions than many of them could ever conceive."

A soldier rode up and nodded to Madrosh. "I'll see you on the other side, My Lady. Squire Brezchwa will accompany you on the barge." Into the looming dusk, Madrosh rode toward the sun setting on the far side of the Oder.

Squire Brezchwa appeared and grasped the reins of Irina's horse and cart. "Lady Irina, you and I, your cart and horse, and two other riders with their horses will be on the first barge across."

"And Velka, my servant, and the two nuns?" A light rain began falling, soon made worse by the quickening breeze from the north.

"That may be too many for the barge, My Lady."

"Velka, at least, must come with us. I may need her."

"As you wish."

The ferrymen hastened in the fading light, and within a few moments, all were loaded on the long, sturdy barge. A half dozen torches cast gleaming shadows on the water's surface. Silky smooth just moments earlier, the river's surface now began to churn with the wind.

Never one to be left behind, Yip slipped aboard and slid under the cart. The ferrymen used what light they had to help them manage the rope as they pulled toward the opposite shore. The barge strained against the wind and water, rougher by the moment.

The rain became heavier. Irina caught Squire Brezchwa's eye, as if wondering about their safety. In turn, the squire grabbed one of the ferrymen by the tunic and shouted words into his ear as the wind began to whirl and whistle, but Irina could not hear them.

The barge appeared to be halfway across the Oder when northern gusts swept across the water and jerked the craft against its only guideline. Repeatedly, the barge bucked and swayed in the wind and whitecaps.

Of the three horses aboard, Jan Brezchwa held and steadied the one leading Irina's cart, but the two horses and their riders in the front of the barge could not hold their charges in place as they danced and whinnied in fear and rebellion. When the horse on the right was hit with a broad splash of water, it shifted its position and weight toward its mate, which clopped perilously close to the barge's low gunwale.

The horses slipped on the wet planks and, in fright, shifted away from the waves and the wind. As they did so, the left side of the vessel began to tip. The ferrymen struggled to keep the barge level and on course as it strained against the heavy rope.

Later, Irina had trouble remembering exactly what happened, but she knew their cart slid to the left gunwale with such force as to snap a wheel from its axle. The sudden tilt of the cart flung Irina into the river as she clutched her blue woolen blanket. For some reason, she couldn't let loose of it. The horse and its cart followed.

In the frigid spring waters, Irina flailed and began to lose buoyancy as her heavy clothes, drenched through, dragged her below the surface. She bumped against something hard, and it seemed as if all time stopped. *Will I see Berek again?*

Onward, she felt herself drifting in the dark, swirling waters, and in moments, she began to lose a sense of having arms and legs, of having a body at all. *I could die to see Berek, but what about our child?*

She felt something grab hold of her arm, and suddenly, she was pushed to the surface and onto the floating carcass of the cart. Gulping air over and over, Irina made herself open her eyes. The fading torchlight some distance away was the only illumination, but she saw little as the distance between the cart and barge began to grow.

The cart's wooden side groaned as someone held her in place. One of the soldiers had acted quickly, she thought. Soon, they were far away from the only light to guide them as the torches winked out. Without a prow, the cart was like a rudderless ship whose resting place would be unknown.

. . .

Tomasz and his compatriot fumbled their way slowly west, gaining on their prey day by day. Despite several wrong starts, dense forests, and frequent spring rains, they managed to follow a blurred trail until realizing they were actually following another group of travelers. Undeterred, Tomasz pushed on, driven to have his revenge.

Although Franciszek made it clear he wished only to be in some quiet barn near Poznan drinking his ale, taking advantage of women and having plenty to eat, he slogged by Tomasz's side because he had no other good choice.

Tomasz had not one but two reasons for hunting down the sojourners, wherever they were. The duke himself, Tomasz could not forgive. Yet he could serve him, and even with some degree of loyalty, if the duke would only see he'd been taken in by the woman and her so-called servant. He knew he needed the blessing of the duke just to remain alive.

As it was, he was an escaped prisoner. He could tell a good lie about what happened to Wojciech and the other one, he reasoned. After all, they were the bishop's men, and as for the lying priest, he would deal with him later. Whatever it took, he had to get back in the good graces of his duke.

The surest way to do that was to expose the woman pretending to be a lady for what she truly was: a servant to Jews! He spat as he envisioned a scene in which he would triumph in the eyes of his master. As he thought about it, his eyes gleamed in a fixed stare.

At one point, Tomasz noticed a stillness in the air that was unnerving. The ground was still damp from an earlier rainstorm that had pelted them for miles, and the leaves, though sodden, began to stir on the forest floor. Looking up, he saw only leaves blinking in the wind, and clouds thick and threatening. Without sun or shadow, there was nothing to guide him. It had rained so hard, in fact, they weren't sure which track to take when it diverged in the forest. Taking the southern or left leg of the road, they began to realize they'd made still another wrong decision.

After two more days wandering in the Silesian Forest, they emerged to find themselves on a rise overlooking a river less than a day's ride away. Tomasz immediately understood their good fortune and thanked God for having brought them to this point. They would spend the night here, he reasoned, and enjoy some cooked meat and a good, dry rest.

"Do you know where we are?" Franciszek challenged him.

"Yes," he responded with a smirk showing the odd, misshapen tooth. "I've never been here, but I know where we are. What's more important, I know where they are!" With that, he raised his arm and pointed. "There. To the north. There we will find our quarry, and there we will find the duke's favor."

What had been a calm, May evening suddenly turned to every traveler's bane. As the sky darkened and rolled with black clouds, Tomasz could see that the entire Oder River valley would be engaged in a battle with the weather. They retreated into the trees. Within minutes, only a few yards around him were visible as they struggled to erect a simple shelter of pine boughs layered over a bent sapling. They supped on a not very tasty hen stolen from a defenseless villager earlier in the day while the flagon of ale Franciszek purloined from a tavern served to quench their thirst and distract them from the storm that howled around them. Their horses bucked against their tiedowns, trying to break their bonds.

"Tomorrow," Tomasz said, loud enough so that Franciszek could hear him over the pounding rain, "we find our way back to grace."

...

At last, the massive cart crashed to a halt on a cluster of giant boulders strewn along the shore.

Irina held on to the craft as it banged back and forth, snagged by the rocks. She had no notion how long she remained there, shielded from the weather only by her protector's cloak. Neither she nor her savior stirred, exhausted and shocked by the cold water and the pelting rain. Her companion seemed deathly still.

In the fog of semi-consciousness, she could discern the muffled shouts of men running, frantic, somewhere near them. The rain slowed, but the wind still buffeted them as Irina clung for life. She could see the blink of torches, and she breathed easier when she realized they were the duke's men, not brigands. For a moment, she thought her imagination had gone awry when she heard the growly voice of Father Martinus Madrosh. *Wasn't he already across the river?*

Irina raised her arm and voice but was not heard immediately as her cries were carried southward in the wind. "Here!" someone shouted. Other voices joined in. Men scampered across rocks while others held torches to light their way. Two rescuers grabbed hold of her and managed to pass her from one pair of hands to others. They secured her in dry, woolen blankets.

"How are you, My Lady?" It wasn't the voice of Madrosh. It was the soft, kind voice of a man she believed a killer. Duke Zygmunt took a corner of the blanket and tucked it more tightly around her.

"It seems I have survived," she said with a wan smile.

"I am so sorry, My Lady. My judgment failed you."

"I thought you and your party had crossed the bridge."

"The bridge, such as it is, threatened to collapse under us. We came back. I wish you had been able to do the same without," he spread his arms in the torchlight, "all this."

"Madrosh?"

"I am here, Lady Irina."

"My Velka? Is she alright?"

"One of the ferrymen—and Yip—caught her as your cart rolled into the water. She seems fine. I'm afraid we're to stay on this side of the Oder until light. Let's get you safe and warm in front of a fire."

As they approached the rest of the company, Velka and the nuns surrounded her, effectively pushing the men aside. They asked her the questions males did not know to ask and to which they shouldn't hear the answers—about her pregnancy, about injury to herself, about miscarriage. Yet chilled from her brief visit to a watery grave, Irina first felt her abdomen, then checked herself for bleeding, before assuring her nurses she was well. Though still soaked with river water, the blue woolen square remained with her, bunched around her mid-section like protective armor.

"I thank you all," she said, shivering in her woolen cocoon. She closed her eyes, uttering thanks to heaven—*Did I just thank God?*—then called out to the priest. "Madrosh—the man who saved me?"

The old priest stepped closer and smiled. "Why, it was Squire Brezchwa, my dear."

. . .

Jerzy Andrezski had never been a religious man. He'd lived as a travelling merchant, taking life as he found it, never worrying about the day beyond the next. He'd seen too much slaughter and pillage, too many crimes too vile to remember, too many people whose tomorrows never came. He'd come to Poznan thinking the God people worshipped was an uncaring bystander, a faceless, heartless, and selfish God who caused nothing but fear. He saw no reason to attend church, but the question of an Almighty was always in his mind.

That was then. That he'd survived was a small miracle, he felt certain, and then, never before had he witnessed the utter self-sacrifice for total strangers that had been shown to hundreds of the dying by the Dominican Sisters. Sister Elisabeth had labored to ensure the poor and the pitied as well as the haughty and highborn approached death with tender hands caring for them. To him, those simple facts moved him to believe there must, indeed, be an Almighty God.

That Sister Elisabeth, too, had died of plague gave him no opportunity to render proper thanks for saving his life. He had pledged to serve her when they first met, but fate did not allow him that opportunity. When he had stumbled away from the caravan, and found himself sick unto death at the church door, he knew that all of his worldly goods would melt into the pouches of those moving on, carrying his wealth along with death itself. But now he had a new chance to build a life pleasing to God.

On the day he felt well enough to leave the confines of the convent, Sister Luke came to bid a plague's survivor a warm farewell. When her words to him conveyed a certain finality, he said, "I'm staying here in Poznan, Sister. In some way, I'll establish myself in a business, I'll be successful, and I will assist the convent and its work in every way possible."

The nun returned his gaze with interest and curiosity. The two had spoken but a few times. "I do not know what to make of you, Jerzy Andrezski. You are so confident of your abilities, but given what has happened around us, what sort of business do you think might be a success?"

"I do not know, Sister. But the answer will come. I am convinced God led me to this place and let an angel quench my thirst. I can't prove that, but here I am, alive, when by all measures, I should be dead and in the pits with all those others."

She smiled. "While you're thinking about it, *Pan* Andrezski," she said, addressing him more formally, "you may have noticed that with all the dead, many of their goods have been left here. You can help us by clearing them out. Perhaps you might sell some items to help you on your feet."

"*Djenkuje*, Sister Luke. I will sell these things, but take little."

As he collected the goods from a shed near the kitchen, he spied Sister Rose and the little girl working in their usual place, and remembered seeing her on the Fareway. He learned from the elderly nun it had been Zuzanna who'd given him water when he was ill, making him wonder how she had come to be at the convent. Too busy to seek an answer, he left, but vowed to take care of his little angel.

. . .

Arriving from the south and moving quietly along the Oder, King Louis's expeditionary force hugged the wood line and approached the shore only to water their horses or to cross back and forth at fording places to take advantage of the terrain. Nearing Glogau, they crossed back again to the eastern shore, climbed the gentle slope forming one rim of the river valley, and slid into the woods.

They continued in that fashion for many miles through a largely uninhabited forest, and the men breathed easily as they rode with little danger of attack. There had been no fighting in this part of Germanic lands for decades, and the Hungarians suspected their sometime enemy had become lax.

It would have been pointless, Sir Bela Kinizsi knew, to attack Glogau or any of its surrounding villages, as such a move would gain the Hungarians nothing of value, and the entire valley would be alerted to their presence. The available maps suggested a much better target. It was lightly defended, yet controlled a critical part of the river. Were they to capture and defend it, why, it would be like cutting a snake in two—Glogau and Breslau. The belly and the tail would wither and die, easy pickings for the larger force to come later.

It was better, he perceived, to control the Oder from that point northward to Frankfort and beyond. All this he explained to one of his officers. "That will be the key we shall turn in the Teutonic lock," he said, confident of his strategy.

As their horses moved through the woods growing thick with bright-green foliage, it occurred to Sir Bela that careless though the Germans might appear, it was better to be prepared. To his field captain, Janos Tomori, he gave orders to send scouts, carefully and stealthily. "I doubt you'll find anything, Timori, but we are within two days of our target—Krosno Castle—and we don't want any surprises, do we." It was not a question.

...

The following morning, a Sunday, Father Madrosh offered a Mass of thanksgiving on the eastern bank of the Oder as the sun cleared the trees and bathed them all in welcome warmth. Given the previous night's ferocity, he expressed gratitude to the Almighty for their party's ongoing safety, and asked all to pray for the eternal rest of the one soldier drowned when thrown from the barge in the squall.

Madrosh then reminded his listeners of John 4 and the Samaritan woman at the well. "Within a few hours, we will cross into another land whose inhabitants are not always loved by Poles or our Hungarian rulers. Just as Christ spoke to the Samaritan woman—ordinarily despised by Galileans—we keep our hearts open to all those of different tongues we will soon meet. It is not enough just to tolerate them. Christ meant us to love all our neighbors as ourselves."

Because they had fasted before receiving Holy Communion, all were ready for a hearty breakfast of eggs, bread, cheese, and a bit of ale. As they ate, they pondered the waters of the Oder, calm and clear, but knew how quickly river waters could change. The shoreline hummed with soldiers and men securing the bridge, though the damage was less than expected.

After the duke's physician had examined her the night before and declared her unharmed by her near-drowning, Irina slept fitfully next to Velka in one of the tents hastily erected for the duke and numerous other nobles. Their clothing dried and they themselves refreshed by a

Mass spent with Almighty God, Irina sought out her confessor and mentor.

"My Lady, Duke Zygmunt wishes you to cross the bridge on horseback rather than walk with all the others. He does not wish you to be over-exerted as we enter Krosno Castle."

"I am so grateful, Madrosh. I am truly exhausted and would rather stay here in rude surroundings than give risk to my child."

"Just so, My Lady. Squire Brezchwa will guide your horse. He, too, is concerned for your safety." The warm breeze quickened, snapping the white and red pennants atop the soldiers' lances.

"That is kind of him," she said, a small smile shaping her lips. "I am curious, Madrosh. You've told me a little about the squire, but there is much I do not know. Why is Duke Sokorski so fond of him? And the duke's wife, what of her? Perhaps these are questions to which I should not know the answers?"

"Oh, not at all, My Lady." He paused to collect his next words. "First things first. Duke Sokorski was married very young to a beautiful girl named Elena. As might be expected, not long after their wedding, it was announced Elena was with child. The duke's parents were yet living, and there was much celebration in Poznan."

"What happened?"

"I have not told you this before because of your own present condition." He looked away briefly. "Pardon me, My Lady. I knew them well—I helped celebrate their wedding Mass with a bishop now long dead. A few months into her maternity, plague struck, and though the Sokorskis fled the city, they could not flee the plague. Elena, the duke's parents, and, yes, Squire Brezchwa's entire family all were wiped away within a week—as if they never existed."

"Merciful God! That must have been truly devastating for them."

"And then, too, the Jews were blamed. Wrongly, of course, but such charges paint a man's memories horrible colors."

After a minute of silence, Madrosh went on, "As you might imagine, Duke Sokorski has never been the same man. He has refused to marry again, but he knew his duty to the Brezchwa family. At once, he took in the boy and has raised him as his own. There will never be a son for the duke but Jan Brezchwa."

"Thank you, Madrosh," Irina murmured in a quiet, thoughtful voice. "In a small number of words, you have told me much about the squire and the man who raised him." The two of them waited for the signal to cross, watching silently as the duke's men heaved and perspired in the morning sun.

"You mentioned Krosno. What is there to know about it?"

"Certainly," Madrosh answered from his reverie, "Krosno Castle is not the largest fortress on the Oder, but it is substantial, nonetheless, and it controls vital lands along both shores. It is an outpost for the Duchy of Glogau, but little else. You can see, Irina, that its two towers are at opposite ends of a long, rectangular, high-walled affair, and it sits imposingly on the river's edge."

"And the narrow bridge helps to defend it."

"Yes. Observe that the castle's towers face the river, and Poland—a warning to our ancestors, no doubt. No such daunting obstacles face the Teutonic lands. It is, if I may say, a bit of German arrogance to state that no enemy could or would ever foray beyond Krosno Castle. "I am told it is a mere country town, unused to seeing large numbers of nobility pass through. Of soldiers and horses, they have seen many over the decades because even peasants know Krosno stands halfway between two important strongholds—both of which had been under Polish rule at one time."

"I shouldn't laugh," Irina said, "but aren't the people confused when their borders change so often?"

"I am sure they are, My Lady, but about the feelings of the people, monarchs care little. As to Krosno, it could have been a powerful town for a military garrison, but large numbers of armed men are not usually billeted here, and likewise, power has never made its home in Krosno. What troops may be there now will be more ceremonial than battle ready."

Squire Brezchwa approached, bowed, and let them know they would cross at last.

Irina looked up at him, gave him her bravest smile, and said, "Without you, Jan Brezchwa, I would not be crossing at all! You will always have my deepest gratitude. If," she added with mirth, "you can assure me we will be dry when we reach the other side."

The squire laughed out loud. "It was my pleasure, My Lady. And yes, I give you my word."

Irina couldn't seem to help liking the sound of his name, and again, she found herself saying both names as one, "Jan Brezchwa." She saw the squire as an attractive, likable young man, but that was as far as she allowed thoughts of him to wander. Irina could not forget Berek, and could not see herself replacing him in her heart and head with anyone at all, certainly not within one lunar cycle of his death.

"My Lady," Brezchwa addressed her with great deference, "when we reach Krosno, we will be there for a few days. You have only to call upon me, and I will see to it that whatever you ask will be taken care of immediately."

"Yes, Squire, that would be very much appreciated," she answered, regaining a certain formality. She would not permit a familiarity she could not welcome in return.

Irina gave further thanks during the crossing, but conversation with the squire was desultory, a relief to her guilty conscience, to be sure, but a puzzlement to him, she could see.

Once across, the travelers landed on a large, flat space paved with cobbles, in the center of which was the town's main well. Surrounding the square was a collection of already ancient dwellings and shops, behind which several dozen more structures of stone and wood tightly strung themselves along the lanes and alleys veining away and up the valley slope.

On the right was the southern wall of the castle, one of its towers cornering the square. A moat of sorts had been dug on three sides so that river waters were allowed to completely surround the islanded fortress. It was an imposing, highly defensible citadel, as Madrosh had intimated.

The duke's entire party was escorted with deference and respect as they crossed the moat's short wooden bridge and paraded through the main gate. The magistrate and commander of the castle, Sir Ortwinus Esel, spoke Polish as he welcomed them in the name of the

Margrave of Glogau, and on behalf of the Margrave of Brandenburg. Sir Ortwinus scowled at the low rumble of muted laughter amongst the soldier-riders.

"Why are they laughing?" Irina whispered to Squire Brezchwa.

Brezchwa, in turn, suppressed a chuckle. "One of the soldiers told me that in German, Esel means donkey or jackass."

"An unfortunate surname, to be sure, and then, there's the man's unusual girth…" whispered Martinus Madrosh himself.

"Father!" Irina covered her lips as she giggled into her sleeve.

"It goes well with his puffed-up personality," said Brezchwa, a broad smile framing his countenance.

"Stop it now, you two," Irina said in mock reproach, then bowed her head so that others would not see her cheeks blush.

Sir Ortwinus cleared his throat and repeated words of further welcome, this time in German, insisting that the duke and his guests dismount and enter for some rest and food. The Margrave of Brandenburg would arrive in the morning or the very next day, Sir Esel assured his noble guests. With a look of poorly hidden disdain, he marched into the keep.

...

Tomasz and Franciszek spent a few hours searching for a place where they could ford the Oder well south of Krosno. Because they were on no schedule, they went about their day with ease, and in mid-morning, they retreated into the cool woods for a catch of small game. As they readied to roast slices of rabbit over a small fire, one looked at the other as they both realized the rustling of leaves and the odd crack of a branch in the woods directly behind them weren't from the light breeze. "We are no longer alone, Franciszek."

"It's just a boar," Franciszek said, turning to stare at the new green of the forest. "If it comes after us, well," he laughed, "that'll be dinner."

"You're right. His or ours?" They howled with laughter.

Another twig cracked.

They sprang simultaneously, Tomasz to grab the reins of their horses and Franciszek to reach for his bow. Tomasz put his free hand on his sword. They froze.

Armed men flew out of the brush from all directions at once. At first Tomasz could not tell if they were highwaymen, but the markings on the light-gray tunics told him these were soldiers. What he saw was a white, doubled cross on a field of deep red, heraldry he had seen only once or twice before.

Believing they were about to die, Franciszek could only mutter, "Oh, for a duck's wing and some cheese."

"No food for us!" said Tomasz in a low mutter.

The captors surrounded their prey, their lances pointing at Tomasz and Franciszek from all sides. The foreigners shouted words the new captives could not understand.

Tomasz spoke his native Polish, but his listeners seemed to understand only a word or two. For some reason, one of the men facing him broke into a broad smile, then dismounted, disarmed their captives, and tied their hands before leading them away. All the while, Tomasz tried to recall where he had seen their tunics before.

Tomasz scowled and swore repeatedly, and as they were jerked along, an image of old Teofil crossed his mind. But only for a moment.

. . .

In the late afternoon, after everyone in the duke's party had taken rest in their assigned spaces for the visit, Irina and Madrosh found themselves together in Krosno Castle's courtyard, surrounded by four stories of timber and masonry, bustling cooks, gardeners, and stable boys. Clearly, all were readying for an important visitor.

"Are you feeling refreshed?" Madrosh wanted to know as they stepped away.

"Oh, yes. Velka has taken care of my needs and our rooms are nicely appointed."

Yip patrolled alongside. They were safe. A long pause ensued while they enjoyed a walk without fear or rain.

Madrosh broke the silence, "Do you remember seeing and hearing the chiming clock in the refectory of the convent house in Poznan?" asked Madrosh. He and Lady Irina strolled slowly around the esplanade, taking in the castle's structure.

Such an odd question! It startled her. She was glad of the walk after so many hours and days in a cart or on a horse—not to mention the time spent in the water. No midwife she, but Irina thought it good for her to walk whenever possible. Riding, her legs became numb, and her intuitive belief was that being out of a natural balance would not be good for the babe in her womb. As she turned her focus on the question, a chill descended upon them. She pulled her cloak more closely around her.

"Clock?" she responded, dumbly. "I've only seen a very few, perhaps just two in all. The one just outside Poznan Castle and the one you mentioned. Why do you ask and why do you talk about so many things other than the subject I want you to talk about?" she demanded playfully, her bright smile underlining her mood.

"You have seen few because there are few. The first timepieces were made hundreds and hundreds of years ago, and they were powered by water. Our word clock comes from the Latin word *clocca,* for bell, because bells or chimes mark the passage of the hours. All of them are vastly complicated. Some even show the phases of the moon and rising and falling tides. While I was at the University in Krakow, they talked about a most famous clock constructed by Dondi in Padua just a few years earlier. It was said Dondi's clock marked feast days of the church and even predicted the times when the moon would obscure the sun."

"That is all very interesting, Father Madrosh. But how does that explain the existence of God?"

He ignored her interruption. "The two clocks to which you referred. Am I assuming correctly you were not able to see what made the timepieces run?"

"You are correct."

"If you were able to examine such a device, you'd probably think it was like a very small mill grinding wheat, only much, much more complicated and intricate. And once you noticed all the gear wheels and springs and levers, would you not conclude that all those parts— like those of a simple grinding mill—could not have come together by chance?"

"Yes. Someone would have had to carefully plan such a device, I would think." After a moment, she went on. "In St. Michael, our mill had to be rebuilt after a fire a few years ago. The stonemasons and carpenters were very careful to place the mill so that the big wheel in the water could turn easiest and fastest for all the farmers in nearby villages."

"You mean it was designed to get the most out of his mill?"

"Yes, naturally."

"But it wasn't perfect, was it?"

"No," she laughed aloud. "After it was finished, they talked even more. They said the next one would be even better."

"Do you think our world as we know it with the stars in the heavens, the sun and moon, the waters flowing through our earth—do you think it all happened by chance? Is our world not a device created by a Master Craftsman much more brilliant than the great Dondi?"

Irina nodded. "I do not mean to be disrespectful, but ours doesn't seem like the perfect world He could create. Does that mean He will make it over again?" she quipped.

It was Madrosh's turn to laugh. "That's an unusual question, and perhaps you are correct, and God will tire of his creation gone awry." After a moment, he added, "but do you realize your question relies on the existence of a Creator?"

"Perhaps," she smiled, "but I am still not convinced."

"Just remember that as complicated as is your mill in St. Michael, and even more so the clocks in Poznan, our very existence, our very bodies, are infinitely more complex—and could not have happened by the same roll of the dice the soldiers use. More to the point, we could not exist without the plan of a Master Craftsman, the likes of whom we can only strive to know."

"So, you're saying God made all of this happen because someone or something had to make it happen by design?"

"What the philosophers might call a Prime Mover, a First Cause. You see, everything we've done in our lives was caused by something or someone before us, like unraveling a ball of woolen yarn that seems to go on forever."

"But even the ball of yarn has to have a beginning," Irina asserted.

"Precisely!"

Irina listened quietly, expectantly.

"And what's so magically brilliant and overwhelming," Madrosh continued, "is that we…"

"We?" she challenged in return, interrupting him.

"Yes, we…the continuing existence of the human race, of all that surrounds us, earth, sky, water," Madrosh said, opening his arms in an encompassing gesture. "We are like your mill in St. Michael, but we are a mill that needs no stream or river to power the grinding wheel. Our universe is like the most complicated clock that never needs winding—because it is crafted by the greatest clockmaker of all."

. . .

Dinner in the great hall had come and gone, and all the while, Irina and Madrosh talked as if no one else was there, paying little attention to the roast venison and the other delights around the table. It hadn't been an intimate talk, to be sure, but it was intense nevertheless. They ceased only when men ran atop the ramparts lighting torches, then in the courtyard and at the gate. Someone said riders must have come to alert Sir Ortwinus of an impending arrival.

By the time they bid each other a restful night, most of their fellow sojourners were well into their first sleep. As she readied herself for bed, Irina had begun to accept the notion of a single Being who founded the world, fashioning the earth and sky from nothing. As she lay resting in her chamber, the notion that stayed with her was the one about an unsprung eternal clock.

I must admit that I have come to like—and trust—this man, this priest, though I am far from convinced of what he says. His avalanche of words about God may be hard to take, at times, but I asked the question, didn't I?

After a few hours, she was startled awake when a heavy sound poured through the nearby open slit in the wall that gave her light and air. It came from beyond the thick stone walls of the tower, from somewhere far below her. Finally, she realized it was the chain's rumble when the portcullis was lifted to allow entrance from the moat bridge.

Irina rose and peered out of the wall's opening. "Ah, the visitor!"

There followed a blast of trumpets announcing the arrival of the Margrave of Brandenburg, Wenceslas the King, and his entourage of thirty or so knights on horseback, their armor glinting in the torchlight, the Teutonic pennants flying their royal colors in the cool May breezes.

Looking down on the scene from her height in the tower, she concentrated her full attention on the margrave himself, a king and prince-elector of the Holy Roman Empire, Madrosh had said; she wanted to see what such a man might look like. She laughed at her silliness when she realized all she'd see from her post was the top of his head! And that in the half dark of shifting images in the torchlight!

The clatter of hooves on the cobbles was deafening. When it stopped, she could hear the high voice of Sir Ortwinus Esel. She smiled delightedly as she pictured him making his welcome speech before the travelers dismounted and marched into the castle's great hall—for refreshment, she guessed.

Based upon what Madrosh had said, the Margrave Wenceslas and Duke Zygmunt would spend time together discussing their business, and she could not imagine their company would rest in Krosno for more than a day or two. In truth, Irina had no idea what to expect.

...

Life was peaceful and plentiful for Bishop Tirasewicz at St. Stephen's. He wanted for nothing. To be so far into the Polish woods was a bit disconcerting, to be sure, but the distance between him and Poznan's plague was comforting. Though the kitchen delights were not as sophisticated and grand as at Poznan, he was well-fed with rustic foods and had a soft bed.

The monastery's abbot, Father Kaminski, kept to his monks, and except for morning Mass and meals, they paid him little attention. It wasn't a matter of disrespect, he knew. It was simply that they were two different kinds of men with very different callings in life, despite their religious vows. *Kaminski can keep to his prayers, and I will keep to myself.*

In the back of his mind, the bishop felt a nagging satisfaction for having rid himself of Tomasz Wodowicz. *Terrible, indeed!* That it was Wodowicz alone who saw and spoke to him on the night of fire and death had been a concern. That the man would soon be dead was most comforting.

Because the monastery was within his See, Bishop Tirasewicz knew everything about St. Stephen's and had ratified Kaminski's election as its rector. He considered the abbot a quiet, contemplative man, ideal to his position as leader of quiet, contemplative men. They worked to sustain themselves, body and spirit, and other than contact with an occasional wayfarer or a villager or farmer nearby, they were content serving God in the manner they'd chosen.

Antony Tirasewicz, on the other hand, had no difficulty seeing himself much like the secular prince he served. Like so many others in his position, he was sponsored by a noble, and had never had any but the most rudimentary priestly training. As bishop, he was a religious administrator with little interest in the mysteries of the church except as to how they might serve his purposes. Court politics suited him vastly more than Catholic doctrine.

In the days of solitude after the duke's party left for Paris, the bishop found ample time to brood. Why was he shown no respect by Duke Zygmunt? Beyond cursory courtesy, the duke had no interest in having him along to see the emperor in Paris. It would have been an easy matter to include the Bishop of Poznan, would it not? Yet the duke chose to take along a pregnant girl of unknown origin! This slight would neither be forgiven nor forgotten.

About a fortnight after the duke's departure, the deep forest repose was disturbed by a local farmer, running out of the woods and calling to the abbot near to where the bishop was taking his morning constitutional.

"Father Kaminski," called Lech Stephanek—so surnamed because he had been abandoned at the monastery when he was an infant—pausing to catch his breath. "My son and I found the bodies of two men in the woods. They'd been dead for some days, and with the smell of blood in the air, the boars and other animals have had their fill."

The bishop stepped closer so as not to miss a word.

"I see," responded the abbot. "How far away is this?"

"A good day's walk. Less on horseback. There had been horses there, as there are still footprints. We covered what was left of the bodies," he said, blessing himself, "with a layering of dirt until we could speak with you. Father, there was one really odd thing."

"And what was that, *Pan* Stephanek?"

"The bodies had no clothes on them but there were clothes nearby—and the clothes had no blood on them."

. . .

Sir Bela Kinizsi set his mind on attack. If King Louis was correct, the invitation to Paris should have already bestirred all the nobles living along the river wealthy enough for a long journey. With any luck, Krosno might be an empty shell.

He strode through his camp considering ways he might overcome what defenders of Krosno Castle remained. Crossing the bridge was out of the question, he knew. Built as it was, the bridge was a brilliant defensive bulwark. He would have to approach from the land side, but even that would be a tricky maneuver.

When he saw Captain Tomori and his men approach with prisoners, he scratched his black beard, and with a chuckle, said to his aide, "Aha! As I thought. One never knows what creatures one will find in the forest." The men were pushed to the ground at Sir Bela's feet.

The captives were wearing the garb of soldiers to some Polish churchman, and as such, they were likely subjects of King Louis. Another of his men was summoned as translator. Through Captain Tomori, who spoke and understood a bit of Polish, Kinizsi said, "You may rise and speak if you've anything useful to say."

Tomasz cowered, obviously considering what words to use, but he seemed to be struck speechless.

"Who are you and why are you here?" Sir Bela demanded, there being no patience to his words.

"We are merely soldiers who became separated from our master, Sire," Tomasz said, his eyes darting left and right.

"Look at me, fool! Who is your master and where is he now?"

"Our master is Duke Zygmunt Sokorski of Poznan, Sire, and we believe he is at Krosno Castle. We were on our way there."

"Your tunics have church markings on them. Do you not serve some bishop?"

"W-why, yes," Tomasz stumbled. "But Bishop Tirasewicz is under the protection of Duke Zygmunt."

"I see," said Sir Bela, who didn't "see" it at all. "How many men does he have there and why is he away from his duchy?"

"Sire, we do not know why he goes there—they never tell us anything," he said laughing haplessly.

Sir Bela did not smile.

"He has about thirty men, more or less, Sire."

"So, you have no idea why your master would be visiting the Duchy of Glogau?"

"No, Sire. When we last saw Duke Zygmunt at St. Stephen's monastery, there were rumors amongst the men about a westward journey of some sort, nothing more. I'm sure Krosno Castle is just a resting place for him. That's all we know, Sire."

Sir Bela knew the reason for the duke's presence, but already, he'd learned valuable information. Indeed, this must be a party on its way to Paris. He looked down his narrow nose at his captives. "We are Hungarians—and, of course, subjects to the same king as your duke." He smiled contentedly. "We would like to meet Duke Zygmunt Sokorski. Perhaps you'll introduce us."

. . .

"Madrosh," Irina addressed the priest, when they spoke again. "I cannot help being curious. Do you have any idea what Duke Zygmunt and Margrave Wenceslas may be discussing?"

Madrosh smiled lightly as he spoke, choosing his words. "My dear Lady, in fact, I do know, as I have been present during their two sessions together, but I would be breaking my pledge of obedience to the duke if I were to…"

She interrupted him with a smile of her own. "Oh, I was hoping you'd respond that way—if you keep your promises to your master, you will keep them for me."

"So it will be. We have but a moment before the feast with our earthly princes. Was there another question, My Lady?"

"Yes, Madrosh, you'll have to do better in demonstrating God's existence, but assuming I take it to be so, my next question is simply this: Is man good or evil?"

"Simply?" Madrosh chortled. "From you, there seem to be no simple questions! At least you've given me time to think how to frame an answer. Come. Let us dine on good German venison."

. . .

When Lech Stephanek, his son, and the abbot's monk returned two days later, they walked slowly, a cortege accompanying the barely recognizable human remains shifting to and fro in the back of their cart. They arrived at St. Stephen's in time to see Father Kaminski bidding a pleasant farewell to Bishop Antony Tirasewicz and his retinue.

The bishop had made it clear, one of the monks earlier informed the abbot, that monastery life was of no further interest to him, and that he had decided to risk returning to Poznan, nearly a month having passed since the plague joined their midst in the city.

"My dear Abbot," the bishop sniffed, "you have my thanks for the hospitality"—a drop of acid on the word—"you and your monks have so graciously provided." For a moment, he forgot what he was supposed to say next. Then he added, "We will remember you in our prayers."

"Your Grace," Karol Kaminski responded, "it has been our honor. May your journey to Poznan be safe and swift." The humble abbot's smile was one of relief.

The bishop cursorily blessed the bodies—without recognizing the remains as men in service to him—and, without further word, jerked the reins of his horse to point the animal toward Poznan. Those returning with him joined in silent procession behind their master.

. . .

In the comfort of Krosno Castle on a windy first day of June, the nobles settled themselves around a table laden with warm breads and fresh cheeses. These they sampled and washed their palates with a strong brew. Huge platters of roast venison and pig followed, their aromas giving those gathered pause to smile in anticipation. Surrounded by their counselors and aides de camp, they began their discussions on a note of pleasantry.

"Your Highness," Duke Zygmunt intoned, bowing slightly, "we are so grateful for the hospitality shown by you and the Margrave of Glogau." Though both Zygmunt and Wenceslas were theoretically of equal rank, the notion of *primus inter primi* was well understood. While Zygmunt was a powerful noble in Greater Poland, the Margrave of Brandenburg was also a crowned King, and son of Charles, Holy Roman Emperor. It had been a slight bow, but one for which Zygmunt hoped there would be a return on his investment.

King Wenceslas smiled in reply, clearly enjoying their encounter. "And how, dear Zygmunt," he finally responded, "may we assist our Polish ally?"

"Ah, Your Highness, I am somewhat embarrassed. I thought it was you who asked for this meeting."

"Indeed. I had heard you'd be making the long journey in response to my cousin's invitation." This was a statement of fact, but one full of implication. Underneath was the implication that since Zygmunt would be crossing Germanic territories, either some sort of tribute was expected, or, at the least, an offer of some other mutually beneficial arrangement.

"Of course, Your Highness. Naturally, I believed your kingdom would graciously welcome and protect favored wayfarers responding to an invitation from the Emperor's own son." Zygmunt knew full well the meaning of the King's parry, as he knew his play was to avoid surrendering a fee for safe passage.

King Wenceslas smiled again in recognition of the delicate situation before him.

To Zygmunt, his host's grin was much like the studied stare of the wolfhound in proximity to a platter of red meat. Zygmunt returned the smile and gave him a nod as a willing and ready combatant. And so the sparring began.

...

Tomasz—not so terrible at this point—fretted. He could no more be part of an introduction to Duke Zygmunt, than a mouse introducing a wolf to a boar. His earlier daydreams about returning to the duke's good graces were one thing. The reality confronting him was another. The duke would give him no time for explanations—a broadsword would be his only and swift greeting. It seemed hopeless.

At that moment, Big Franciszek appeared, blocking out the sun. As he stared up at his companion, he thought to himself it was easy to see how he earned his name. Franciszek was at least a foot taller than most men around him. His flaxen hair allowed friends to easily hail him from a distance, while giving enemies more time to flee. As Tomasz waited for Franciszek to form his words, an idea began to form in his own mind—an idea that would lift him out of the barrel.

It would mean he would have to abandon pursuit of personal revenge on the duke and his troublesome charge, Irina Kwasniewska. At least, for now. Franciszek, however, could help to make the introduction happen without danger to himself, Tomasz realized.

"What are your plans, Sire?"

"A very good question, Franciszek. I'm not sure, exactly, but I think you will play a very important part in them."

CHAPTER VII

1378

Following a night's rest, Madrosh found Irina in the gardens studying the basil, marjoram, and scented mint that filled the air. "And are you well today, Lady Irina?"

"Yes, my dear Madrosh." She patted her belly. "The old ones tell me this baby is not ready to kick, but it won't be long before I will surely feel its presence."

"You continue to be content with your circumstance. That pleases me. And what do the old ones say about the child's soul, eh? There are many who think the child had life when you conceived, and it was then that God gave it a soul. There are others who think the child will not be truly alive until it grows into a form familiar to us. At that time, they believe, its soul springs forth from God. An interesting question, *nie?*"

"I do not know what to think. I'm not sure what the soul is all about. And there you are again. We were supposed to be talking about good and evil, Madrosh!" she said in mock consternation.

"Ah, good and evil," intoned the priest. "At the Joselewicz house, perhaps you heard names like Plato and Aristotle, or Augustine and Aquinas?"

"No, Madrosh, I did not. Who are they?"

"When you ask about good and evil, the answers are many. Great thinkers have pondered these questions for thousands of years. The ancient Greeks, including Socrates, Plato, and Aristotle, were, of course, not Christian in their beliefs. Christ did not exist on earth when these men were living. Augustine was an African who became Bishop of

Hippo over eight hundred years ago, and Thomas Aquinas was an Italian priest who died just about one hundred years ago. Different though these men were, they thought and talked much about the idea of a soul, and in consequence, about good and evil. Another large topic! How large is your appetite?" He chuckled.

"Did these foreigners look like us?"

"The Greeks? Yes, they look very much like us, but Augustine was African. He was a black man."

"A black man? I've never seen a black man, or heard of one, for that matter."

"Do you remember the old ones in Poznan and around the farms ever talking about the Mongols? Their skins were much darker than ours, and their features, different as well. Augustine, they say, was even darker, nearly black as soot."

Irina took this in while they climbed to the parapets, where the stonework was just wide enough for the two to walk side by side. The night had been cool, but the morning sun warmed them both. It took away Irina's shiver, allowing her to concentrate on the kettle of knowledge Madrosh was about to pour out for her.

"We have some time today. Tell me a bit about these men, and about our souls."

"Of course, we do not know who might have been the first to talk about it. When Plato wrote about Socrates and his thinking, they talked about the soul as if it were a part of you, but an invisible part.

"Most interestingly, when the ancients talked about civilizing one's soul, it implied that man is on a continuum of development. That is to say, ideas of good and evil may be different now than they were a thousand years ago, and even more so, a thousand years from now."

Their animated conversation about the philosophers went on for over an hour. Irina nodded throughout, attempting to take it all in.

"I'm sorry, My Lady. I'm telling you what I understand about this topic because I think you are interested and can comprehend it. Not many of our time, men of the cloth or the sword, have either quality. Please pardon me. You have asked me about things I love to talk about."

Irina smiled. "I would not have guessed." Catching a warming ray of sun, she found a place to sit where the stone had already taken in the heat. She invited Madrosh to share the space from which they could see over the town and across the river, well into the distance. Yip, who never left her side, lay down at her feet, the warm stone a welcome treat for the old dog. Irina studied him for a moment, wondering if Yip had a soul and whether he would find his purpose, like Plato's acorn. "Since you don't mind my questions, my wise Madrosh, please continue."

"As you wish, Lady Irina. It was Aristotle who felt that all behavior is guided by its own end—a particular good."

"Just what good is Tomasz the Terrible seeking, Father Madrosh?!"

"One must wonder. Yet we have to believe good will come of Tomasz's evil." Madrosh paused to let that thought find rest in Irina's keen mind.

"So, if I could sum up these three thinkers," Irina ventured, "it sounds like they were attempting to find a reason for our existence, perhaps seeking a purpose for us. And they thought it was our duty to seek the good in whatever we did or became."

Madrosh sat silent, smiling in appreciation of her mental acuity. "But in this regard, they could take all their brilliance no further, my dear. It was not until Christ came on earth, that it all began to make some sense."

"The laws of the Jews did not make sense?"

"I said nothing of the kind. Remember, the Jews escaped their bondage in Egypt hundreds of years before the Greeks began to think about a soul. The books of the Old Testament tell us about the history of God as the Jews knew Him over the centuries. And that is what it is, essentially, a history of God's experience with the Jews. Later, the New Testament of the Bible explains why He sent his Son, to take the next step in the development of man's soul and his relationship to God."

"I am not sure I understand."

"The books of the Old Testament speak of God's laws and the desire to hew closely to the letter of those laws. Christ came to show that it wasn't a distant, fearful God who ruled the universe, but one who loved us as much as his own Son. Because God's Son came to live amongst us and set a human example for all, his victory over death made it clear there was more than just this life on earth. Each time we say the Mass, we celebrate and remember Christ's promise of eternal life, if we but believe in him."

"But what about those others you mentioned, Augustine and Aquinas?"

"Ah. My stomach tells me we must eat before we think more. Shall we meet in this very spot after our mid-day meal? The sun will continue to warm this place along the wall."

Irina stopped him from leaving. "If Christ had not existed, do you think we would understand who and what we are?"

Madrosh stood, pondering. "I am sure not, My Lady," he said with finality. "In my humble view, it was Christ's existence which taught us about loving our neighbor as ourselves. Until that point, even though the religion of the Jews held us to the right path in preparation for His coming, the world was just a collection of warring tribes that lived and died into nothingness, no closer to an ultimate peace than they were thousands of years before."

Irina thought a moment. "And now we are somehow different?"

. . .

In the afternoon, Captain Tomori returned to the Hungarian encampment after several hours with Franciszek, and made his report to Sir Bela.

"Sire," he said, unable to restrain a chuckle. "These two are no soldiers. They were raised in Poznan and have had a soft life. The smarter one is the duke's castellan and does the dirty work for which his knights will not soil their hands. He is called Tomasz the Terrible and carries out the spoken and unspoken wishes of his master, while this one, Franciszek, just does what Tomasz tells him." Tomori chuckled again. "Terrible, indeed! About a month ago, these two burned all the Jews they could find, and for some reason, they are not in their master's favor at the moment. That explains why they are separated from the main group."

"Interesting. There seems to be a piece or two missing, however. The duke would not just leave them. There's something else. Tell me what else you learned."

"Yes, Sire," Tomori began, and recounted his observations about the route of travel and what his prisoner had told him. "These two," Timori chuckled yet again, "actually got lost—that's how I knew they'd never soldiered in the field before." He laughed. "That Franciszek proved a source of much information!"

"If our intelligence is correct, between the duke's men and those already billeted at the castle, there couldn't be more than fifty or sixty fighting men. Do you agree?"

"Yes, Sire. We outnumber them and to be sure, we have the advantage of surprise."

"If we need it, Tomori. Zygmunt is a Pole, don't forget, a subject of the same king you and I serve. If he is loyal to Louis, he should be our ally."

"Yet many Poles are not the loyal subjects they ought to be."

Sir Bela thought further in silence. Finally, he said, "Tomori, we will have to find out just what goes on inside those walls and whether Zygmunt is for us or against us. We must have Krosno Castle and everyone in it." He paused and added, emphatically, "One way or the other."

. . .

The plague vanished as quickly as it came. Thousands had perished, Jerzy Andrezski learned, as he noted the many houses left empty in every lane and byway. The squire who ruled in the duke's absence ordered everything touched by the plague to be burned: bodies, clothes, and cartage.

Naturally, the order did not apply to items in the church's possession. This revelation caused him to scurry to every church in Poznan. In each, he made a fifty-fifty arrangement for all the goods he could sell. He assured one and all the goods had been blessed by the church, and therefore were quite safe. It was not the entire truth, but if it was safe enough for him to touch, he reasoned, it must be safe enough, indeed.

To the Church of the Heart of Jesus, on the other hand, Jerzy

Andrezski was as good as his word. He returned 90 percent of his earnings to Sister Luke. For the next weeks, Jerzy made a good deal of money on scarce goods. The detritus—the unsalable goods—he gave away to the poorest in the city. Too, he used his keen eye to select a number of good properties for purchase knowing there would be a demand for them sooner or later. In a short time, he became one of Poznan's respected men of business—one of few remaining.

. . .

As Bishop Antony Tirasewicz made his way back through the woods and fields, he found it remarkable how few people he encountered. In the little village of Wozna, he was stunned by the utter quiet as he dismounted and walked, slowly, from house to house. He touched nothing, but peeked in the doors and windows, open to the air. Not a whisper of breath.

Wozna had always been a good stop to water horses and have a bowl of soup at the largest structure, an inn of sorts where the couple and their children served travelers at all hours of the day, and sometimes the night.

This day, he saw only an old man and a child. "*Pan,*" he addressed the man quietly and respectfully, as if in the presence of the dead, "where is everyone? Surely..."

The old man stretched his arm in the direction of a blackened pile some one hundred feet away. Through his missing teeth, in broken Polish, he mouthed a few words. "There. Three weeks ago. They are all there. And their things. We," he said, his other arm around a boy no more than ten years on the earth, "we are left. No food for us. No food for you."

Astounded by the human devastation, the bishop reached deep into his cold heart and blessed the two wretches in front of him. He turned and said to his companions, "Give them some food!"

After a few moments, he climbed back on his horse, his chilly composure having quickly returned. "To Poznan we go!"

Upon his arrival in the city, he realized Wozna had just been a taste of the bitter meal to come. Whole streets and alleys were abandoned.

People had simply vanished. He suspected that many of those alive had left and returned as he himself had done.

Spent fires were everywhere, sodden black masses blotching the landscape. The air carried a roasted ugliness he could not wave away. At his own residence, a palace next to the Cathedral of Sts. Peter and Paul, the doors remained tightly shut.

He had left instructions that his house not be used in caring for the diseased, but that God's house could be used for that purpose. All seemed quiet now. The flowers drooped from lack of care and water, and what grass there was had grown knee high with the weeds. No servant came out to greet them. It seemed strange, but perhaps they were out provisioning the palace.

He had the door broken in, and as the disgusting odor rushed out, the bishop and his party found them, dead for weeks, mouldering in the dusty, foul air. The looks on the man and his wife were a mix of surprise and horror, as if the plague would not have dared cross the bishop's threshold.

Bishop Tirasewicz could not stay there now, he saw. Turning to the others, he gave his orders: "I will go to the convent of the Dominicans. You will remain here to purify this house so that it will be of use to me again."

At the convent, he encountered another shock in the person of Sister Luke, who introduced herself as the new Mother Superior, pending his approval. As they took each other's measure, she spoke of Sister Mary Elisabeth's death and the convent's current circumstances. Half of the nuns there had also perished, she reported.

Despite his shock, the bishop remained true to himself. "I am truly sorry about the loss of Sister Elisabeth," he said, "and you may consider yourself ratified as the new Mother Superior by the See of Poznan, my dear Sister Luke. I will send the official proclamation forthwith." Then, he cleared his throat. "However, Sister Luke, you must not count on your bishop for financial support. See to your own needs the best way you can."

Sister Luke bowed in submission, as he expected, but, he noted, she offered no plan for the Dominican Sisters to support themselves.

...

Still perplexed, Sir Bela had the prisoner brought to him. Tomasz quivered. The Hungarian lord watched his captive for a long, silent moment, much as the cat eyes an unsuspecting mouse.

"What do you have to say to me, Tomasz, my fellow subject?"

"Sire?" Tomasz asked, bewildered, yet attempting to fathom the Hungarian's meaning. "Fellow subject?" He stopped. "Did you not take me prisoner?"

"Indeed, you are my prisoner. What do you have to say to me, Tomasz, about your master, Duke Zygmunt?"

Once again, Tomasz responded with the same question. "Sire?"

"Tomasz, Tomasz, we are brothers, you and I," Sir Bela said, smiling, his voice cordial, belying the circumstances of their conversation. "We serve our masters. One is like another, wouldn't you agree? Your king just speaks a different language than you. Come now. What does Duke Zygmunt think about this?"

"Truthfully, Sire, he would never discuss such a thing with me."

"Indeed, not, Tomasz," Sir Bela jousted. "He may not have spoken to you, but surely, the duke's men have an idea what their lord thinks of his king—and they talk around his castle where you can hear them." Deliberately repeating the man's name, he said, "Yes, Tomasz?"

Shaking, Tomasz lowered his eyes briefly, the reflex contradicting what he was about to say. "Of course, Sire, my master is loyal to the king."

"Tomasz, I believe you have some reason why you do not want to see your master. I don't know what it is. Perhaps I do not care. Do you understand me?"

"Yes, Sire. The Duke is a Pole, not a Hungarian."

"Simple. Truthful."

"You need not make an introduction, after all, Tomasz. You will be there at the right moment to say farewell."

Uncomprehending, Tomasz was led away.

...

164

With the sun's radiance his first companion upon leaving the great hall after the mid-day meal, Madrosh found Irina awaiting his return up on the parapets. As always, Yip sat at her feet watching, ever listening. "I trust you ate well, My Lady? I'm so sorry not to have been with you, but there is something I want to ask you. By now, you have formed an impression of the margrave. What might that be?"

"In answer to your first question, yes. As to your second, we've met and spoken twice—you were there the first time. I do not understand his tongue, and so our contacts are necessarily brief. That is the way I prefer them to be," she said, eyeing him carefully. "I will do what I need to do so that Velka, Rosta, the Sisters, and I—and my child—have safe passage to Paris, not back to Poznan."

"Do you intend never to return?"

"We shall see, Madrosh. We shall see." She paused, smiling back at him. "Now, back to good and evil?" The early afternoon sun brightened their otherwise drab surroundings of gray stone and aged timbers, giving new attention to the lustrous greens of the treed hills around the castle's landsides.

Madrosh nodded. "First, allow me to reinforce one of your strongest qualities, My Lady."

Surprised by his words, Irina merely raised her eyebrow.

"It is a simple one, and for most, not so easy to master." He paused. "You say little at court, my dear, and that one trait makes you both interesting and unassailable. May I respectfully suggest you continue that habit," he said without a question in his voice.

Irina nodded, adding the smallest smile of thanks.

Warming to the topic on Irina's mind, Madrosh cleared his throat. "I want to mention some of Aristotle's thinking about the soul. He is said to have believed that when a baby is conceived, it has a vegetative soul, that is, the essence of a senseless entity. When the baby grows a bit, it receives an animal soul, and finally, when it achieves its humanity, a rational soul."

Irina's gave him a look of impatience.

Madrosh held up a finger to forestall her complaint. "Just a moment, my dear. Do you see where that thought might take us?"

She said nothing.

"I mention this to explain why in our time some men of the church, even Augustine, have not objected greatly to the deliberate loss of an unborn baby." He said this and lowered his eyes.

"What are you trying to tell me, Madrosh?" Her voice was a harsh whisper.

"At the present time, the church may condemn relations outside of marriage, but not a deliberate miscarriage, as long as it happens before the baby becomes ensouled."

"Are you suggesting that I find a way to miscarry, Madrosh?" Irina felt color rising in her cheeks. "Is this your way of telling me it would be better, more convenient for me?" she demanded, anger claiming each new syllable. Do you not yet understand what I am about? Would I have gone to this extreme," she said, extending her arms to show where they were, how far they had come, "to rid myself of a child I did not want?"

"I am so sorry, My Lady," the old counselor hastened to say. "Truly, I admire you for not having done what many have done."

"Madrosh, understand me now! This baby means everything to me, and I will carry it as long as God wants it so. This child also carries Berek's spirit, and that I will never forget."

"I understand perfectly," Madrosh said, realizing he had touched a most tender spot in Irina's emotional well-being.

The spring air became heavy with their silence. Irina swallowed hard. Finally, in an attempt to put the exchange aside, she asked, "Are you saying that how each person's soul is made up determines whether a person is good or evil?"

"That could be one answer, yes, Irina."

"Might you be saying, then, that a creature like Tomasz may have very little of a rational soul?"

"That may be what the Greeks would say. As Christians, we have a different view of the soul. That's where Augustine and Aquinas joined the reasoning."

Irina sat, absorbing the sun's caress for another moment or two. Without thinking about it, she stood and took the two steps to the crenellated wall, where the incredible view from so high up on the castle wall presented itself. Suddenly, she caught her breath, her hand over her heart, as if it had stopped.

"What is it, dear Lady?" Madrosh rushed to her side, the breeze rustling his beard.

Irina was trembling. She pointed. Yip climbed upon the bench, put his paws on the wall, and began a low growl. "Look down into the square. Do you see who it is?" She breathed heavily, deeply. "How can this be?! How can it be that evil's altar boy is here to pay us a visit?"

. . .

Just after making a substantial payment to Sister Luke's good nuns, Jerzy Andrezski sought a place to rest his heavy frame. Later, he said it had been just a coincidence that the place of rest happened to be in the Church of the Heart of Jesus. For a good part of his life, he had worked hard to deny that God could possibly exist. Now, he worked hard resisting the pull of God's presence around him.

He sat in the coolness of the stone building, always drafty, no matter what time of day or night. Rubbing the bristles of his unshaven face, he looked up into the unlit gloom of the church's cavernous interior, and noticed something about the small lancet windows high above his head. They provided thin slices of light in the high side walls, but also let in the wind and the rain. The openings were small, as required by the architect, supposedly, since larger openings would have weakened the walls and let in more weather. They were in contrast to the one large glass window above the church's main doors. Something about the arrangement drew Jerzy's attention.

Seemingly alongside his thoughts of church architecture was a strong feeling of gratitude for his very existence. Yet he refused to admit he was praying. Then he laughed at his own foolishness. As he argued with himself about the God he'd long denied, something about the openings in the walls nagged at him. He tried to swat away the idle thought, but before he realized it, he was walking quickly, out of the church, through the square, almost trotting across the city to the cathedral.

At the great cathedral of Sts. Peter and Paul, he pushed open the stout wooden doors and strode down the nave's center.

"Here now!" called Father Shimanski, who had been kneeling at a side altar. "Show some respect to the house of God. Close those doors!"

Ignoring the order, Andrezski approached the priest. "Father, forgive my manners. I wanted to see something here, and the open doors will give us more light. Could you help me?"

Curious about the clean, pleasant giant of a man before him, the priest changed his tone. "Aren't you Andrezski, the merchant?" Without waiting for an answer, he asked, "How can I help you, my son?"

"Tell me about your windows."

"Our windows? Well, yes, they are made from what is called stained glass. We've had them for about twenty or thirty years, I'd say, and very expensive they are. The glass came from Italy with great effort. It was very hard to transport the pieces across the Alps, there being no good, safe land route most of the time."

"The glass was brought here in pieces, then?"

"Yes, a craftsman came along with two assistants. They spent many months heating and molding great quantities of lead strips to hold all the pieces together. The pictures in them are, of course, religious, and help the people understand Christ and the figures in the gospel. See, over there, the great windows showing Saints Peter and Paul as earthly shepherds of the flock?"

"Yes, Father, but can you tell me about the clear glass, how it's made."

"The clear glass?" the priest asked in surprise. "Yes, well, the Italian craftsman and his helpers actually made the clear glass here in the city. There were also two apprentices they trained who, along with their own assistants, watched and learned a bit of glassmaking from the Italians.

"*Prosze*, Father. Go on."

"I do not know much, *Pan* Andrezski, but it has always been manufactured along the Mediterranean, and mostly in Murano, an island near Venice, where the secrets of glass are jealously guarded. And so the price of its beauty and novelty has remained high."

"And that's why there are few glass windows around here?"

"Yes, my son, that and the fact that earlier outbreaks of plague took so many who knew its secrets."

"I don't understand, Father. Why didn't the Poznan apprentices trained by the Italians keep making glass here?"

"I am certain they would have, but," Father Shimanski said, lowering his eyes, "they are dead and buried in the plague's great lime pits—they died when the Great Mortality first visited a generation ago. Now, *Pan*, tell me why you want to know about the windows?"

"What other glass is to be found in the city?"

"Oh, there are a few pieces in the castle, and one beautiful window in the Church of the Heart of Jesus. It was Duke Zygmunt's father who arranged for this gift to the church just before he died, and as his own reward, he had the Italians make him a few small pieces to show to visitors who came to the castle. It is wonderful, *nie*? To be able to look through something clear and not feel the wind and snow in your face?"

"And what happened to the Italians?"

"Those who did not die of plague, could not stand our frigid winters and returned to Italy, taking with them all their knowledge. No one else in Poznan had the money to bring back the glassmakers, and no one left alive here knew enough to make the glass."

"The families of the dead men, their sons. Where are they to be found?"

"Let me think now," the priest paused. "Of course. One of the sons has survived. His name is Pawel Tokasz. Everyone knows him."

Large man though he was, Jerzy Andrezski loped out of the church, shouting a loud *"Djenkuje!"* over his shoulder, while Father Shimanski remained thoroughly mystified.

...

At the other end of the city, Sister Luke's convent prepared itself for a refectory dinner with Bishop Tirasewicz, which she hoped would mark the close of his week-long visit while his palace was swept free of death. They had spent little time together and had little conversation—all to their mutual satisfaction, she surmised.

The bishop seemed to have enjoyed the well-tended gardens and courtyards but was noticeably ill at ease in the quiet solitude usually found within the convent walls. For his entire stay, Mother Superior's goal had been to let the bishop feel free to come—and go—as he pleased. When he announced his stay had come to an end, there was noticeable joy amongst the convent nuns as they made certain the church and convent were spotless, the linens white and crisp. From the kitchen delicious aromas alerted them to the feast about to be served—a feast of farewell.

At the dinner itself, the bishop seemed to be contemplating a topic for discussion. After many pleasantries about the work of the good sisters and careful commentary about the absent Father Rudzenski, he set about it. "Sister Luke, I was curious about the woman and her servant girl your Mother Superior sent along with me. What do you know about them?"

Caught by surprise, Sister Luke prepared her words carefully, not knowing why he would ask such a question. "Why, Your Grace, so much has happened since they left I had all but forgotten about them. I know little, to be sure. Mother Superior found them in church praying. She talked to them for some time, took a liking to them, and when she discovered Lady Irina was with child, she decided to do what she could to spare them from the Great Mortality."

"Do you know why she was called Lady Irina? What was her surname again?"

"Lady Irina Kwasnieska. She came from elsewhere, possibly Gniezno, I think. In truth, Bishop, that is all I remember."

Sister Luke closed her eyes momentarily to remind herself to confess the lie she had just told—and she would wait to do so when another pastor was assigned to them. She did not understand the bishop's intense interest in the young woman, and could think of no reason to tell the man across from her that Irina's little sister was in the convent at that very moment.

"Ah, thank you," he said. "No matter. We won't be seeing her again,

I venture. She and the serving girl have continued on to Paris, France, and I cannot imagine she'd ever come back here."

The women maintained an impassive, almost uninterested demeanor during the brief time he spoke about the lady from the east. Sister Luke, for one, thought he regretted that Sister Elisabeth was no longer able to answer his questions. Her heart pounded, and breathing became difficult, but with great poise, she asked the bishop if there was anything more he cared to ask.

"No thank you, Sister Luke. Let me thank you and the good nuns for hosting me while dispossessed of my own home. I wish you all well, indeed, as you raise the funds to sustain yourselves." The bishop eyed Sister Luke carefully, then rose from the table, gave the nuns a slight bow of thanks, and proceeded to his waiting horse for the short ride to a better bed.

...

Captain Tomori and Franciszek Montowski rode their horses into the large square fronting Krosno Castle's imposing entrance. In the early afternoon quiet, little else was happening. A few merchants were speaking in low voices and there was the idle noisemaking of little children, but the two horsemen turned heads.

Tomori noticed that many of the townspeople looked at them warily, no doubt curious about tunics of different markings than those ordinarily seen in the Duchy of Glogau. Surely, they eyed the very tall man in garb far better than that of a peasant, but not as finely spun as that of a knight or wealthy merchant. The Hungarian smiled as he saw them pointing at Franciszek's large head covered with a shock of yellow hair.

The riders carried themselves as if returning to their own castle. Tomori shouted for the gate to be raised for him.

"Who comes!" demanded the guardsman at the gate.

"Janos Tomori from the King of Hungary," the knight expressed with a confidence he did not completely feel.

The heavy iron portcullis rumbled off the ground as if by invisible hands, but the heavy chain clanking against itself drowned out all other noises. Tomori noticed every detail.

Once inside, they were led, first, to Sir Ortwinus Esel, who challenged them to state the purpose of their visit. In return, Tomori demanded to see the duke.

Sir Ortwinus, apparently considering their request, displayed a welcoming demeanor. "The duke?" he asked finally, confusion in his voice.

Tomori wondered if there was something wrong with the man.

Big Franciszek could not help himself. Despite instructions to be silent, he mustered his best voice and said, "Yes, Duke Zygmunt, of course."

"Of course." Sir Ortwinus responded with a smile, as if a burden had been lifted from him, and at once, he turned, leading them deeper inside the walls of the fortress.

...

Madrosh and Lady Irina had come off the parapet and were halfway down when she grasped her belly, telling the priest she felt dizzy. Asking Velka, who was coming up toward them, to lead Lady Irina to her chambers—with Yip close behind—Madrosh then hurried toward the great hall where he knew Duke Zygmunt and the Margrave, King Wenceslas, were in quiet, private, and earnest discussion.

Taking his usual position behind his Polish master, Madrosh listened as the clatter of Ortwinus Esel's boots joined with the clang of his scabbard against the light armor he wore. Their concentration broken, the nobles looked up at him with a mix of amusement and annoyance. Madrosh observed carefully as the appearance of the men they had seen from above portended something very unexpected.

Bending low, Sir Ortwinus said, "Two men say they're from the King of Hungary, and the big one spoke in Polish, My Lords. They asked for you, Duke Zygmunt."

The margrave glanced at the duke, a question in the lift of his eyebrow, and the duke nodded in assent.

Sir Ortwinus beckoned the intruders who had been kept waiting at the entrance to the hall.

"Just what is it!" spoke Duke Zygmunt, making his demand with force, yet respect, and completely ignoring the surprising presence of his own minion.

Captain Tomori bowed, not deeply, but enough to show respect in return. "The King, Louis of Hungary and of Poland," he added with emphasis, "sends his compliments and requests a private audience with Duke Zygmunt." He did not acknowledge the man seated with the duke.

Madrosh bent to his master and they conferred in low tones. Duke Zygmunt, a guest at Krosno, chose not to introduced either his royal companion or Madrosh, and waved everyone else away.

"You have it. Speak, Captain Tomori," the duke said at last. "What is it that King Louis could want of me?"

"Duke Zygmunt," he began, speaking in halting Polish, "King Louis would be most pleased to know that you are here at Krosno," he said.

It was clear to Madrosh that no one would fully understand the Hungarian, and Tomori's presence augured a conversation not to misunderstand. Gently, he put his hand on the duke's shoulder and once more, whispered a few words. At once, Duke Zygmunt signaled for an interpreter, apparently not trusting the niceties to the oaf, Franciszek.

When one of Wenceslaus's men appeared, the duke said, "We may do without the pleasantries, Captain."

"As a Pole, and as a subject of His Majesty's, he would want to believe your loyalty to him supreme. That said, Excellency, you should know that the king has a plan to secure a water route to the Baltic."

The interpreter's presence gave everyone the opportunity to absorb the words of the other.

"And so?" Duke Zygmunt asked, glancing at his companion at the same time.

"And so the king expects your unequivocal support in winning control of the Oder and its military strongholds."

Duke Zygmunt and the margrave sat stone faced. Madrosh remained impassive to the man's words, as he was well aware the margrave understood Polish. When Tomori paused, Zygmunt chose not to respond immediately. Instead, he turned his head, slowly, to look directly at Tomori's accomplice. "And you, Franciszek Montowski, am I looking at a dead man? Why are you here? And with Captain Tomori?"

Madrosh could see that Tomori was taken aback at the duke's tone and apparent contempt for Franciszek. Too, he wondered if Tomori took the duke's companion to be someone in the duke's service.

"D-duke Zygmunt," Franciszek stammered, "we were set upon in the woods by robbers who killed the soldiers you sent with us. Tomasz and I killed our attackers, Sire, and we could have run but chose to rejoin you and show our true loyalty."

"I'm beginning to understand your true loyalty," the duke responded evenly, the irony apparently lost on his visitors.

Taking no notice of the duke's irony, he said, "Sire, Tomasz has something of importance to tell you, something that will change your view of us when..."

Tomori cut him off, apparently having concluded things were not going well.

Whether it was the difficulty of language or the demeanor of the conferees, Madrosh could not fathom. What he could understand was that Tomori made a very wrong assumption about the man seated at the duke's side.

Although Tomori attempted to speak in Duke Zygmunt's native tongue, it was the interpreter who made the meaning clear. "Sire," he began, his voice laced with respect, "we found your two men in the woods. They were on their way here, we believe. We chose this one to come now, believing you would recognize him and not think us an enemy. In truth, Sire, I apologize for this man's brash manners."

"Brash isn't the word," the duke responded slowly. "Please get to it, Captain Tomori. What is it you want of me?"

"Sire, we understand," Tomori said as if speaking with a conspirator. Nodding at Franciszek, he continued. "You have enough men for control here. As a subject of His Majesty the King, you are to join our forces and take command of Castle Krosno for Hungary," he said, then added, belatedly, "...and for Poland."

Madrosh could not believe Tomori would seek Zygmunt's aid in overthrowing control of a Teutonic castle in which they were guests. It seemed the duke wished to draw him out.

"Control? What does that mean, exactly?" he inquired further, equally careful not to glance at the margrave immediately to his side. The fingers of one hand found the ring on a finger of the other and began to turn it round and round.

"You, Sire, would allow our troops to enter the fortress and in an act of fealty, submit to the King's personal representative on this expedition, Sir Bela Kinizsi." He waited until the interpreter repeated his words to the duke.

"Submit? Hmmm. I think I understand what you mean. As a loyal subject, I must consider my duties to *Wielko Polska* and my king!"

Tomori beamed with pleasure at the duke's response. "*Bardzo dobrze*—very good, Sire!"

"I bow to your counsel, Tomori," the duke said slowly, his mind working. "You must give me time to quietly secure the castle and the town for you. Why should Sir Bela's men shed blood unnecessarily? Let me think about this for a bit," he said as he looked down at his hands and twirled the ring on his finger. Finally, he grasped it in two fingers, looked up, and said, "Yes, in three days' time, with trumpets sounding, your entire force will be welcomed into Krosno."

The interpreter's words evinced a broad smile. "That will be most excellent, Sire."

Madrosh watched Brandenburg's margrave intently. Earlier, he thought the margrave ready to explode, but now, the man seemed to relish the drama unfolding. The margrave kept his silence, a very slight smile arcing his lips.

"Oh, Tomori, when you return, I would be most pleased to see Franciszek Montowski and the other brash one, Tomasz Wodowicz, in a place of prominence amongst your troops. They should be properly acknowledged for service to me and King Louis."

Tomori beamed. "As you wish, Sire."

. . .

At the Hungarian captain's departure, a tense silence enveloped the chamber. Afternoon shadows lengthened, and the hounds stirred in their soft spreads of straw along the wall. Tan, with droopy ears and lips, they raised their heads, fixing their stares. One stood, walked to a corner, and relieved himself, but no one paid attention to the animals. Still standing, Madrosh knew it was not his place to break the silence.

Duke Zygmunt turned to his host and said, "Sire, this must surely have sounded strange to you."

"To say the least." The margrave's tone was even, expectant, the thin smile still on his lips.

"Despite what Tomori thinks—and will carry back to Sir Bela Kinizsi—it is to you I have pledged my loyalty in this matter." Zygmunt noticed he was turning the ring on his finger. He made himself stop.

Incredulous, the Margrave and King, Wenceslas, interrupted Duke Zygmunt's next words. "My dear Duke, I will hear your words, most certainly, or battle you to the death right here in this hall, but first, explain to me why you are willing to risk all in an act of disloyalty to your king."

"In spite of the fact that he is the King of Poland by agreement with *Kazimierz Wielki,* Louis is no king to true Poles. We are not Hungarians. We are Poles!" All this, he said simply but not without passion. Behind his master, Madrosh nodded in firm agreement.

"And neither are you Teutons, Zygmunt," noted the margrave, surprisingly affable, using his companion's given name without his title for the first time.

"True enough, Sire Wenceslas, but at present, the bonds between us are not dripping in Polish blood."

The margrave sat silent for a moment, acknowledging the truth of Zygmunt's words. "Evidently, you have a plan?" His smile was broader, one of warmth for a friend.

...

Within hours of the strange visit by the Hungarian, there was little else but hurry and bustle as the men and women of Krosno Castle began preparations for what was to come. No one was told much, but each group of laborers was given a single task to accomplish.

A cadre of Castle Krosno's defenders made ready an official

welcome at the foot of the moat bridge. Their role would be important but brief. Others polished their armor and readied their finery while still others focused their entire labors on the large courtyard just inside the heavy gates.

Few of the men at Castle Krosno belonged to its keeper, the Margrave of Glogau. It fell, therefore, to soldiers in liege to a Polish nobleman and the neighboring Margrave of Brandenburg to satisfy the Hungarian's demand.

. . .

The growing warmth of early June made the unshaded parapets an ideal place for Irina to enjoy the balmy air while waiting to discuss with Madrosh the mysteries of their existence. The skies were blue and dry, making the hours she and Madrosh spent together all the more pleasant.

Irina's thoughts drifted to the image of the young squire, Jan Brezchwa. Her contacts with him were usually fleeting, about some task or duty, but they seemed more and more cordial, their voices to each other less impersonal and not at all brusque, as when they first met. *Yet my loyalty is to Berek—I cannot think of anyone else.*

When Madrosh made his appearance, his demeanor was somber, and Irina did not know what to make of him. She had never seen him so discomfited.

"Madrosh, what has transpired that affects you so?"

"I should not say, My Lady," he said, looking away, "but you should be prepared for whatever might come. You need not be concerned for your safety. Duke Zygmunt has a devilish plan, the outcome of which the Hungarians will not have time to remember." He stared into the distance.

Though Irina blanched at his words, she had come to trust him. "Devilish, you say?" Seeing no reaction, she added, "I will not press you on it if you keep me interested in good and evil," she said, trying to keep concern from her voice. *What will Duke Zygmunt do?*

Madrosh sighed. "Yes, I suppose it is." He turned to her. "Let's talk about the good Augustine, then, and the opposites of good and evil."

It was amazing to her how he could change in an instant. *No wonder the duke prizes him as his counselor.*

Madrosh warmed to his subject. "The question often arises, Lady Irina, if God knows that evils will occur, is he God? If God does not know, how can he be God? And if he knows and does nothing, is he a God without power? Or an uncaring God? And if he has no power or does not use it, how, too, can he be God?"

Madrosh had wasted no time laying out the challenges to the very essence of the Creator. Irina nearly regretted having asked the question. "You are making me dizzy, Madrosh!"

"I apologize, My Lady. Free will can be dizzying. You see, it is not God who does and permits evil, it is man. When you lived on the farm and your mother left butter and sugar on the table, she probably told you not to touch it. She knew, however, that you would be tempted, and that when she was not looking, you might take a taste with your finger."

Irina started to laugh.

Madrosh chuckled. "Do you remember, Irina? Whether you tasted it or not, your mother did not *make* either choice for you." He paused. "God knows about men's deeds, but he does not make their choices for them, and we earnestly believe God will hold them accountable for what they do! Augustine further believed that once one knows the truth, one is responsible for the truth."

Irina interrupted. "Forgive me, Madrosh, if I am speaking sinfully, but what does God think of Bishop Tirasewicz?"

Madrosh laughed heartily. "I do not know what God thinks of him, my child, but Augustine gave us some thoughts on this as well. He believed that it is Christ only who determines whether a sacrament is valid. That means that when our bishop performs a baptism or a marriage, or forgives someone's sins in Christ's name, his personal behaviors, as we may judge them, are separate from the acts he performs on Christ's behalf." After a moment of reflection, he added, "That is not an easy garment to don, is it? It is a simple reminder for us that while we may make our own judgments about someone, in the end, it is solely the judgment of God that matters."

"Just like Father Rudzenski?" she asked, but did not wait for an answer. "And in the end," she taunted Madrosh, "is man judged good or evil?"

The priest nodded, pensive. "The ancients believed that man is intrinsically good—that all natures are created by God and therefore could not be evil in themselves. There are some who think God may have created Adam and Eve as innocents, as intrinsically good, but because of their sin, we are born with varying degrees of good and evil in us—you'll remember we spoke of this earlier."

"Intrinsic?"

"It means the very core of something. Deep inside an apple, the very center of it has the seeds for another of the same, and those seeds have within them the power to grow an apple tree that produces apples, sweet or sour—the vegetative soul, remember? What's in the heart or core of the apple is not what we see by its skin, but it is what makes the apple what it is. Underneath, where you cannot see or touch, is this essence—our nature.

"Think about it this way," he went on. "If man, king or servant, is born with evil in his soul but overcomes it by his free will, then he will become the person we may not want to judge harshly. If a man overcomes his evil desires and seeks what is good, is that not what God wants?

"What about someone who seems by nature a good person?"

"God may judge such a person on a different plane. One has to think that a person who has not been tempted by sin cannot claim virtue."

"I see."

"Think about man from our earliest history. Have his urges been to benign behaviors or have they tended toward the evils of greed, covetousness, lust, and murder? God's gift to Moses of the Commandments helped to civilize our souls. God's gift to us of his Son helps to educate our souls to choose what is good."

"You're saying God judges us by what we do with our lives, not by what we are at our borning."

"Well said, Irina."

...

"*Pan* Tokasz?" Andrezski shouted out to the man leading his cow into the meadow.

"Who calls me?"

Jerzy tied much of his hope to the simple farmer who turned and walked toward him, a man wearing gray woolen leggings and a brown tunic stained with barn work. Like nearly all other Polish men, he was topped by a mass of brown hair unused to a brush and facial hair unused to a blade.

So excited Jerzy was about his idea, he didn't take time to introduce himself but began talking about the farmer's father. His listener took a step backward. And when he asked the farmer to tell all he could remember of his father's work with the Italian craftsmen of so long ago, the man called Pawel Tokasz reacted in shock.

"Do you realize my father has been dead for some years? And why should I tell you, a stranger who comes without a name?"

"I am Jerzy Andrezski, and if you will help me, you may be glad you did."

"*Pan* Andrezski? The man so many talk about since the plague?"

"You embarrass me, *Pan* Tokasz. At the moment, however, you are the most important man in the meadow."

"You honor me much, sir. Let me pasture my cow and we can talk a bit."

They found a large elm tree and sat under its new green leaves, taking in the cool shade. For some time, Tokasz talked and Andrezski listened as the man struggled to remember the many things his father had imparted to him. Some were secrets, Tokasz recalled his father saying. At one point, he leaned his head against the trunk of the huge tree and suddenly opened his eyes wide.

"What's the matter, *Pan* Tokasz?"

"Come with me. I have something to show you." After rummaging around a battered wooden chest in the back of his cluttered barn, he handed to his visitor a long cylinder of some kind wrapped in dusty, parched leather.

"Be careful unrolling the skin as it is very dry," said Tokasz.

"What is this metal tube inside the leather?" queried Andrezski, not much interested in its covering.

"My father said it is what the men used to blow and spin the glass. I don't know how it's done, exactly." He then reached back into the chest and brought out another package. Carefully unwrapping it, he held in his open hands a piece of glass slightly larger than the hands that held it. He passed it to his visitor.

Andrezski held it to the light. There were little pockets of air in the round pane of glass, but it was otherwise clear and caught every speck of light. Andrezski held the small pane in front of his face, looked through the glass at the face of the farmer, and laughed with childlike delight. Tokasz laughed too, as if they were boys with a plaything.

"This, *Pan,* is the most important piece."

"The leather wrapping? Why?"

"See the etchings on the skin? My father said they represented letters and numbers, but I cannot read them. He said whoever could read it would know how to make glass."

CHAPTER VIII

1378

In the gray dawn, Irina awoke to sheets of rain slapping Castle Krosno's outer walls. The heavy cloth covering the opening, even when tied down, was effective in keeping out the weather only when there was little or no wind. What's more, the leather thong to tie it was missing. Free to join the wind, the woolen cloth, damp and dank from the blowing rain, flapped and snapped like an unlatched door. The small fireplace, kept alight by Velka, did little to warm the apartment.

Irina stepped off the high bed onto the stone floor and made her way closer to the fire, wrapping herself in the large blue square of wool she had taken when she left the Kwasniewski farm. She lowered herself onto the floor next to Yip and rubbed his neck and back as the old dog brushed the hearth with his tail. As she hugged herself in the scant warmth of the fire, she wondered if the love of a good man would someday be hers again.

She began to cry softly. Within moments, her shoulders heaved in deep, heartful agony as she thought about Berek and the family she would never see again. Remembering her conversation with Madrosh the afternoon before, she grasped her belly as if by doing so, she could keep her baby always, never to be truly alone again. Being lonely and alone were far different words, each having its own kind of terror. Her sobs continued in waves, like the storm outside the walls.

Velka ran from the little anteroom where she had been mending a torn garment, and knelt by her side. "Lady Irina," she said very softly, having come to address her by Irina's self-given title, "what is troubling you?" Putting her arms around Irina's shoulders, the two rocked back and forth, Velka quietly humming an old hymn. After several minutes, Velka said in her country Polish, "My Lady, look! The rain is stopping and the sun has come out for you. It will not be such a bad day, after all. You must welcome it with dry eyes."

Velka's caress carried with it a tenderness Irina had not felt for several weeks. She held her head to Velka's breast and let her breathing keep time with the tune Velka hummed for them. Soon, she lifted her head and a ray of sun caught and glinted in her damp eyes before the window covering flapped shut once again. At the same moment, the image of evil entering the castle in the person of Franciszek made her both fearful and angry. Irina sat fully upright, and seeing Velka's bright smile, resolved to meet the day and whatever it might bring.

By mid-morning, she had bathed, donned fresh clothing, and readied herself to spend another day with her mentor. She knew that listening to old Madrosh was the best thing she could do for herself. Not only did the bits of education he offered help her live the role she now played, she found the intellectual challenges as tasty as a warm apple tart in late summer.

On her own, she made her way up the uneven steps to the upper battlements, occasionally looking down to see the curious preparations underway below her. The air was heavy with the smells of humans and animals living and functioning in close quarters. She noticed that the higher she rose, the clearer, cleaner, and sweeter the air became. She instinctively took a deep breath, reminding herself not to lose her balance as she slowly conquered each step upward, Yip her only escort onto the heights.

With the sun full on the high stonework, she found the bench she and Madrosh had claimed for themselves all but dry, the steam rising as it began to absorb the warmth of the day. She sat for a time thinking about the morning, and what had transpired in the weeks before. It was hard to escape thoughts of her beloved Berek, but she noticed that when she became tearful, it was more about her loneliness. It was as if her inner self had finally accepted the fact of a void in her heart that would not likely be filled.

She was surprised when an image of Jan Brezchwa suddenly appeared in her mind's eye. There he was. Standing, not speaking, just smiling at her. She felt embarrassed by her own smile and fought to compose herself as Madrosh, breathing heavily, crested the top step.

"My apologies, My Lady, I am behind my time this morning, and I see," he said, noticing her demeanor, "you have been enjoying my absence."

"Not at all, Father Madrosh. It was merely a moment of pleasant solitude."

The two spent many minutes catching the other up on the latest bits of court drama, and more than once, laughter broke out in in the early summer air.

Madrosh saw fit to ask another kind of question. "And so, Lady Irina, what did you observe at last evening's meal?

Surprised, Irina turned to face Madrosh directly and said, "I saw two noblemen enjoying each other's company. They seemed to share a secret, Madrosh!"

"Just so, my dear." Madrosh concluded the sentence, and the subject, with a twist of his lips that was more a grimace than a smile. Irina could not tell what he was thinking, but the old man seemed preoccupied with a special unpleasantness.

For the next hour and more, the two discussed further the teachings of the ancients. "The writings and teachings of the Greeks evidently had a great influence on Augustine and Aquinas, and taken together, they have helped me further understand a progression of thought about the soul that goes back over fifteen centuries," Madrosh said.

"So now we come to this man Aquinas?" *I do not know how much of this I can take, but if I show no interest, what will I miss?*

Madrosh cleared his throat. "Now, My Lady, we come to the midday meal, and if you choose, we will meet here again where the air itself helps to clarify thought!"

Thank God for food! "Ah, Madrosh, why is it that the very thought of food is so powerful a distraction for you?"

"Only food for thought, My Lady," he said, smiling at his own attempt at humor, and led her down the steps.

. . .

"And what do our spies tell us, Captain Tomori?"

"Sir Bela, I am pleased to report very good news. Our observers report that many are working to clean and dress the large square in front of the castle—out of respect for our visit, I'm told. The townspeople do not seem to know the purpose of our coming, but they are happily making ready for us."

"What about inside the castle itself? Are they preparing a proper welcome for the representatives of King Louis?"

"Yes, Sire," he responded with a bright smile. His bushy, blonde beard shone in the sunlight. "All is as it should be. We understand that soldiers of all ranks are polishing and brightening their weapons and mail, and the local major domo, Sir Ortwinus, has ordered large quantities of hay for our horses. It bodes well for a pleasant conquest, does it not, Sire?"

"We shall see, Tomori. We shall see. Ready a messenger to carry news to his Majesty. He can leave as soon as we've raised our flag over Krosno. Make certain too that our two Poles look presentable. Oh, and Tomori, see that our own troops look their very best tomorrow. They will not have many easy victories on this expedition, and I want them to enjoy this one."

Tomori chuckled with agreement and pride. "They will enjoy themselves, Sire, but I venture to say, they'd rather do some killing— they would have been just as happy if we had to fight our way in."

For a few minutes, the two soldiers recalled for each other earlier expeditions in which each had served, their many conquests drenched in the blood of the hapless. They relished the beheadings, the quarterings, and the burnings.

"Not to worry, Tomori, we will see plenty of good killing!"

. . .

Bishop Tirasewicz sat at his desk, brooding. Who is Irina Kwasniewska, he continued to wonder, but thus far, his inquiries in wealthier circles had gone unanswered. Summoning his principal minion, he determined to satisfy his curiosity, one way or another.

"Father Shimanski, I want you to ask our cathedral staff of priests if anyone knows of a Kwasniewski family, possibly of minor nobility, living in Gniezno." He saw the puzzled look on the priest's face and made a shooing gesture to the man, much as he would brush away a gnat. "Don't ask me about this, Father. Just make the inquiries and let me know what you find."

"Yes, Bishop," Shimanski added obediently, casting his eyes downward.

Tirasewicz knew Father Shimanski to be a very thorough man who would, in turn, pass along the instructions to his staff. In truth, he did not expect any of his own people to produce an answer. He had, after all, selected his men of the cloth because they and their families were local and known personally to the Tirasewicz family.

Just as his family had no relatives in any distant city, he doubted any of his staff would have such connections. He was well aware that except for people in his position, soldiers, or nobility, almost no one traveled beyond a small circle of land where they were born. Tapping one of the leather-bound ledgers with his bejeweled fingers, he slapped his hand down in frustration, and said to the empty room, "Something does not ring true about Lady Kwasniewska from Gniezno—and I will find out what it is!"

. . .

Pan Tokasz and Jerzy Andrezski sat for the longest time over a common meal of ale, cheese, bread and a bit of red *kielbasa*. The longer they talked, the more *Pan* Tokasz had to say. For one thing, Tokasz remembered an old man who had been a helper to his father and the Italians on the church project.

"But the priest said that all the men were dead!"

"Not all. Jan was one of the men from Poznan. He is old now," he said, pausing to reflect. "He himself has always been a decent man, my father thought, but we will not trouble ourselves to meet his son, Tomasz." Tokasz told what little he knew of him. "Tomasz the Terrible, they call him."

"Of what concern is this man, then?"

"You are not from here, *Pan* Andrezski. Tomasz Wodowicz is, indeed, a terrible man. If Jan Wodowicz is able to assist us, it will be best to tell no one."

...

"My Lady Irina," Madrosh announced after their mid-day repast of roast rabbit, a few dried fruits, and various breads. "We should walk, should we not?" Not awaiting her response, he continued, "Let's cross the moat bridge and navigate the square. In your gentle condition, fresh air and a bit of exercise will do you much good."

"As you say, Madrosh. You are now a physician of the body as well as the soul!"

"Since you speak of the soul," he said with a wink, "let us talk more about Thomas Aquinas. He, too, spent much time satisfying himself that it wasn't just by faith alone that one can know God exists. Of course, he believed, fundamentally, that faith alone is sufficient, but for those"—and here Madrosh cleared his throat—"who want something more substantial before investing in faith, he offered five proofs of God's existence. Three of them we've already discussed somewhat because they are based upon Aristotle's thinking of over a thousand years before."

"Oh, refresh me a bit, won't you?"

"Aquinas focused on the notion of a first mover," he began in answer. "By this, he did not mean the idea as action, but instead, as *kinesis*—Greek for 'movement'—of potential to actual existence. If you have an idea, for example, it is not the idea to build a mill in St. Michael that makes it real. It is the action of the builders that makes it real. The act is totally separate from the idea, do you see?" He went on. "We cannot assume an infinite series of preceding movers without accounting for the existence of the First Mover. That must be God."

"Preceding movers?"

"Yes, Irina. Your parents and theirs before them, and so on, all the way back to the first of our kind."

"Our kind?"

"The first of us who thought about who they were—not plants or animals. The first who pointed to the sky and wondered, who asked questions and sought answers."

Irina's brow wrinkled. "And?"

"Another proof would seem obvious: if the very fact that an Original Being must exist leads to the conclusion that there is only one, this Being must be the one and only God."

Irina nodded.

Madrosh inhaled deeply before resuming what philosophers believed about God's existence. She and the old priest strolled across the cobbles and made a circuit of the broad square, busy with shops and the noise of sellers, much like the Fareway in Poznan. Despite the tempting goods offered, she kept her focus on the words flowing to her like sips of hot soup on a cold evening.

After a minute or two, he continued, "The last argument has to do with something I said earlier. Our world is not totally random. Just as the Old Testament says God created the world in a particular order, there must be such an order in what we see around us for it to make sense. The foundation of the castle walls is on the bottom, never on the top, you see?

Irina smiled. At the butcher's stall, she stopped and asked for a bit of fat for Yip, who kept them quiet company throughout their saunter. His bushy white tail, topped with a black tuft of fur, wagged furiously as Irina bent with a treat for her ever-loyal friend.

"We'll close this topic with one additional idea offered by Aquinas about God. You and I and all other things pass away. Trees rot and disappear, and over time, even stone crumbles. Rivers, too, change course. It is our nature to pass away, and thereby, we change. God's nature does not change. It is always the same. That means that God's nature is, simply, to be."

Irina shook her head, as if dazed by a difficult notion.

"Because we're walking on real ground and not high on the parapets, I can risk making you a bit dizzy with such thoughts," he chuckled. "Here's another: To Aquinas, it was inconceivable for God to have created the world and everything in it out of matter that already existed. If this matter already existed, he wondered, then where did it come from? What made more sense to Aquinas is that God created the first bit of unshaped or unmolded matter, and by sparking it into life—*kinesis*—brought forth what we see around us—the sky, the sun, water, earth, and so on, and, more recently, intelligent beings—us."

"Intelligent? I'm not always so sure. Just how far have we really come, good Father?"

"A very good question, Irina." Madrosh paused, acknowledging her insight. "Do you remember our discussion about free will? God created us and, as such, moved his thought into reality, prompting untold 'motions' ever since."

Irina remained silent.

"Many in the church talk about free will," Madrosh continued, "but they believe that every single thing that happens is controlled by God, yet we should pray for him to make something happen the way we would wish it, almost as if we're praying for God to change his mind."

"Are you saying, then, there is no need to pray?"

"On the contrary, Irina. If, indeed, God 'let go,' then he allows his Creation to grow and blossom like the flowers in the forest. In that case, there is all the more reason to ask him to intervene on our behalf. Sometimes he does. And sometimes he answers our prayers by doing nothing at all."

"Now that, Madrosh, is a mystery, *nie*?"

"I do not want you to walk away from our talk thinking that God, like a clockmaker, wound up his creation and 'let it go.' Many think God is always involved with his creation, shaping us, guiding us."

"Guiding us?"

"Yes, Irina, it is the power of God's grace. It is His gift to us, and it never stops. Another way to think about it is that because God knows how everything will all turn out, he knows the end of all things—his plan—but he does not make all the things happen in between even though he knows they are happening, and He is guiding us as we go. Like your mother and the butter and sugar on the table, eh? More often than not, it is we who make our worlds, not God—even though

God always knows exactly what we will do. If only…"

"Only what?"

"If only we would follow His freely given guidance."

"This leaves me much to think about."

"Precisely, Lady Irina," he said, addressing her formally to under-score the point.

For many minutes, the two sat in the shade watching in silence the ongoing groundwork for the visit of the Hungarians. In the latter part of the afternoon, they returned to where they started—the moat bridge.

"By the way, child, I might point out not everything I've said is doctrine of the Church. Some in Rome might consider my interpreta-tions of these matters as, well, shall we say, flawed."

"I must ask you, Madrosh, why is it such a concern for you to hold a view not quite the same as the Church itself?"

"I will answer you this way. There was a man from England, a thinker by the name of Ockham. Ockham challenged the church less than a hundred years ago. He was excommunicated for his outspoken stand, then died during one of the first attacks of the Great Mortality. So, you see, my dear, having one's own thoughts is not always easy."

"And so it appears it is one thing to have free will, but quite anoth-er to act upon it. Eh, Madrosh?"

His answer was a long, simple chuckle.

"It seems you would rather not be the one to carry a flag, then?"

"For now, that is so, My Lady. With Ockham and others, there be-gan soft breezes of change coming to the church, and I firmly believe great upheaval will come when those breezes whip into winds of both change and destruction. Understand me, Lady Irina. This will happen whether I carry a flag or not."

Pausing to take in the last of the afternoon sun, Madrosh decided to change the subject. After a bit, he started with, "Our discussion is far from complete, of course. It means little without some further un-derstanding of the soul."

As they walked on in silence, Irina thought more about what they had just discussed. Soon they crossed the moat bridge and reached their starting point. As they passed under the raised portcullis, Irina said, "Madrosh, there's something about which I'm curious."

"Yes, My Lady?" Madrosh waited, expecting a difficult question. Instead, he found himself surprised.

"Why have they spread all this hay on the ground in the courtyard? It is laid on a bit thickly, don't you think?" Madrosh said nothing.

She went on. "They say there will be one hundred hungry horses in here tomorrow, and so many animals will turn the courtyard to mud and muck."

Madrosh stared down at the strewn hay as if he was praying.

"Still, it's strange," she said. "Do you not think so?"

Madrosh stopped walking. Lost in thought, he stared at the hay, his eyes moist and sad, and then, looking back at Irina, he said, "Tonight, we must pray, Irina, for all the souls in hell, for those already there, and," he paused, "for those about to go."

. . .

Jerzy Andrezski wasted no time pursuing his idea. He had sold every unclaimed item in Poznan, and to him, ideas were but idle dreams if not propelled by action. That, he understood, was what competition was all about. He knew, too, his idea would require everything he owned as an investment, but he was always willing to take a risk, to invest in himself.

The next day, he walked as fast as his long legs would carry him from his cot behind the convent at Heart of Jesus to the land farmed by Pawel Tokasz. On the way, he couldn't help noticing the city was in many ways different without Jews. Somehow, it was not as alive, as rich, as substantive as it had been. Because Jews had occupied key business positions, commerce without them was like a ship without its ballast—yet, to hear people talk, it was as if the killing of the Jews and the Great Mortality had never happened. It was as if whatever had lingered in the communal conscience evaporated like a rain puddle in the sunshine.

People went about their business, glad to have lived to see a beautiful June day. What was striking, however, was there were so many fewer people about and the shops of many craftsmen stood hollow, their window openings like dead eyes on the world. It was as though the city had taken a step backward in time. Shaking his head in dismay, he reminded himself he could do nothing to bring back what had been.

"Let's find *Pan* Wodowicz—he gets older every day," he called out to Pawel Tokasz, who was in the midst of pitchforking manure out of the cowstall.

Together, they hurried themselves to a hut on the edge of the city, where the old man sat whittling a walking stick from a branch of white birch. Introductions over, Andrezski began talking about the making of clear glass. He could see the old man's eyes come alive and twinkle as he recalled a time when he was a part of something important.

"How hot must the fires be?" asked Andrezski. Old Jan Wodowicz took a deep gulp of ale, both to clear his throat and to command the attention of his two listeners.

"You are impatient, my friend. In due time. We will not be making glass the Italian way."

"Is there another way, *Pan* Wodowicz?" asked Tokasz incredulously.

"When the Italians came here," Wodowicz began, "they brought with them great bags of sand they'd collected from the seashores of their country. They said the sand had to be very fine. For the cathedral, the Italians made the glass their way. Then they left and took nearly everything with them, including their secrets." His face broke apart in a wide, toothless grin. "But not all their secrets," he added slyly.

"You, *Pan* Tokasz, have a few, and I have a few others," he said, pointing to the dome of his head, out of which grew a very few thin gray hairs. The etchings your father had are for Italian glass, and they will help, but there's more to know."

"*Pan* Wodowicz, is there anyone else in Poznan who could help us?"

"Not in Poznan, but deep in the woods," he said, pointing westward.

"In the woods?"

"Yes, and that is where the glass will have to be made, so that people in the city don't complain about the smoke."

"Who is in the woods, then, to help us?"

Old Wodowicz laughed and slapped his knee. "Why, the monks at

St. Stephen's, of course—and one in particular."

. . .

In the morning, fog shrouded the Oder River valley and refused to release its grip. The bout of sunshine from the day before had warmed the earth, but when the light, cool rain came overnight, it produced a tenacious mist hovering near the ground. By mid-morning, the already dark day wore a gray gauze preventing Madrosh and his companion from seeing much more than a dozen feet in front of them. He wondered how the day would progress.

"This day does not augur well for the visit of the Hungarians. No one will be able to see them, nor they, us," Irina observed, and began to walk along the second-story gallery where they'd agreed to meet.

"It may not matter, My Lady."

"You seem so sure of things, Madrosh. How much time do we have until they arrive?"

"An hour, perhaps more. So, we have some time to talk. What might be on your mind today, my child?"

"Madrosh," she began diplomatically, "you have done your job well. I think I understand some of what you have so patiently explained to me, and using reason, I see why great thinkers have come to believe there is a God. But for me," she said, her voice breaking, "my heart still aches so for what Poznan did to my Berek and to so many good and innocent people."

She stopped talking and turned her face away. Though never married and never a father in the physical sense, Madrosh had seen and learned much in his life, and one thing he knew for certain was that a woman with child tended to emotional surges he neither understood nor experienced. Thus aware, he let Irina spend her tears and held his words. Finally, she found her voice once more.

"It may be a while before I can embrace the God that let this happen."

Madrosh did not argue. He knew she would remember what he'd said about free will and that what had happened was not God's doing. He knew, too, that grief and motherhood were a powerful combination for unsettled thinking. He had come to like the pretty young woman and wanted to provide the best guidance to her. He just wasn't sure what the right way might be.

When she spoke, it was with a clear voice. "Madrosh, can you tell me why the world is better off because of God and religion? With all the wars and violence, does the church do more harm than good in representing God to the people?"

"As always, you ask no small questions, my dear. I will do my best for you. You may remember me mentioning that God's gift of the Commandments brought greater goodness and peace to those who believed in him. It is fair to say the existence of the Commandments amongst Jews and Christians propelled mankind forward beyond explanation."

"What if it had stopped there, Madrosh? What if all we had were the Commandments?"

"Remember, that's all we did have for over a thousand years before Christ. While the Commandments helped to improve the behaviors of those they touched, they did nothing for the rest of mankind. We are beginning to learn that many ancient kings, emperors, and even pharaohs had developed codes of laws, but there too, they did not touch enough people to make any real difference. And as for the Jews, they have never been a people to seek others to join them as Jews. As a consequence, the beauty and effect of the Commandments would likely have stayed with them alone." He cleared his throat and squinted into the mist as they walked, so as not to crash to the floor over an unseen obstacle.

"One might guess that life today, almost fourteen hundred years after Christ, would be the same as it was fourteen hundred years before Christ had he not come. With his coming, Christianity has spread the idea of one God—even the Muslims believe in the same God—but it has also spread other new commandments, one of which comes to mind now."

"And that is…?"

"To love thy neighbor as thyself. When people remember to apply it, it brings changes never seen before. In simple terms, it means each man must respect—and love—a being other than himself.

"That may be true, Madrosh, but it doesn't explain why we still have whole peoples murdered because they are somehow different."

"My Lady, you have come to it. Man's nature, perhaps. Man's soul." Somewhere nearby, through the now lifting fog, trumpets sounded an eerie welcome. "And today, I'm afraid, you will learn more about it."

. . .

Sir Ortwinus Esel knew others must have thought him a large mouse caught in a trap as he skittered about Krosno Castle, but he preferred that image to the other four-legged creature with which many others associated him. When he thought about it, he laughed, then forced himself to concentrate on his task.

It was all too strange. Why had the Hungarians come here instead of Glogau, some thirty miles to the south, where that duchy's margrave resided? Would his Teuton master not be insulted at having been overlooked? To what arrangement had the Hungarian come with the Duke of Poznan and the Margrave of Brandenburg? Why would two subjects of King Louis of Hungary meet with King Wenceslas? What details of this arrangement could possibly have made all three men appear content? Why were the Hungarians coming back again this very day? Most importantly, why had he not followed his instincts and sent a messenger to his master, the Margrave of Glogau? Had his hand not been stayed by King and Margrave Wenceslas himself, he would most certainly have done so. Then, of course, responsibility for whatever happened in Krosno would not be his.

And now, Sir Ortwinus could hear the trumpets he had directed to sound a short while earlier. Ordinarily a beautiful, clear sound, the trumpets' blast now seemed to fall to the ground like the fog lying so heavily there. Worse, the sound seemed distant and forlorn, as if heralding a state funeral. Upon orders of his guests, Sir Ortwinus had applied the full force of castle and town residents to ready themselves for the most unusual visit. Why they were to give so royal a welcome to the emissaries of King Louis of Hungary, rarely a friend to the Teutons, he could not imagine.

In the eerie quiet of the late morning, he felt the faint rumble of horses' hooves—hundreds of them—clomping the hard earth, knowing they would soon thunder on the cobbled main roadway leading to the vast square in front of the castle. He hurried to the main gate, passed through it under the portcullis, and crossed the moat bridge to stand at his assigned place.

He had been tasked with greeting the new guests, but the instructions to him were as strange as the entire affair. He was to warmly welcome the Hungarians and wave them across the bridge, but he and his men were not to follow. None of it made sense, but he knew that in this time and place, he was nearest to last in the pecking order of nobility, and therefore, last in the knowledge chain. His grasp on the position as Krosno Castle's ceremonial functionary was at times tenuous, and he would do nothing that might give his guests reason to carry an unfavorable report to his margrave. He did exactly as instructed.

As he positioned himself near the trumpeters at the foot of the moat bridge, he could dimly make out details of the buildings at the far end of the plaza. The fog was lifting rapidly. Soon, the rumble of horses, leather against hide, metal slapping against leather, light armor clanking along, made the ground vibrate. Sir Ortwinus began to tremble with the ground, concerned as he was with the happenings around him, despite assurances of his noble betters.

The first horses came into view, and Sir Ortwinus thought he recognized the Hungarian, Captain Tomori. Next to him had to be Sir Bela Kinizsi, and behind them, two men unlike all the others. When the horses came to a stop not many feet in front of him, Sir Ortwinus cleared his throat and began to speak.

. . .

Madrosh suggested they climb back to their perch on the parapets where they could get the best view of the day's events. At first, the priest's invitation mystified Irina a bit. *Wouldn't we get a better view at the courtyard level? Or on the first gallery?*

The fog was beginning to lift, and a few details lower down came into view as they mounted the curving stone steps. They quickened their pace when they heard the sound of horses on cobbles signaling the imminent arrival of the Hungarians. The whole enterprise caught their full attention, and Irina wanted to catch every bit of the pageantry, though a sense of dread shadowed the moment. *Will Franciszek make another appearance?*

From their high redoubt, Irina could make out Velka, Rosta, and every manner of class and person within Krosno Castle who stopped to watch, but they, too, were not in the courtyard but in the galleries above it. She looked everywhere for the face she wanted to see. It was that of the young, innocent, and very appealing Squire Jan Brezchwa. They had had few occasions to speak since their arrival at Krosno, and about that, she was of two minds. On the one hand, she felt alive and content in his company, and on the other, she wished no man to intrude on her memory of Berek. Jan Brezchwa was young, handsome, and attentive, but she didn't know what to do about him.

In reaching their high place, they could look across the square and begin to see the long line of horsemen coming from the south. At the very front of the column were two men expensively garbed and armored, their metals giving off a soft gleam in the low, misty light of the approaching noonday. There were two outriders just behind carrying pennants dressed with a gold edge surrounding a gray field bisected with a red cross. The colors of the first two riders and their flag-bearers were in stark contrast to the two men immediately behind them. Not soldiers, they were dressed well, but seemed shabby by comparison.

All along, Yip remained at Irina's side, and she was pleased to see her beloved sheepdog wanting to protect her and her child, almost as if he had certain duties to perform, and this was one of them. As she and Madrosh peered through openings in the castle's battlements, Yip scampered on top of the stone, sat on his haunches, and watched every movement below with the utmost concentration. Irina wanted to laugh at her dog's behavior, but cast her gaze in the same direction catching Yip's attention.

The mist and the civilian garb fooled the pair on the parapet for a moment. Then Madrosh put his hand on Lady Irina's arm and said, "Be calm, My Lady."

At the same moment, she saw, too, and with a gasp, inhaled deeply. "Yes, it's them! I thought we were rid of them—forever. First the big one the other day, and now the castellan himself is here!" Yip uttered a low, menacing growl.

"Perhaps not for long, My Lady."

"What do you mean?"

Just then, they heard the high thin voice of Sir Ortwinus Esel pierce the air around him, the fog parting before him like the Red Sea before the Israelites. All leaned forward to hear his words.

...

It was earlier in the day, when they left camp and all the horses were in formation, that Tomasz felt the growing terror deep within him. It was the kind of dread that rumbles up from the soul and makes breakfast yearn to make the wrong exit.

He swallowed hard. There was no way, he knew with a cold finality, that Duke Zygmunt would ever believe him, would ever take him back, no matter what he might say about the two women pretending to be a lady and her servant. He knew it when he splashed his face with frigid water early that morning and tried to put his concerns aside, allowing arrogance to overpower reason. But when he looked at his hands they couldn't stop shaking.

Despite his innate bravado, Tomasz's voice had become nervous and uncertain. Franciszek looked at him, frowning and wondering. Incredibly, Tomasz finally concluded—laughing out loud when he realized it—Franciszek had been right. Running to Poznan would have been the smartest thing they could have done. He now knew Zygmunt would have been gone for at least a year and, with luck, might never be coming back. In Poznan, he could have lived near his father and made a life somehow.

Tomasz calmed himself, and as they joined the Hungarian formation and rode toward Krosno, he knew that he had to escape before meeting face-to-face with Duke Zygmunt. Just that prospect renewed his shivering on the warm June morning. Bile climbed to his throat. Whatever opportunity arose, he knew he'd have to take it, no matter what the risk.

Crossing the river and moving through the woods was an orderly, controlled affair, and despite the low fog, there was no chance to break from the formation of twos. Any of the fifty pairs of armed men would ride him down and kill him if he jerked the reins of his horse left or right. Sir Bela and Captain Tomori kept him hemmed in like a garment too tight around the neck. His nerves jangled all the more as they rode closer to Krosno and a fate he did not want to imagine.

Within two hours, the troupe reached Krosno's town plaza, the clomp of horses' feet on the cobblestones intimidating the small party waiting at the moat bridge. Townspeople had gathered to gawk. Tomasz's eyes darted everywhere, but no escape presented itself.

They stopped several feet short of the rather plump fellow waiting there to greet them. He appeared more the jester than the general, and he waited for the cascade of sound from the arrivals to come to some quiet. Then he spoke.

"I am Sir Ortwinus Esel and on behalf of the Duke of Poznan, Zygmunt and the Margrave of Glogau, whose duchy you visit, I extend their greetings and welcome to you, Sir Bela Kinizsi, Captain Tomori, and the soldiers of King Louis of Hungary!"

His face glowing with the words he heard, Sir Bela bowed in acknowledgement, and Captain Tomori followed his lead. Sir Bela spoke for them all: "We are honored to represent his Highness, Louis of Hungary, on Teuton soil and look forward to a long association with Krosno Castle and its people."

Just behind the parade's head, Tomasz was in full panic. He watched the plump Ortwinus bow in welcome, and apparently following a protocol, make a grand gesture signifying that the guests should ride ahead.

At that moment, the four trumpeters, in a line but a few feet away, issued a further welcoming blast that pierced the misty air.

Sir Bela and his men had not anticipated the blare of the trumpets. Startled, the horses bucked and whinnied, their hooves climbing high in the air. When the first horses began their fearful dance, many horses behind them joined in the chaos, so much so that the men and their mounts in the first dozen ranks had great difficulty maintaining order. What had been a neat column of two's was now bedlam in the mist. Ranks broke and men shouted commands to their horses.

Tomasz saw his chance, his one and only chance.

. . .

From atop the castle wall, Madrosh, Lady Irina, and all the duke's soldiers stationed there were taking in the light pageantry somewhat comically and pompously carried out by Sir Ortwinus. When the trumpets sounded their overwhelming blast, Irina heard several on-lookers begin to chuckle at the embarrassed Hungarians.

Irina could not laugh. As they watched, Irina pointed and tried to cry out, but her voice died in her throat. She caught Madrosh's atten-tion, and at once, he leaned forward to study the melee below. When she could speak, she said, "See him? It is Tomasz." As if there were no other riders there, she focused fully on Tomasz the Terrible as he pulled his reins sharply to his right and bolted into the grey shroud that still lingered. She shouted in a most unladylike manner, pointing at the man and horse galloping toward the long, narrow bridge across the river. Her voice, and the man's escape, were lost in the ruckus below.

Irina then fixed her eyes on the two men in the lead. As they strained to control their mounts, they did not realize what had hap-pened behind them. When the horsemen regained hold of their reins, but barely, their animals sprung forward with even more energy. The Hungarians bolted past the immobile Ortwinus. Across the moat bridge and through the castle gate they clattered, Franciszek in his place amongst them.

Irina and Madrosh looked down in both fascination and horror. Yip was so agitated, Irina grabbed him by the collar and held him as best she could. As she did so, she wrestled with the emotions welling up inside her.

She had begun to feel at ease with the world as it was after St. Stephen's. When Tomasz and Franciszek were led away, she was certain they would face a horrible death, and that thought gave her some sense of satisfaction. She held that cold comfort until three days earlier, when Big Franciszek reappeared and it became known Tomasz the Terrible was yet alive.

At Krosno, either one of them would present a deadly danger to Irina and Velka. She clutched her belly to protect the baby she was carrying. Hers was not just any child. It was one with Jewish blood, soon to be born to a world where death and horror came more often to Jews merely because they existed. *Would the duke believe what Franciszek might say about me?*

With anger in her voice, she turned to Madrosh and demanded, "Will that man never meet God?"

Madrosh looked back at her, said nothing, but on his face there was a most mournful expression.

As she spoke the words, Yip broke loose and bounded from the parapet. She called to him, but in a flash, he disappeared down the narrow stone steps.

CHAPTER IX

1378

Sir Bela smiled as he rode through the gate with anticipation of so easy a first victory on the Baltic campaign. Under the broad stone arch of Krosno Castle he rode with his one hundred heavily armed men, and what an impression they had made. It was majestic, he thought.

Soon he would exult to King Louis as his messenger was sent forth with news the first fortress west of the Oder was his. What was more, the traitor, Zygmunt Sokorski, would—in the end—be executed and all his lands and titles forfeited to the king. By two hours past noon, he guessed, his messenger and two soldiers would make a fast ride toward the homeland.

When the last of his men completed their entry into the vast Krosno courtyard, the clank of the portcullis chains filled the air as it dropped with a heavy thud. Sir Bela was at once struck by what he saw—and what he didn't see. No one was there to greet them. All openings on the lower levels were shuttered. The quiet was eerie. No welcoming crowd. No birds singing. Only a single dog's menacing bark broke the stillness.

At the very least, he expected Duke Zygmunt to personally welcome the king's emissary. Uneasily, the horses pranced in the hay, gnawing what they could. Sir Bela turned to another noise, that of the inner gates swinging shut on great iron hinges.

...

In the second-level galleries some twenty feet above the courtyard, soldiers of Zygmunt and Wenceslas ringed the inner ramparts, their polished armor and weaponry glinting in the brightening sun.

From her perch higher up, Irina watched in fascination as the Hungarians looked at each other, their horses a-skitter. She wondered where Yip had gone, and hadn't noticed the duke and the margrave had taken positions a few paces from where she and Madrosh stood. Irina stared at the nobles, her eyes wide seeing they were not down below greeting their Hungarian guests. *Why are they up here?*

Instinctively, Irina leaned closer to Madrosh, grasping his arm. She had not noticed that her breathing had stopped, and in an unconscious act, had focused all her attention on the men there with her as well as those penned below. Just as the fog had blanketed the ground, a dread crept over her. Her lungs heaved, frantic for air.

Zygmunt's voice boomed out, "Welcome, Sir Bela. The Margrave of Brandenburg and I tender our regrets that we were not in the courtyard to receive you personally."

"The Margrave of Brandenburg? What are you doing, Zygmunt? Do you realize you are insulting your king? Do you understand what will happen to you and your estates in Poznan when King Louis hears of this?"

"Yes, I do, Sir Bela. I informed Captain Tomori I was a Pole, not a Hungarian. And your king, Sire," he said, pausing, "will never hear of our meeting."

At that moment, Zygmunt raised his arm in a command signal and dropped it. An archer to Zygmunt's left shot an arrow that dug into the ground just in front of Sir Bela's horse. It had not been the bowman's intent to strike soldier or horse. His task had been simpler, Irina realized. It was to shoot a flaming arrow into the hay.

She could see the Hungarians were confused by what was happening, but the shooter had mastery of his weapon. Smoke curled into the air. In a moment, a dozen fiery arrows injected themselves into the courtyard's yellow carpet, flames sucking on the hay.

"Trample them out! Fix your bows! Shoot at will! Aim for them!" Sir Bela shouted, pointing at Zygmunt and Wenceslas.

Irina could see Franciszek's head shifting from side to side, apparently looking for Tomasz. He appeared ready to spur his horse in any direction. Through the spreading smoke, the perspiration of fear matting his yellow hair to his head was easily visible.

Franciszek called for Tomasz. He looked upward and despite the distance, his steady, dumb eyes found Irina's on high.

She returned his glare. Unlike in another courtyard not long before, this time he sought only pity. She gave none. From nowhere, a dog appeared and nipped at the shanks of Franciszek's horse, snarling without relent.

"Yip!" Irina called to her beloved guardian. Her voice bounced off the stone walls of the castle. "Yip, come back!" She was desperate, but the dog paid her no heed. Yip bayed, barked, and bedeviled Franciszek's horse until it reared in the air and threw its rider onto the burning floor. Yip leapt upon his prey and went for Franciszek's throat.

Arrows rained upon the Hungarians, each hitting a satisfactory target: man, horse, or hay. Through the growing smoke, the horses took fright and tried to run. There was no place for them to go. Riders lost control of their animals, falling to earth only to be crushed by others before being set alight. Soon, the small flames grew into a bonfire, licking, then consuming pennants, horse blankets, tunics, hair, and flesh.

Irina put her hands to her mouth and tried to scream out again, but could not. She saw her beloved sheepdog on Franciszek as the man struggled with the dog and the flames washing over him. Soon, they were engulfed. Tears froze in the corners of her eyes. She could not move or speak.

Irina turned and stared at Zygmunt in revulsion as he and Wenceslas watched men and horses die a most gruesome death. She could see in their eyes that these men clearly enjoyed the glimpse of hell before them. They held the same gleam of excitement she had seen from another holocaust. In a courtyard in Poznan.

Within a few minutes, the horses ceased their cries, their riders already having lost their own voices. The fire had not been long burning, but the stench of scorched flesh and emptied bowels soon became unbearable. The conflagration slowly subsided, and after a long while, during which no one moved a step, the thick, black smoke drifted upward, like a pitiful, dark prayer. Everyone with the courage to look saw empty eye sockets staring heavenward in reproach. From the watchers above, there came only a funereal disquiet.

Irina's hand was on her heart, her emotions running from horror and revulsion to satisfaction and justice rendered. She wanted to vomit but refused to let herself do so. This day recalled too vividly for her the fate of the Joselewicz family, and it frightened her that the looks on the faces of the men controlling these events were not unlike those on that earlier, terrible night. In Duke Zygmunt she saw something she knew was there but did not want to see.

She began to moan with great, heavy spasms, her whole being shaking. First Berek and her Joselewicz family. Now Yip. He'd had his revenge. Love for her and hate for her enemy had determined his fate. Finally, her tears ran freely and she didn't care that her lords, her hosts, were watching her.

Irina knew that in war, cruelty was commonplace, but there was something dishonorable about what she had just witnessed. Even so, emotion triumphed over more sensible instincts. Though Madrosh taught her not to make judgments about others, she was pleased that Franciszek had died with all the brutality she thought he deserved. She stopped her tears, swearing to herself she would mourn for Yip, but no others who died this day.

Madrosh held her, and as if divining her thoughts, whispered hoarsely, but gently, "Remember to pray for the souls in hell, Irina."

She turned to him. Coughing through the wisps of smoke, Irina choked out words she wanted to shout but could only whisper. "Yet one man has escaped this hell, Madrosh!" She collapsed.

When she fell, it was not into the arms of her teacher, but into those of a patient, waiting squire, Jan Brezchwa.

. . .

For nearly an hour, Tomasz spurred his horse to a full gallop, and dared not look back. Even the wind against his face and chest could not dry the sweat born of fear. Having crossed the Oder to the eastern shore, he rode straight over the plain, and only upon reaching a stand of birches did he turn to check behind him.

In the distance, he saw a large black cloud rising from the castle, and the very sight made him smile, but because Sir Bela would likely send riders after him, he turned eastward once more and drove himself deeper into the thick tree line. He had no idea how far he had gone, but his horse could go no further without water and rest.

Surrounded by oak, birch, and elm, he dismounted onto a pair of wobbly legs. He let himself fall next to a fast stream where he and his horse quenched themselves in the cool water, and when his breathing returned to something akin to normalcy, he lay back, staring at the sky through the green canopy. He surprised himself by laughing out loud, but then no one could possibly hear him. "They're all dead! That bastard Duke Zygmunt and his pet bitch—they're all dead, and I don't care that the Hungarians did it to them!" Saying the words aloud made it all seem more real.

"Hah!" His guffaws went on, and he rolled onto his side in laughter. Ah, lucky Franciszek, he thought. He was there for all the fun. Perhaps some good had come of this, after all. He would miss having Franciszek around, but he had no doubt his man would find a place for himself in Sir Bela's service. After a few minutes, he thought he heard horses, but it was merely his imagination.

The thought of capture made him rise and take to his horse for another hour or so before he halted in a sunny glade where both could water and he could nap. Closing his eyes, he took a hard look at his circumstances, but in truth, he had no plan because he had never expected to survive Krosno Castle.

Franciszek had been right after all. It would have been foolish to think he could return to the duke's good graces and enjoy revenge upon the two impostors who had accused him. His desire for vengeance had overridden good reason. He had, indeed, turned over all of the goods he'd taken from the Joselewicz house—and from the twenty-odd other Jewish homes and shops he and Franciszek had pillaged that night! He was guilty of many things, but never of disobedience to the duke's demands.

It made him angry still to think that the jewelry and trinkets in Franciszek's pocket had likely come from the Joselewicz house. It was treasure never once in his possession, yet it brought him a death sentence. As he drifted into unconsciousness, he satisfied himself on two counts. There was no reason to spend time thinking about what the two girls had taken for themselves. It must have been a great deal to give them their new life—and at Krosno Castle, their sudden death. He giggled at the thought of it. Second, Poznan would be his next destination. On his way, he'd seek food and rest at the one safe place he knew.

...

Codes of honor were to be respected. In battling one's enemies, a knight gave his opponent a fair contest. Exceptions to the rules of engagement were few and rare. Two reasons to force such an exception were convenience and secrecy. If no one knew a knight broke the rules, then the matter might deserve no further judgment.

Duke Zygmunt felt his conscience bore no extra weight because of the day's events. Had the Hungarians prevailed his life would have been forfeit—of that, there was little doubt. The Hungarians were quick, clever, and cruel, and he harbored no feelings of dishonor. Indeed, he carried feelings of relief and satisfaction.

From his vantage point, he could no more have submitted himself, a proud Polish noble, to his nation's ancient nemesis than he could have disavowed his church. Nobility was one thing. Protecting one's future was another. He had no choice but to annihilate the Hungarians once he committed to link battle arms with Wenceslas and the Teutons. Zygmunt did not know whether he'd see his native Poland again in his lifetime, but he did not want his name ever to be spoken by Poles as a betrayer of his homeland and his people.

At the evening meal, Duke Zygmunt and Margrave Wenceslas dined in an awkward silence, but in the full certainty that by the day's action, a serious threat had been thwarted. The margrave finally spoke. "And so, Duke Zygmunt, I and the Duchy of Brandenburg are everlastingly in your debt. How shall I repay the succor you have so freely rendered on my behalf?"

Zygmunt bowed in gracious acknowledgment of the day's most obvious outcome. "Your Highness, there is no need. We share borders and a love of peace between us."

After a pensive moment, the king said, "That is all true, Zygmunt, but my gratitude must go beyond a word or two. It is personal with me, and I do not like to be indebted to anyone. For all that you have done, you and your entourage shall be under my care and protection as we journey to Paris."

"Ah, Your Highness, that is most gracious and generous of you."

"It is the least I can do. We will have a fine time together and further bind our relationship. I already have in mind a plan that will include a rest at Tangermunde, about three days' journey west of Berlin. It will be good, I think, for the women and, in particular, the one with child to take their rest for a few days before we go on to Paris."

"In truth, Your Majesty, my original plan of travel was to Brandenburg, where I had hoped you and I might meet to discuss matters of mutual interest. However," Zygmunt paused, smiling, and throwing up his arms in a gesture of surrender to fate, "what has occurred could not have served us better. And so, Your Majesty, it will be I who is in your debt." He bowed his head slightly and brought it up again with a broad smile.

In the beginning, when the invitation to visit Paris had arrived and the meeting with Wenceslas arranged, Zygmunt wanted merely to forge a friendly alliance with his neighbor to the west. When the Hungarians presented themselves, they brought with them an opportunity Zygmunt could not let pass. It was the chance to secure his future, and that of the Duchy of Poznan. Yet it was this second objective that, ironically, was now in jeopardy.

King Wenceslas gazed at him and said, "You smile, and yet there is concern in your face. What troubles you?"

"My dear ally," he addressed the king, "I must also seek your counsel on how I might deal with the possible, though distant consequences of my act in your defense this day. Not one of Sir Bela's men escaped, and so we do not know what Louis will conclude when he does not hear from his expedition. We must give incentive to Ortwinus Esel and the Margrave of Glogau never to speak of what occurred here.

"Also, gracious Wenceslas, I would not want to return to my native Poznan a year or more hence only to be marched to the axe man's block. I would want to ensure the security of my family and my duchy in the years to come. What advice might you render to help me achieve the peace for which I long, and freedom from the Hungarians, Your Grace?"

Wenceslas hesitated. "Let me ponder this most interesting problem, Zygmunt. In the meantime, let us raise our goblets to a military victory with no loss of men to our side, and to an uneventful expedition to Tangermunde!"

. . .

Jerzy Andrezski made a brief stop at the convent to inform Sister Luke he would be leaving the city for a time. His newest associates, Pawel Tokasz and Jan Wodowicz, stood by, both impatient to head west toward the edge of *Wielko Polska* and the forests of Silesia.

"Why are you leaving Poznan, *Pan* Andrezski?" the young Mother Superior asked.

"To explore a better future, Sister."

"I thought you began a good business here."

"Yes, Sister, I thought so, too," he answered in both gratitude and humility, "but it will not sustain us, and I want to provide for you and the other nuns here, and for the little angel who gave me to drink when I had a great thirst."

Sister Luke smiled. "Dear friend, we will be grateful for whatever you do for us, but you have given us bounteous thanks many times over."

At the sound of his voice, Zuzanna ran into the room and hugged Andrezski's leg, her tiny arms barely able to circumnavigate the big man's thigh. "*Pan* Jerzy, I missed you! When will you take me with you?"

"Someday, Zuzanna, someday. That is, if you don't join the convent and become like Sister Luke," he said, laughing and picking her up in the air.

The nun smiled and recaptured her charge. "First, you must grow a bit, Zuzanna!"

"Yes, and then, *Pan* Jerzy, you will take me to see my sister, Irina!"

...

Two full days of hard labor by the townspeople and men of the castle were necessary to remove the remains of the funeral pyre to a great pit north of the castle.

A brilliantly sunny day greeted Wenceslas of Brandenburg and the Duke of Poznan as they preceded their large entourage out of Krosno Castle down to the river's edge. There, all of the men of noble rank and their squires, as well as all of the women and their attendants, boarded the barges tied up along the banks. In the shadow of the bridge they had crossed many days earlier, the barges were released from their moorings, and they began their drift with the river's flow, ever northward toward a distant sea. Meanwhile, most of the troops and all the horses and carts would make speed overland and meet them in Frankfort *an der* Oder.

"And a good morning to you, My Lady," Madrosh said.

"Indeed," spoke Duke Zygmunt, who joined them. "How are you faring, my dear?" Without waiting for an answer, he continued, "I trust we will all be more careful on the waters than when we arrived at Krosno, *nie?*"

"Most certainly, My Lord," Madrosh said, answering for both.

"Well, at least we will not have them to concern us," he said, gesturing toward the place along the river where the charred remains of the Hungarian invasion force had been interred. "They are all safely in eternity," he added with a slight smile on his lips.

"Not all, Your Grace," Irina said, but immediately wished she hadn't. Having spoken and seeing the query etched on the duke's countenance, she had no choice but to go on. "Perhaps you weren't able to notice, but Tomasz Wodowicz did not die with them. Father Madrosh and I could see from the parapets that he rode off when the trumpets first blasted, and no one rode after him." All color drained from the duke's countenance

"Then there is someone left alive who…" He stopped short, as if he had no more breath for words.

Irina could see the duke's entire demeanor had changed in an instant. From a smug satisfaction there came something else. *Was it fear?*

Duke Sokorski stared blankly at Irina and Madrosh, but could find no words. With a whisper, he said, "Excuse me," and walked slowly to the front of the barge.

Irina and Madrosh exchanged glances.

"I hadn't thought to tell him," Madrosh said. "I'm so sorry it fell to you, my dear."

"No matter, Madrosh. Perhaps I learned something, but it is too disturbing to think about now."

Turning her vision to the present, Irina was pleased to see that Jan Brezchwa had somehow managed to be on her barge, within earshot, as if waiting to be summoned. They began to exchange more than greetings, and while their brief conversations were, to Irina, charming, they did not discuss the weighty topics she and Madrosh had thus far chosen.

What she and Jan spoke about Irina could never seem to remember. Like the river beneath them, their talks flowed and turned as did the beautiful shorelines on either side. It didn't seem to matter what their conversations entailed. They were exactly what Irina needed to help blur the horrific events so recently refreshed in her memory.

All the while, Madrosh stayed close by, never interrupting, never breaking their growing bond. He smiled all the while, his broad cape billowing in the breeze almost like a shielding cocoon allowing the young people to deepen their acquaintance without distraction. He enjoyed the role of grand protector.

The river itself turned sharply west some distance above Krosno, and the passengers could hear the boatmen chattering in a German dialect about the city ahead of them. Madrosh explained that Frankfort, already a member of the Hanseatic League, dominated trade between Stettin and Breslau. They would overnight there, then pass by the little village of Berlin before reaching the favorite fortress of the Emperor Charles and his son Wenceslas. Tangermunde, it was said, would be a great place for rest, refreshment, and final preparation for the long journey west.

...

Having heard nothing from the parish priests in and around Poznan, Bishop Tirasewicz decided brooding over the mystery was an empty exercise. To quench his curiosity, he concocted a plan to serve his purpose well. A journey to the east would be in order. Oh, not for himself, of course. Such journeys could be perilous—especially if plague continued to lurk there.

Over several days, he observed his staff closely, in search of one who could be trusted with the delicate mission of a visit to the Bishop of Gniezno. Having made the best choice, and barring an unforeseen event, Antony Tirasewicz would have the answer to his question in a matter of weeks.

To his private audience chamber, he summoned young Father Ryzard Michalski and provided, without much in the way of explanation, the reasons for a sojourn to Gniezno, *sulla rosa et sub rosa*, a mission best kept secret.

...

Toward Poland's western woods, Jerzy Andrezski, Pawel Tokasz, and Jan Wodowicz rode from Poznan in spirited anticipation. Jerzy was pleased that Tokasz had decided to leave his farm in search of something better, and his family did not object since much of the planting had been done and he could be spared for a time.

Andrezski wasn't so sure about his feelings for Jan Wodowicz, who subtly let them know that qualities such as loyalty and honesty were distinctly relative. They knew, however, that the old man's cooperation might be necessary for the success of their venture.

They made the trip in a few long days, traversing the roads and faint forest tracks with the speed that only three unencumbered men could achieve. What they saw along the way served to confirm what they already believed. The plague's visitation had been just as severe in the outlying villages—like Wozna, where they stopped briefly—as it had been in the city, and they encountered few people, fewer still who welcomed contact with strangers.

Arriving at St. Stephen's at mid-day, Jerzy was astonished to learn that none of the monks there had been touched by the plague, according to a surprised but welcoming Father Kaminski. "And what brings you three so far into the forest to this place of God?"

"Good Father," Andrezski began, "we come in search of knowledge and resource, but perhaps not of the kind you might imagine."

"I have heard of you and your generosity, *Pan* Andrezski. You have my ear."

Jan Wodowicz spoke up impatiently. "Father Abbot," he began, "many years ago, there was a man who worked in Poznan with the Italians from Venice." He caught his breath. "They made the glass for Sts. Peter and Paul Cathedral, but this man left Poznan shortly afterward, when the Great Mortality made its first visit there."

"And what does that have to do with St. Stephen's?"

"That man became a monk, Father, but I no longer remember his name."

"Father Abbot," Andrezski said, taking control of the conversation, "it is very important to us—and perhaps to you—that we speak with him."

"Important to me? How?"

"To you and the monks here at St. Stephen's." Jerzy took in the surroundings and continued. "You men of God have had to work exceedingly hard to wring substance out of your prayers to the Creator," he explained as diplomatically as he could.

Karol Kaminski nodded, his bare forehead gleaming in the June sunlight.

"One might imagine," Jerzy said in his most empathetic merchant's voice, "the men of God at St. Stephen's must live a sometimes-meager existence, *nie?*" He could see the abbot was deep in thought. "Perhaps we might be able to help."

After some moments, while his guests waited patiently, the abbot conceded, "The man you seek is Brother Heidolphus Brotelin. I will bring him to you."

...

The more he thought about it, the angrier Bishop Tirasewicz became. His eyebrows arched like bristles over the cold stare he cast across the empty room. He had long made it his business to keep an ear to Poznan's ground—for the good of the church, he told himself—and often, the things he heard paid dividends. And then his face turned upside down and his smile became like a cat's grin over a mouse.

"Father Shimanski! Have my horse brought round." Despite the June warmth, he threw the black cape over his shoulders and splashed himself with the scarlet piping and cap of a bishop of the church. In a short time, he found himself at the convent gate, where he demanded an audience, unannounced, with Sister Luke.

"Why yes, Bishop Tirasewicz," the Mother Superior said, surprised at both the visit and the bishop's distinctly cool manner, "how can the Dominican Sisters be of help to His Grace?"

"Let's be seated, Sister Luke. Where we can talk." He followed the silent, obedient nun to a small parlor.

"I have become aware, Sister Luke," he said, repeating her name so as to command her full attention, his voice like an insistent drumbeat, "that your convent has sought to profit from the misery of the people. Much gold and silver has come into your hands from those of one Jerzy Andrezski, is that not so?"

"With all respect, Bishop Tirasewicz, many goods were left here by the dying, but little silver and no gold," she carefully stated. "I merely engaged *Pan* Andrezski to sell the goods, and return to us what he thought reasonable."

"What he thought reasonable, Sister Luke?" he said, the words carrying both contempt and sarcasm.

"Yes, Bishop, and *Pan* Andrezski has been very generous to us."

"Generous. Surely. I am deeply disappointed you haven't decided to share your bounty with your bishop."

"You had just returned to the city, Your Grace. There hasn't been time to apprise you of our good fortune. And I might point out that with the loss of so many priests and parishioners, *Pan* Andrezski's

214

generosity has been most timely. We have very little."

"Your bishop, too, has little, Sister Luke. My needs are sparse! You must consider giving half of what you receive for the needs of your bishop and the cathedral." It was clear this was not a suggestion.

Stunned by the bluntness of his greed, Sister Luke said, "But Your Grace, such a subtraction from our treasury would present a great hardship to us."

"Did you not take a vow of poverty?"

"We did, Your Grace, and we are poor, still, and only following your instruction to fend for ourselves and the city's poor. The sisters and I," she said, bowing her head, "never thought of you in those terms."

The bishop slapped the arms of his chair and rose, his temper at its edge. "Well, now you can think of me in terms of half your income," he snarled. "Is that understood?"

Sister Luke dipped her chin. "I certainly understand your position, Bishop."

CHAPTER X

1410
GIVERNY, FRANCE

"I have seen so much death in my life. I caused it to others. Now," she whispered to no one, "now, it comes for me."

That death had found Big Franciszek caused her little guilt. That it eventually found Tomasz Wodowicz—after all the murders she had learned he committed in his pursuit of vengeance—caused her none at all.

Irina's mood shifted with the charcoal clouds crowding out the spring sun. The past month had become a pageant of bitter memories come to haunt her. She shivered. *It seems I must live those days again! But not for long, nie?* For some time, she stared into the chateau's shading meadow, where she knew other life would soon do the work of the night world.

Finally, the well-padded chaise enveloped her into a fitful state, neither awake nor asleep. Though wrapped in the folds of a long nightgown, she could not shake the chill. She reached for the cape lying across the nearby chair where Velka often sat to keep her company. Forcing her lips into a smile, she thought about the cape made of farmer's wool, yet handsomely sewn and dyed a brilliant blue. She pulled it over herself, clutching tightly the last relic of her youth, and awaited the warmth she hoped would soon caress her. But the wool's feel against her cheek drew her further into the past.

Pain brought her back to the present as it grabbed her once more, then left, leaving her to await its return. The ache in her belly wasn't from bad food or impure water, and neither was it from despair over a long-ago loss. It was something else. *But will I have long enough?*

For herself, another kind of death would be her visitor one day, but not before, she hoped, there might be an answer to her most ardent prayer. *What has become of you, my son?*

Velka's soft whisper stirred her. "My Lady, is there something I can do for you?"

"Where did the sun go?" Irina asked drowsily, as if the day's earlier warmth might still caress her, ease her discomfort, and shield her from her own memories.

"You needed your rest, so I didn't wake you. Would you like some broth?"

Irina shook her head. "You are thoughtful to ask. Later, perhaps?"

"Just call out, My Lady. I will come." Velka backed away, her felt slippers shushing on the polished wood floor.

Cold rain began to pelt away the day's remainder. Soon, its tattoo upon the chateau's wavy windowglass seemed to insist she not brush aside all that had happened in her life. It had all started in Poznan, a place so far from where she rested, yet the images of what happened seemed to surround her—like the clouds hovering outside her window.

Irina clutched the cape, and as her eyelids fluttered in surrender, she turned her mind's eye to another time and place. Over the years, she had become less certain of her memories, and some, she supposed, were the recollections of others she had woven into her own. It no longer mattered. The year 1378 was one of upheaval and adventure.

1378

Teutonic Lands

Jan Brezchwa hurried to be at Irina's side as she disembarked the barge at Frankfort *an der* Oder for the day's travel overland.

"How can I be of assistance, My Lady?"

"Do you not first attend to your master, Father Madrosh?"

"I have been ordered to see to your needs first, My Lady."

"Did you require such an order?" she asked, mischievously.

Brezchwa's face burnt itself red in an instant, and he said nothing.

"Tell me, Squire Brezchwa," Irina asked, ignoring his discomfiture, "what details have you learned of our journey to the west?"

"I am told, My Lady, we will be on the River Spree for a few days. We will pass by the village of Berlin—there is not much there, it is said—and we will meet up with the Havel River. I understand it is beautiful as it changes from river to lake and back again many times over. Then we will cross overland to the River Elbe, near which is Tangermunde." Brezchwa chuckled. "Father Madrosh told me of an earlier Margrave of Brandenburg who buried his treasure in the parish church there, and passed his secret to his son, the Margrave Otto. When Otto was taken hostage, he recalled his father's treasure and was able to ransom himself."

Irina smiled at his boyish enthusiasm for a good story. "My, you are a waterfall of words today, Squire. And the journey?" she asked, unable to still a pleasant smile.

"From there," he said, clearing his throat in embarrassment, "much of the trip will be slow going as we climb up into the mountains. We will be many weeks yet in Teuton lands before crossing the French frontier. We should be in Paris, they say, sometime in the early fall."

"A long journey, *nie?*"

"*Tak*—Yes, My Lady."

She thought for a moment. "That should give me some weeks of rest before my child comes."

Brezchwa lowered his eyes.

Irina realized she had never spoken to him of her child, a much more intimate matter amongst nobility, she had come to understand, than amongst farm people, where conception and death were an everyday occurrence.

Brezchwa stammered. "You will need help, then."

"Yes, Jan. I will." As he walked away, she realized she'd just called him by his first name.

...

In the Silesian shade, Jerzy Andrezski was able to ignore the full summer weather. He made himself remain patient. Within an hour, Abbot Kaminski strode in followed by a truly ancient specimen of man. Nearing eight decades, Jerzy had been told, Heidolphus Brotelin had already been an old man when he worked on Poznan's cathedral some thirty years before.

He could see the monk eying him and Pawel Tokasz with both interest and suspicion, but seemed to show some recognition for their old companion, the one with the crafty smirk.

Brother Heidolphus looked directly him and said, "Jan Wodowicz! I'm truly surprised you're alive."

Wodowicz shrugged and gave him a crooked smile in return. "It's been many years, Heidolphus. And I am here because we both remember something of value to these men."

Brother Heidolphus looked back at Andrezski and asked, not unkindly, "What do you want of me?"

"We want to make glass, Brother, and with your skill and memory, this may now be our time to do it."

Brotelin nodded and seemed to search his mental shelves for the knowledge they were seeking. "That is a worldly skill forsaken by me decades ago. Why would I resurrect it now?"

"Because what you know, Brother, will help the monks of St. Stephen's and so many others," he said.

Brotelin pondered further, then looked to his superior, silently seeking permission. Father Kaminski accommodated him with a nod.

As he spoke, the elderly man lost years from his face and the infirmities of age as if by some magic. "Here, we could make what is called Forest Glass," Brother Brotelin pronounced. "It had not occurred to me earlier, but I am aware, as is Abbot Kaminski, that other monks, particularly the Germans who live not many days west of here, have perfected a method using beech trees to make the ash we will need." He saw the question in his listeners' eyes. "Ah! The German method is a bit different from that used by the Italians, you see.

"This particular part of the forest is ideal for the production of glass, as I think about it. We have all the resources here we need but one: sand. You will have to bring me the cleanest sand you can find. Then we can make glass!" The old monk exhaled, as if he'd used up all his air.

Andrezski was quick to reply. "I will provide the monies needed to start. Sand can be brought from the Warta or the Oder, whichever is finest. If you oversee us in the glassmaking, I will sell it. In return, you will have what you need to live God's word here in the forest."

The old monk let go of an unseemly giggle. "A moment," he said. "There is much work to do. In a few weeks' time." Thinking out loud, Brother Heidolphus began parceling out the work to be done by each of their party. Brother Heidolphus took a deep breath of satisfaction, as if his entire life's purpose, after almost eighty years, had just been presented to him.

As he finished speaking, a young monk strode into the room and whispered into the abbot's ear. Father Kaminski shifted his gaze to Jan Wodowicz, and in a tone of astonished surprise, said, "*Pan* Wodowicz, it seems that your son is here to see you."

...

The expedition had been tiresome, but at last, the Margrave and King led his troops and his guests up the road to Tangermunde. What Duke Zygmunt, Madrosh, and Irina could see was, indeed, impressive. The thick, pink-red brick walls of the castle were at least three, perhaps four stories high and the main gatehouse itself, square and solid, stood even higher. The roof rose from all four sides and reached a point—in the Teutonic style—from which the king's colors flew in the July sun.

King Wenceslas was proud of his domain and was gratified his guests were impressed with the signs of prestige and power. They marched into the castle's courtyard with great relief. Those who were not soldiers, especially the ladies, were glad to be at a place where rest would likely take precedence over balancing themselves on the un-clean river boats. Waiting for them in bright daylight were two rows of knights, fully garbed in small-link chain mail said to weigh at least forty pounds. Plumed crimson feathers rose from their dress helmets while emblazoned on their chests in a field of deep blue was a white cross. Armed with swords and halberds, they were less a formidable force than a king's talisman.

Irina and Velka, with Rosta in close tow, were escorted to a pleasant set of rooms lodged high in the inner wall of the castle. At once, she was confronted by a device she had never seen before. Instead of a woven mat or leather covering, she could open a glass window that swung in on the kind of hinge upon which a door might hang. Her whole life she'd been used to openings in a wall covered by an oilcloth, if that. To be able to look through the glass, wavy and bubbled here and there though it might be, was a great pleasure. She longed to share this wonder with someone she loved, and could almost imagine Berek at her side enjoying her excitement. At once, she was desperately sad without him, but infinitely glad to be safe with their unborn child.

As her emotions ran between extremes, she realized her helplessness in discerning the why of things. As a female, she had always been told to bother herself with things of importance to the men in her life rather than what was important about life itself. To Irina, that would never be an answer. *I cannot help what I am, but that fact will never stand in my way.*

One of the qualities she could not change about herself was her growing regard for personal cleanliness. Of all the discomforts of road and water travel, going without a morning washing all over made her skin itch just thinking about it. Almost as bad were the other members of the party from king to caretaker who saw no use in washing their hands and faces, removing the grease and oils from their hair, or changing their clothes with some regularity. Never mind the other parts of their bodies that, left untidied, made one grateful for outdoor encounters. At Krosno, she had the last full bath since leaving Poznan, and she would not permit another hour to pass before enjoying one again. *Do the Germans use soap, I wonder? I will have Velka find out!*

Thus far in their travels, the seemingly endless hours of thoughtful conversation with Madrosh were the greatest gift—and distraction— anyone could have given her. Believing much of what she'd heard from him, she wanted to explore further some principles that God Himself must have laid down but that had thus far eluded her attempts to perceive them. She would, she told herself, have to find out just how far Madrosh could take her.

That evening and the next morning, she rested at length, then spent her energies directing Velka and Rosta in organizing their things and preparing for what would be a long summer's land and river voyage. The castle had grown warm, and few breezes disturbed the air. After the mid-day meal of roast venison from a freshly slaughtered stag, along with bread, greens, and berries, Irina sipped from a flagon of ale. She did not know whether Madrosh was available for a good walk in the parklands surrounding the castle, but she held out hope.

As if he had divined her thoughts, Madrosh found her. "Come, My Lady, and we shall see what this countryside may afford two Poles who are strangers in this land."

"Yes," she responded with delight. "I, too, am ready for what might await."

They descended from the great dining hall to the courtyard and walked out the main gate itself, giving themselves another opportunity to admire the interesting and massive scale of Tangermunde. After some light conversation about meetings between the duke and King Wenceslas, and the developing schedule for their departure, Irina broke her silence and asked, "Madrosh, when God created the world and then, us, didn't He also give us the rules that govern?"

"You mean the Commandments." It was a statement, not a question.

"No, I don't mean rules that we must follow. I mean rules we are born with. When I bake a morning cake, I put the raisins in the dough before the loaf goes over the fire. When the cake comes out, the raisins are baked in. Do you see? What rules are baked in us?"

"You have broached this topic already, My Lady. Do you remember?"

She looked at him quizzically. "Have I?"

"On the walls at Krosno, as the trumpets sounded, you commented about man's murderous impulses, and I said, 'You have come to it.' So, yes, there is such a rule as you call it. We call it man's nature or natural law. We have come near it with our talks of Augustine and Aquinas." He smiled broadly. "I see, however, your thirst was not quenched. Perhaps, we will attempt to drink a bit more deeply."

Quietly, as if preparing to jump a high hurdle, she said, "I am ready."

"Mind you, My Lady, you might be surprised to learn that it has been with very few people now living that I have had discussions about nature and its laws—except at Krakow, of course, and to no one have I thought to reveal my own views on the matter."

"You mean, Madrosh, that once again, you might hold a view different than that of the Church?"

Madrosh inhaled deeply. "Alas, my dear one, once again, it may be so. You see, in any given age, what the Church has come to believe is what she insists her children believe. Those of us gifted—or cursed—with an inquiring mind, however, must be very careful with whatever thoughts or views might be uttered in query but received as heresy. You'll remember what I said earlier about the Englishman, Ockham!"

Their slow pace near and into the woods around Tangermunde proceeded enjoyably. The soft July breezes brought the fresh scents of new green amongst the trees with animal and plant life propagating profusely from the life-giving force of spring rains.

"What you mean to convey to me—once again, Madrosh—is that what we talk about is not for the ears of another."

"Not any other, My Lady, and while I regret my fears, they are, indeed, real."

"Enough, Madrosh!" she said, not unkindly. "The sunshine awaits your secrets."

"Dear Irina, you have developed such charm. It is hard to resist your entreaty."

They walked on a few more steps. Without further encouragement, Madrosh began speaking, his thoughts streaming like a rain-fed brook, undammed and unbound, "Nearly all of the ancient philosophers believed there was a core of principles common to all persons, a system of right and justice no earthly power had a right to take away. Aristotle and philosophers known as the Stoics held what to them was obvious: natural law is often different enough in practice from man-made or what is called positive law. Laws and rules decreed by princes, kings, and even popes are in themselves subject to the influences of those who make them. They are often motivated by self-interest and therefore do not bind one's conscience when they are in conflict with God's eternal laws."

Madrosh looked over at his partner. She was deep in concentration.

"When Augustine came along, he was amongst many Christian thinkers in the west who tied the natural to the divine. They believed the core principles—the rights of man—were all bestowed by an eternal God, and thus immutable, and eternal in themselves. He insisted that natural law was what existed before man's fall from grace in the Garden of Eden. After the fall, living in strict accord with natural law was no longer a possibility and man could seek salvation only through divine law and the grace of Christ. We must come back to this point, Irina. It is where the implications in Augustine's reasoning are most startling.

"Aquinas felt that even if natural law was the perfection of human reason, it fell short of an understanding of, and an equality to, the divine law. In his *Treatise on Law,* Aquinas described it as humanity's participation in God's eternal law."

Irina laughed quietly. "Oh, Madrosh! It's as if you are in a race, and I am struggling to keep up with you!"

"My Lady, I have no doubt you are mentally running right at my side." He, too, laughed lightly, then turned his mind once more to a topic he hastened to pursue. "And so, my dear, Aquinas sliced the bread even thinner when he said that the natural law could never be blotted out from the heart of a man, but applications of that law might be suppressed in conscience. That is a nice way of saying a man may ignore what is right in order to justify what serves him best. Tomasz the Terrible would understand that."

"But Madrosh," she interrupted, "just what is this natural law you're going on about?"

He chuckled. "I suppose I have been dancing around it. It could be defined in different ways, many of them found in the Commandments themselves. To kill another, to rob him of his possessions, of his wife, to lie to him or about him—these are all rules that all must abide by so that each one of us may enjoy the peace of his own life."

"Animals kill and rob, do they not?"

"Yes, they do, and that's the difference. Remember when we talked about a vegetative, animal, and human soul? It is the nature of animals to do what they do. It should not be the nature of man."

"But isn't it?"

Madrosh paused to take a breath. "Let's continue for a moment," he said, ignoring the riposte. "All the great thinkers have agreed that these fundamental, natural, and moral principles must underpin positive law. It is these core principles that apply to all, Christians and non-Christians, but as Aquinas might add, it is divine law that gives us as Christians further guidance in our actions."

"Your words weigh heavily on the shoulders of this poor farm girl, Madrosh. Are you not simply trying to say that what basic rights God has given to man, each man must give to every other? What lies behind those eternal rights must be applied in the same way by those with an earthly power to give? Are you not saying that while man may change his laws with the seasons, God's laws are permanent and unchanging? And are you not saying that because they are God's laws, we must obey them first and last?"

It was as if the summer air had evaporated, and everything came to an eternal quiet. As if the trees stopped to listen, the birds perched to cock an ear, as if the blades of grass stood themselves straight in respect.

Catching the old priest's eye was a giant stag that appeared over Irina's shoulder less than fifty feet away. Standing tall as a man with antlers wide as a cart, it stood stock still and watched the human pair intently. Madrosh himself could not speak for several moments, and when he did, he was largely incoherent.

"My Lady," he said, bowing his head slightly, "it is you who should have taught in Krakow while I should ever remain your student."

"Do not go on so, Madrosh," she said with an honest blush. "I only gave back to you what you so thoroughly laid out for me. You gave meaning to the raisins in the loaf!"

"Ah, but now, I know not what or how much more I can teach you."

"Bah! I am but the moist clay in your potter's hands, Madrosh. You have said nothing thus far to propel you toward the axe man. What is it you are afraid to say?"

"Let's go back to Augustine's insight about natural law in the Garden of Eden. He said it was there that natural law existed in its purest form, as a model of perfection, perhaps, but when man was expelled from Paradise, it was no longer possible to live according to the law."

"Yes, that's what I understood you to say."

"That's true as stated—and by the way, my dear Irina, what I have said to you about the philosophers and the view of the church is all *my* understanding of their teachings. If someday you learn that I spoke in error, I do hope you'll forgive this old man."

"You were saying...as you approach the hangman?" She laughed merrily.

"It is not you dangling there, my dear! What I was saying was if Augustine's insight is correct, it means that even in Paradise, man's nature, which we thought had been uncorrupted and incorruptible, compelled him to grasp what was not his—the apple of perfect wisdom.

"Do you see? If even in a state of grace in God's special Garden, a place where Adam and Eve wanted for nothing, if even in such a place, man's nature prevailed over the so-called perfection of natural law, then man never had a perfect nature at all.

"He was never destined to live in Paradise because God knew that with Adam's free will, he would defy God's commandment about the forbidden fruit. God knew all along that Adam and Eve would leave and propagate the earth. The Almighty didn't make it happen, but he knew it would happen. Some would interpret those events as God's plan, after all."

"Madrosh, how can you be condemned for this thinking?"

"You must take it a step further, Irina. Aristotle, Plato, Augustine, Aquinas, Christian and non-believers alike, have all held that at base, man's nature is good, always seeking the good. Remember our talk of the soul?"

"And you believe what?"

"There are only two other possibilities. Man is by nature evil, or man is by nature neither good nor evil."

"And so, master Madrosh, what are we?"

"One is easily tempted to think of man's nature as evil. When you consider that from the beginning of time, man has controlled his impulses only when under the forceful eye of another, that fact is telling. Only when men formed into groups for protection and the peace that comes from kinship, did he learn he could not do whatever he wanted with whomever he chose. He was no longer free to take any woman for his own, to take another man's animal, to kill or rob—when those transgressions were made against those in his group. These rules did not apply—and still do not, as we can see daily—when the women, the animals, or possessions belong to another group." Madrosh paused so that she could think about what he'd said, then continued.

"And in each group, who rules? The strongest, the biggest, the one others will support with arms and fealty—and the one they will fear."

"I'm not sure I understand your conclusion," Irina said.

"From ancient times, kings imposed rules of their own making. These could be laws about how a man goes about buying a goat, how he must pay his taxes, and so on. Laws would be made without relevance to God or religion. Rarely was there a moral underpinning of right and wrong until the Commandments came to Moses."

"And those same Commandments have been used in conquering and killing other peoples, Madrosh!"

"Exactly. A group with commandments is sometimes no different than a group without them."

"So, if you believe that man is basically evil, why would God create us?"

"Another marvelous question, Irina! Yet I did not say that man is evil—it is, merely, one possibility. We are now led to the proposition that man is neither good nor evil. Upon reflection, I would contend that no man is born the same as every other man, his stewpot having varying proportions of good and evil in it. And yes, he is a child of God, made with all the potential to be in the image of God. The man grows up to be what he wants to be—good or evil or, likely, at times one or the other—in spite of his parentage and upbringing. You yourself know of persons like Sister Mary Elisabeth and Tomasz the Terrible—both children of God, yet one grew to be decidedly good, and the other, decidedly evil."

Irina nodded. "If God is just, how could he judge a man or woman if they were raised to steal and kill, if that's all they knew in life?"

"God is just, my dear, and it is my belief that in his truly infinite wisdom He judges of each of us based on what we were born to, and later, how we were able to exercise our free will. The most important words here are 'how we were able.'"

"Do you think God gave us the Commandments and, later, Christ His Son to balance the evil in the world?" Irina asked.

"From time's first flash of light until July in the Year of Our Lord 1378, we haven't come very far, have we? If man is by nature good, the Joselewicz family would never have encountered the terrible Tomasz." Madrosh exhaled, surprised, perhaps relieved that at last, he had spoken his notions aloud.

Irina observed the priest carefully, but said nothing. *Now I begin to understand.*

Madrosh smiled to himself, adding for her ears, "And yet, my dear. God always seems to offer us a way to salvation."

...

Jan Wodowicz's reaction to the news of his son's appearance could not have been more profound. Instead of pleased surprise and a broad smile, there were emotions everyone in the room could easily read: concern, distrust, perhaps even fear. All the words he could muster were, "How is that possible?" His voice stammered.

The abbot said, "I was wondering the same."

At that moment, Tomasz pushed through the heavy oak door and planted himself squarely in front of Jan Wodowicz. "Ah, *Ojciec*, you are not happy to see me?"

Barely controlling his voice, the elderly man said, "My son, it's just that I would never have expected to see you here in the middle of the forest so many miles from Poznan!"

"Well, here I am, and now," he chuckled, "and I'll stay to help you in your last years. You should be glad."

"Tomasz, I heard you'd left the city weeks ago when the plague was upon us. I myself never expected to survive, much less see you again. How did you come to be here?"

"It was the burning fires of hell that drove me back to Poznan, and now here you are," he said, a smirk twisting his lips. "And so, Father, I might ask you the same question—how is it that you come to be here?"

"Well, my son," Jan hesitated, "these men remembered my work on the glass for the cathedral so many years ago, and they want to make it here. St. Stephen's, it turns out, is a fine place for just such an enterprise."

"That's wonderful, Father," he said. As he paused, it was apparent he was considering something, as warped wheels turned in his head. "When I return to Poznan, the bishop himself will be delighted to hear of your endeavor."

It was Abbot Kaminski's turn to join the conversation, mincing no words. "I thought you had already returned, *Pan* Wodowicz. Were you not sentenced to servitude there by Duke Zygmunt? By all rights, you should be dead!"

"Yes, Abbot, of course you are correct." Tomasz began speaking more excitedly. "When the bishop himself returned, he found evidence of my innocence and released me on his own authority. He sent me here when he learned that something of interest might be afoot."

His listeners looked at each other in disbelief, and could see Tomasz's eyes darting rapidly, as if he had just told a lie too thin to believe. Gone was the smirk.

Before anyone could speak, Tomasz looked at his father and said, "And so, dear *Ojciec*, how can I help you?"

The abbot began to respond, but the older Wodowicz interjected quickly. "That is a kind offer, Tomasz," he said, purring like a contented cat, "but I see no place for your skills in this labor. Perhaps the bishop will find other uses for you in Poznan."

"I take your point, *Ojciec*. Nevertheless, I will be sure to look in on you. You should be treated well by your new partners." Tomasz smirked, eyeing each listener in turn.

CHAPTER XI

1378

At Tangermunde, the bustling activity of the castle's serving class dwarfed what they had seen at Krosno. Everyone in Duke Zygmunt's entourage noticed it, and though rumors flew, no one knew exactly what was afoot. Obviously, the staff and even the nobles, including King Wenceslas himself, were preparing for a visitor. Irina kept out of everyone's way.

Before long, the trumpets sounded their clear, high notes, and the very ground seemed to tremble as crowds of well-scrubbed and well-dressed castle folk cheered wildly for Charles IV, Holy Roman Emperor, returning home, the same home where his son Wenceslas was Margrave and King.

If there had been any questions about travel plans and protection for the sojourners, they evaporated in the summer sun. The Poles beamed. It would be different now, they all whispered amongst themselves. Now their travel would be a bit slower, but it would likely be more comfortable, especially for Irina, who, as it turned out, was not the only woman with child to embark on their journey. There would be others, including several children. There would be Madrosh, of course, but Irina knew his duties—and his time spent with—Zygmunt would increase dramatically. That meant, unfortunately, scant time for their own talks.

Yet there would also be Jan Brezchwa. Over the previous weeks, their time spent together seemed to grow longer and more frequent. Feelings of guilt over Berek remained—*I will never abandon you!* But

---

at some point, she knew, their child would need a father.

After a week of rest, heavy dining, and much revelry amongst the nobility, it was on a note of heartful anticipation that Irina and the huge party of royalty, nobles, advisers, families, staff, and heavily armed soldiers departed Tangermunde in early August. They began what she had learned would be a serpentine journey, again traversing long stretches on river barges, followed by monotonous days in airless carriages.

"Shall I be sure to travel on the same barge with you, My Lady?" Jan's hopeful smile always charmed her.

"Most assuredly, young Squire," she said, laughing with encouragement, even as her baby gave a good kick. *Might Squire Brezchwa, a good man with an easy smile and a boyish humor, bring a fast beat to my heart once again?*

...

Jerzy Andrezski could not have been more pleased. With a new reason to live, Brother Heidolphus took his task seriously and well. In short order, everyone had as much new work as each could handle.

Jan Wodowicz quickly burned off all the grass, and gathered huge piles of clay and stone for the three large furnaces built upon a large, flat stone platform. From sunup to sunset, he and the brothers performed the heavy labor, stopping only for prayers and meals. Not one man had trouble sleeping.

Pawel Tokasz used another part of the same clearing to harden a clay floor so that when they burned the great beeches, the ashes they collected would not pick up mud, dirt, or pebbles of any kind. Brother Heidolphus insisted that the ashes be as free of unwanted matter as possible. The men laughed at the notion of clean ashes but worked all the harder, burning cut beech logs and letting the low fires dry but not completely consume them.

Jerzy Andrezski organized the remaining monks into two groups, each taking carts and pack horses, one to go west to the Oder and the other, east to the Warta. They were to find the best sand they could, as pure as possible. Once they dried it, they were to haul it back to the clearing near the monastery. In short order, the monks agreed. The sand from along the Warta, several miles south of Poznan, was the best, the most plentiful, and the easiest to transport.

Jerzy also made sure to follow Brother Heidolphus around, much like a puppy dog after his new master. He guessed the days left on earth for Heidolphus Brotelin were relatively few, and as their enterprise progressed, it became clear the knowledge held by old Wodowicz was both rudimentary and, in part, inaccurate, the elderly monk thus becoming his only hope to understand the ways of glassmaking, with every nuance he could remember to impart. *As it turns out, old Wodowicz's only contribution has been to lead us to Heidolphus, but thank God for that!*

"By September we should be ready," Brother Heidolphus proclaimed to Andrezski one early-August day.

"Once we have fashioned samples to take to Poznan and Gniezno, I am sure to sell all you can make. The weather will be turning cold just as I come around and offer a means to keep warm for those who can afford our prices." He laughed. I suspect there may be many, don't you think, Brother?"

The old monk smiled in return. "Yes, Jerzy, you will be giving them a way to see their world in a different way."

Just then, a young monk came running from the monastery. "You should return to the monastery right away," he said, gesturing to both the old monk and Andrezski.

"Is there something wrong?"

"With all respect, Brother," the young monk said while bowing his head and hiding his eyes, "there is always something amiss when Bishop Tirasewicz pays St. Stephen's a visit. In the end, it is we who pay." Andrezski's hearty laugh did not lift Brotelin's frown.

. . .

On the Elbe, the royal entourage moved slowly against the river's natural flow. The rowers strained to move the heavy barges up river, and when possible, sails were employed to take advantage of the breezes to push them along. Soon, they passed through the little village of

Magdeburg and debarked for a day off the water. One of the little boys on the journey who caught her notice was ten-year-old Mattias—Matti to most—who was son to one of the king's retainers.

"Matti, you little rascal," she called, laughing and holding her belly, "be sure to stay close. Squire Brezchwa cannot be chasing after you." The boy giggled, pretending to wield a knight's sword, and ran off into the woods. His father, *Herr* Schoenist, laughed in turn and said, "Don't mind this boy, My Lady, he always comes back." The people in their little knot of sojourners had become close as they battled the heat, the insects, and the dirt that clung to them all.

The long days on the barges left much time for rest and conviviality. Daily life was somewhat eased by the fact that Irina and others of her station were not on the same barge as the royals. Because there was little chance to be in their company for whole days at a time, dress and manner were somewhat more comfortable when the heat encased them like a funerary shroud. Irina couldn't help but notice that the hotter the weather, the more aromatic were the people around her.

Madrosh stayed with his duke and only when the barges banked themselves for one purpose or another—a meal or a tented overnight— were Irina and Madrosh able to exchange a word or two. At one point, she beckoned Madrosh to one side. "I am so glad not to be on the duke's barge, good Father. After our last conversation about Tomasz, I have no idea what to expect. Has the duke said anything about it to you?"

"Except to chastise me for not having mentioned Tomasz's escape sooner, well, no, he hasn't referred to it. Now that you mention it, he has been much quieter of late. He is bedeviled by something to be sure."

"Good word for him, Madrosh."

The priest arched his eyebrows in question.

"'Bedeviled.'" Irina paused. "It will be much harder to be in his company now, I'm afraid."

"He's been very kind to you, you know."

"Only because he thinks I'm of monied and noble blood, like him."

"And?"

"And because he thinks I am not a Jew."

Madrosh nodded. "You are reminding me my role as counselor to the duke has not been very successful."

"I am so sorry, Madrosh. I didn't mean it that way. Remember what you said about people and their proportions of good and evil? Perhaps our duke is a perfect example, *nie?*"

Irina missed their deeper conversations, but she finally admitted to herself she was beginning to enjoy the increasing and welcome attention given her by Squire Brezchwa. Their conversations, while not weighty in nature, were pleasurable.

Now more a warm memory than a bitter loss, Berek yet filled her mind. Still, she could not fathom how in less than three months' time, so much could have happened to her. And yet all that had occurred made it easier for her to think about a future. *Has what has happened all been just chance? Could it have been the hand of God?*

Leaving the Elbe a few days later, the company continued to sail on the Saale until reaching Naumburg, a pleasant town of some three thousand people. There they saw another cathedral named for Sts. Peter and Paul. To Irina's untrained eye, the church was similar to the one in Poznan except that even from the river, she could see many more spaces filled with both clear and colored window glasses.

Soon, however, the river became too shallow for travel, and they debarked for land travel. After passing through the university town of Jena, where Madrosh begged a few hours' leave to visit with scholars, they forged on, steadily rising higher in the heavily forested hills. Reaching the river's head at Hof, they felt fortunate to enjoy the cooler breezes comforting them at the higher elevation. Mid-August in Germany was no different than mid-August in Poland. In their heavy clothing, no one moved with any speed. Unfortunately, few bathed, but Irina and Velka kept to their habits of cleanliness as best as they were able.

For the slower pace, Irina found herself most grateful. Slower travel may have been more practical for all, but for Irina, five months into her pregnancy, it was far more comfortable. As she dripped with perspiration, each rock in the cartpath jolted her and her baby in ways she could never before have imagined. For Irina and the other two expectant women—with whom she commiserated often—Rosta had prepared what amounted to a wooden chaise mounted on each cart so that the women could at least recline somewhat while their party trudged up and down the river valleys. While the contrivance eased their discomfort to a great degree, Irina had no trouble daydreaming about a long rest in a shaded glade next to a cool brook. Quiet conversations with Madrosh became a sought-after distraction.

One of the hopefuls—a German woman in the margrave's family—had not fared so well, as it turned out. The constant bumping prompted a miscarriage, some said, along with copious amounts of blood. Their company stopped for a day, but no longer, while a midwife named Kalmus was found to tend to her needs.

While the woman and her family were saddened by the loss, it did not seem to deter them. A heavy woman who wore her experience in childbirth like a tunic, Kalmus reminded everyone that miscarriages were extremely common and the young woman's good health augured well for many more children to come.

Irina understood Kalmus's meaning. Indeed, on the farm and in the village of St. Michael, she'd often heard of maternal misadventures—it was all part of nature, people said—but she knew how she'd feel if she'd lost her child, and she went out of her way to give the woman special words of comfort. Care had to be taken, Velka told her, because Irina's—thus far—successful pregnancy must not be a daily reminder to the other woman of her loss. She was at first taken aback by Velka's view on the matter but found her advice both thoughtful and accurate.

Travel on land and uphill much of the time became even slower as they followed mountain roads heading toward the River Main. Six days past Jena, the party halted when it became clear that little Matti, son of Squire Schoenist, was nowhere to be found. On behalf of his man, King Wenceslas sent searchers, first to look into every cart and trunk, and then, into the surrounding trees and hills. When Matti did not reappear, the king directed his men to return to the place where they had last rested.

In the meantime, the entourage abandoned their conveyances for what shade they could find. Many prayed. Others reminded Irina what voyagers should always remember. Whether it was disease, loose bowels, bad food, fevers, storms, or drownings—not to mention enemy attacks—almost never did a group beginning a journey have the same number at the end of it. Already a soldier had drowned crossing the Oder and a mother had miscarried. Except for Krosno, there had been no force of arms against them.

Irina was one of those who sat quietly and waited. Although she had come to believe much of what Madrosh had taught her, belief in prayer was not yet part of it. As the hours wore on, she fretted. *What happened to little Matti?*

Near sunset, the answer came with the return of the horsemen. One of them, she saw, had a small bundle tie to his saddle's pommel. Only an eerie quiet accompanied their return. Their grim faces told part of the story. The news passed in hushed tones. Little Matti had wandered off once too often, it seemed, and he'd been caught by what they'd supposed to be a gray wolf foraging for meat. Little remained of the boy, who had been found by the dogs accompanying the men.

At once, the king commanded a Mass be said for the lad and immediately, what little remained of him was buried by the roadside, his grieving mother not the least bit comforted by the heartfelt words of those around her. It seemed as if the entourage had been schooled by the words of Irina's mother. They wasted no time on sadness, but set up camp for an early morning's departure.

Though the next day's journey began in a somber mood, it changed once again when the travelers learned that once they reached Bamberg, life would become much easier for all. At that point, they would board barges and catch the current down the Main for many miles. While the summer heat would once again prevail, they would be freed from the cruel bounces the carts offered.

By the end of August, when the party came upon the mighty Rhine at Wiesbaden, to Irina, all seemed right with the world.

...

"I am most displeased, Father Abbot!" Bishop Tirasewicz said, his voice shaking, the nostrils of his long nose flaring.

Keeping close eye contact, Father Kaminski thought the bishop's pointed nose was aimed like a dagger. "I do not understand, my dear Bishop. How could I possibly have displeased Your Grace?" The abbot believed he had nothing to fear from the Bishop of Poznan, so why did he now feel afraid?

"Why, dear Abbot"—the last two words uttered sarcastically as if in riposte—"do I have to hear about your great commercial undertaking from common gossip around Poznan, and not from your own lips?" The bishop's eyes were as demanding as his voice, the tone of which seemed to condemn his listener to an unhappy fate.

Father Kaminski steadied his eyes on the hawk-like face in front of him, and waited a moment before answering.

"Bishop," the abbot responded with no formality or concession, "you are aware that I make trips to Poznan every three months or so. It is not yet September, when I customarily make such a journey, and at that time, I would have given you a full report on the activities of St. Stephen's."

Mollified but little, the bishop's voice remained firm, yet now more petulant than peeved. "Father Abbot, it is more than a mere report that interests me, but now that I have come to you, you may deliver it."

"I am not prepared to do so, Your Grace, but if you'll dine with us this evening and enjoy a good night's rest in our most comfortable quarters, I will provide any information you wish in the morning, before your departure." The abbot knew his words were presumptuous, but he'd made a decision.

"As you wish, Father Kaminski. I look forward to it."

Despite the summer evening's heat, the atmosphere had been decidedly chilly. Nevertheless, the morning's sun seemed to grant fresh dispositions to both oral combatants. A hearty breakfast went even further to fuel their exchange.

"As you may have heard, dear Bishop, the monastery is fortunate to have the special skills of a glassmaker in our midst, and that discovery, coupled with the know-how of a Poznan merchant, will allow us to make a better living for the monastery and for the people we serve around us."

"What about service to your bishop?"

"How do you mean?"

"Surely, Father Abbot, there will be financial rewards. What were you planning to offer the Diocese of Poznan?"

The question was not totally unexpected. "Ah, of course. Let's work this out together. We don't know to what degree we'll be successful, naturally, but we will need to pay our workers, our own expenses for materials in the manufacturing process, and the costs of selling and transporting the glass. As well, the man who sells the glass will expect his own profit. It was his idea, after all. He brought together the means to make it happen, and it is his energy that will make it a success."

"Never mind about him and his problems—or yours, for that matter, Father. I want 50 percent of what you receive for the needs of your bishop and the cathedral."

"No." There was no courtesy, as in, "No, Your Grace." Only finality. The single word hung in the air like a large icicle suspended from a roof, ready to drop. The silence was not reverent.

The bishop's face purpled in rage as the color rose in his cheeks and enveloped his forehead. He could barely speak. "What did you say?" Tirasewicz demanded, taking a full second for each word.

Father Kaminski glanced around the simple room, then rose to ensure the two doors were closed and that no one was attempting to eavesdrop. The bishop's impatience pervaded the air.

"I think we should understand each other, Bishop. As Abbot of St. Stephen's, I report to my Order, not to the Diocese of Poznan. The resources of this monastery are at my disposal and for the use of this Order and the poor around us. What proceeds come to us are intended to go for the propagation of the faith and the needs of the people, and not for the luxuries of any one person. Because *Pan* Andrezski intends to sell what we produce in this duchy, I am sure he also intends to make a donation to the Diocese of Poznan, and I'm sure he will be generous."

The bishop's countenance remained no less royal in color as he asked, quietly, viciously, "Andrezski? Did you say Andrezski? The same profiteer,"—his voice rippled with sarcasm and climbed higher with each syllable—"who has been dealing with the Dominican nuns in Poznan?"

"One and the same. Surely, you knew that from your informer. In fact, I feel sure that *Pan* Andrezski's donation to the diocese would be directed to the convent, not elsewhere. The Sisters saved his life and he feels grateful to the Church."

Bishop Tirasewicz gathered his black robes and rose to his full height. "I could have you removed," he hissed. "I could have this stinking pit closed for all time."

The abbot stood to face him, finding his full voice. "Bishop Tirasewicz. Our understanding is not yet complete, it appears. Should you take such a foolish action, you will only bring upon yourself the wrath of Rome. The new pope, Urban VI himself, is a personal patron to the head of our Order. Like the Holy Father, our Founder, you know, is Roman, not Polish or German. I think you can imagine the events to follow as they would concern you."

All color drained from the bishop's face. Pretense of power was unmasked. He had been brought to the level of a deposed tyrant by a mere abbot.

"One other matter," Father Kaminski added. "I have been courteous to you because you are the bishop. Outside this room, I will maintain my respect for the See of Poznan. In return, you will never attempt to take advantage of this monastery again."

"You will regret this," Tirasewicz rasped, no longer seeming quite as tall.

"Bishop Tirasewicz," Kaminski addressed him, "there is no need to be unpleasant. Our enterprise will bring monies to the city and the convent will no longer be a financial concern to you. You—and the Diocese—will benefit enormously."

For several seconds, the bishop's composure seemed frozen. His contemplation complete, a slow smile came to his face. "You are right, of course, Father Kaminski," he said with a full reversal of demeanor. "I was, indeed, hasty. That the convent will soon be financially sound is of great interest to me. Naturally, I will do all I can to further the success of your venture. My man, Tomasz Wodowicz, will be directed to see that the right things happen for you and this merchant, Andrezski."

The turnaround in Tirasewicz's demeanor was so swift, so sudden, it gave the abbot pause as he forced out his next words. "Tomasz Wodowicz? Hmmm. A perfect man for you. Many will hold you to your word, I feel certain, Bishop," he said with a slight smile. "Let me see you to your horse."

. . .

Jerzy Andrezski spent the balance of the summer transfixed by the prospect of making and selling glass. Because of Brother Heidolphus Brotelin's extraordinary labors, the gathering process for clean ash and the construction of the furnaces was completed, but the last major component required gentler hands.

In conversations with the abbot, Father Kaminski had been careful not to divulge many details of his conversation with the bishop, but he had said enough. That the younger Wodowicz, dark side and all, found shelter under the bishop's mantle was also cause to be careful.

Andrezski became even more concerned when he met up with Sister Luke. She had become apprehensive about the order's ability to support itself in consequence of the bishop's demands, and unlike the monastery, her convent was under the direct control of the Diocese of Poznan. As a consequence, the thumb of the bishop was always upon them, his hand always in their coffers.

"Sister Luke, now that all of the goods you gave me to sell are gone, just what does the bishop believe he is entitled to?"

"I am not sure, *Pan* Andrezski. Somehow he has the idea you will continue to sell what may be donated or left with us."

"You can assure the bishop, Sister, I will continue to provide the same service to the convent, and on the same terms. As you wish, he can have half of all the money you receive from any goods I sell."

"But..."

"That is correct, Sister. There will be very little."

"Then how are we to live?"

"There will be another source of income for you," he said with a grin. "What and whether you report so to the bishop will be, of course, your own affair."

"And what would that be, *Pan* Andrezski?"

"As I recall, some of your nuns have experience as potters, and that you made all the platter ware for the churches and rectories in Poznan. Hasn't that been a small source of income for you?"

"Yes, but there has been less call for our pots, jars, and plates since the plague."

"Now there is more. I am bringing to you your first order. These pots are unusual and must be made carefully because they are special white clay pots necessary in the making of glass. We will need many as replacements on a regular basis, and as our business expands, so will your orders."

Sister Luke stared at the humble merchant in front of her. "You are not a simple man, indeed, *Pan* Andrezski." Her composure gone, she caught her breath, inhaled deeply, and through her tears of gratitude, stammered, "Tell me more."

Jerzy relayed what Brother Heidolphus had described to him in great detail. "We will need six of them to start, Sister, and it would be best to make an additional pair, just in case."

Sister Luke paid careful attention to the requirements and took the drawing Jerzy had brought along. "You shall have the jars you require," she said, now a vendor in a new business.

"That will be fine. You must pack them with straw in wooden chests that we will cart to the monastery. When we need more, I will let you know. In the meantime, I will stay in Poznan."

"*Djenkuje bardzo*—Many thanks!" Sister Luke smiled in deep gratitude for the work. "I feel truly blest."

"There's one other thing, Sister."

She raised her brow in expectation.

"It's Zuzanna. That little angel saved my life, and to her and all of you, I'll be always grateful. I feel a responsibility for her. Perhaps, in time, she might come to think of me as her benefactor." Andrezski stopped himself. "Oh, I know, Sister. I have no right to presume so. Her own parents may return to claim her."

Sister Luke hesitated, and sighed deeply. "Alas, *Pan* Andrezski, I fear her parents are gone from us. Someone would have come to collect her by now. As to your spending time and getting to know her, I think Zuzanna would like that."

A cluster of intertwined thoughts swirled in his head. Guilt claimed companionship as he realized prospects of commerce took more of his attention than Zuzanna's welfare. While the bishop's conivings were one thing, and much about the man remained unclear, of one thing Andrezski was certain: his religious beliefs were simple, and his leanings toward faith in God did not lead him to fealty toward Poznan's worldly prince of the church.

...

After weeks of relentless heat, rock-strewn roads, and winding rivers, the Emperor halted the royal tourists at the frontier between Germany and France. His Excellency commanded a special Mass be said for his party and all those who cared to gather from the countryside. Rich and poor celebrated the relatively uneventful crossing of the Teutonic lands, and prayed for an equally quiet entrance into a new land.

On the bluff overlooking the French countryside, Father Madrosh sang a traditional Latin Mass as hundreds uttered the words of confession and the Apostle's Creed, then stood silent to receive Holy Communion from the priest's hands.

By this time, Madrosh had performed his pastoral work well, as everyone in their party had come to know the tragic story of Irina's widowhood. The valiant death of her husband was the epitome of chivalry in the eyes of all and earned him prayers for his eternal rest.

Too, Madrosh was aware all noticed the bond forming between the two youths, Lady Irina Kwasniewska and Squire Jan Brezchwa. From king to cowherd, they all knew that long life was always in question, and no one of marrying age remained long alone. Irina was expected to find a man for herself. If she did not, her liege, duke, king, or emperor would make the match for her. The budding relationship between Irina and Squire Brezchwa was seen as a natural solution to a small problem. All the better that they appeared to have chosen one another. Madrosh was content.

CHAPTER XII

1378

"Humor me, Madrosh," Irina exhorted her mentor as they bumped along the road to Paris some days later. "Explain to this humble country girl a bit more of the complex royal maneuverings that brought us here in the first place," she said, holding her belly with both hands as she spoke.

"Are you truly interested, My Lady?"

"Not particularly, my dear friend, but I am now entering my seventh month, and if this road does not become less of a jolt to me and my child, I will be forced to have it in this carriage! And no woman should be pregnant in late summer heat." She laughed—wearily. "Please talk, Father Madrosh, as it will take my mind from this present discomfort."

"Shall I have Velka sit with you? Or shall I find Squire Brezchwa?"

Irina smiled, mostly in acknowledgement of the twinkle in his eye as he asked about Jan Brezchwa. "You may, but I fear their presence will not remove the ruts along the way."

Madrosh chortled. "I am so sorry, My Lady, and can only wish you were in a better state to attend to my meanderings. You and I enjoy this kind of thing, so where do I begin?" It did not take him long.

"This is what I understand the history to have been. The present king of France, Charles V, was crowned some fourteen years ago, and ever since, one war after another consumed the resources of the realm. On the surface, my dear, the country was at peace but like a large cauldron of thick soup ready to boil, there were deep and hot issues beginning to bubble."

Madrosh looked over at his student. "Is this what you were asking about?"

"Perhaps. Yet I have wondered all these months why the invitation went out to the nobles of Europe."

"Ah! Let me see how I can explain this. What you may not have perceived is that for some seventy years, the pope has resided at Avignon, but Pope Gregory XI insisted on moving the official residence back to Rome. Charles's attempts to persuade the pope to remain in France, ostensibly under the protection of the French monarch, were refused. Then poor Gregory died this past March, and his passing ignited a fuse."

"In March of this year? His death has something to do with the invitation, then?"

"Yes, but the answer is not quite so simple. For political reasons, Charles wants the pope to remain at Avignon, and it was in this environment that Charles V launched his invitation for royalty and retinue throughout Europe to convene at Paris under the auspices of his uncle, Charles IV, the Holy Roman Emperor." Madrosh saw that Irina was about to interrupt. "Let me continue, and perhaps you will understand it all."

He cleared his throat. "What made his invitation most sensible politically and serendipitous religiously, was what occurred in Rome after Gregory's untimely death. Because the papacy had been housed in France for so many years, the College of Cardinals, the body that elects popes, had become dominated by Frenchmen. In Rome, mobs overcome with the notion that a new French pope would take the papacy back to Avignon, demanded election of a Roman and no other. In April, the Cardinals selected a commoner who chose the name Urban VI. The new pontiff quickly distanced himself from his former brethren by demanding from them virtuous and religious behavior, decrying their vices and restricting their sources of income."

"I bow to you, Madrosh. You are correct. It is never simple."

"As the summer's heat invaded Rome, the riled French Cardinals decamped the city and returned to Avignon, where they immediately declared Urban's election invalid and elected another Pope, Clement VII. We have only just heard of this, but it happened a number of days ago."

"You mean, while we've been crossing France, they elected another pope?"

Laughing into his words, Madrosh tried to compose himself, "Yes! Charles had not expected the election of a second living pope. When he thought about it—at least that is what the margrave has confided to our Duke Zygmunt—Charles did not regret the bothersome pomp, pageantry, and exorbitant expense of having his uncle and a good bit of royal Europe as his guests. They could help him further solidify French power, along with a new French pope. It was an opportunity not to be lost!"

"So, now there's one pope in France, and another in Rome?"

"I could not imagine such a plot myself, dear Irina. It is into this roil we find ourselves." Suddenly, he stopped speaking. "Ah! Look ahead! There! Can you see it? It's the wall of Philip II Augustus, built by him some two hundred years ago to protect his city." They could see crowds gathering and cheering.

And so, in that dry, balmy time of year, the vast procession approached and were met by emissaries of King Charles, then directed through a gate three times the height of a man, where throngs cheered them on. Atop the rapidly decaying wall were squads of workmen performing necessary repairs. To a man, they looked down from their lofty perches and as instructed, no doubt, raised lusty cheers and waved their caps in honor of the rich and colorful royal parade.

Despite the no less bouncy carriage, Irina could not believe what her eyes were seeing. The great walls, the tall buildings, the masses of people. "All on a perfect day," she voiced.

"You said something, My Lady?"

"I am taking it all in." She could hear the pealing of bells throughout the city. One in particular was throaty and deep, its toll seeming to rumble the very avenue on which the visitors rode. "Such a sound, Madrosh! Like thunder itself."

The priest said they were hearing the Bourdon Bell, called Emmanuel, being rung for them—for the Emperor, really—from the Cathedral of Notre Dame.

"Just how can you know so many interesting facts?" Irina exclaimed.

"Just so, My Lady," he said smiling. "It is true that my studies at the university in Krakow included many subjects." He then pointed out that the great cathedral had been finished when he was a boy. He had wished to see it, he said, ever since hearing about its great buttresses and colored glass windows.

As the procession moved further south, they enjoyed the swarms of people pressed against the stone and timbered buildings along the roadway. They actually looked fed and healthy, and the streets—paved in stone—weren't carpeted with filth.

The party paused when they reached the River Seine. From their vantage point, they could look across the river at the *Île de la Cité*, and see the entire majesty of *Notre Dame* itself. Irina had never seen anything made so beautiful or reaching such heights. The cathedral's stone catching the morning sun took her breath away.

"One can only pray nothing ever happens to *Notre Dame*," Madrosh whispered to himself.

Someone bade them cast their gaze to the west where the new *Palais du Louvre* gleamed like a fortress built of snow. Madrosh explained that King Charles had directed a great architect to add strength and beauty to the original arsenal built by Philip Augustus, remaking it a stunning royal residence. No longer would French monarchs reside on the island in the middle of the Seine, but in the Louvre.

"How did they come to name it so?" Irina asked, practicing the sound of a name so unusual to her tongue.

"Actually," responded the encyclopedic Madrosh, "it comes from an old Frankish word, *louwer*, meaning fortress, but you can see, as Charles decreed, it is now much more than it had been."

"Will we be staying there, Madrosh?"

"No, My Lady. I understand the Emperor and his family, staff, and soldiery will make it their residence. That would likely include King Wenceslas as well."

Looking a bit disappointed, Irina rejoindered, "And us?"

"Do not look so, My Lady. We will be staying on the island itself, in the *Palais de la Cité,* next to the church called *Sainte-Chapelle* and not far from the beautiful cathedral I have waited so long to admire. Be assured, dear Irina, we will be most comfortable."

Irina herself cared not where she stayed. Her concern was for the new life she carried.She estimated she was but six to eight weeks from delivery of Berek's child, a child impatient to be born, judging by the amount of kicking and turning inside her. She was glad to be at journey's end, not only because it had been long and arduous, but because she needed time to prepare for the rigors of birth.

"Will there be room there, Madrosh? With all the nobles of Europe coming, I mean."

"High royalty will be welcomed to the *Palais du Louvre*. The rest of us will find comfort on the island. Being somewhat apart from those on high will have its advantages, I assure you," he said with a broad smile.

Irina looked toward the island and again at the distant castle. "Madrosh, why are there so many castles in the city?" she asked in all innocence. "Why would the king want to move from such a beautiful place?"

"My Lady, as you know, there's a story behind every story, isn't there? Here is what I understand. Many years ago, the monarch created a position called the Provost of Paris—a man who represented the king and managed the affairs of the city. Over the years, the provost accumulated much power, and about twenty years ago, he led a merchants' revolt against the monarchy. The crown initially conceded a few things the provost demanded, but after a year of wrangling and bloodshed, the king's forces crushed the provost, and he and his men were executed."

"I am not sure I take your point, Madrosh."

"As a guest here, My Lady, I wish to be careful what I say. The French are not a calm people. They are not easily put down. I suspect the king thought the island too hard to defend and too easily surrounded. The old fortress *du Louvre* presented itself as a much more viable stronghold. That's why the king began its redesign not long after the uprising ended."

"I see!"

Madrosh chuckled, "I am sure you do, My Lady. It is the same everywhere, *nie*?"

"Yes, Madrosh. Safety and comfort go to those who hold power."

. . .

At St. Stephen's, Brother Heidolphus Brotelin's broad smile earned the attention of his abbot.

From his place across the refectory table, Father Kaminski said, "Brother, you are to be permitted a moment of satisfaction, and I shall not remind you about the sin of pride."

Brother Heidolphus bowed in respect to his superior. "It was not pride, Father," he said to Abbot Kaminski. "Truly it was not. My smile reflects my deepest thanks to the Almighty for having provided so many beech trees."

"Why beech trees, Brother? I never asked you," asked Jerzy Andrezski, who had been asked to join in their celebration.

"Beechwood has a chemical property that gives us not only clear glass but shades of gold, yellow, reds, and purples. The glass we make will be beautiful, indeed, once we have mastered the timing in the fritting process. I remember the Italians also said the clay used in the pots had something to do with the coloring. We have much to be pleased about, but there remains much more work to do."

It was the third batch of glass panes that had been perfectly executed, or nearly so. The white clay pots fashioned by the Dominican Sisters were exactly what he had requested, and once they arrived at St. Stephen's, the entire process had begun in earnest.

With the process mastered, the molten mixture was poured onto a large stone, ground perfectly flat. When cooled, what remained was what the monk called a "round" of new glass that could itself be ground, polished, and cut.

"When will samples be ready?" pressed Jerzy, the anxious merchant.

Brother Heidolphus exhaled, "Very soon, Jerzy."

"Actually, my Brother, I will need extra pieces to cut in addition to a quantity of sample glass." In response to Brother Heidolphus's raised eyebrow, Jerzy added, "I'd like to install a few small glass panes for the

Sisters at the Heart of Jesus. They will be my first customers, then others will see the windows in the convent and the church, and become my next customers." At that, everyone laughed at the earnest man of business.

After another ten days of experimentation, Jerzy had all the glass rounds he could manage. In the same cart used to transport the clay pots from Poznan, he and his helpers packed the pieces of glass in layers of straw. With Father Kaminiski's prayer and blessing, Jerzy and his men departed for the city, and Brother Brotelin found time for prayer—and rest.

· · ·

Father Michalski finally left Gniezno, his departure delayed by a fever keeping him abed for a fortnight. Bishop Gromek had insisted the he remain until well enough for travel, and promised his visitor he would send a message of explanation to Bishop Tirasewicz. Father Michalski, though grateful for the gesture, knew the bishop's note would make little difference.

It was with some dread, then, that the priest began his journey home. His own master was not the kind, gentle churchman he had observed these past weeks in the person of Bishop Gromek. It would be generous, indeed, to describe Bishop Tirasewicz as a churchman at all.

How the bishop would feel about the report he would offer would be another matter entirely. He loosened his Roman collar, shuddering when he imagined the conversation.

· · ·

Less than a week later, Jerzy had several clear and golden-hued panes secured between lead muntins in the convent wall facing the square. He then installed the new devices as windows in the very room where he had survived the plague. The Sisters were especially pleased by their new ability to see outside without the rain and wind coming through the openings, and to enjoy the sun's warming rays.

One of the older nuns, who had survived the plague but was never content, said in a high, shrill voice, "This is so nice, *Pan* Andrezski, but when we want a breeze come next summer, how will we let it in?"

That stopped him cold. "You know, Sister, I never thought about that. Perhaps we could make a window swing like a door. Would that do it?"

"Most assuredly, young man, but summer will be here before we know it. You'd better hurry."

"I'll have to think how best to do it, Sister Agnes. Let's now enjoy the fall weather."

"Now don't delay, kind sir. The hot days will be here soon enough and these woolen habits make me think of Purgatory!"

Thinking he was glad to have never married, he said, "Yes, ma'am. I'll get to work on it." As he walked away, he thought about her complaint. It would be a wonderful way to improve the value of his product—and create a need for more skilled workers.

Jerzy carted his samples as far east as Gniezno and found immediate demand for his glass wherever he went. No longer was it a magical luxury seen only in great churches and palaces. To accommodate the demand, he knew, the monks would build more furnaces and cut more beech trees. *Ah, poor Brother Heidolphus—no rest for that man."*

As fall winds pulled the last leaves from the trees, Jerzy's work crews retraced their earlier journey and began to make and install the clear and colored windows their customers had purchased. Theirs was a craft requiring much careful work, and when finished, they left behind delighted nobles and churchmen.

Everyone involved in the business was overwhelmed with their success. In all their labors, they had overlooked nothing. Or so they thought.

. . .

In the old *Palais,* arrangements and accommodations were quickly made for nobility and those further down the ladder of both regal and social importance, all in accord with a strict code. Nevertheless, Irina's pregnancy worked to her advantage. Courtesy of Duke Zygmunt and King Wenceslas, two older men who oversaw her maternity with grand-fatherly concern, Kalmus had been assigned to oversee her journey to motherhood. Recruited to join the company at Tangermunde, and seemingly ever-present ever since, Kalmus was a plump woman with iron-gray hair always in a tight bun that seemed to pull the wrinkles from her face.

Still with child were Irina and another woman from King Wenceslas's party. Kalmus kept herself busy tending to each of them, and her stern personality ensured her "ladies" took no risks to themselves or the lives they carried.

Irina had Velka and Rosta to care for her, and, importantly, Jan Brezchwa made it his concern to stay close at hand. She and Jan talked for hours, their acquaintance having developed into a friendship, and then into something else.

She found herself caring for Squire Brezchwa in a way she never thought would be possible after the loss of Berek. Her affection grew to the point she longed to hear his words of fondness, feel the touch of his hand on hers, his lips on her lips. When that had not occurred as she might have expected, she came to the conclusion he simply did not know how to say what he was feeling and thinking. She determined not to fret about it. *And do I really want this now?*

Irina was further comforted to learn that Duke Zygmunt and her beloved Madrosh were housed a stairwell away on a level just above them in the truly charming, but very old, *Palais de la Cité*. Safety was uppermost in Irina's mind as she contemplated her place in a strange but beautiful city.

"Madrosh," she commented two days later as they began one of their many tours of Paris, "how is it that these people, these French, seem so much more advanced than we?"

Madrosh smiled before answering. "Don't let their buildings and clean streets alone impress you, my dear. They are people just like those we left behind. In time, they will prove that to you."

Irina chuckled. "You always have to be mysterious, dear Madrosh! Speaking of buildings, is that yet another huge new fortress they are constructing?" she asked, pointing. "Don't they have enough of them?"

"That, my dear, is to be called *la Bastille*, and someday soon, if I may say, it will house those who demonstrate themselves insufficiently happy under the rule of Charles V."

"Do not speak in riddles, dear priest."

"Please remember what I said about care in the words we use here. We will not have the protection of the emperor or the margrave if we are bad guests in the eyes—and ears—of the French king."

"Thank you for the kind reminder."

"As to *la Bastille*," he continued in a lower voice, "they tell me it was originally the gate of Saint-Antoine in King Philip's wall. Not too many years ago, sometime after the revolt I mentioned earlier, it was extended as a fortress for the defense of the city, but remember what I said. The French cynics and I agree—discreetly. One day, it will make a fine state prison."

Irina wrapped herself more tightly in the great cloak she wore. She wasn't sure if it was the weather or the new Bastille in front of her that gave her such a chill. "Must you be a pessimist, Madrosh?"

"Things are not always as they appear, my dear. Those we've seen are apparently content citizens—or perhaps wise enough to restrain themselves—but they are heavily taxed to fund the king's military endeavors, as well as his lavish palaces. Underneath the smiling and cheering crowds, there is a tension, growing by the month. I fear what the future holds for a French monarchy."

"When you talk about these things, I am confused. How can one tell good from evil in such a complicated life?"

"I do not always know, Irina."

. . .

"What do you think will happen to our little Zuzzie?" Jerzy asked Sister Luke.

"What is it that so concerns you so, *Pan* Andrezski?" she asked, gently, without answering his question.

"I am unsure about what is right for her. At the moment, I am not in a position to give her a home or raise her. Even a young boy would overfill my days! Someday, if she is willing, and if I have a family and a household for her to join, she would be welcome. I continue to feel a great obligation toward the little one who saw my thirst and gave me drink. And for now, I hope you and the good Sisters will keep her."

Sister Luke offered him a look of warm understanding. "*Pan* Andrezski," she began most kindly, "with Poznan being a center of your new business, you may come by and rest with us often, spending as much time as you wish with our little angel."

"Sister Luke," he said hesitantly, "Zuzzie always speaks of her family, but, especially, of her sister Irina. Once, when I was here, Zuzzie mentioned her name, as if she knew Irina was alive." He arched his brow in a question.

Sister Luke's face reddened, caught off guard as she was. "*Pan* Andrezski, you have not been alone in thinking about the right thing to do for Zuzzie." She paused. "In that regard, I owe you an apology, good sir, because Irina may, indeed, be alive. I didn't know how to tell you because I'm not sure it makes any difference."

Andrezski looked at her, attempting to absorb what she had just said.

"Incredibly, Irina Kwasniewska was here—perhaps days before you. It was clear that she needed to leave the city for her well-being and that of the child she carried. Sister Elisabeth sent her away in the care of the bishop, but Zuzzie was not found until afterward, and so we did not realize they were sisters until it was too late."

"She was with child, you say?"

"Yes, just a few months along. When she did not return, I learned she had gone on to Paris with Duke Zygmunt. That was in the spring. What has become of Irina is a mystery, I'm sorry to say."

Andrezski looked off into the distance. "That changes everything, does it not?"

"Perhaps. Perhaps not. Paris is not Poznan, and they tell me it is a very long way from here. Zuzzie may never see her sister again."

"Or maybe she will! May I see my little angel?"

Sister Luke nodded. "Of course." She smiled broadly, relieved of her burdensome secret. "I believe she is in the courtyard. There is one other thing, *Pan* Andrezski," she added, in a different tone of voice.

Jerzy stopped and turned, caught by the change in her voice. "What is it, Sister?"

"When Irina was here, she was finely dressed, not a girl from the farm at all. What is more, she had a servant—Velka, I think her name was—and Irina claimed to be a gentlewoman from Gniezno." She paused. "Yet there can be little doubt she and Zuzzie are sisters."

Jerzy's face became a blank.

"None of us understands, I'm afraid." She smiled. "Perhaps someday you'll go to Paris to solve the mystery!"

They both chuckled, but Jerzy knew laughter could not brush away all the questions in his mind.

The sun shone brightly, highlighting the few remaining leaves on the trees, as if to mark the fall day with a special brilliance. "Zuzanna Kwasniewska!" Jerzy Andrezski called out when he first he spied his charge in the convent yard.

"*Pan* Jerzy, you remember my name! Did you find my parents? My brothers and sisters? Irina?" The look on her face was one of excitement, anticipation.

Jerzy's expression changed in an instant. "No, I did not, little Zuzanna, but I am certain they are looking for you. How could they not? They would never leave such a pretty little girl with an ugly old man like me." He laughed.

"You are not old or ugly. You are special to me," Zuzanna said in her very small voice.

"It is you who are special, little Zuzzie. You are the angel who saved me when I was thirsty."

She smiled. "I did little but give you water."

"No, little Zuzzie. You gave me life and I will always owe you mine."

...

"Ah, dear Bishop Tirasewicz," breathed Father Michalski. "At last, I am back in your care."

"Never mind that, Father." The impatience in his tone evident with every syllable as he tapped a fingernail, fortified with everyday grime, on the wooden table. "You've taken a very long time to answer a simple question. What might that answer be?"

"Your Grace, you know I had been taken very ill. Had Bishop

Gromek not insisted…"

"I said, 'Never mind that,'" the man of God spat. "Tell me what I want to know!"

"First, I can assure you, Bishop," Michalski responded, quivering, "we searched every record, every possible baptismal entry, and spoke with many of the learned ones of Gniezno. What we found is absolutely nothing. There is no record of a Berek or Irina Kwasniewska, or any Kwasniewski for that matter. The Kwasniewskis seem not to have existed in that province."

Speechless with anger, the bishop stared at the young priest. His mouth snapped shut and opened again. "Then, this Irina we carted around like royalty is nobody! The so-called Lady Irina I foisted off on the duke is likely no more than some merchant's daughter, or worse," he exclaimed further. "Surely, someone must know who she really is!"

"Did you not say, Bishop, that this young woman seemed to be of some means?"

"Yes, Father, I did," the bishop rejoindered, pensive. "And that is most interesting. Just how did she come by those means?" Tirasewicz looked into the distance, and after a moment, said quietly, "The fact that she is not who she says she is could be valuable in itself. I must think how I might use this information to advantage."

. . .

"It is now time, Madrosh." In her voice, there lingered the small triumph of decision matched by unforgotten despair.

The old man smiled, rising from his chair, as he felt sure of what he was about to hear. Nonetheless, he played along. "Time, My Lady? The child comes?"

"No, Madrosh," she said, laughing. "I know you spoke with Jan Brezchwa on my behalf." She became serious and looked into his eyes.

Madrosh cleared his throat. "I did so, My Lady, only to nudge things along, perhaps. Your present condition suggests that a husband would be highly desirable." He looked away, embarrassed.

Taking his meaning, she smiled. "Words escape me, Madrosh!"

Madrosh laughed—relieved—and blushed under his gray beard.

"Then you've had a meeting of the minds?"

"My dear friend, there is no meeting of the minds because there have been no words—or anything else," she said with emphasis. "It is what I wanted to talk to you about, as my priest, confessor, and counselor." She lowered her eyes, reflecting. "Berek Joselewicz was the first man I loved, and I know that despite our youth, he loved me and his child with all his heart." In turn, her anger showed itself. "What happened to him and his family was a sin and a crime. There is not a day that I do not think of him and what might have been!"

Madrosh faced her directly, letting his eye take in every nuance of her expression.

"I am sorry, Madrosh. I have not yet learned to hide my feelings—and my bitterness."

"What you feel, I cannot even imagine. What I do know, my dear Lady, is that with few exceptions, like me," he said gesturing to himself deprecatingly, "our lives are short, indeed. Your memories of young Berek are precious to you, but so is the life of the one to come." He paused, then added, "and so is the life you have yet to live."

Irina looked up at him, her eyes wet with tears and anger.

Madrosh inhaled deeply and continued, his listener desperate for every word. "Jan Brezchwa may not be your lover and hero, but he is a wonderful match for you. He comes from good Polish stock in the ranks of lower nobility. He will provide you a life that would be hard—now—to find otherwise."

"You are right, Madrosh," she said, exhaling fully and taking more air before continuing. "How much does he know?"

Madrosh shrugged his shoulders. "He knows what you have told him, and what very little I have told him. I would never betray your confidences, My Lady," he said, and bowed slightly. "Because you are with child, and with whatever knowledge you have given him, he is, perhaps, fearful of rejection. I believe he has come to care very much for you, my dear."

"He has said nothing."

Madrosh nodded. "As I said, he may not know you are, shall I say, interested." He cleared his throat.

Her anxiety dissipating, Irina laughed. "Oh, don't go on so! I suspect, Father, that a few more words from you might serve as an encouragement."

"And I suspect, My Lady, that perhaps a few words from you will matter much more."

"My head and heart needed to hear those words. The truth is, part of my agony has to do with guilt. There is Berek, high on his horse, and beautiful in memory. And there is Jan, a man for whom I have developed a deep affection, perhaps more." Irina blushed, wanting to let her words end there. She cleared her throat of emotion and asked, "And so, Father Madrosh, what do we do now?"

"You two should talk again. What I perceive is that all the ingredients are here for a good marriage, except..."

"Except?"

"Except the right words between you and..." Here, the old man stopped, hardly able to say the next words.

Irina waited.

"And some, some, ah, action," he said, reddening, "to seal the arrangement."

Irina lowered her head, put her hands up to cover her face, and laughed out loud.

"There is nothing to laugh about," he said, still discomfited.

"You are such an old innocent!"

"I'd say, knowing the two of you, what happens next is up to you."

...

The fall days in Paris alternated between brilliant sunshine and drenching rains. Luckily for those blessed with the comforts of an easier life, there were distractions most memorable. One of them was a royal gathering in the *Palais du Louvre,* where fresh tapestries hung heavy with their woven histories beautifully colored to enrich every tale they told.

Madrosh had prepared her well. As Irina surveyed the throng of glittering nobility, everything the old priest had described seemed to fit together, much like the stories threaded into the tapestries. In her brief time in Paris, she had learned much, and not just from Madrosh.

Surrounded by beauty and bounty, Charles V reigned in relative contentment, it seemed. Royal onlookers would have celebrated his many accomplishments for his country, if not his nation. Under his reign, the borders of France were largely regained, many fine cathedrals, fortresses, and palaces were constructed, and at the moment, the people were at peace, laboring mightily to enjoy great harvests.

Yet those same observers might have noted there was a price to be paid. To achieve the greatness in mortar and stone, the nobles and the people were taxed heavily. Charles depended upon the French language and culture to unify his people. Moreover, he counted upon his small army of Catholic Cardinals to arrange Sunday support for his kingly visions.

What might have been an ordinary time was not permitted by fate. When he issued his broad invitation for the nobility of Europe to come to Paris, Charles was at the peak of his reign. His uncle, Charles IV, was Holy Roman Emperor, and his cousin Wenceslas was King of the Germans. In his worldview, the only cause of distress was the inexplicable decision of Pope Gregory XI to return the papal court to Rome after some seven decades in Avignon, under France's most protective roof. Even so, Gregory was a good pontiff, according to Charles, and at least there was stability in that corner of the king's universe, even if that corner had now been removed to the Italian states.

Jostling the king's view, Gregory's death, and the debacle of two popes more than blurred the original reason for a royal gathering in Paris: strengthening borders and alliances. Now it took on an entirely new dimension, one of supreme importance given that the Catholic Church served as the one and strongest common thread amongst all peoples and kingdoms of Europe and, particularly, of the king's own France.

Such complexities and eventualities consumed every conversation within every palace and royal residence, and while Irina relished the talk as a diversion from her maternity, for her, it was only that—a grand diversion. Her more immediate concern involved the future of a fatherless child. On this occasion in the Great Hall, the panoply and pomp served to distract her from thoughts of familial fullness.

All around them were men and women dressed in the richest of scarlets, the truest of forest greens, and the deepest of blues. Velvet and damask prevailed, all trimmed in fur of the lynx. There was silk, tinseled cloth, and pearl embroidery aplenty, and enough enameled buttons and clasps to make a country woman's eyes grow large. What took her breath away, however, was the bobbing sea of diamond- and ruby-encrusted headpieces, each one of them catching its sparkle from the hundreds of candles lit around the audience room. There were many kings and queens, it seemed, and Irina worked hard to follow court protocol.

As always, Irina and Jan, along with Father Madrosh, were placed deep in the masses of the entitled, but near to their patron, Duke Zygmunt. After nearly a half an hour awaiting the king's entrance, the hall's glitter could not take Irina's mind from her condition, after all. She began to tire of standing, and begged to be excused. People made way for her and Squire Brezchwa to make a quiet exit.

Descending the broad marble staircase to the palace's main entrance, Irina made for a carved stone bench on which to rest, when Jan said, "All of this is so pleasant, but so momentary, *nie*? It's not real."

It was such an unusual thing for him to say, Irina looked up at him and waited.

"I mean all the glitter, all the wealth in the world, means little in the dark of night when one is alone."

"What are you getting at, Jan?"

"In the Great Hall up there, most of them mean little or nothing to one another. They're all about position, power, and show. It's a very thin covering for people fearful of what the next day may bring to their status and fortune."

"Why, I've never heard you speak that way," she said, suddenly finding still another reason for kinship with Squire Brezchwa.

"It seems people are better off when they have much less to lose. Then the people around them mean so much more to them. It's then about family, the people they love."

Irina felt herself tingle with affection she didn't think she'd ever feel again. "If that's important to you, you should do something about it." Her voice was thick, throaty.

He beheld her, his eyes suggesting he was not sure if she meant what he might only hope was true.

"Yes, Jan, I—I mean, we," she said, touching her bulging midline, "can be your family."

Jan looked as if lightning had struck him into utter silence.

"You have only to ask."

He knelt beside her, grasped her hand, and without a moment's hesitation, said, "I thought you would never allow me to love you, and yet, I do. Would you allow me to be your most fortunate husband?"

. . .

A day later, when Irina and Madrosh had an opportunity to stroll the palace's long halls while rain pummeled the windowpanes, she said, "Well, Father, Squire Brezchwa has asked me to marry and I have gratefully accepted."

Madrosh paused them in their progress and touched Irina's forearm. "Do I perceive in you a note of happiness or victory?"

"Both! Don't ask any more questions, Madrosh. Time hastens! Now how do we do this," Irina said, laughing, "before another blessed event intervenes?"

Madrosh offered her a conspiratorial smile. "We need not make this complicated," he began. "You and Jan are two young people who wish to wed. In the eyes of the church, you present yourself as the widow of Berek Kwasniewski. The banns will be published, and in a few weeks' time, you will be married here in Paris."

Irina's eyes became large in astonishment. "Madrosh, you devil, you have already thought this through, and unless I'm wrong, you and Jan have already discussed the details!"

Madrosh did not answer, but smiled mysteriously. "With your permission and that of the Bishop of Paris, I would be most honored to say the wedding Mass."

. . .

Weeks had elapsed from the time the Poles and the Germans made their entrance into Paris, followed by fifty dozen others in royal pilgrimage to the French seat of power. For the sojourners, it was a time to regain the pleasures of earthly comforts in what was for many a center of culture and civilization. Along with quiet conversations, arrangements and manipulations large and small, and diplomatic drama in every castle, the wedding banns for Lady Irina Kwasniewska and Squire Jan Brezchwa were published in good form.

And so when the leaves had finished their aerial display and carpeted with color the beautiful, cobbled streets of Paris, and as the winds and rains of October demanded the attention of everyman, the Church of St. Denis became the scene of a serene and proper wedding of two young wayfarers. The Margrave of Brandenburg, King Wenceslas, insisted on giving the bride away while Duke Zygmunt smiled delightedly as sponsor of the groom. Many Poles and Germans from their long journey were there to wish them well, along with the church bells pealing their tonal joy.

Atop the gold-threaded robes of the church, Madrosh wore a chasuble of white with a red cross, colors of meaning to the religious, and of national pride for Poles. Beginning with the words, "*In nomine patrie...*," he blessed the wedding couple and all those present with the goodness of Almighty God. The Mass, laden with readings from the Old and New Testaments, told the story of sacrifice and remembrance, of abiding, eternal love.

Showered with best wishes and purses of gold coins to help them on their marital journey, the pair had special words for each other.

"Jan, I am so happy you have come into my life. I will always honor and love you for that."

"Oh, Irina," he responded, "I am the fortunate one in finding someone like you. I will love and take care of you always." Their kiss was long and loudly applauded.

CHAPTER XIII

1378

Within days of their nuptials, the Brezchwas were flattered to have been invited to yet another grand gathering one late afternoon in the Great Hall of the *Palais du Louvre*. As always, Madrosh was there to accompany Duke Zygmunt and the small entourage from Poznan. Irina was allowed to be seated while they waited for the king, and from her vantage point, she enjoyed what pleasures her eyes revealed.

For Lady Irina and Squire Jan Brezchwa, merely being in the same grand room again with Europe's nobility, high and low, was living a child's fairy tale. With its high, vaulted ceiling, a weave of stone arches and wood, the Great Hall sheltered all within from the rains without. Though Irina had heard much of foreign lands around the Joselewicz dinner table, the reality was far richer. Even on a gloomy day such as this, the hundreds of lit candles splayed their flickering streams on the jewels and rich brocades of the well-dressed women and men. More interestingly, the light made the gold and silver threads in the wall hangings seem to dance, their dazzle springing to life the woven stories of biblical times.

The notion of two popes dominated everyone's talk. Already, there was subtle pressure not to make a hasty decision about the counter-pope, Clement VII. Whether to remain loyal to the Church before their own culture, the Parisian clerics had yet to publicly express their views. They were waiting, no doubt, for a signal from their sovereign.

Trumpets sounded. For a few moments, Irina and others in her circumstance stood as King Charles entered, greeting favorites on his march to the throne. Once seated, His Majesty surveyed the assembled mass of princes of the earth, all the while gently massaging the ever-painful lump that dominated all feeling in his left arm. He had lived with the discomfort for some twenty years, Madrosh had told her.

Having a reigning pope in France had its advantages, Charles was heard to say, though most discourse from the throne could be heard only by those within earshot. Though Charles's voice was but one, all knew his decision, once made, would bind all French subjects. After a short while, the king rose to leave. Men and women bowed until he'd left their assemblage. For herself, Irina was glad to be dismissed so that she might rest before the next day's event.

For the public ceremonies, Charles the King deferred to Charles the Emperor in hosting the continent's royalty choosing to attend. Those not formally in the procession, including Irina, Jan, and Father Madrosh, positioned themselves along the route for the best view of royalty on display.

The grand parade was the most spectacular event Irina had ever witnessed, imagined, or dreamt about. The emperor, along with kings, queens, and other high royalty, departed *le Louvre* early on a Sunday morning for Mass at Notre Dame Cathedral, rode up *l'Escolle S. Germain,* crossed *le Pont Neuf,* and paused at *le Palais de la Cité.* The gilded carriages were driven by men so richly dressed they would be taken for kings in other settings. The bright-white steeds pranced with red ostrich plumes fluffing the air above their heads, their bridles guided by other men equally well dressed and powdered. Onlookers could see glittering jewels through carriage windows, and for open conveyances, there were men on the running boards shielding passengers from the sun with highly decorated umbrellas.

From their vantage point high on the steps of *Sainte-Chapelle,* Irina missed nothing. Then Duke Zygmunt fell in line behind King Wenceslas. The Duke, along with hundreds of men like him, honored their host by walking behind the carriages of their enthroned sponsors. Madrosh explained that had King Louis of Hungary and Poland chosen to attend, the duke's place in line would have been different. "It's a good thing King Louis chose to stay home," he had said.

As Irina took in the splendor of the event, she could not help but make silent note of several points for further discussion with her mentor. Among them was the great disparity of wealth between those in the parade and the thousands of ordinary Parisians gazing at the spectacle along the way. She also wondered if there were any Jews whatsoever in Paris—she had seen not a sign of them anywhere. It was one subject she could not wait to bring up.

"Madrosh! There are two very black men walking behind that carriage there," she said, pointing at the same time.

"Are you asking me a question, My Lady, or providing me information?"

"I've never seen a black man before, Madrosh," she answered in mock reproach. "Are they like Augustine of Hippo?"

Madrosh chuckled. "Not quite, my dear. They belong to the King of Naples who rides in the coach just ahead of them."

"Belong?"

"Yes, Irina, 'belong,'" said Jan, speaking for the first time. "You see, they are slaves."

"Slave is a word I do not understand, husband," Irina said. Out of habit, she turned to her other companion. "Madrosh, what does this mean?"

"Slavery has long existed all throughout Europe," he sighed, "just not so much in your lifetime, and even less so in Poland at present. Yet you know from our own history that when the Mongol hordes from the east came so many years ago, those they did not slaughter, they enslaved to work their farms, tend their animals, and serve their households. Before the Mongols, and for thousands of years before Christ, slavery was commonplace. It was never thought wrong to own the body of another. Holy Scripture itself refers to slavery without condemning it." He paused, but neither of his listeners made comment.

"The Mongols are gone now," Madrosh continued, "but slavery remains, though it has changed somewhat. Now most Christian men believe it a sin to own men of their own kind. But to own men, women, and children of another religion or color is another matter altogether." Casting his glance downward toward his young companion, his tone gave away his own view of the matter.

"I'm not sure I understand exactly what you mean.'"

"Those black men there," he pointed, "are Africans, of the black race—like St. Augustine, in fact. By Europeans, they are considered inferior. They were captured on another continent not very far from here, enslaved, and made to become Christian. In Africa, slavery was not based on race, but on the strongest overlording the weakest, one tribe over another, so it is also true that black men own other black men."

Irina found herself shocked that men owned other men like simple possessions. Despite the rough and cruel times in which she had lived in rural Poland, where men and women might be poor, and have to serve or soldier for their duke, they considered themselves free by God's grace and under no other. "Why does this have to be, Madrosh?"

"No matter what the circumstances or who enslaves whom, it has always been about simple greed: taking a man's freedom or his labor or his skill and paying nothing for it. In that way, one man prospers over another man's sweat. I must point out, dear child, that what happened to the Jews in Poznan and elsewhere was just a more brutal way to steal another man's property and, indeed, his life!"

"Then these men are...?"

"They are in service to the king, or their owner, and will remain so, until they die. They have no freedom to leave, marry, or labor where they choose. The king provides them a place to sleep and gives them food. He does not need to give them anything else." Jan nodded in assent, an acknowledgement of the ways of *noblesse oblige*.

"I have to say, Madrosh, the Africans look well-fed and well-treated. Slavery may not be so bad for them. Could that not be so?"

Madrosh shot her a look of patient rebuke. "As I have said many times in our talks together, appearances are often deceiving. In fact, if these two men are well-fed and well-treated, they are a rarity. Most often, slaves are chained to their work and fed as little as possible. There is nothing at all appealing about their lives. They are no better off than oxen yoked to a plow!"

By this time, Madrosh and his young companions had fallen into the long train of the pageant, near its end. Irina held tightly to Jan as she walked, her time of delivery near. She laughed and observed that their lowly status had earned them the best and most complete view of all, except that they and all others on foot had to dodge the horse droppings. They had not missed a single gilt-appliqué, bejeweled head-piece or facial expression of sublime superiority. All in a long line, they moved slowly toward the twin towers of the great cathedral dedicated to the Blessed Mother.

After some silence, Irina stretched up to Madrosh's ear and whis-pered, "What about the Jews? Where are they?"

Madrosh glanced around in quiet alarm, and with his cloak as a protection, brought Irina closer. "This is a topic we should discuss at another time, when no other ears may hear us."

Irina and Jan both nodded. Looking more closely at the Parisian spectators along the way, she could see not all were washed or pros-perous. "And what about them?" she asked, turning to her friend and priest.

"Them?" He nodded thoughtfully. "Their chains are not so visible," he muttered in a low voice, "and someday, they will throw them off!"

. . .

Irina thought the end of November to be her time of delivery and was pleased she and Jan would have several more weeks before another event commanded their attention. And so, on a brilliantly sunny, but cold day in late October, they took a carriage ride into the countryside near the village of Giverny.

Their short drive was Jan's suggestion, as he had come to loathe the machinations of palace life, yearning to discover more ordinary pleasures. Toward that end, they stopped at a glade just off the road for a respite and picnic lunch. It was too chilly to sit on a blanket, so they remained in the covered carriage as they supped and the horses grazed on field forage. After a repast of cold chicken and sliced apples, Jan moved to step out of the carriage.

"Are you leaving your bride already?"

"Ah, you are so charming I could never leave your side, but I must stand for a bit, and besides, there's an interesting shop over there. Can you hear them working on something?"

"Of course, but if you don't mind, I will remain right here."

He bent to kiss her and said, "I am too curious not to find out what goes on there. Certainly," he laughed, "it is not palace politics." Jan left the glade and was gone for some minutes. When he returned, he carried with him the boyish excitement Irina had come to love. "You must come, my dear. Wait till you see!"

"What is it?"

"Oh, be patient, and you will find the whole business most fascinating."

On they walked to the shop with a worn-down sign out front. "Antoine Chevalle Woodworks." That was all it said. Once inside, they saw a cavernous building heated by roaring fires under steam devices the size of two men. "What are those?"

"They capture the steam to bend and shape wood for furniture and building frames," Jan said.

A man not much taller than Jan, but stocky, bearded, and bald, walked up, his body mostly covered by a worn leather apron. "How can I help my visitors from the city?" His tone was not entirely welcoming.

"Tell us about your work here if you will, *Monsieur* Chevalle," she said.

"Your speech tells me you are not Parisians, I am glad to hear. From where do you come?"

Irina blushed as she thought the peasant's behavior outrageous until she remembered her own background. She chuckled and immediately responded in her French tinged with Polish, "We are from Poland in the east. And soon, we may be seeking lodging out of the city. We will need furnishings, *Monsieur,* and so my husband seeks to find out how good you are!"

"I am a master at what I do, *Madame,* and what I do is make furniture for people of means."

"To be honest, *Monsieur* Chevalle, your business does not look prosperous," Jan said, reminding the man of their respective positions in the social scheme of things.

"It is prosperous enough, *Monsieur.*" Still grumpy, he added, "You may look around, if you wish."

They were intrigued by Chevalle's work, the artistry of veneering that, he said, had been in use for thousands of years. It was not in fashion now, Chevalle explained, and thus practitioners were destined to a craftsman's genteel poverty. French acquisitors were demanding solid, hardwood furniture, finely wrought, and no other, it seemed.

What caught their most immediate attention was not the beautiful work that materialized from Chevalle's clever hands. It was the trio of black men, barely clothed, who performed the hardiest labors for the shop.

"Who are these men, *Monsieur* Chevalle?" Irina spoke impulsively.

"Eh, you who are from the city ought to know," was the riposte.

"Why do you say that, shopkeeper?"

"It is Parisian wealth that buys slaves from Africa."

"What has that to do with you?"

"This shop was owned by a nobleman. I was indentured to him myself. It was he who purchased the slaves to help with this poor business. When the owner died, he left it all to me. What am I to do with them?"

"Free them!"

"*Madame!* I earn little to eat as it is. These brutes are the only way I can make things go."

"And so, Chevalle, is it thus that a master would enslave you, so you would enslave others?"

"Is it not always so, *Madame?*"

"Eh, shopkeeper," she said, "you who are *not* from Paris must know. Perhaps we will stop again. Perhaps not."

On the ride back to Paris, Irina thought about what she had seen. The images in her mind were not beautiful wood pieces, however. What troubled her was the reality of good and evil before her eyes in the grand procession to Notre Dame, and in the lowly shop of Antoine Chevalle. She thought, too, about the shackles of her own sex. Although Madrosh showed her respect, she never forgot she was a woman with certain duties expected of her. It wasn't her sex that bothered him, Madrosh had said often enough. The rules of their society were like iron, and neither of them had the strength to bend the metal. *Perhaps someone should try. Someone like me?*

...

"Today there will be a conclave of great interest," Madrosh intoned as they walked along, once again near the towering walls of *Sainte-Chapelle*. He paused and let his eyes rise ever so deliberately to the very peaks of the majestic structure in front of them.

Irina and Jan, his usual daily walking companions, could not help but ask the obvious question, taking the words from each other's lips and speaking as one. After a playful laugh, Irina spoke the words, teasing the old man ever so gently. "And what will the royal ones meet about, wise Madrosh?"

The smile he gave in return quickly turned to stone, "They will be meeting to discuss the matter of two popes. The outcome I fear will be an unwise one that in the end, will have an effect on all Christendom."

"I do not understand, Madrosh," said Irina, puzzled. "Why do we still have two popes? Can they not decide who is the right one?"

"As always, my dear one, you manage to ask the only question that needs to be asked. And the answer is, of course they can decide the matter, but will they have the courage to decide rightly is yet another question. My thinking is this will not be their last meeting, I'm afraid."

Suddenly, he clasped her arm just above the elbow and steered her, slowly, up the steps of the beautiful church. Irina's movements were halting, but steady. "You want this child to arrive sooner rather than later, eh, Father Madrosh?"

"It will wait a bit longer, My Lady." He chuckled. "We did not chance to see this the other day, and today's sun will light the world inside. Come, Jan."

They crossed the threshold of *Sainte-Chapelle* and passed through the darkened vestibule before stepping into the nave itself. "How clever was Cormont!" Madrosh whispered. "He leads us from the outer world, lets our eyes adjust to the shadows, then thrills us when we step into his paradise of glass and color."

At that moment, it was as if the trio lost their voices in the glorious beauty around them. Stretching to the very end of the church, behind the altar, were column after column, not of stone, but of the most beautiful stained glass either had ever seen. It appeared as if there were no walls at all except for the stunning windows of amazing color that seemed to dance on the floor and make the entire room shimmer in glistening light.

Irina broke their silent reverence with a whispered question. "Is it true what they say about this place?"

"Yes, it is true. This chapel—a cathedral in any other place—was built to house relics of Christ's crown of thorns and what remained of the true cross. I was told the windows behind the altar tell the story of the relics, how they were found and how they came to be in this special place."

For several minutes, Madrosh stared at the scene before him. At last, he continued in hushed, reverent tones, "You recall our conversation the other day? It seems to me this chapel is an allegory about our civilization. Here, on the inside, amidst the great beauty of design and purpose, we enjoy what seems like perfection. These thin walls of stone and glass, strong and fragile at the same time, are all that separate us from the ugliness of the world beyond this fortress of faith.

"Inside, we delude ourselves into thinking we have come far from the days before Moses. Outside, we are reminded just how very few steps we have taken these thousands of years. We have not come far at all, my young ones," he said, looking at each of them in turn. "I sometimes think that beneath a very thin coating of civility lies the ugly inner layer of jealousy and greed marking the false gestures one man offers another."

Irina, unlike Jan, spoke to Madrosh with familiarity. "You are showing yourself to be as cynical as your pupil, Madrosh, and I must say that most peasants would nod their agreement to your words. Their daily lives cannot have changed much since the time of the Bible."

"It depends upon one's point of view, *nie?* Outside this jewel box it is not nearly so pleasant. Is it?"

Jan hung back to study the stories in glass. The other two made their way to the long kneeler facing the great altar and genuflected there in deep respect and silent prayer. The amber and rose lights cascaded upon them, warming their devotion.

After a long moment, Irina spoke once again, this time with urgency. "At the moment, Madrosh, my attention is directed entirely toward the baby within me who now wants to be born!"

Startled yet not surprised, Madrosh called to the new husband, and led his companions to the main doors, where *Madame* Kalmus waited with servants and a litter, as Madrosh had fortuitously directed.

Irina grasped the old man's hand and exclaimed, "God has already answered so many of my prayers!"

With her other hand, she reached for Jan Brezchwa, her eyes imploring him to be for her now the man she so desperately needed. This, while she cried familiar tears for Berek, the man whose child she would soon deliver.

. . .

On the western edge of Poznan, just before the road steeped downward into the river valley, Jerzy Andrezski rode ahead of the two horses yoked to the heavily laden, four-wheeled cart. Its driver was a young monk dispatched by Father Kaminski to assist Jerzy in delivering the goods, as it were. Or perhaps, thought Jerzy, he was sent to keep an eye on business! In any event, Paulus Ossowski was an enthusiastic young man who had shown himself to be careful and protective of the load he carried.

Before they'd left St. Stephen's, Brother Paulus had listened closely to the tutorial offered by the elderly Brother Heidolphus. Carefully, he demonstrated how the glass must be stacked and packed in the cart, with straw between each layer and all around. Though the thirty rounds of glass, many clear and others colored in stunning hues, shifted themselves many times over the course of the journey, they were totally intact upon entering Poznan, or so Brother Paulus assured Jerzy Andrezski.

Just as they neared the Church of the Heart of Jesus, a lone rider galloped toward them. Aggressively, the man reined in his horse just short of Andrezski's own mount, blocking any forward progress. For a moment or two, they exchanged words, none of them agreeable, before the rider turned and rode back to Poznan.

Andrezski turned to see that Brother Paulus was curious about what had just transpired. "Yes, Brother?"

"It may not be my concern, *Pan* Andrezski, but who was that very unpleasant man whose every word carried a sneer?"

Andrezski laughed. "Brother Paulus, you do not mask your observations. You must learn to do so! That man, Tomasz Wodowicz, is the son of our own *Pan* Wodowicz at the monastery.

He is not like his father, as you have seen!" Andrezski laughed again.

"And what did he want? Are we in danger?"

"I think not, Brother. This man, Tomasz—Tomasz the Terrible, they used to call him—is in service to Bishop Tirasewicz now, and at the moment, he thinks it his task to harass us. Why? Because we share no profits with his master. I think your Father Kaminski might tell you a thing or two about that," he said, then thought to add, "Watch out for him. He will lurk in the shadows. Do your good work of protecting our wares, and all will be well."

...

The solemnity and civility of the wind-swept November days in Paris were shattered with just a few words from on high. Once again, Europe's nobles gathered in the Great Hall of *le Palais du Louvre* immediately after their mid-day repast. The Emperor convened the group with a prayer for resolution of the papal imbroglio. It was a nice touch, Madrosh thought, but misleading in the extreme.

Everyone attending glittered, or thought they did, in all their finery. Varying shades of royal purple abounded, and those without crowns made sure to show off brocaded, tinseled damasks abundantly ornamented with lynx or civet furs. Dotted throughout the throng were elderly men dressed entirely in scarlet tinged with gold piping. Atop their heads were deep-pink zucchettos, a symbol of rank for the princes of the church then present.

According to all that Madrosh had learned—and later relayed to Irina and Jan—the French king's own theologians had decided that the election of the College of Cardinals in Rome was sacrosanct, and therefore, the only valid pope was the Archbishop of Bari, Prigamo Bartolomeo, as Urban VI, who had been selected on April 9 of that year. Yes, they acknowledged, Urban was a man of the people, a man of God, who, in its wisdom, the College chose to remedy the ills of Holy Mother Church. Most certainly, his election to fill the shoes of the Fisherman, the unbroken line of succession from Peter the apostle, could not be overthrown just because some of the French cardinals wanted to protect their wealth. Moreover, such a precedent of electing a pope of convenience caused them all a shudder of despair.

Still others argued that the election by French cardinals of Robert of Geneva as Pope Clement VII, only two months before, was the only valid expression of the holy men free from the mob intimidation that marked the earlier Roman election. Moreover, they pointed out that politically, it was much more to French advantage to have a direct influence over a pope on French soil, Clement or any other.

It soon became apparent to all that Charles V, King of France, had already pondered these arguments, and made his own decision. Amongst most of the heads of state present, there appeared to be consensus for Urban, but at that time and place, the most important national voice was commanded by Charles of France rather than that of his uncle, the other Charles and Holy Roman Emperor.

Keen observers would have noticed men at arms posted every ten feet or so the length of the hall. Each man wore mail and polished armor, carried a short sword at their waist belt, and held a lance with a tip honed to a fine point. Madrosh thought them there not just to display power, but to remind Charles's guests to conduct themselves with care.

On his throne, Charles spoke, as always, in the third person. As he did so, he cradled his aching arm in hopes of alleviating the pain. "His Majesty Charles, King of all the French, has decided that Cardinal Robert of Geneva, recently elected at Avignon as Clement VII, is the legitimate Pontiff for all Christendom. In this nation and in all its territories, counties, and states, now and in all those that shall be under the reign of Charles, Pope Clement VII and no other shall be recognized by any or all persons giving homage to the King."

At that, the chamberlain struck the floor with the Great Scepter. There were no cheers. Instead, there were murmurs amongst the assemblage, all present knowing there could be no opposition. Those from other nations might protest with impunity, but those within the domain of France kept a stoic, stony silence. The King stood and, with quiet dignity, left the hall, his fateful decision deadening the already chilled air around those remaining.

Dismay and confusion reigned thenceforward. Within weeks, one by one, the monarchs and, eventually, the emperor himself, departed for home, leaving behind a deep wound dividing their only unifying force, the one church of God.

...

Tomasz Wodowicz knew the bishop would be angry, and to a large extent, it bothered him not at all. Though he was now the bishop's man, he hadn't forgotten the so-called man of God had forsaken him at a time when he needed it most. His loyalty to the Antony Tirasewicz was barely skin deep.

As he had expected, Bishop Tirasewicz fumed, his nostrils flared. "How dare they!?" he shouted, challenging the only other man who could feel the hot breath of his anger. "For weeks, I, Antony Tirasewicz, Bishop of Poznan, have had to listen to churchmen, nobles, and petty merchants talk about the marvel of plain and colored glass fashioned in frames used to keep out the weather."

Wodowicz stood mute.

The bishop mimicked Andrezski's admirers: "Why, these new windows not only keep out the rain, the wind, and the snow, they also let in the light! Just think," some have said to me, "we'll save on candlelight, and this winter, we will be warm by our hearths!"

"Those vile bastards," he went on, letting Tomasz Wodowicz see a side of the churchman few outside the man's study would ever glimpse. "Your harassment has had no effect, Wodowicz! I thought you were the one they called 'Terrible,'" he said, mocking his underling.

"Your Grace, everyone has come to know I am in your service now that the duke is gone. How would it be for people to see me interfere with a man and an invention so popular with so many? My doing so would only make you enemies, My Lord Bishop!"

"You have failed me, Tomasz Wodowicz, the not-so-Terrible," he said, mocking him again. "You have done nothing to add to my—er—the church's coffers and neither have you elevated my prestige in any way."

Wodowicz said nothing.

"Here is something else you should know. It is now November, and I suspect, given what I hear from Paris, Duke Zygmunt and his people will return here in the spring."

"Return in the spring, you say?" Wodowicz went cold. *The duke should be dead or in a Hungarian prison!*

"Yes, my good man, and you know what that means. You give me no reason whatsoever not to turn you over to him so that at last you will enjoy the earthly punishment you deserve." The bishop stared at his prey. "Can you give me one good reason I should not do so?"

His heart beating fast, Wodowicz decided two could play that game. Cocking his thumbs in his sword belt, he displayed his infamous smirk. "Perhaps I can, Bishop. How can I be sure you'll keep your word?"

"Don't be insolent with me, you scoundrel. If you have something of value for me, say it—and take your chances." Seated at his desk, he looked up at the man before him, the set of his jaw framing the challenge laid upon his minion.

Wodowicz nodded. "I'll wager you'd like to know about Irina Kwasniewska, now wouldn't you?"

The bishop's jaw dropped. He stood, his hands on his desk to balance his anger. He inhaled deeply. "So, Wodowicz, you have me."

He nodded, wary.

"What is it, then? I have learned there is no noble family with that name from Gniezno. Your information had better be good."

Wodowicz laughed. "Your information is correct, Your Grace. It was much simpler, after all," he said, pausing for effect. "I'm quite sure she was a serving girl in the Joselewicz household."

"Nonsense. The girl is Catholic—I gave her Holy Communion myself."

"That's because she comes from a peasant family in St. Michael," he said, "so of course, she is Catholic—but she worked for the Jews."

The bishop pounded the desk, staring into the wall past his bargainer. Then, slowly, he sat down. Nodding in understanding, he said, "So she somehow pilfered some of the Joselewicz gold! How else to explain her wealth!? Madrosh, that scoundrel, must have known!" He was breathing hard, his chest heaving.

"*Tak!*"

"Well done, Wodowicz." He paused, catching his breath. "St. Michael, you say! Shimanski! He should have known, too. I'll deal with him later," he snarled. He turned to Wodowicz. "Very well, you'll be spared—but you'll have to leave the city. I do not want to have to make explanations to the duke." Then, apparently, he remembered the other reason for his anger. His voice rising along with his frame, the bishop demanded, "Where is this man Andrezski now?"

"Your Grace, they are not far away. I am told they are cutting and installing new glass in the house of Henryk Mazurski, the leather dealer."

"Mazurski! A leather scraper?! A mere peasant in new clothes with new money? This rectory has not been windowed as yet, and the skin man is getting them?" His rage grew. Tirasewicz stalked out the door even as he called for his horse, his furor growing by the moment. Once mounted, he clasped his riding crop and trotted up the lane. "Come along!" he commanded Wodowicz.

A few minutes later, the bishop rounded the corner of a new street called Merchants' Row. All the shops and houses had been built in the last year or so, and were of the latest designs with large rooms for living. It was the perfect place for Jerzy Andrezski to market his wares, Tomasz knew. Installing such glass in one house would soon mean cries for the same luxury from all the others within view. As his master galloped ahead, Tomasz hung back.

His long black robes flying behind him, Bishop Tirasewicz cropped his black horse. Just ahead was Andrezski's four-wheeled cart, and Tomasz held himself close enough to see the man perched atop the driver's bench shiver in the November cold.

...

The bishop's horse clattered across the new cobbles and came to a sharp halt near the glass maker's cart. His face sheened in anger, Bishop Tirasewicz dismounted and took a few steps closer. "Where is Andrezski!" he demanded of the driver who yanked the reins to steady the horses.

"Why, Your Grace," the driver began with a half-smile, his full attention still on the horses gone skittish in front of him. Finally, he said, "He is inside with Master Mazurski. If you'd be good enough to wait…"

"Wait! Wait? You insolent bug. You'd make your bishop wait?" He swung his riding crop at the driver. Missing his target, he began striking out wildly in his anger. The crack of the leather against the air resounded in the street, as another of his lashes missed the driver, but struck one of the horses. Steam filled the air as the horses lurched and panted their warm breath into the cold day. A small number of people had appeared, including Jerzy Andrezski and his newest customer. Seeing the bishop's frenzy, their mouths hung open.

Struck again, the animal closest to the bishop snorted and leapt ahead, yanking the other horse along with it. The driver used all of his strength to control his startled animals and managed to keep them from going more than a few feet, but the violence of their movement was enough to loosen the leather thongs used to secure the large glass rounds to the wooden ribs on the cart's upper level.

On racks below were two more layers of rounds to be cut and installed, all in a particular order to keep the load in balance. As they had been cut to size for Mazurski's windowpanes earlier that morning, the remaining edge pieces, each shaped like a quarter moon, had been tossed loosely on top of the rick. These leftover pieces, unsecured, had no value and would be returned to the monks for a second melt.

As the horses jerked to and fro, two of the quarter moon pieces left their nests and took flight.

One of the projectiles landed harmlessly onto the cobbles, shards tinkling the air. Not so, the other. Where Bishop Tirasewicz had positioned himself foretold his fate. The second quarter moon, a weapon on its own path of destruction, pierced the churchman's richly embroidered black garments, wedging deep into his chest.

The bishop stumbled backward, surprise frozen on his face as he struggled to remain upright. His lips moved, but no sound came. Grasping the quarter moon with both hands, he wrenched it free, granting the air a gush of red to match the buttons on his cassock. He looked up only to glimpse his own demise.

In a wink of time, a full round slid free of the cart, and like a shining, sharp-edged platter, it caught the bishop's neck, partially separating his head from the rest of his body.

The crowd gasped, their breath taken away by a life lost at no hand but the dead man's own. The mass of black stained by a stream of scarlet suggested not the end of a man's life, but the essence of his soul seeping into the dirt between the cobbles.

Tomasz the Terrible saw it all, and while he would not have wished such an end on any man, he felt a certain satisfaction about the churchman who denied him at St. Stephen's. Quietly, he backed his horse away and faded from the gawkers around the corpse. To himself, he muttered, "Tirasewicz may be finished, but I will have another day."

. . .

In early December, the name of Stanislaus Brezchwa was entered into the baptismal records of the Church of St. Denis, the infant having entered the world in the morning hours of All Saints' Day, 1378—several weeks earlier than expected. Kalmus had done her job well as a midwife, and so mother and child were healthy and strong. With blue eyes and soft, auburn hair, little Stashu reminded Irina not of Berek, she said, but of his parents—there was a glint in the baby's eye one could not mistake.

Overjoyed to have become a husband and father all in the same month, Jan Brezchwa could not have been happier had the boy been his very own. He had no desire to ask Irina about Stanislaus's forebears, savoring his own secret in the matter. His new wife was comely, he had a handsome new son, and Irina had months before made him aware of the fortune she carried with her. It was he, in fact, who'd arranged to have her ball of melded metal cut for her use. Although Duke Zygmunt, his patron, had been most generous with him, a squire without patrimony could not have asked for more.

The duke was a proud substitute grandfather, and both Zygmunt and Jan remarked just how fair, how "Polish" the boy looked. The duke was even heard to say he'd be delighted to have him as a knight in his own household. Throughout it all, Irina kept her thoughts to herself, and never considered sharing with Jan her conclusions about the duke's role in the slaughter of Poznan's Jews.

As Father Madrosh washed Holy Water across the infant's forehead and pronounced him a child of Christ, Little Stashu Brezchwa looked up at his admirers with a faraway gaze suggesting a vision far beyond his age.

. . .

Charles IV, Holy Roman Emperor, was one of the first to leave the city of Paris. Though he departed with disappointment and reproach, he was powerless to change the king's ruling on the papacy, which reminded everyone how little real power the occupant of the Empire's throne enjoyed. One thing was certain to him, however. His position was secure, and he believed that though his nephew had made a very wrong decision in supporting Clement, it would soon sort itself out. Before he left France, there was one thing in his power he would not forget to do.

On their travels west from Tangermunde, the emperor had had ample opportunity to observe the members of his large party, and had taken a somewhat distant interest in one of the women with child. He watched with both pleasure and admiration when Madrosh, counselor to the Polish nobleman, quietly and gently brought her together with a very eligible young squire. In an age of arranged marriages for convenience, power, and greed, a marriage for love proved a rare thing—of that he was certain, and it gave him great pleasure.

About to take his leave, the emperor made a point to summon the young couple into his royal presence, and he arranged the audience to be a private one.

The surprised Brezchwas had been asked to bring along their little Stashu, barely a month old. In the best finery they could manage, they met Charles IV in his chambers. There, too, purples and blues decorated the walls and even the chairs on which they sat. Because they had become so used to light, highly sophisticated court conversation, they were again surprised when the Emperor spoke to them in Polish, and complimented them on their decision to wed.

It was a short visit, ending only when the emperor made them a special presentation. "I give to Master Stanislaus Brezchwa this token of my hope for him and his descendants." It was a small cross of gold, faced with brilliant white diamonds. The Emperor pinned it on the baby's gown himself and said to the wide-eyed infant, "May the light in the eyes of God himself guide your way."

. . .

Jerzy Andrezski had been profoundly affected by the bishop's grisly demise. Those who had been gathered around, including the Mazurski family, all blessed themselves in true Catholic fashion. Yet Andrezski had to admit he wasn't sure if people were asking blessings for the soul of the dead man before them, or thanking God for having taken this particular creature into eternity.

Stories of his gory death were passed from mouth to ear in hundreds of ways over several days. It gave them a sense of awe and even fear, believing that God could strike a man down in an instant. So seldom did the God in heaven choose to intervene on behalf of the righteous, the religious men and women of the city publicly expressed appropriate grief at the bishop's demise, but privately thanked the Father of all for having ended the Tirasewicz reign.

Men and women of the cloth waited for a new bishop to be appointed while they continued the business of saving souls in the ways Christ himself had intended. Their attention was further diverted by rumors of two popes, and by Duke Zygmunt's impending return home from

Paris. The people of Poznan, from serf to squire, monk to merchant, were exalted by the news of a return to normal, of life before the plague.

. . .

Tomasz Wodowicz remained around Poznan for a few weeks, going from one alehouse to another, from one brothel to another, pursuits funded by none other than the church—in a manner of speaking. Had he been asked, he would not have recalled much of what he had done during that time, but he remembered one thing.

While it appeared that all of Poznan had run to gape at their bishop's headless corpse sprawled in the street, Tomasz turned his horse back toward the bishop's palace, where some recompense for his labors might be found.

Once inside, he knew where to go. Whatever the bishop might have had, he kept it near, within his grasp. To the dead man's study he went, but this time, to the side of the bishop's desk where he had never been.

Smirking with irony, he quickly found his quarry. Noticing that dust had not been disturbed on and around the bishop's illuminated parchment copy of the Bible—because the man would never bother himself to seek its knowledge—Tomasz decided to lift the heavy tome and shoved it to the floor so he could inspect the desk's wooden surface where the book had been. Not until he lit a candle and brought it close did he spy the carefully carved square of wood laid into the polished surface.

Slowly, he ran his fingers over the surface, pressing here and there. Finally, he found the right spot and the entire lid lifted. Inside the space, about the size of a man's two hands, there were a pair of satisfyingly hefty leather pouches, sewn tightly and thonged together at one end. Both gave him the warming jingle of coins—pure gold coins. Quickly, he put them under his tunic and determined to search the rest of the room, but then he heard voices from the palace's grand entryway.

Smiling, he whispered to himself, "Why be greedy?" Silently climbing through the window space, he ran to his horse, mounted, and guided the animal to an out-of-the-way alehouse he knew. Swaggering in, he thundered to the innkeeper, "I'm thirsty!"

CHAPTER XIV

1378

"Good afternoon, Squire and Lady Brezchwa," Madrosh teased his audience when he joined them in their apartment in the *Palais de la Cité*. High enough in the castle to have a view of the city, but with no buffer to winter's blows, all were more heavily clothed as the days hung dark and gloomy, and the bare trees readied themselves for a burden of snow. It was the week after little Stashu's baptism.

"As always, Father Madrosh, we welcome your visits. You have news for us?"

"You have been aware, no doubt, that all the while we have been away, messengers have gone back and forth between here and Tangermunde, relaying news from Poznan and other places as well."

"Yes?" both of his listeners asked—like anxious children. Jan and Irina exchanged glances.

"News from other parts of the Empire I have not come to talk about. From Poznan, however, I do have something to report. You have already heard of Bishop Tirasewicz's most unusual departure from this life. While we must pray for his soul, I must say"—he spoke carefully— "his absence will do much to lift the religious and moral fervor of the Polish people in Poznan. His demise, I hasten to add, has had a chastening effect on Duke Zygmunt, it appears. Perhaps I judge unwisely, but the man has been especially devout of late, and I believe his awakening, shall we say, may be genuine.

Jan began to speak, but Madrosh kept on.

"I can assure you there has been a distinct change in his personality

282

and outlook, but I claim no role in this change. Much to the contrary," he said, in a rare exposure of his inner feelings, "I myself have felt a total failure to the men I have counseled. The choices and the behaviors of the bishop and the duke have often saddened me, and as to the bishop, my chance to be of some good is gone forever. This change in the duke, however, renews my hope."

"I remain a cynic, Father," Irina said quickly. "I may never know to what degree Tomasz was carrying out the duke's wishes that night in Poznan." She paused, apparently taking care in what she said in front of Jan, and swallowed hard. "You remind me often that I am not to judge. I am, however, human, and actions will say much more than prayers."

"Please, Irina," Jan said, "the duke has been so good to me, and has done so many wonderful things—for you as well, to be sure."

"Yes, dear Jan," Irina said, her hand resting on his forearm, "you have seen one side of him, and I, another. It is that other side that will always trouble me."

At that moment, Irina saw that the old man's eyes had glistened over. "I am sorry, Father. Perhaps I am too harsh." She continued, ever so tenderly, "but after all these months of comfort to me, I cannot now believe it is I who seek to ease your pain. Why do you weep so?"

"Because I have failed."

"But," Irina protested, "you have saved so many souls. In very real ways, you have saved me and my child." Irina stopped herself for a moment.

The old priest smiled in gratitude, then seemed embarrassed to have shown them so much of himself. "Now it is I who must ask a question. Jan, have you spoken to Duke Zygmunt about your desire to stay here in Paris with Irina and Stashu?"

"I have not, Father. I hadn't thought there was a need to be hasty."

"This is now the time, Jan. And there is reason not to delay."

It was not just his words but the tone of his voice that caused Irina to back away in concern. She waited, expectantly.

Madrosh proceeded. "The duke will leave for Poznan immediately after the Feast of the Epiphany. And I must go with him."

"No, Madrosh!" Jan said.

"Ten times no!" said Irina.

"You two now have each other, and you have little Stashu. Your need for me," he said, looking directly at Irina, "has ended. I must go where there is a flock to be tended—in Poland. You see, Jan," he continued, now looking at the young father and bridegroom, "there is no day to waste." He saw the concern on the faces of the couple. "I have reason to believe," he said, gesturing with his hands to calm them, "that approached properly, Duke Zygmunt will release you from your obligations. It will, however, be with reluctance, Jan, as you have been very much a son to him."

Irina and Jan held each other's hand, relieved to have some clarity about their future. They intended to remain. In the weeks they'd been in Paris, they'd found the city much to their liking, and Irina, in particular, saw no reason to leave. For her and Stashu, in so many ways, Poznan meant nothing but danger. Jan could have insisted she accompany him back to Poland, but given a choice, she knew he would not do so. Except for the duke's paternal feelings, there was little in Poznan for either of them.

Silence took over the room. Irina blinked, as if to will away the news not to her liking. Then, as so often occurred, her voice filled the air. "Why, Father Madrosh, here you are on *Dzien Swietego Mikolaja*— St. Nicholas Day—and you have had not one iced cookie Velka baked knowing you would come!"

Spirits returned, Madrosh accepted one of the *piernicki* with child-like glee. "Yes, My Lady, you can tell dear Velka I have now enjoyed her baked treats well—too well, I might add—but for the final time. Even the best things in life have an end, do they not?"

"You mourn too much, Madrosh, and there is so much we have not discussed," she insisted, as if their conversations trumped all else. "There is so much you have not answered, and I will not let you get away without good answers," she teased.

Madrosh stood, his eyes dry. He put his hand on her shoulder. "We have some weeks left, Irina. There is much we can talk about in that time. There is much, also, that you already understand. In you, I perceive one who has the ability to discern many answers even when there is no one to give them."

Not one to let time slip by, Irina said, "Tomorrow then?"

Madrosh nodded. "As for you, young Squire," the satisfied priest continued jovially, his goals apparently accomplished, "you must see Duke Zygmunt very soon!"

. . .

Jerzy Andrezski, the former caravan merchant and scoffer of all things religious, converted himself to a prosperous city tradesman with a newfound respect for the mysterious ways of the Almighty. Though he was quickly becoming wealthy, he had not built himself a town palace, and neither had he become a devoted churchgoer, though he was becoming richer in faith by the day.

He continued to believe—and he would not be convinced otherwise—that nothing short of a miracle kept him from a death by plague. That a small child would pay attention to him, quenching his thirst when he cried out, was part of that miracle. His inspiration for the making of glass came to him in a church. His discovery of God's man in the woods, Brother Heidolphus, a master of the art with a willingness to work its craft, all struck him as works of the divine.

Yes, of course, he told himself many times over, all were pieces of strange luck, but he knew much more than luck was at work, and he never forgot the old man's gift of knowledge along with his parting words. "It is now for you, Jerzy, to give Poles a view of life they've never had."

Within weeks of the first clear glass window fittings in Poznan, and the sampling of stained windows in chapels and churches, people came from the north, south, and east to marvel at his inventiveness with the new luxury—including new hinged windows. More importantly, they came to place orders. It occurred to Jerzy that interest in his glassware was in some manner a way for people to let their memories of the plague, the bishop, and all the other ills of their time fade away into a view of their world the glorious windowpanes revealed.

In his bounty, Jerzy never forgot his promise to Sister Luke, and as a consequence of his generosity, the nuns were able to increase fourfold their services to Poznan's poor and outcast. No one was ever turned away from their doors. The more the sisters did in service to the least of the people, the deeper in devotion to their cause Jerzy became.

The Church of the Heart of Jesus itself never looked as wondrous and beautiful as after his gift of biblical stories in stained glass for every opening in the church. The colors playing on the walls and the altar on a sunny Sunday morning were truly sublime. Soon pilgrims for miles around came to bask in the glories of God's work—and Jerzy's as well.

As for the monks at St. Stephen's, they, too, prospered with success from their glassmaking skills. Even though many local men appeared to work in the business, Father Kaminski had to restrict his own men's labors in the endeavor as it consumed so much of their energies, leaving little for their true service to God.

"Father Kaminski," Jerzy said in his hearty voice, after a good meal with the brothers, "I am so glad that you have found ways to keep up with the making of glass rounds. I cannot tell you how well it has been going. My greatest fear, however, is that St. Stephen's will not be able to provide all that we can sell!"

...

It was a sunny day in Paris, near the end of Advent. A light snow had fallen the night before, but most people out and about ignored the chilled air, as they seemed to enjoy the Christmas season. In the world of Paris and France, it would be a season of peace. Despite the papal imbroglio, the visits of the emperor and much of European royalty had been a huge success. Their stay of many weeks had been expensive, no doubt, but so much gold and silver moving from one pouch to another helped to employ and feed the populace. The rumbles of disquiet seemed to have evaporated.

In their palace apartment, life was just as peaceful for Jan and Irina. Their rooms were comfortable and noisy, the new infant's needs loudly and often expressed. Irina and her coterie of servants attended to little Stashu throughout the day. Her Jan occupied his time doing the bidding of his duke, and though his master had released him from fealty, Jan assisted Madrosh in preparing for their return to Poland. Grain goods would not be plentiful in the countrysides of France and Germany during the months of January and February, they knew, and so the gathering, sacking, crating, and carting all manner of foodstuffs occupied many waking hours.

Irina treasured her times with Madrosh. Her mood would lighten the moment Velka opened the large wooden door at the old man's arrival. That he would be leaving her life—undoubtedly forever—was a prospect she worked to put out of her mind, but could not.

"I am so glad we have this opportunity to visit," he said. "With all the Christmas duties and activities, I feared we would not have time for other than public pleasantries. The duke is insistent we be prepared for our departure after Three Kings."

Irina smiled, immediately cheerful in the presence of her closest friend, "Well, dear departing one," she responded teasingly, "I am likewise glad you have found time for me." She laughed, seeing the effect of her words on his expression.

"Yes, My Lady," he said sheepishly. Madrosh continued, his expression turning somber. "Unfortunately, I must begin our talk with the sad news that Emperor Charles has died. From what the messengers tell us, His Majesty spared nothing to reach Prague and settle some important business with his three sons. Within days, he simply died in his sleep." He paused. "I mention this because I know his gesture to little Stashu meant a great deal to you and Jan."

Irina blessed herself and bowed her head, whispering a prayer for the emperor's eternal rest. She remained silent for some moments. Then she blinked her eyes, as if the simple physical motion would clear her mind.

"May we finish a discussion point of some weeks ago?" she asked without a trace of emotion left from the earlier topic. "You remember, Father. It was the time you became so alarmed when I asked you about the Jews in France?"

"Yes, I recall it well. I hushed you because unlike Poland, the Jews have had a much harder time here. It is not a subject for discussion in public, to be sure."

"When you say 'unlike Poland,' you cannot be referring to what happened to Berek and his family!" Hearing her own impulsive words, and the tone of them, she was grateful only she and Madrosh were in the room.

He did not answer her directly. "In the meantime, I have discreetly asked a few questions. To a sufficient degree, I can assure you, My Lady, the Jews in Poland have had much longer lives and deaths that have been more natural than brutal."

"Yes?" she said, quietly and respectfully.

"I remember you mentioning," Madrosh began, "that on the night Berek and his family were slain, you thought a priest might save them if they gave up their faith."

"Yes, everyone thought that."

"There's a reason. It has happened many times in the past. Here in France, for example, it was in the city of Limoges, I believe, that all the Jews were rounded up and given exactly that choice. At the end of a month of intense discussion and debate, only a very few wished to convert to Christianity. Of all the rest, those who did not flee to other cities, killed themselves." Shocked, she clasped her hand to her heart. "Was there no other way?"

"Robert the Pious conspired with his nobles to destroy all the Jews who would not become baptized. A rich Jew from Rouen travelled to Rome and begged the pope to intervene. In fact, the pope sent a high churchman to the king in an attempt to stop the persecutions."

"Yet they continued?"

"Most assuredly. At some point not many years later, the Jews were accused by many of being in league with the Muslims when the Church of the Holy Sepulcher in Jerusalem was converted to a mosque."

"Could such a story be true?" asked an incredulous Irina.

"Whatever is repeated many times over is almost always believed by those who do not search for the truth. Whether any of this is true is often irrelevant. Even so, it aroused strong feeling throughout Europe. While crusading against the Moors of Spain, it has been said the soldiers killed every Jew they met along the way. This happened despite the fact that Pope Alexander had praised the nobility of Narbonne for having prevented a massacre of the Jews in their district. You see, my child, in France, the hatred of the Jews by the monarchy goes back at least four hundred years."

"Father Madrosh, it cannot still be that way, can it?" Her breathing quickened and became uneven.

Madrosh lowered his head, as if the shame was his own. "You may recall that when we entered the city, we passed through the wall built by Philip Augustus. Upon his coronation, just about two hundred years ago, he issued an order compelling the arrest of all the Jews in France. It has been said the arrests occurred on a Saturday, when the Jews were in synagogue. Everything they owned was confiscated. Their valuables, their investments, their precious metals—all of it went into the king's treasury. Their lands, houses, and barns were all converted into gold and silver, and all of it went to Philip."

Irina sought a place against which to lean, the weight of Madrosh's words pressing her hard. *Have we made the right decision, then?*

"Then, not twenty years later, he reversed his thinking when it occurred to him that the financial skills of the Jews would be even more valuable to him. At once, he issued edicts favorable to the Jews— similar to the ones in Poland. This was not done because Philip had become penitent. Rather, his reasoning was that it would enable him to tax all their activities. In effect, he made them serfs. The Jews and their possessions were the property of the king and his barons. The king even had a separate treasury account recorded and called "*Produit des Juifs*—Proceeds of the Jews." That is why so much is known about this period."

Irina shook her head, as if in disbelief. "And still today, Madrosh?"

"In the same years the Council of Vienna met, France's King Philip the Fair exiled all the Jews and put himself in their place. That is to say, he commanded that all the proceeds from their financial dealing be given to him. It is true that King Louis rescinded those orders not many years later, but there were many conditions attached. The Jews had to pay the king a substantial fee just to return, and only a small percentage of their business profits could remain with them. They were required to wear a circular badge which would identify them for all. Yet it is always the same. It is always about greed."

"But today, Madrosh?" exclaimed Irina with impatience, searching for a different answer.

"I know, my dear, that your impatience is not with me. In your voice, I hear you searching for some hope your chosen home will not be like Poznan. Yet I should tell you," he said, placing his hand over her forearm in a most gentle way, "never be deceived by the looks and charm of a place. The more gild, the more guilt, I have come to believe."

"It's just that..."

"I know, dear Irina, it's just that you have a concern about your son." He lowered his eyes. "I am given to understand that the laws remain in effect today," he said gently. "That is why you see no sign of Jews in Paris. They simply do not exist here."

"What is it about the French?"

Madrosh shrugged. "I do not know the answer, My Lady. The French, the Germans, the Poles—they all have a distaste for the Jews in one way or another, but the Poles seem a bit less so."

"Why is that?"

"Poland, whatever it is today or will be tomorrow, has been conquered by so many, the race has melded like so many metal nuggets over a hot fire—they are tempered and strong, not by force of arms, but in their faith and perseverance. The Jews will exist there forever, I suspect."

"My little Stashu exists here," she said defiantly.

"Yes, he does, Irina, and that is why you must forever keep your secret."

. . .

Father Taddeus Shimanski found himself the center of all activity at the Sts. Peter and Paul Cathedral as the Advent season progressed. There was much to do, after all. The people of the city wanted to celebrate as never before. They had lived to the end of a year that had brought the Great Mortality, the departure of their duke, and, more recently, the death of their bishop.

As he walked through the nave of the great church, a familiar figure entered the main doors. This time, Father Shimanski thought to himself with a smile, the man was not running, and he knew to shut the cold out behind him.

"Father Shimanski," Jerzy Andrezski called out, "a word with you."

"Yes, *Pan* Andrezski." He laughed. "Now all of Poznan knows why you were so curious about our glass!"

"Hah!" Andrezski chortled. "I've not forgotten how helpful you've been, Father, and I've come back to receive your counsel once again."

"Oh?" responded the surprised but flattered priest.

The two of them moved toward the sacristy at the rear of the church and found seats next to the glowing embers in the fireplace there. "Father Kaminski, Abbot of St. Stephen's Monastery in the Silesian woods, suggested I see you."

"Ah, yes! My friend Karol. But why to me?"

"Father Kaminski has become concerned the glass work is taking his men from their mission of prayer and service to the poor. You see, Father, orders have increased and the monks cannot keep up with them. They cannot take on any more work even though workmen and artisans have appeared to help them. They are not enough."

Father Shimanski laughed. "But I have no monks for you, *Pan* Andrezski!"

Jerzy chuckled in return. "I understand, Father, but your friend believes you may know of an area somewhere east of the city where I could establish another factory."

The Vicar did not respond immediately, but asked a few questions about the requirements of such a project. Upon a few moments' reflection, he said, "Why, of course!" Then he was silent for a moment remembering the lie he told the bishop—or, rather, the information he kept from him.

"Of course?"

"The Great Mortality spared nearly all of those in my home village, but the dry summer brought them a poor harvest there. With the beech forests nearby, and plenty of sand within a day's walk, the men might be happy for a new trade. Your business would be a godsend."

"Just where might this be, Father?"

"Why, just a few miles east of Poznan. In the village of St. Michael."

...

Christmas in Paris had been magical for the Brezchwa family. High Mass, with glorious choirs singing the joyous hymns of the season, thrilled Irina like no celebration before it. For the first time since she discovered she was pregnant, she felt safe. Though she missed Berek Joselewicz, the hole in her heart was at least partially filled by the delightful infant he had fathered and the man now beside her. That she loved her husband was not in doubt, but he was not her first love, and for reasons she could not understand, Berek was still with her, as if he would return someday. That she was content with her circumstances was what she made those around her world believe.

It should have come as no surprise to the Brezchwas, however, that their comfortable surroundings could not be theirs indefinitely. A polite messenger from the Vicomte D'Orléans, the king's chancellor, paid the apartment a visit a week before the great feast and informed them with the greatest regret and courtesy they would need to vacate their chambers in the *Palais de la Cité* one week after the departure of Duke Zygmunt for Poland.

Then the young messenger delivered better news. The Holy Roman Emperor had done more for them than present little Stashu with an expensive bauble, it seemed. His influence had secured for their use a small chateau and farm in the village of Giverny, north of Paris. It was a part of the countryside she and Jan had come to love. True, they could use the residence for but a year, but it would be just what they needed to establish themselves as citizens of France.

No small consolation was the final announcement from chancellor's messenger. The pair had been nominated to become *le Comte* and *la Comtesse* Brezchwa at Christmas season ceremonies.

It had been a remarkable day, but as she thought about her new national home, her feelings were truly bittersweet. Though she loved her native Poland and its people, she could never erase what had happened to her there, that love for the Joselewiczes had no more depth than the thickness of their skin. She was happy in this land new to her, and despite what Madrosh had imparted about the Jews, she did not foresee a fearful future, her constant vow being that nothing would happen to the infant she now held close.

Whatever misgivings she might have had, she dismissed, literally, with the blink of an eye. She picked up the large blue square of wool and smiled as she surveyed its new countenance. A clever seamstress she'd encountered in the palace knew exactly how to make a peasant's cape into a noblewoman's wrap. The older woman seemed curious about what Lady Irina was doing with such a piece of material, but she worked magic incorporating it into a beautiful garment befitting the beautiful young woman from the distant east.

As Irina and Madrosh stepped through the *porte cochère* of *Le Palais,* she wrapped herself tightly so that she might not chill. They spoke with each other warmly and in the spirit of the season as they began one of their last hours together.

"Madrosh," she began, as they crossed into the *Jardins du Roi*—Gardens of the King, just on the point of the island, "I have told myself I must ask you large questions, monuments to your wisdom!"

"My dear Lady, you embarrass me. None of our talks have centered on the trivial. You have always managed to ask very large questions and have summed up my words with great insight. It is in your presence that I tremble," he added with a benign smile, "because I never know how you might challenge me. I'll wager, you have one of those questions for me now. So, come now," he teased, "out with it!"

Also embarrassed, she hesitated. "It's not so much a question, really," she began. "We started out talking about God, and yes, you have convinced me there must be such a being. You have explained to me about the soul—my soul—and yes, I begin to understand what that might mean. I might also consider that man may not be intrinsically good—otherwise, God would have a very easy time of it, would He not? And there would have been little point to His creation."

She raised her hand, wanting to continue. "It seems, then, that if man is truly an infinitely varied mix of good and evil, the gift of the Commandments has forced men to make a deliberate choice toward the good—out of fear, if nothing else. What that means," she continued, as Madrosh eyed her in astonishment, "is that man is either intrinsically good with an outward appearance of good or evil, or he is intrinsically evil but doing good only for the observation of others. Or perhaps, Madrosh, there is that third choice to which you apparently subscribe—man is a mix of good and evil at his core and how he comports himself in his everyday life." She paused for effect. "So, Madrosh, which is it? More important, why does it all matter?"

Madrosh laughed out loud. Seeming to spill into the Seine itself, his laughter carried across the beautiful, leafless gardens of the king. Irina laughed too, though she wasn't sure why.

"You have listened well, My Lady. And it appears that in the countless quiet hours of caring for your infant, you have thought much about our conversations. Let's consider."

They walked and talked, their faces reddening in the cold. The winter air did nothing to impede their footfall or intrude upon their words. If anything, their spirited talk brought them immense warmth.

"Remember, Irina, I did not say my view was correct, nor is it one necessarily upheld by the church. Yet, in my limited understanding, what you yourself have concluded seems to make the order of things more sensible. You asked why it is important.

"It all matters," he went on, "because we are not talking about some fairy world that is not real and does not exist. We are real and we exist. The same is true for what surrounds us. It matters because it helps us make our way through life if we can discern even a glimmer of why things are the way they are.

"I believe that just as man is the mix of good and evil you described, in all spaces around us, God and Satan constantly battle for our souls. I happen to believe most fervently it is God who triumphs over evil in the long run of things, but in day-to-day life, evil wins many skirmishes. How can that be? It is not because God is weak or impotent against evil, but because we freely make choices for evil."

"And you said," Irina hurried to ask, "that we are accountable for the choices we make when we have the ability to see what is right?"

"Yes, and I believe that is most important. God cannot expect us to be perfect as He is perfect. Yet He expects us to live up to what we understand, fighting our own battles against the corruption of evil.

That is why scholars say we are created in God's image and likeness."

"Is that hesitation in your voice that I hear, Madrosh?"

"Yes, My Lady. Most church theologians abide by that view because it's in Scripture."

"Yet?"

"You see, original Scripture was in Hebrew or Greek, and Christ spoke in Aramaic. The church speaks in Latin and at this moment, you and I are speaking in Polish.

"A tower of Babel, wouldn't you say?"

The priest chuckled. "Indeed, My Lady. Some words in some languages do not easily pass into other tongues with the same sense, the same meaning. I can, however, agree with the church because the word 'image' most certainly could be translated by the word 'intelligence.' That is to say, when God created man, in his image, that does not mean we look like the Almighty, of course. That would be an insult and truly arrogant of man to think so."

"Just a moment, Madrosh. You mentioned Scripture, yet in all of our talks, you have rarely seasoned your words with those of the Old and New Testaments. Why is that?"

Madrosh threw his head back and once more, laughed heartily. "Ah, My Lady, you have caught me!"

"How so?"

"Our conversations started because you had serious questions about the existence of Almighty God. It would have been too easy to spout lines from the Bible and dare you to contradict them. So many times, churchmen make grand biblical pronouncements and expect their listeners to accept them without reservation—without a moment's further thought. So, you see, I thought it best to talk about our God in everyday terms—hopefully using the power of reason to clear your thinking. *Nie?*"

"A good answer, good Father." Irina smiled broadly. "Now let's see how you grapple with the question of our being created in God's image and likeness."

"I can see you won't let me escape so easily. Here's what it gets down to: God gave us the power to think and to reason, however imperfectly, so most assuredly, he did not give us a duplicate of his own intelligence, did he? Yet that power to see things clearly, to discern right and wrong—well, that is an ability given to no other living thing, so when we talk about being in the image of God, we must think in terms of 'intelligence.' That's the only way it all makes sense."

"And?

"Ah! Now we come to the notion of God's 'likeness.' Just as the word 'image' doesn't necessarily mean what the word ordinarily conveys to people, the same is true with the more troublesome word 'likeness.' If 'likeness' means God gave us the additional gift of a love of virtue or righteousness, that may also be true, however imperfect once again." He paused. "And therein lies the problem. You and I seem to have understood that man is born with infinitely varying degrees of good and evil. Man's individual nature, his or her individual self, and in that respect, our resemblance to the Almighty must be like a very poor reflection in an infinitely rippling pond. By definition, God is perfectly good. Alas, we are not."

"And man's soul?"

"If we are like God in any way whatsoever, it is nothing less than the soul reflecting the essence of God. The soul is where we may find the beauty of man in God's image."

. . .

Not for the first time did Father Shimanski wrestle with his instincts. For the decade he had served under Bishop Tirasewicz, Shimanski knew his earthly master was ill-suited to the church, yet he had taken a vow of obedience, not to the bishop, but to the church. That in itself helped the vicar define his role. He'd made his own vow to become the bishop's softer face to the people of Poznan, but most often, his plan failed, inasmuch as the bishop's vile disposition managed to show through any guise his vicar might put forth.

On the one hand, he could follow the late bishop's example and enjoy an earthly life of ease for as long as he dared. On the other hand, he could do what he knew he should do, and that was to serve God and his people in the best ways he knew.

It was the latter instinct that moved him to assist Andrezski, the man whose wares destroyed his bishop, however much at fault he was for his own demise. Andrezski was obviously well-skilled in mercantile pursuits, Shimanski had to admit, and his generosity to the Dominican Sisters and many others in the city was already well known. The man's desire to expand his business could only serve to better the lives of more people.

And so the day after Christmas, Father Shimanski and Jerzy Andrezski, along with a few others, including old Wodowicz, crossed *Ostrow Tumski,* passed over the Mary and Joseph Bridge, rode up the Fareway, and along the road to Gniezno. Their horses turned on the road to St. Michael and within a short time they reached their destination, winter winds howling across their path a good part of the way.

Father Shimanski conferred with the parish priest there and led his group to a farm on the edge of the village, where his cousins were at work in the barn. Within minutes, Andrezski was introduced to Edouard and Peter Kwasniewski.

Andrezski was dumbfounded, and for the moment, completely forgot why he had come to St. Michael. "It cannot be!" he exclaimed, his tone of voice catching Father Shimanski unawares. "Is this the same Kwasniewski family to which belongs a little Zuzanna Kwasniewska?"

"Indeed," Father Shimanski said, satisfied with his conscience.

As if by magic, the faces of the Kwasniewski brothers lit up like candles at High Mass. Edouard spoke first. "Zuzanna is our littlest sister. She left here in May with our parents and the rest of the family, and we never saw them again. The Great Mortality did not take them, then?"

Andrezski was as direct as he could be. "I met your family on the way to Poznan. We talked and laughed for several miles, in fact. The last I saw them—though I never learned their name or where they were from—they were in Srodka walking toward the bridge, and...and I never saw them again." He took a breath and cleared his throat. "The nuns at the Church of the Heart of Jesus found Zuzanna wandering in Srodka, they told me, and they took her to the convent. When I lay sick in the same convent, it was little Zuzzie who gave me water when

I was thirsty. Your littlest sister saved my life!"

The brothers tried to smile but seemed to grapple with the other reality. "Little Zuzzie will have to be our miracle," Edouard asserted.

"You came here to tell us about her?" Peter inquired, incredulously.

"No," Andrezski responded sheepishly. "In truth, I did not know of a tie between Father Shimanski and you," he laughed, "and then, between you and Zuzzie."

"When can we see Zuzzie with our own eyes?" asked Edouard.

Peter held up a hand to get their attention. "*Pan* Andrezski, do you mean to say only Zuzzie survived?"

"You have a sister, Irina, *nie?* She also survived, the nuns have said."

Peter and Eduoard spoke, one interrupting the other. "Irina alive? Can it be?"

"Yes," Jerzy assured them. "Mind you, I have not seen her myself, brothers. According to the nuns, she came to the convent on her own and expecting a child. After she left, Zuzzie appeared, and sometime later, one of the nuns realized they were sisters."

The brothers sat down, disbelieving their ears.

Andrezski told them what else he had heard.

Peter spoke up. "But why would anyone take a simple farmgirl to Paris?"

Jerzy shrugged his shoulders, acknowledging his own lack of answers and understanding. Then he remembered something else. "Sister Luke did say Irina appeared to be a woman of wealth, and that she had her own servant girl with her."

Edouard's face defined disbelief.

Peter said, "That couldn't have been Irina, then. I just don't believe it was her." To him, it was final.

Andrezski then explained to the brothers the real reason for his visit. Over two hours and a bit of bread and cheese washed down by a home brew, they discussed the possibilities, and everyone agreed St. Michael could be an ideal place to make glass.

By mid-afternoon, the visitors needed the remaining light to return to Poznan. They parted, but not before assuring the Kwasniewskis they would be back—with little Zuzzie.

CHAPTER XV

1378

No Christmas season would ever warm Tomasz Wodowicz. He'd long before abandoned faith in man or God, and his dealings with his supposed representative here on earth—as Bishop Tirasewicz was wont to remind him and everyone else—gave him the all the proof he needed that the world he knew was all about might and money. Nothing else mattered.

This had been the first Christmas, however, that he could provide a feast for himself, thanks to the departed bishop. In an out-of-the-way inn on the edge of Poznan, he had supped well and paid for the best ale, despite curious stares from the innkeeper. He had done all of this in solitude, a state in which he'd spent most of his life.

While he enjoyed the companionship of Big Franciszek, it was true, he never felt he was with someone. Franciszek was a gamepiece to play with, maneuver to his liking, and otherwise pay no heed. Where was the big man now, Tomasz wondered? And what about Duke Sokorski. The duke being alive and expected in Poznan in the spring suggested the Hungarians never existed, that he and Franciszek had just imagined them. *And that can't be!* Sokorski and the impostor of a noblewoman should be dead! He scratched his head and ordered more ale.

As he fell asleep that night, his saddlebag clutched to his chest in what passed for a private room at the inn—something he'd never experienced before—his head swirled with all sorts of notions, and by the time he woke the next morning, a plan had already begun to take form. If that peasant woman, Irina Kwasniewska, could pass herself off as a minor noblewoman with a little money and better clothing, couldn't he do the same?

Retrieving his horse from the inn's stable, he mounted up and continued to think about how he might change himself. Oblivious to the cold and the wispy flakes of snow filling the air, he set out for St. Stephen's. As his horse trod on, the snow thickened and deepened, so much so that if he hadn't been traveling a well-worn track, he'd have lost himself within the white unknown.

By midday, concern edged its way into his thoughts. The notion of making a shelter of pine boughs and building a fire in the snow had no appeal whatsoever. Resting alone in the woods was an invitation for a wolf pack to sup on him, and that thought alone spurred him to keep going. He did not stop, and as the snow rose nearly to the horse's knees, concern turned to alarm.

He had no choice but to plod on. Before daylight began to ebb, however, he began to believe in the God he had forsaken. There could never be a God, he'd learned to believe, who would let him be born into squalor, and live no better than a barnyard pig. No matter what the priests said, God was just something to fear, and in his everyday life, there were too many others to fear. And yet, unless his senses betrayed him, he felt sure he was inhaling wisps of chimney smoke. Smoke from a cookfire. Smoke from a dwelling.

He kept going, letting hope and horse guide him as the heavy snow dragged the smoky air closer to the ground, closer to him. A miracle! Or perhaps it was just luck. Finally, his horse led him to a wide clearing and he could just make out a line of huts in the disappearing light. All were dark and quiet but one. On his right, there stood the village's largest building, and from a window opening, a soft glow peeked around the waxed cloth used to keep out the weather.

Deep snow silenced his movements, giving him the advantage of surprise. He dismounted a few feet from the only entry he could see, and without thinking twice about it, pounded on the door just as someone with authority might do. In a moment, an old man leaning on a stick peered out.

"Open up, old man! Don't you see I am a traveler in need of shelter?"

"Indeed, sir. Come inside. *Prosze.*"

Wodowicz pushed past the man and saw he was not alone. A young boy stood close to the fire glowing on the hearth, fear a gleam in his eyes. He ignored the boy. "What is this place, *Pan?* Where am I?"

Apparently surprised by his question, the old man said, "Why, you are in Wozna, good sir, except that this boy and I are the only ones left from the plague."

Wodowicz took a step back, remembering his death sentence from Duke Sokorski.

There ensued a small conversation about the place before the old man said, "And you can see, good sir, we have little food to offer, but there is shelter for you and your horse."

"Never you mind, my man. I am provisioned."

The boy ran to the door.

"Where are you going?" the old man asked through his broken teeth.

"To get the man's horse, *Dzjadzja*—Grandfather," came the respectful response.

"I'll go with you," Wodowicz said quickly. "You see to the horse," he spoke, ordering the boy, "and I'll see to my saddlebag."

Returning within a few minutes, they were warming themselves by the fire, when the old man said, "I am called Jozef and the boy is Padasz. He is my grandson."

"Padasz?"

"Yes, he was born in a rainstorm," he chuckled. "And from whence do you come, good sir?"

"From Poznan. I remember your village from another time, Josef, but did not recognize it in the storm, and," he hesitated, "without people."

"Yes. It has been hard, but we scavenged what dried vegetables were left by the others, and since the spring past, we've had a bit of grain brought to us by the monks and their merchant when they pass through."

"Merchant, you say?"

"Why, yes. *Pan* Andrezski and his men come through here with their glass wagons. The monks are generous to us."

"Why, of course!" He thought a bit. "How often do they pass?" he asked with the same interest any passing traveler might have.

"At least once a week, but with this weather, it may not be for a while." The old man cleared his throat, politely. "And you are, sir?"

"I am," Wodowicz stopped, unsure what to say next. "I am," he repeated, "Squire Krawcyk." It was a name he'd heard was used by people living east of Poznan, and probably unknown to the old man.

"Then welcome, *Pan* Krawcyk. You may stay as long as you wish."

"Indeed I will, Josef. I will stay the winter and pay you well—on one condition."

Surprised, Josef stammered, "To be sure, Squire. To be sure."

"I seek rest and refuge and don't care much for socializing with travelers, no matter who they are. From time to time, I may break my silence and converse with those passing through, but only at my choice."

Josef nodded.

"Are you sure you understand? Make sure the boy does, too."

"Indeed, Squire." He nodded again, resolutely.

Wodowicz liked the sound of the title. In a moment, Wodowicz—Tomasz the Terrible—had become Squire Krawcyk. He decided to be magnanimous in sharing a bit of veal and pork with his innkeeper. The old man produced some ale and stale bread, and given what would have been his chances in the snowstorm, Wodowicz—Squire Krawcyk—relished the feast before him.

1379

Winter never seemed an auspicious time for travel, but the day had arrived for Duke Zygmunt Sokorski to depart for Poland. Along with the Feast of the Three Kings culminating the Christmas season, the Poles who had come to know each other intimately over eight months now had the far less joyful duty of bidding each other farewell.

In their time and place, Irina—and everyone else—commonly understood life was indeed, tenuous, and one must make the most of every moment. Sudden death from an unseen malady, from the violence of battle, or from the vagaries of cruel injustice—was an everyday occurrence. And so it was such a reality that came to Irina and Madrosh when, two days after Epiphany, after all the religious symbolism and pageantry had concluded, the caravan of horses, carts, and carriages was readied in the courtyard of the *Palais de la Cité*.

Wrapped in the repurposed blue woolen cape that reminded her of when she and Madrosh first met, Irina stood in the stone archway observing the leave-takings. They were intense and laborious with every precaution being taken for the safety and survival of the travelers. There had been thought of waiting until spring to make their journey, but the season of new life was also a time for battle and death. Though the weather might be treacherous for them, it would be less menacing than men lying in wait.

Men stamped their feet in the packed snow and horses pushed out great cloudy breaths while they awaited their masters' commands. The duke, Jan, and all the others savored their partings, often teary-eyed and sentimental, as they bid one another, *"Bonne chance!"*

Although Irina had developed warmer feelings for the duke, the man he had been in Poznan and the good Christian he seemed now gave her pause. There was something about him that made his repentance seem a shallow pond, not the deep lake it ought to be. Even so, they embraced, and she thanked him for his generous patronage.

Then she watched as Duke Zygmunt mounted his horse at the same moment Madrosh came out of the keep and faced his protégé. The two eyed each other like a pair of pups happy in the presence of one another. Their relationship had been natural and proper, but deep, even though they knew they were an unlikely pair.

"Words do not come to me, Master Madrosh."

"Ah, Master it is now, is it?" Madrosh riposted as lightheartedly as his emotions would allow, his voice quavering.

"Of course it will always be you who is truly master to me and many others. And so, Madrosh, with what words will we part?"

"I could have many, my dear *Comtesse,*" he said with a broad smile, "but many we have already had, have we not? We have exchanged more in months than many do in years." After a moment, he continued. "Aside from all the warm compliments I might pay you this day—and which you know are in my heart—I do have one thought to leave you that might sum up so much of our many talks."

"We shall exchange the same compliments in the same way, then." She bowed in sincere humility. "And what are the words that flutter over this farewell, then?"

"When we last talked, that cold day in the gardens by the Seine, you'll remember we touched on God's eternal battle with evil."

"Yes, I recall it well. It seemed we were not quite finished."

The priest nodded. "It is just this—not an answer but a question." He looked directly into Irina's bright blue eyes. "If we agree that evil exists only because we *let* it exist, then could it be true that God must contend with it *because* of us?" He let the question hang.

Madrosh placed a hand on each of Irina's shoulders, bent down, and kissed her on the forehead. "It is a terrible question with which to leave you, but having come to know you, I suspect you equal to the challenge. You will understand the answer when it comes. May God bless you, my child," he intoned, his right hand raised, and made the sign of the cross over her. Just then, Irina reached out a hand and placed it on his arm. "Wait, Madrosh! I know that answer. It leaves me no hope. There must be more you can say."

Already turning, Madrosh checked himself. He looked deeply into her eyes. "If one accepts the existence of God, then one must accept the reality of hope. It is why we talk about salvation, in part through the sacrament of confession. We acknowledge our sins, accept responsibility for them, and pledge not to sin again. This is the central tenet of all belief in God, Irina: We must try to be good, be better than we are, and we so commit ourselves. Yes, it is that. We can be better than we are."

Irina nodded. She remained quiet, and smiled in both gratitude and sadness. Tears streamed down her cheeks, but she said nothing, her silence sealing what was in her heart.

Jan and Madrosh held one another in warm embrace. Then Jan

stood next to his wife and held her tight.

Light snow fell as Madrosh mounted a beautiful white mare and steadied himself. Then Duke Zygmunt clasped his heavy cloak around him and together, heading their procession, they rode slowly away from the palace, toward the same gate through which they all had entered Paris months before.

. . .

With little time after the holidays to pack their things and make final arrangements for their move from Paris to Giverny, they were at the mercy of the bitter weather descending upon them. What they soon came to know was that the small chateau and farm at Giverny was in a poor state of repair and hardly a residence, except for the four-footed kind. The previous occupant, Jan had been told, had so angered King Charles that he paid for his insult to royalty with his head, and the poor man's family had to leave hurriedly.

Yet the place was theirs—even if just for a year—and they were glad to be gone from castle intrigue, infidelity, and indolence. With Rosta, Velka, and a team of workmen, they spent two months in the biting cold restoring the interior to a level of civility and cleanliness acceptable to *Comtesse* Brezchwa.

In the unheated January air, Irina and Velka were vigorous in their labors, making Chateau Fournier both habitable and clean. Once, sitting near the one small fire they built for themselves, they were sipping tea when Velka said, "I want to tell you about something that has bothered me."

"Yes? Rarely do you *ask* to speak—usually, you blurt out what bothers you."

"Be glad they are gone, My Lady."

"What? How can you say that, Velka? Madrosh is very dear to me."

"Not the good Father, My Lady. Not Duke Zygmunt."

"Then what? Or who?"

"King Wenceslas. Or rather, one of his knights."

"What about him?"

"You and the other one great with child—you had little to fear.

And I, plain looking that I am, also had little worry, but not so other women, married or not."

"What do you mean, Velka?"

"You are naïve, if I may say so, Irina. One of the knights was like a wolf in the woods where women were concerned and he did not care whether they were interested in his attention. His king, Wenceslas, seemed not to notice. Or care. Many are glad to see their backs, but will not speak of what they were made to do."

. . .

Another problem Irina had not wished to face presented itself most clearly as the year began. The weeks of basking in royal largesse were over, and the couple needed to find a prosperous livelihood as their wedding gifts, along with Irina's cache of Joselewicz gold and silver, would not last forever. Continued court life would be costly, especially since Jan preferred to remain a military professional in service to royalty, but Irina discovered that often, such was a poor existence. All the more so, she came to understand, because they were living in France—but were not French. She and Jan complemented each other well, but because of who they were and where they were, *livres* were not going to grow in their orchard.

They had to find some venture in which they could invest, yet manage its affairs closely, using their talents accordingly. Weeks went by while Irina and her reluctant husband debated the possibility of a business with Antoine Chevalle. One conversation stood out.

"Irina, he is rough, uncouth—unsuitable to represent the pieces so beautifully wrought by his hands," Jan had said. "And you, my dear, object to his use of black men so."

"Yes, but perhaps we can change some aspects of his business—a craft you found fascinating, as I recall."

"I did, indeed, but as you'll also remember, Chevalle said his business was not doing well—a fact he did not care to hide."

"Do you suspect it is doing poorly because he has one little sign off the road in Giverny? No one of wealth would find him, or having found him, venture into his shop—except someone like you, dear husband."

"You are *correcte, Madame,* and I bow to your observations. I must admit he has no one like us to present his work in the right royal circles."

"And there is one other thing, *Comte* Brezchwa," she had said with a charm she had almost forgotten, "and that is this: He is French, and his name will be important for all the wrong reasons."

"I bow once more, my *Comtesse,*" he said, and leaned closer for a most passionate kiss.

With Velka there to care for little Stashu, she and Jan repaired to their chamber for an afternoon of lovemaking neither had yet experienced with one another. Alone and in the great bed, it was clear to her the boyish Jan had never been with a woman before, but somehow, he knew exactly how to please her. His hands were soft and knowing, and his lips had their own knowledge. Later, they saw one another in a different, most fulfilling way for the first time. Their smiles, their tender words spoke volumes—without words—to tell each other there were no regrets.

· · ·

St. Michael lay quiet as heavy flakes began to cover the deep layer of snow already there. The horse made the sleigh's polished wooden runners glide across the packed surface, and the ride from Poznan went quickly.

Zuzanna sat snuggled next to *Pan* Andrezski in a large, thick blanket, and only her little face poked out to meet the wind as the horse pulled them along. Soon, they were in sight of the Kwasniewski farm, and Jerzy could see she had not forgotten her home. "My house! Is Mama there? Papa?"

Hearing the horse's bells, Peter and Edouard came running out. Jerzy stayed in the sleigh watching as the brothers hugged and kissed their only link with a family now vanished. All three of them little children again, they ran around making circles in the snow, laughing and crying all at once.

Jerzy tried to smile, but his feelings were mixed, as he knew his own relationship with Zuzzie would change. In truth, he was jealous, but it had been his own long-ago choice not to marry and have children. He refused to look back.

All went inside and sipped a boiled chicken broth by the fire. The Kwasniewskis continued their playful reunion and Zuzzie seemed happy to find the crude wooden toys all the children had used, dirty and wet from the weather though they were. Then she seemed to lose herself in her memories, wondering aloud where everyone had gone. Though in her childhood home, she walked the two rooms as a stranger, looking and poking around, but not wishing to return to its emptiness. Though warmed by the fire, she seemed chilled.

The men pushed melancholy aside and turned to business. It was Eduoard who spoke first. "Peter and I have talked with the others around St. Michael about what you propose. My grandfather told me about the times when summers were long and warm with just enough rain. Those were good times for farmers, but not so much now. The growing months are drier than in times past. Winters have become harsh and long. It's not the same now. So, for us, your proposition makes sense. We agree on the partnership we discussed, and despite the weather, we will begin the work you want us to do." Peter nodded.

"That is good news, indeed," Jerzy said with a smile. "Will it be alright, then, if I send *Pan* Wodowicz back next week with a few others to make preparations and give instruction?"

"That will be fine." Both brothers laughed. "Felling beech trees will keep us warm! There is little to do here in winter, so the work will fill our days."

"*Bardzo Dobrze!*" Jerzy gave them his broadest smile.

"The old man Wodowicz and the others can stay with us," Edouard added. At that, all three men remembered Zuzzie, playing quietly near the fire. The question hung in the air, unspoken.

"As to little Zuzzie," Jerzy volunteered, adding a smile to his words, "this might not be a good place for the little one. The nuns will keep her when no one is here to watch over her."

"No fear there," Eduoard said. "When I am here, she will be fine."

"And she will grow up soon enough," Peter added. "*Pan* Andrezski, I still find it hard to believe what you told us the last time—that our sister, Irina, a wealthy woman with child, can be one and the same."

"Peter! Edouard!" Zuzzie called. "Where are *Matka i Ojciec*? I want to see my brothers and sisters," she cried plaintively.

"Ah, little Zuzzie. They are not here," Peter said truthfully. "They went to heaven."

Zuzzie stared at them, thinking. "But not Irina?"

. . .

As a married pair, *Comte* and *Comtesse* Brezchwa lived a comfortable but hardly lavish existence in Chateau Fournier—still being renovated—and Irina, for one, knew time was not their true friend.

When a brief warm spell appeared, the two of them gathered a picnic lunch, and coached the two miles or so to the road on which Antoine Chevalle kept his shambling business. As always, little Stashu was with them. Chevalle did not warm to the boy, they noticed.

Before then, Jan and Irina had visited with the crusty Chevalle on several occasions, and he always refused their offerings of cheese, bread, and a jug of table wine. Nevertheless, the pair enjoyed seeing the men at their craft. They kept their welcome by buying several pieces of their work.

Keeping his distance from what he often referred to as "Paris wealth," Chevalle refused them contact with his men, the blacks who kept his fires going in the steamers, hauled his wood, and performed tasks at an apprentice level. "Don't want to teach them too much, or let them get the wrong idea," he had once said.

At one point in the visit, Jan cleared his throat over the hammering and chiseling, and said, "*Monsieur* Chevalle, Lady Brezchwa and I believe there may be a possibility for an arrangement of mutual satisfaction were we to partner with you."

As if struck, Chevalle took a step backward and shook his head with some vehemence. "What could I possibly gain by an association with the likes of you?"

"No need to be rude, Chevalle," Irina said with a brusqueness that shocked her listeners. "My husband and I have been by here seven or eight times since our first meeting, and except for one occasion, we have yet to see anyone here to buy."

"You are wrong, *Madame*. As I told you, my business is my business and it is just fine."

"Have it your way, Chevalle, and we will watch you slowly starve. And these men?"

"They will starve first."

"And that will satisfy you?" Irina paused to let her words settle in to the cabinetmaker's hardwood head. "What should satisfy you will be food on your table, a woman who will put up with you, and more than a few *sous* in your pocket."

"And what would you have to do with what's in my pocket?" He smirked.

"When you stop being an ignorant fool, I will tell you." Irina sat on the only stool within reach, pulled Stashu up to her lap, and waited.

As if the air had deflated a giant bag, Chevalle shrugged his shoulders and said, "What is it that you want with a poor carpenter?"

"You are no poor carpenter," Jan said, looking around his shop. "You are a master at your trade, but no one knows of you."

"What we want," Irina said, "is your skill and your French name."

"And what do I get for that?"

"You get to live a decent life with a full belly in front of a warm fire when winter comes. In trade, Chevalle, my husband and I will sell your work to those who will appreciate it and can afford it."

"You will sell my cabinets to royalty?"

"Don't be silly, Chevalle! You are good, but not that good—yet. There are many in the nobility who seek fine furnishings at reasonable prices and together, we can satisfy their needs—and our own at the same time."

Chevalle found his own place to sit, and as Jan and Irina could see, he slowly thought through the words he heard. Finally, he stood and offered his hand to Count Brezchwa. "I can agree to that."

"And you can take my hand as well, Chevalle, because you will have to deal with me just as often as my husband."

For a moment, Chevalle didn't know what to say or do, but then he smiled and said, "For us, it is a new day, then. Are you satisfied, *Madame?*"

"Not completely, *Monsieur* Chevalle. We will have no slaves in our business. You must free them."

Chevalle blanched, then inhaled deeply, and finally, shrugged his shoulders, as if in agreement. It was that easy, and Irina wished that all of life's troubles were so readily settled. Their conversation continued for some time, with few details left at issue.

As she and Jan rode back to their residence, they spoke of their concerns about Chevalle, but put them aside in the hope that a real business venture, properly played, could make them a good living—at least one good enough to enjoy their lives in a setting like Chateau Fournier. As they strolled on, Irina said, "This will not be as easy as we first thought, my husband."

"Why do you think so?"

"He will be stubborn about his men, I think—until he has enough money for himself to be comfortable."

"That I see—and it is likely true of most of us, I'm afraid."

"You are wise to understand that, Jan, but there will be other difficulties as well—though we have many court acquaintances, there are few we know well enough to have them introduce us. Sadly, our best friends went back east. We must think of a way to advance our business without being seen as doing business. Do you see my meaning?"

"Yes, I think I do."

Nearer to Chateau Fournier, she had to admit she wasn't sure if she was attracted to the venture because of its promise of success or because it offered the opportunity to exact a justice. As for the first, she needed the business to live. As for the second, she needed it to live with herself. For the Jews, for the blacks, for those spat upon everywhere. As she considered much of mankind's lot in servitude, she vowed to live Madrosh's commandment. Chevalle's slaves made her understand natural law, but for her, divine law was a matter of simple accounting: *What have you done,* God might ask, *with what I have given you?*

...

Two weeks passed with little respite from the storm. Squire Krawcyk made certain the boy cleared a path to the waste pit on a daily basis so that when the denizens of their snow-laden dwelling needed to relieve themselves, it was not impossible. Each morning, he had watched the boy pitchfork the heavy snow over his shoulders, left and right, until the top of the snow cover was chest high.

It was enough time for his beard and moustache to grow sufficiently thick to nicely mask his appearance. Because woodsy residents often did the same, the old man appeared to think nothing of his guest's gradually changing appearance.

When the snow finally came to an end, so did the reserves of food the old man had been hoarding.

"Well, Josef, that's a problem, *nie*?"

"Indeed, Squire."

"As innkeeper here, how do you propose to feed me?"

"As you see, sir, we have nothing now to feed ourselves."

Silence hung heavy in the smoky room.

"Perhaps we can come to an arrangement?"

"An arrangement?"

"Let me buy your inn, and I will let you and the boy have some of what I still have in my saddlebag. It will be little, but it may see us through."

The old man remained quiet, though the two men knew there was little choice.

Krawcyk laid a gleaming silver coin on the hearth, and the old man stared at it.

Finally, Josef picked it up, his simple action all that was needed to seal the bargain.

Within days, the sun shone bright and clear, and steadily, the outline of the road began to appear. A few days later, the early afternoon brought a sound none had heard in a while: the rumble of big wooden wheels along with the clink of iron rings and leather, the whinnying of laboring horses and shouts from the drivers.

Josef and Padasz stepped out of what had become their cave to greet the familiar faces coming up the road.

"We tarry but briefly," one of the monks shouted as he and his companion descended from the glass-laden rick. "The weather has delayed us for too long, and with a bit of a repast, we will be on our way."

"We have nothing to offer, I am sorry to say, Brother Marcus."

"Not to worry, Josef! We have been worried about you and the boy, and have brought a sack of grain and a few potatoes and another with some salted meat."

"Ah, you are our saviors once again, Brother."

True to their word, the men warmed themselves and enjoyed a bit of food and conversation before relieving themselves and climbing aboard their wagon and waving a farewell.

Squire Krawcyk appeared and said, "You did well, Josef."

"*Djenkuje,* Squire. As it turns out, sir, the monks have saved us and I do not need to sell my inn. Let me return your silver, sir."

"A deal is a deal, Josef. The inn is mine."

"But sir!"

"But nothing, old man. I am not one of the monks who gives you something for nothing. You will adhere to the terms of our arrangement or pay the consequences."

"Yes, Squire," he said, bowing in submission.

"When will they return?

"The monks, sir? Uh, perhaps in a week or ten days."

"Ah! Now I can make my plans."

. . .

Irina came to understand that principles of conscience are easy to fashion, to mouth noble words even, but to practice them, often difficult. What she had also come to believe from the moment she and Velka left the Joselewicz house was that luck went to those who made their own, even though the price of luck was sometimes dear.

Chevalle & Companie was not a success. The parties did not fully understand their roles and what was worse, Jan and Irina did not know the first thing about selling anything to anyone, much less savvy Frenchmen at court. They had no showplace for Chevalle's skills to be on display in a setting most comfortable to the demanding sorts even at the lower rungs on the royal ladder. They were embarrassed at their own arrogance—and ignorance—and Chevalle snickered his disapproval as only he could do.

Although Jan proved himself a fine father—and husband—he was not so diligent a man of business. Stashu was his principal interest, and as the months flew by, he spent less and less time furthering the interests of their struggling firm, much to Irina's disappointment. While she'd have preferred to be the lady of the chateau, she knew the viability of her family—and of the business—would be hers to ensure.

...

Cold sunlight threw itself upon the snowy ground day after day, the result being a shrinking mantle of snow everywhere Tomasz Wodowicz cared to cast his eye. He could hear and see tiny rivulets of water etch the bare spaces on the ground, and noted the icicles clinging to every roof edge in what remained of Wozna. The nights remained bitterly cold, and he was grateful for his lodgings and the old man and the boy he'd made his serfs. He owned them just as he owned the inn.

Out of the frigid, thin breeze, he tried to warm himself where the sun washed the wall against which he leaned. It was a good time to think. Already, he smirked, he'd vastly improved his station in life. When a boy, he had nothing. His mother and the two younger sisters in the family were taken with a bout of plague when he was but six or seven years of age. He had few memories of his childhood, or, he occasionally reminded himself, few that he cared to recall. His father had no interest in him or anything other than his own memories of working with Italian glass men. Whether his father slept at their hovel or elsewhere, Tomasz was left to fend for food, bits of clothing, or sticks for a fire. The assorted rags he'd gathered became a blanket of sorts when he stitched them together using a de-feathered goose quill and yarn he'd stolen.

Some life, he grunted. Not until he ran away and found work at the castle did things begin to change. He thought he'd done pretty well for himself, having risen to become the duke's castellan, but posing as Squire Krawcyk with sufficient silver to speak for him was a much better arrangement.

In the weeks at Wozna, he used the skills of his youth along with cloth scavenged form Wozna's empty buildings to dye and fashion for himself clothing reasonably akin to what a country squire might wear. Leather boots with hose and a linen tunic topped by a hooded shoulder cape would serve him well in Wozna, but in a city like Poznan, he'd have to secure clothing of a costlier kind, including a soft, felt toque to wear in fairer weather. There would be time to obtain accoutrements more authentic, but for now, his nicely trimmed beard and moustache below a clean face and washed and brushed hair above made Squire Krawcyk's presence different, but real.

Wodowicz had been sunning himself for some time when he heard a familiar rumble of wooden wheels slicing their way through the softened earth and making for the inn. Within a few minutes, an empty rick came into view, the horses pulling it producing plumes of warm air from their nostrils as they panted from their labors. Two monks covered in a brownish grey wool sat above them in full control of their beasts and burden.

"Whoa, my mares!" one of the monks shouted, pulling to his chest the four long strands of leather knotted in the horses' bridles. "Where's our Josef?" he asked, giving his listener a curious smile along with his words.

"Josef and Padasz are inside warming the good barley soup we have for you, Brothers."

"And you are?"

"I am Squire Krawcyk, and have sheltered here over the winter, Brother. And what's more, in order to help our two friends inside, I have traded ownership of this humble inn for a piece of silver," he said smiling with pride for their benefit.

The monk who had spoken wrinkled his brow, seemingly dubious of the words he'd just heard. "We didn't know Josef was so much in need," he ventured, choosing his words.

"Most certainly, good Brothers," he said, nodding to both travelers, and changing the subject. "Come inside and warm yourselves."

Once seated with his guests around the one table near the fire, but not the door, under and around which the outside air crept in to steal their meager heat, the men talked while Josef and Padasz served them a hearty soup, bread, and warmed ale. The monks ate with gusto, their heads bent to their bowls, and used chunks of bread to soak up what remained.

"What news of the glassmaking, then?" Squire Krawcyk asked politely.

"Sire Andrezski does well for us," said the taller of the two, much too thin and nearly swallowed by his woolen cocoon. "Not only has he found another place suitable for such work, it is nothing less than a miracle that he and the Kwasniewski brothers found each other."

The squire's ears perked up, like a hunting dog's to a rustle in the leaves. "How so?" Krawcyk leaned toward them, playing with the bread in front of him.

"Do you not want your bread, Squire?" Rotund and not shy, the other monk eyed Krawcyk's doughy possession hungrily.

"It's yours, good Brother—to keep you warm on your journey. You were saying? A miracle?"

"Indeed," the empty-handed monk said while his brother fairly inhaled his quarry. "It must have been the hand of God to bring little Zuzanna together with her brothers."

"Zuzanna?"

"Yes, Squire. Zuzanna gave water to Andrezski while the man lay dying with the plague at the convent. As it happens," he went on with enthusiasm, "she is also sister to Irina Kwasniewska!"

The "squire" was hardly able to control his breath and, in turn, his voice. "Why is that so important?" He knew the answer, but it appeared there was more to know.

"Because the woman, Irina, presented herself to the Dominican Sisters as Lady Kwasniewska from Gniezno. How that could be true no one knows, but there is little doubt, she and the little girl—and the brothers in St. Michael—are all of one family."

Krawcyk's head spun with savory possibilities. "Most interesting," he murmured. For the next part of an hour while the monks rested and thoroughly warmed themselves, he hardly noticed what was happening in the small room daring to call itself an inn.

Over the weeks, he'd thought through his plan over and over. Once satisfied that he could pass for a nobleman's squire—and when the weather had cleared for travel—he would leave Wozna forever to hunt down his first prey: Duke Sokorski. Then a journey to Paris for the prize: the bitch herself, Irina Kwasniewska! She was the impostor, the lover of Jews, who had taken what should have been his.

The monk's revelation changed everything. When he heard the merchant Andrezski had somehow connected himself with two brothers of the same name—and the girl, Zuzanna!—he thought it was too good to be true. He tried not to smile. Big Franciszek had always told him his smile—his smirk—was a dead giveaway.

"By the way, Squire," began the monk too thin for his habit. "Squire Krawcyk?" he repeated when the man across the table seemed lost in thought.

"Yes?"

"You look very familiar to me. Were you by chance a squire in service to Duke Sokorski?"

Krawcyk's heart thrummed with excitement and fear. "Whom did you say, good Brother?"

"Duke Sokorski. Your voice. So familiar to me."

"Surely you're mistaken, Brother. I am from the east, near Gniezno."

The monks merely smiled.

Krawcyk made a note to be very careful with these men, but immediately was drawn back into labyrinth of his mind where a feast of possibilities lay before him. He realized the snowstorm and the inn at Wozna had been his own miracle, one he could not proclaim to the men of God or anyone else. He had been given the gift of time to hide, to rest, to consider—and to change. He couldn't explain it to himself, but knowing now of the little girl's existence made his new plan irresistible.

The bishop's death had given him pleasure, but when it came to settling scores, it was not enough. He noticed the monks eyeing him curiously, and so he raised his cup of ale and toasted Merchant Andrezski's success. Now he had a plan, and as soon as the monks were on their way to St. Stephen's, he would head in the opposite direction.

CHAPTER XVI

1410

As the days marched into summer at Chateau Fournier, longer hours of light meant Velka keeping up with her mistress's standard of cleanliness in all their surroundings. There were no exceptions. Floors, windows, furniture, bedding, and kitchen in particular, where the mice always seemed to find a home.

Irina's challenge was to keep up with her daily routine, yet she had less and less energy to expend on it. Today, Irina lay abed on the main floor, gathering in the chateau's morning sounds, when there was a hard rap at the main door, the head of a metal cane, she thought. Velka's leather shoes clacked across the foyer floor. Then, with the latch undone, the beech door creaked as it opened. Two rooms away, she felt the air move.

"*Monsieur le Docteur Bernard,*" said Velka in a language she never desired to master, "you must speak to her. *Madame* is ill. She fights it."

Irina smiled as she listened to her servant's loud whisper. She could imagine, too, Velka fighting a physical reaction to the doctor's bodily aromatics. In seconds, she would rush ahead to make certain all the windows were thrown open.

The mistress of Chateau Fournier knew she was pale, her vigor at a low ebb. As the doctor entered her private chambers, she motioned him to come closer, much as she detested his lack of hygiene.

At one glance, the portly, aging doctor said, "Have I not told you, *Madame*, that too much personal scrubbing would be dangerous for you?"

"*Monsieur,* you should live in such danger."

The healer shrugged off her sarcasm, said something about the body's defensive layers, and asked after her well-being, then waited.

Irina's breathing came slowly, heavily. "You asked, *Monsieur,* and I will tell you, not that it matters. For the last few months, my stomach has given me some discomfort, but it is not important."

"You must tell me more than that, *Madame,*" he said with impatience.

"When I eat," she sighed, "even a little, I feel very full. It stays with me. And yet I have no appetite. My whole life, *Monsieur,* I have not had this problem. Now it is here—every day."

He nodded, then shrugged his shoulders. After a few more perfunctory questions, he mumbled something to the effect that he had nothing to tell her at the moment. "But I will return," he said cheerily. He gave her no potion to ease her discomfort.

The interview, though short, exhausted her, but upon his departure, the air cleared. With help from Velka, she moved to the chair by the window and gazed across the meadow. At least, she thought, the smelly old man had not asked her to make a life or death decision. She had already made too many of those in her forty-seven years.

She laid her head back, and her eyelids became heavy. She knew she would soon return to an earlier time of both pain and joy. The more she thought about Chevalle, the more she thought about the Dampierre affair and, too, what she later learned happened to Zuzzie. *Ah, Zuzzie!*

1379

The partnership between the Brezchwas and Antoine Chevalle had barely begun when all of France erupted, just as Madrosh had once predicted. The forced but troubled peace ordering their daily lives evaporated when riots began in Paris and did not end for months. Charles's taxes to support his wars against the English had greatly alienated the laboring classes, who, as always, bore the brunt of imperial ambitions.

The people were starving and had no more *livres* to give.

Even so, the king and his nobility suffered little, as Irina and Jan discovered most clearly on one of their visits to court. Neither of them enjoyed their encounters there, especially since marital fidelity, amongst other virtues, seemed to have no place in the royal environs. It was not unusual for each of them—a fresh and attractive young people—to be solicited, even pressured, to surrender their fidelity to one another. Because Irina's natural beauty shone through what little adornment she allowed herself, even at court, her appearance and demeanor seemed to attract men—and women—with little restraint upon convention.

Now that Irina was no longer pregnant, but married, she would be considered a safe conquest by those courtiers who preyed on women like her, wife to a minor noble. Should a pregnancy occur, she was warned by others, the cuckold would take quiet responsibility. She—and Jan—wanted no part of such arrangements.

It wasn't long before one of their court encounters nearly brought about their undoing.

. . .

For Tomasz, the road he'd taken from Wozna was easy for a man on horseback, and south of Poznan, downhill to the cluster of small houses nested along the river's edge. There was a rude inn there where he nighted and made sure he knew the way to St. Michael.

His hope went a bit awry when the innkeeper explained that a person whose skills he sought did not exist in his village. The small, unusually fat and balding man took some time to admit he knew of a woman fitting his need, but she lived a few miles downriver. There, he would find a seamstress to his liking, the man had said after Tomasz purchased bread and sausage to go with his ale.

Upon meeting the woman, he took in her diminutive height and wondered if a race of dwarfs lived in the area.

"What troubles you, good Squire?"

"It's just that so many around here are so small, *Panie.*"

"So be it, then," she said, her thin lips tight. "What can I do for you?"

"Ah! As you can see, I've worn these clothes to their end, I fear, and soon, I will be required to make a more suitable appearance before my duke." The woman took it all in with nary a reaction. "And so I shall require you to fashion me a good set of clothing along with a feathered toque, if you please."

"That will not be a problem, good sir, but not for a 'small' price," she cackled at her own little joke.

He chuckled, but weakly. "But can you do it in the next two days?"

"But sir, that would prove difficult, I'm afraid."

"Just as difficult if I were to pay you double—in good silver?"

She stood, as if in triumph. "Let us make the measurements now, then, and I will work through the night. Extra candles must be included in the price."

"As you say. I shall return in two days' time, then."

He found himself spending a second night in the nameless river village. Well-rested after two sleeps, he rose long before the cock crowed, and downed bread and cheese purloined from the larder. Dressed warmly with a lambskin cape over his back, he secured his horse, crossed the plank bridge over the Warta, and climbed out of the river valley toward St. Michael. All in all, it had been a successful though tedious stop in his journey.

At St. Michael, Tomasz Wodowicz surveyed the snow-covered terrain, taking in its stark contrasts, even in the colorless landscape. The day proved clear and windless, and remained so through noontime when he neared the place where the local priest told him the Kwasniewskis farmed. He was surprised to find whole stands of beech stumps but then remembered someone telling him how important their ashes were to glassmaking.

Reining his horse to a halt, he leaned forward in his saddle to hear the whip and pull of the large two-man saws and the shouts of men at work on the trees. Though some distance away, the sound carried across the flat, barren fields, as Tomasz whispered to the cold air, "If they're in the woods, the girl will be in the farmhouse, *nie?*"

Taking refuge in an apple orchard, he watched and listened intently, as his ruminations centered on acts against him requiring revenge.

For those transgressors, like the bishop, the Kwasniewska woman or any member of her family, and Duke Sokorski, retribution was his dream and obsession. Nothing else mattered.

The bishop, he laughed to himself, had not only done himself in, but had provided a silver stake for him to proceed unhindered in his other quests.

"What shall be, shall be," he murmured. Looking toward the farmhouse, he could see the chimney smoke still drift into the sunlight, and that meant someone was there, perhaps preparing food. And the girl?

It was time.

He took a slow, circuitous route to place himself behind the farmhouse, out of sight of the men working several hundred yards away. It was a mean place, yet he marveled that the bitch, Kwasniewska, had come from such a mud-colored shed not unlike the manger mindless priests told tales about at Christmas.

Near his horse was a copse of bushes, bare of leaves, surrounding the outdoor waste pit where everyone relieved themselves. Behind it and about thirty feet away was another pit, long and rectangular, in which beech logs burned golden hot. He waited.

Within a few moments, he heard the door to the farmhouse, a planked affair on leather hinges, slam open, then closed.

"I'll be right back, *Pan*."

"Don't go near the firepit, little Zuzzie!"

The voice was sweet and gentle, but to whom did it belong? Tomasz keened his hearing, but no other sound came. Around the corner appeared Zuzanna Kwasniewska, wearing nothing but thin leather booties and a woolen shift. Her auburn hair lay still on her shoulders as she walked toward the waste pit.

Tomasz could feel the tingle. The vengeance he'd carried for so many months was about to be satisfied, and he could feel it as fully as he felt the winter air in his chest.

"Why, hello, little one," Wodowicz said, in the warmest voice he could muster.

"Who are you, sir, and what do you want here?" she asked, her tiny voice hinting fear.

In a blink, Tomasz grabbed her and said, "I want you, Zuzanna! Just you. Let's get you warm," carrying her toward the pit aglow with a glimpse of hell.

Zuzzie shouted, "*Pan* Wodowicz! *Hoch tutai*—come here!"

Confused, Wodowicz said, "I am here, little one, just for you." He took several more steps to the edge of the pit and with both hands raised the little girl above his head.

Something jerked his shoulders from behind. He lost his balance and began to fall backward, the girl flying out of his arms and into those of another. Relieved of her weight, he regained his balance and turned to face his attacker.

Holding Zuzzie next to him, the old man said, "Who, who?" then stopped. "It's you! You, Tomasz! You have come to harm this little one?"

"So, *Ojciec*, doing for this little nothing what you never did for me?!" He lunged, grabbing his father by the throat. "You miserable bastard! You have gotten in my way."

Zuzzie fell to the ground and ran while the two men grappled. They stayed upright, turning and turning, neither man having the advantage. They were at the very edge of the pit and finally, youth won out. Without hesitation, Tomasz managed to grab the elder Wodowicz by his waist sash and collar, and flung him upon the pyre below. He saw the old man's mouth open to scream as he landed on the glowing hot logs, but no sound came as he was quickly engulfed. Within seconds, he was a black lump, barely distinguishable from the logs becoming ashes there.

Tomasz stood open-mouthed. That he had just murdered his father mattered not at all. What mattered were the sounds of running, angry men.

. . .

One frigid February day, as Jan and Irina cuddled with little Stashu, Velka brought in a piece of folded vellum stock sealed in red wax and a silver ribbon. Because of the time of year, the invitation's arrival surprised them. At that point, with all the dust and wet plaster at Giverny, and a little boy they would be loath to leave with a wet nurse, they preferred a glowing fireplace by a toasty bed to travel of any kind.

Nevertheless, winter's boredom and social etiquette overcame their love of home and hearth. They bundled up and bade their coachmen to brave the snowy roads to Paris, where they were to be hosted by *Monsieur le Duc et Madame* Dampierre, a man whose rank at court might prove important given the frustrating launch of their business with Chevalle. On the ride to the city, they agreed to determine—with circumspection—what level of interest there might be amongst those present for fine wood furnishings.

During the mid-afternoon soiree, the well-gowned and furred ladies, powdered wigs and all, clustered around each of the four fireplaces, one on each wall of the ballroom, and gossiped amiably, the focus of their chatter being who in the room was a cuckold and who was not.

The Brezchwas disdained the sexual fantasies that seemed to take over nearly every social gathering, but protocol required they not parade the ballroom together, and so each found the cluster of sophisticates where they felt most comfortable.

Unnoticed, Irina soon wandered away, and found herself admiring a beautifully crafted, highly varnished and gilded breakfront sitting under a room-sized mirror composed of many smaller squares of silvered glass. Jan, she noticed, was otherwise engaged with gentlemen at the other end of the room, and she hoped he hadn't forgotten the purpose of their visit.

As she surveyed the piece's many details, the mirror reflected the image of an older man approaching. He stood close to her and, without introduction, expressed his own admiration for the workmanship of the piece. She could feel his breath.

"We've not been formally introduced, *Monsieur*, yet I agree with you." She held out her hand.

"The piece is only beautiful next to you, *Madame*. I am Maurice Dampierre at your beck and call," he said, bowing to kiss her hand.

Irina laughed in embarrassment. "So it is your piece I've been admiring. Your words are too kind, *Monsieur le Duc*, and I am *Comtesse* Irina Brezchwa," she said, holding her hand to be kissed.

"I have seen you at court, *Madame,* and have been wanting to make your acquaintance. May I ask, what appeals to you about—my piece?" He bowed to bestow a lingering kiss upon her extended hand.

"My husband and I have just begun an arrangement with a fine craftsman in Giverny whose work, we believe, has been overlooked by people of means," she said, giving her listener a coquettish look.

"I myself never wish to overlook an opportunity," Dampierre responded, a sly smile sliding across his face.

Irina returned his gaze. So intent was she in pursuing an important entrée into French court life—unlike the relatively inconsequential place she and Jan occupied—she failed to absorb the meaning of Dampierre's suggestive comments, his casual touches.

At the same time Irina weaved through Dampierre's maneuvers, Jan stood in the circle of nobles answering questions about the wilds of western Poland. His keenest inquirer was a man ten years older than he named Auguste Sainte Tellier, son and deputy to the king's minister of finance. Later, when the Brezchwas compared notes on their experience, each seemed delighted with the interest shown in them.

"Perhaps your instincts are *correcte*, my dear wife," Jan said, once tucked into their coach for the long ride home.

"Indeed, *Comte* Brezchwa," she said formally, teasing him. "Maurice Dampierre may be the key to everything."

. . .

Tomasz Wodowicz raced away into the frigid afternoon air. That his father was dead at his hands was of no consequence. What angered him was that he'd failed to kill a little girl, and now he'd be hunted.

The last time his chest heaved in fear was when he escaped Krosno. Then, he'd galloped for miles until his horse could go no further. Today, at least, it would be different. Had the woman enough time?

He reappeared at her dwelling along the river. In fact, several hours had elapsed since his flight from St Michael's, and it was after dark. Candleglow filtered from the window opening. He banged on the door until she answered it.

"Not until tomorrow, good Squire, as promised."

"But I have been called to duty, woman, and I must have my clothing now."

"There is something about you, Squire, that I don't like." Her statement was an arrow bolt in a conversation between a peasant and a person of purported nobility.

Wodowicz placed his hand on the court sword scabbarded in his belt for emphasis. "Do you know you're talking to Squire Krawcyk of Gniezno?" His voice rose an octave.

"I do not know who I am talking to, my good sir. If you want your costume, you may rest here by the fire, but several hours remain, and the more you torment me, the longer it will take to finish."

Wodowicz began to withdraw his sword, then slammed it to its seat. "Just so, good woman. I wait, then." In any other circumstance, he would have slammed the sword up her breastbone and laughed while doing so. However, this insolent woman was key to him fully shedding the appearance of the man soon to be pursued. "Let them look for the castellan known as Tomasz Wodowicz," he muttered to the fire warming the room.

"Did you say something, Squire?"

"N-no. How much longer?

"Be patient and be pleased, good man."

Squire Krawcyk fell into a fitful sleep, only to be awakened by the urgent sound of hoofbeats passing near. "W-what, who, who is out there?"

"Only soldiers would ride through at this hour," she said.

Krawcyk slept no more, but waited, perspiring, even as cold air fought the warm in the stifling room. He watched the woman's fingers move with lightning speed as she sewed a tunic of fine wool, its sleeves and collar decorated with dark-blue piping. He wondered where in this godforsaken place would a woman find the materials she needed, but put the thought out of his mind.

Two hours later, she held the garments to the best light in the room and smiled. "Whoever you are, Squire, take these and go—and remember, I'm not the only one who saw you come here." Quietly, quickly, he folded his new clothing. She produced a linen sack and held it open for him. She waited for him to acknowledge what she had said, then held out her hand. "You may pay triple the rate, good sir."

Krawcyk's jaw dropped.

She smirked.

"Your reputation is well-earned." He flipped her the coins and turned.

Ignoring the coins on the table, she stood stone-faced, ready for him to leave. Surprise came to her face when she fell to her chair, unable to breathe, as Krawcyk's short sword cut through her lung, piercing her through.

Krawcyk retrieved his silver pieces, then waited until he was sure she could not cry out. He turned and left, but not before wiping his sword on a piece of fabric. "You won't be needing this cloth, eh, *Panie?*"

. . .

The Brezchwas decided to move quickly with Chevalle, encouraged as they were by what they'd seen and heard at *le Duc* Dampierre's soiree. At the workshop, they framed satisfactory plans with the craftsman, and all in all, thought the morning went well. Making ready to depart, Jan asked him, "And so, Chevalle, now that your black men are free, how much do you pay them?"

"I pay them nothing, *Monsieur* Jan. You have made so few sales, I have only a bit more than before with which to support myself." His tone, more than his words, scoffed at the notion of freeing and paying his men—to him, little more than nameless brutes. Despite their words of agreement, Chevalle had kept his men in bondage. It was not that he mistreated them. Indeed, not one of the four had want of shelter or food, but they were not free. All of Chevalle's arguments washed away with that simple fact.

Irina and Jan stood there, their silence a contempt for his excuses.

"Why free them? They are no better than animals, no better than Jews!"

Irina could feel anger's heat rise to her face. Despite her fine dress and refined manners, she picked up a barrel stave and took a step toward him, a man twice her size. "Did we not have an agreement?" It was less a question than a statement, and it was backed up by a woman with a weapon.

"Ah, more silliness from the Parisian wealthy," he spat. "You two know nothing of business, and you know nothing of how the poor are forced to live."

"Oh, I know about being poor, Chevalle, but poor as I once was, I enslaved no one."

"Do your part," he said, bowing mockingly, "and I will do mine. Now leave me to my work!"

Irina took another step, her arm raised, ready for the attack.

Jan did not intervene. He leaned against a large work table, folded his arms in front of him, and smiled while he enjoyed the show. The three black men shrunk in the corner, their eyes unbelieving.

Chevalle took a step backward. His hand searched for something on the bench behind him but found nothing. Irina could see him swallowing hard, and in a moment, he changed his demeanor altogether. "My deepest apologies, *Madame* Brezchwa. I had no idea you felt so strongly about these heathens."

"When!" Jan would not allow a discussion about the matter.

"Tomorrow," he tried.

"No! Today," Irina commanded. "Now! Free them now, Chevalle! We will all prosper or starve together, but we will all be free!" In the silence, punctuated only by the hissing pressure in the steamer, she added, "We will wait."

Chevalle summoned the three men with a jerk of his head and said, "You are free men now. You may go, if you wish." Chevalle choked on the words, a jumble of French and some other tongue.

The men looked puzzled. In broken French, one of the men, Phillippe, said they knew nothing of freedom, that no one of their kind had ever been free.

"It is different, now," Jan explained kindly. He went on to tell them that they could go where they pleased and live where they chose.

Phillippe spoke for them. "*Monsieur.* What is freedom if we are hungry? We know nothing else. *S'il vous plaît,* we will stay here and work for you if you feed us."

For herself, Irina could feel her eyes well up, but smiled at them.

"For now," Jan said, embarrassed, "that will be acceptable. When we are successful, we will pay you well." Out of a large basket at his side, he produced breads, cheeses, grapes, and cold, boiled chicken. Offering the food and a cup of wine to Chevalle and his men, they all ate in nervous silence, but with pleasure.

The three freedmen, slaves only moments before, nodded happily and presented their broadest smiles.

Irina motioned to Jan, who pulled from a pouch attached to his tunic a gold sovereign, which he handed to Chevalle.

"This is what you will pay yourselves until the spring," Irina said. "It is more than enough for all the bread, sausage, cheese, and ale to strengthen you—all of you—for your labors at *Chevalle & Companie.*" It was her turn to smile.

Three of her listeners beamed. Chevalle bowed, bitter, but richer, in defeat.

The Brezchwas departed open-eyed about life's realities, and dejected at the same time.

"Irina, they are free!" Jan seemed self-satisfied.

"*Mon Dieu,*" Irina said. "We are just like them," she added, gesturing in the direction of Paris. "These men will be comfortable only after we are comfortable!"

. . .

As he rode hard and fast on the back road toward Wozna, the only image in Squire Krawcyk's mind was the look of surprise on the old woman's face. "Who was she to be threatening me?" he spat into the wind cutting against his teeth.

Wozna came into view as rain began to fall, its drops like cold daggers cutting through his lambskin cape. There were other travelers, he noted, and he'd have to be careful in his words and mannerisms. Tomasz Wodowicz is dead, he reminded himself, and only Squire Krawcyk lives.

Dismounting, he led his horse to the lean-to serving as a barn, and tended its needs. Still in his country squire's garb, he slipped around to his own lodgings and was glad to see it had not been ransacked. He lit a small fire and, drying himself as best he could, changed into the beautifully sewn clothing the old woman had bequeathed him. He laughed at the thought of it.

Into the inn's main room, such as it was, he was greeted by two men at table who had already visited Josef's ale barrel many times over. Sodden and surly, they sat with their eyes empty of thought but ready to close. One looked up and said, "Well, who do we have here?" his words slurred almost beyond recognition.

Josef spoke. "Mind your manners, you. This is Squire Krawcyk of Gniezno, and this is his inn.

Krawcyk was surprised at the old man's loyalty, but quickly discerned why. To him, Josef turned and said, "These two men are soldiers from Poznan in search of Duke Sokorski's castellan." He stopped, then continued. "And they think it is my duty to feed and water them as a courtesy!"

"You men are from Duke Sokorski?"

"N-no, Squire," one hesitated. "We are sent from the castle, to find the man who was castellan there, Tomasz Wodowicz."

"Why are you here, then?"

"It is said, Squire, this man Wodowicz may have stolen some valuables from the bishop's palace when he died."

"Josef, didn't you tell me of the bishop's death some time ago?" The old man nodded, his silver forelock dangling near his eyes.

"Then why are you here now, my good man?" Squire Krawcyk addressed the one who seemed most capable of answering.

"We were told to search everywhere before the castellan could go far. Some say he murdered someone at St. Michael just two days ago and we are to find him."

"But why here?"

"It was thought he would ride west, Squire. It is well we are here to protect you from this evil one."

Squire Krawcyk smiled broadly. "Perhaps you are right, soldier. Josef," he said, turning to the old innkeeper, "give these men more to drink. No doubt, they will guard us through the night and tomorrow.

They can resume their search for this man, Wodowicz." He smirked.

Surprised at the turn of events, Josef did as bidden. "Your horse, Sire?"

"All is done for the night, Josef. You and your lad may bed down if you wish. I will rest here for a day longer, then make my own way west."

"But Sire, what of your ownership of the inn?

"The inn will be yours, Josef, along with my lambskin cape."

"Then why, Sire, did you buy my inn?" he asked, clearly confused.

"So that I was assured of a place to—to rest." Krawcyk knew he was tired. He had almost said, "to hide."

Josef bowed. "Very good, Sire. And if I may be so bold to ask, Sire, where will your journey take you?"

"I am said to have cousins at Krosno," he lied, "and I've been invited to visit. I'm told it will be a fine place to spend my summer."

CHAPTER XVII

1410

On a sweltering August day, Irina braced herself when Velka poked her head in and said someone was riding up the lane. *Is it Stashu?*

But it was *Père* Alexandre Dubois who deigned to darken the morning hour. Irina noticed Velka's wrinkled nose, a signal to her mistress that inhaling deeply might not improve her disposition. The windows were already opened as far as possible.

Irina's habit of keeping one's person free of the muck of daily living was shared by few others, no matter their place in society, she had come to learn. It caused her—and Velka—no end of amusement when so-called learned men like *Monsieur le Docteur* Bernard seemed content to live within a cocoon of dust.

"*Père* Dubois, how good of you to call. How may I serve you today?"

The young cleric smiled in response. "*Madame,*" he proceeded, "*Monsieur le Docteur* Bernard mentioned that you continue to feel unwell. It is true that I have not observed you at Mass on Sundays, and so it is I who come to find how I might serve you."

Irina smiled her best client smile. "I hope the good doctor did not send you to offer me the Last Rites, *Père* Dubois, but I am glad of your company, in any event. Could we pray together, Father?" And that they did for some minutes, the priest administering Holy Communion and concluding with a blessing.

Irina spoke again. "I should not ask this, Father, but I must." She paused. "Have you ever doubted God's existence?"

"Ah, such a question," the cleric exclaimed. "It is a matter of faith!

332

And it is a matter you should never question," he scolded her gently.

She smiled when she thought about another priest she had known. Madrosh was a man who seemed to believe every question was, in itself, an answer. For *Père* Dubois, apparently, there were no questions. "Ah, you are so *correcte.*"

After he departed, Irina's attention shifted to the business she and Jan had managed for nearly two decades. To their great fortune, they had revived an artform in wood relatively unknown for hundreds of years, and introduced the wealthy classes to the beauties they had mastered. Veneered furniture, unknown amongst commoners, put their company name on the lips of many in salons across France. Was their discovery luck or providence? Irina came to feel it was the latter, but early on, the Dampierre affair seemed only like bad luck.

1379

The Brezchwas were invited to yet another soiree, this time at the palatial estate of the minister of finance, and there both Irina and Jan met again with their contacts, but on this occasion the four of them were in the same conversation, both nobles, as if competing with one another, expressing interest in seeing Antoine Chevalle's work. It was an uncomfortable circumstance inasmuch as Dampierre and Tellier were mortal court enemies. Any attempt to work with the two of them would be a disaster, she had been advised.

All in all, the afternoon event could have been counted a success. As the sun moved toward the western sky and the afternoon air became frigid, Irina sought Jan to make their departure. Duke Dampierre cornered her once again, suggesting a showing of her wares. Though she was becoming attuned to the duke's double meanings, she brushed them off, suggesting in turn that Chevalle needed many months to prepare a variety of pieces for Dampierre's viewing. She detailed the demands of design, wood preparation, and manufacture, not to mention the staining and varnishing processes. Late summer, she said, after everyone returned to Paris from their retreats in cooler climes, was the earliest a viewing could be arranged.

"Will you display these pieces in your chateau, then?"

"What a most wonderful idea, *Monsieur le Duc*. I hadn't thought to do that, but that will give me time to ready Fournier for your visit."

"Ah, wonderful, *Comtesse* Brezchwa! I am certain we will see more of you this season, but I will not forget seeing what you might offer me even sooner—I am sure you will let me know of a date?"

"Most certainly, *Monsieur. Au revoir*," she said, her parting smile belying her apprehension.

Once inside the carriage, Jan confided to her that Auguste Sainte Tellier seemed more interested in him than in furniture. Irina laughed out loud and gave him an impish smile. "Don't you dare let him take you from me."

"Rest assured," he answered and gave her a passionate kiss that led to much else on the long ride to Giverny.

"It is a good thing this is a closed carriage," she laughed, "and that the driver is hard of hearing."

Back at Chateau Fournier, she and Jan made plans to visit Chevalle the next day with more ideas for him. At the same time, they discussed how they might turn their large parlor—indeed, a small ballroom— into a showplace of sorts. "Whatever else Dampierre may be, he gave us a wonderful idea, and with luck, he will spread the word about our enterprise."

The social season progressed as the Brezchwas might have expected. They were invited to more events, their attractiveness more an asset to them than their rank, and each time they saw Dampierre and Tellier—separately—they exchanged many pleasantries, always to be reminded of a future rendezvous at Chateau Fournier. Irina and Jan began to realize Dampierre and Tellier were courting them, but for what, they chose not to imagine.

. . .

Leaving Wozna, Squire Janusz Krawcyk accepted Josef's gratitude and wished him and the boy well. "I doubt I shall return, my good man. The inn proved a perfect refuge for me, but I am called to the west."

"Why, Squire, do you not return to *Wielko Polska* with your own kind? if I may be so bold."

Krawcyk did not answer immediately, but then said, "I fear there is little for me here." The inn had been a stage upon which he practiced his performance as a country squire, nothing more.

What he could not tell Josef was that he had developed a taste for killing. He had bashed in more than a few peasants' heads in his time, to be sure, and had never been called to account for it. Despite admonitions of the church and its commandments, it seemed killing was only a crime when a peasant committed the act. True, there were rare exceptions, like the priest, Rudzenski, but for the most part, forgivable killings were permitted by the overlords or their minions.

Killing the Jews was a good example. It was his duty to the duke to rid the city of them, one way or another, and he had no regrets. Burning so many had given him immense satisfaction. And until he had flung his father into the flames, he had never realized how much he hated him. Seeing him lie helpless and forever stilled in an instant had been a pleasure. Doing away with the seamstress was purely a matter of self-defense. No moment of sleep would be lost over any of them, and neither would there be any hesitation over the coming death of Duke Sokorski, the one man who should have stood by him.

For weeks, he urged his horse through the woods, retracing the same steps he and Big Franciszek had taken so many months earlier. It snowed and rained, but he felt himself an accomplished man of the woods. The endless stands of leafless birches were empty of robbers and Hungarians, and for that he gave the Almighty his thanks. "*Boze,* are you there?" he once shouted to the trees.

At last, he found the broad span of sunlight signaling his arrival at the river valley of the Oder. And ahead, to the north, was Krosno. It looked the same, but as he squinted in the afternoon glare, he noticed the flag above the castle was German, not Hungarian.

"Now I'll know what happened," he muttered to the bare brown and black limbs of every plant and tree.

. . .

335

By Ash Wednesday, the flow of invitations to Chateau Fournier and other homes of the lower nobility began to slow, and as the days warmed, there would be fewer still. For that, the Brezchwas were relieved. Being seen in one salon after another was an expensive proposition, and their once grand pile of gold and silver had now dwindled; there remained but half a year's subsistence for them and their now extended family at the Chevalle workshop. Easing the financial strain were the occasional sales of a piece or two for someone's country estate, and the proceeds served to feed and shelter Chevalle and his men. Just as important, the sales helped finance the purchase of fine woods and other materials for the pieces they'd designed.

Much work remained to be done. Chevalle's nimble fingers were busy making miniature versions of the large pieces, replete with tiny brass fittings, like armoires and side tables for silver servings and fine cutlery. The miniatures could be carried easily at the back of a coach and four so that interested parties had something to see before agreeing to buy.

For the larger pieces, Phillippe and Etienne, two of the freedmen, were trained to shape and bend the slim boards of oak, elm, hickory, and cherry, but Chevalle's steam presses were ancient, and plagued with breakdowns in the piping system. The pipes, short sections of hollowed oak four inches in diameter, were wrapped and sewn tight with leather, then slathered with a black pitch found lying in puddles on the ground at the foot of the Pyrenees and brought eastward for sale to purveyors such as Chevalle. When the system worked, it was efficient and effective, and over the years, Chevalle, the master cabinetmaker, had learned many tricks to obtain the gentle and perfect curves he sought.

Just how fragile the steam presses were became evident one day when Jan stopped by for a visit.

While Jan and Chevalle were talking above the shop's din, there was a sudden snap and hissing of steam clouds. Then Etienne shouted, "*Mon Dieu!*" in great agony and emerged from the cloudy hiss holding his right hand in the air with his left. The man's black skin ended below the elbow where it had turned pink and bubbled.

Chevalle rushed to the man, grabbed his arm, and, drowning it in one of the buckets of ice cold well water, held it there for some minutes, until some relief appeared on Etienne's face. Phillippe could do nothing with the pipe until the water stopped boiling.

Later, Jan told Irina he felt guilty because he might have distracted the men with his questions, causing poor Etienne to react instinctively rather than thoughtfully when one pipe section separated from another. In only a few days, the men would have the steam press repaired and in full operation, he reported, but it would be many weeks before Etienne's severely scalded right hand would be fit to use.

The Brezchwas had their very surprised young *Docteur Bernard* look after the man, but aside from some poultices and cold-water soaks, there was little to be done.

Chevalle swore mightily, and the quiet industry prevailed, but at a slower pace.

...

The ride into Krosno proved uneventful, fear Squire Krawczyk's only companion the entire way north along the river and up to the bridge to Teuton lands. He could not shake the memory of the last time he'd crossed the river.

On the one hand, he felt satisfied to have escaped the Hungarians, but on the other, he would be crossing into lands not always friendly to Poles, and there would be no welcoming arms at Krosno to greet him.

Perhaps there will be no enemies either, he thought, and with a deep breath of resolve, spurred his horse to cross the bridge at a brave canter. Though he'd had several weeks since leaving Wozna to think about things, to concoct a plan of sorts, once seeing the place again, he had no idea what to do or what to expect.

Landing on Krosno's cobbled stone square, near to the moat bridge from which he'd made his dash, he looked the square over and let his eyes settle on a prosperous-looking building. He made for it at the slowest pace his thumping heart could manage, and found that he'd guessed correctly. It was an inn for travelers of means.

He decided to stay in place a few days to learn what he could before riding another mile. Information was what he wanted. One item was simply a matter of curiosity: What happened at Krosno with the Hungarians? The second piece of information was vital: What might people have heard about noble travelers heading east, and what route would they take? What better place to hear such things, he concluded, than an inn where ale and talk flowed freely?

. . .

Warm weather would soon sweep across France, the Brezchwas knew, and nearly everyone of standing at court would adjourn until cooler evenings would allow gatherings at which both men and women were once again clothed in heavy, brocaded layers of finery. Irina and Jan breathed easier, and looked forward to a long summer with little Stashu. Pressure on them to host Dampierre, Tellier, and their friends would evaporate with the heat.

Weekly, one or the other of the Brezchwas visited their furniture manufactory to monitor progress. Etienne's hand had healed, and he proved an eager apprentice, much to Chevalle's surprise, and eventual pleasure.

They'd been careful to sketch pieces that would show off Chevalle's talents for fine engraving and edgings, and gilded paintwork equal to that in demand amongst wealthy Parisians. One feature they liked to mention to their bejeweled friends was their ability to design and execute skillfully hidden secret spaces, sized to suit the needs of courtiers at any level of royal society. The women, especially, enjoyed hearing about a space where their most precious jewels—love letters, perhaps—could be safely hidden away.

The Brezchwas enjoyed their own secret in this regard: An unintended consequence of what they called their "special" feature was a competition that developed amongst a certain class of nobles as to which of them needed the largest compartment—suggesting ownership of the largest cache of gems. "Such fools," Jan had said to Irina, and she replied, "And from these fools *livres* flow!"

Their respite ended when a note arrived from *le Duc* Maurice Dampierre. It was polite but pressing. The duke said he'd been singing their praises all over Paris and he wanted a firm date for a showing at

Chateau Fournier.

After intense conversations with Chevalle and his freedmen, and consultation with the French court's keeper of the calendar, Jan and Irina settled on Sunday afternoon, the 21st of September.

"This will be 'do or die,' my dear *Comtesse* Brezchwa," Jan said.

"Such an interesting turn of phrase, but not to worry, my darling," Irina said, "we will have all summer. We have just enough money, and the men have just enough time."

...

One particular voice drew the Squire Krawcyk's attention, its timbre piercing the din of hearty revelers a few evenings after his arrival. It was a voice that gave him both a frisson of fear and a feeling of familiarity.

He stood on his stool to find its source, and when he did, laughed out loud, but in the crowd of bone-weary men drinking away their ailments, no one paid attention. He climbed down, grabbed his stein, and pushed his way through the gentry of the peasantry, as it were. They parted for the man dressed in garb reserved for the nobility; in their society, everyone knew his place, never to change from birth to death—unless by deception.

All week long, the squire had worked to perfect his role. He postured and demanded, and—despite surly looks from many—his costume and his supply of silver spoke for him. No one challenged his questions, but answered him with respect. Yet no one seemed to know anything. He did not bring up the Hungarians directly, and dared not, yet to his surprise, no one seemed to recall any excitement ever happening in Krosno. It was as if everyone had lost their memory, as if what he had seen and experienced had never happened.

He saw that tonight would be different. Holding court in the company of knights and squires was none other than Sir Ortwinus Esel, his high voice commanding the attention of all. "Aha!" the man boomed as he stood, "now we have another Pole come to make our lives interesting. And who are you, sir?"

Squire Krawcyk made his practiced introduction and bowed to the man in front of him. "At your service, Sir Ortwinus!" he bellowed over

the noise around him. "As one of those interesting Poles you mentioned, let me stand for your next stein of beer."

"Indeed, good Pole, and I mean no offense by what I said. Let us,"
he said, his voice still high but slurred, "be done with these people so
that we can build a bridge between our two nations." He laughed at
his own silly words, and added with a further laugh, "and if you have
the silver, I will be your friend." He draped his arm around Krawcyk's
shoulder and led him to a small table in a part of the room beginning
to clear with the hour. Dropping heavily onto a stool, Sir Ortwinus
signaled the barman for replenishment.

"You must be an important man here, Sir Ortwinus. Everyone
gives heed to your words."

"Indeed, you are correct, good Squire. None of these people," he
said, waving his hand over the crowd, "knows what I know."

"And I am a mere squire who knows so little."

"And a Pole at that!"

Krawcyk fought the urge to ram the baked clay stein down the
man's throat—in pieces—but he knew the Teuton's knowledge was
worth more than gold. "Ah, but allies—is that not so?"

"A most interesting word, that."

"How do you mean, good sir?"

"The Germans and the Poles have always been like two lovers who
spend more time quarreling than loving, eh?" Sir Ortwinus sipped his
beer and smacked his lips. "What happened here last year was when
we were allies, but it sickens me to this day."

"How's that, my friend?" Krawcyk had spent enough years as
a castellan around nobles to learn how to work them with the right
questions.

"I am forbidden to talk about it, and the townspeople have been
warned."

"Then, perhaps, we should not talk about it," Krawcyk said, eyeing
his opponent warily.

"But if I can't talk about it to the king's ally, then who can I talk
to, eh?"

"King?"

Ortwinus either ignored the question or simply couldn't hear it. "Good that you do not know any of these people, Squire. Then you will have no interest in repeating what I may tell you."

"You are correct, Sir Ortwinus. This is my first time in Krosno," he lied.

The Teuton twice slapped his stein down on the table, apparently a signal for the barman to bring more beer. While they waited, Krawcyk could sense the man giving him careful scrutiny. "And yet there's something familiar about the way you carry yourself, good Squire." Then he guffawed. "But perhaps you Poles are all the same!"

Again, Krawcyk counseled patience. He would have loved to squash the fat German sausage, but more, he needed what the man had—information.

When Sir Ortwinus quaffed another deep swallow of beer, he said, "The Hungarians. Hah! They came here thinking they could take Krosno Castle from us—and with the help of your Pole, Duke Sokorski." He paused, remembering. "Good God! What a mistake they made. Every one of them, including the big, yellow-haired Pole who had come to negotiate—they were all burned to death. All of them!"

"You mean the one they called 'Franciszek,'" Krawcyk said, regret and fear accompanying his words as they flew from his mouth.

Sir Ortwinus took another long swallow and was halfway to putting his stein on the table when the squire's words registered. He stared directly at Krawcyk, examining every feature of his face. He stood, hands flat on the table. Then he pointed at his visitor. "It's you! You are the one who escaped. No one was to escape!"

"Y-y-you are mistaken, Sire." His tone was pleading, abject.

Sir Ortwinus turned and shouted to his men at the other end of the room. "Come at once. Arrest this man!"

· · ·

At the bishop's palace in Poznan, Jerzy Andrezski and his crew prepared the many window openings for new, fitted and hinged glass windows, each with red, orange, and yellow panes mixed with clear. The work was strenuous, with dust and bits of glass filling the air.

"I know you'll be most careful, Jerzy," Father Shimanski said to his friend, the glass merchant.

"Indeed, Father. We know you want the palace readied for the new bishop. Have you had word on his appointment?

"There have been rumors, but I am not at liberty to say, my friend." He smiled with pleasure knowing something the very knowledgeable merchant did not.

"So, you are taking care of things until then, Father?"

"Yes, that is correct. I do not know if you've heard, however, that Duke Sokorski has suffered an injury on his return from Paris."

"An injury, you say?"

"Unfortunately, yes. He is an older man, as you know, and perhaps he could not react quickly enough when his horse stumbled descending to a river barge in Germany. He will have to heal in the village of Berlin, but most of his entourage is with him."

The two continued to talk while Andrezski and his men went about their work. Father Shimanski asked about the business in St. Michael, the Kwasniewski brothers, and, with a broad smile, about little Zuzzie.

"Everyone is doing well now," Andrezski said. "Zuzzie stays with her brothers from time to time, but otherwise, she stays with Sister Luke at the convent, where she is safe."

"Safe, you say," Father Shimanski said. "It is sad she had to witness Tomasz—who is, indeed, a Terrible one—murder his own father." The priest made the sign of the cross. "What could possess a man to kill his own blood?"

Andrezski had been guiding a man planning a window frame to fit, when he said, "Oh, my good and gracious God!"

"What is it, Jerzy? Did you injure yourself?"

"No, Father. You said something—something like, 'What could possess a man to kill his own blood.'"

"And so I did. What of it?"

"It ties to something Zuzzie said at the time and we all ignored the words of a frightened little girl. I don't remember exactly her words, but it makes sense now.'

"What's that, my friend?"

"Wodowicz had not come all that way to kill his father in the middle of nowhere. He had no reason to."

"What did Zuzzie say?"

"We thought she was confused. She said Tomasz had lifted her over his head, then his father. It made no sense then. But now it does."

"And what does it mean, Jerzy?"

"It means, Father, that he was there to kill Zuzzie. The old man must have tried to protect her, eternal rest be unto him."

The priest mouthed a silent prayer.

"And it means something else. Wodowicz ran away, some say, to the west." He paused. "Didn't you tell me once, Father, that Bishop Tirasewicz and Duke Sokorski had condemned him at St. Stephen's?"

"Yes, for stealing silver and gold from the Jews."

"From the Jews?"

"Yes, it appears that when Wodowicz and his men sacked the Joselewicz house, they kept back some of the booty for themselves."

"Isn't the Joselewicz house the place where Zuzzie's sister worked? Irina?"

"Yes, my son. What are you thinking?"

"I'm thinking Tomasz Wodowicz means to kill again. I'm sorry, Father. I will have to leave this work to my men and your good supervision."

"But…"

"I must see Sister Luke. Too much time has been lost. I must hurry."

CHAPTER XVIII

1379

Two soldiers dragged the erstwhile Squire Krawcyk across Krosno's square, across the moat bridge, and into the castle. Once inside, with the portcullis slammed to the ground behind them, Krawcyk began to sense what had really happened in the courtyard, lit only by torchlight at that time of night. He walked into an airless wall of stale smoke and burnt flesh he could smell but not see, and for that, he was grateful.

"You will enjoy your stay with us until I can learn what to do with you." Sir Ortwinus was displaying the most pompous version of himself, exaggerated, no doubt, by the vast volume of beer he'd consumed.

"Ask someone here at the castle. You are mistaken about seeing me here. I'd only heard tales about the giant of a man some in the alehouse said was called Big Franciszek." He tried the lie because it was all he had.

"There's no one to ask. Everyone decamped shortly after the royal party itself left on its journey west."

"Where—why did everyone leave?"

"Wait until you see the courtyard in daylight, my good sir. If the stench took your breath away tonight, light will make you think this place is hell, baked to cinders." He nodded to the soldiers. "You may as well put this sod up in the gallery where the stench is worst. I'm doing you a favor," he said turning to look at his well-dressed prisoner. "Down below, the air is better, but the rats are hungry. Take him!"

"Wait! The duke you mentioned—Duke Sokorski?—he will stand for me. I'm certain he knows my people."

"Hah! The duke is laid up with a broken leg. He won't 'stand' for anyone!" The man's jowls shook as he enjoyed his joke.

Krawcyk made a face of disgust as he was led away, but called back to his warden. "We must talk, Sir Ortwinus. I can be of service to you!"

The words caught the noble's attention, but he did not turn around.

A week went by, during which the prisoner remained confined to a small gallery apartment with little else to do but think. He chastised himself for having been so stupid as to mention Franciszek by name, but there was a chance the fat and lonely Ortwinus would want to believe him.

The apartment's entrance was off the second gallery overlooking the courtyard, and with a window opening in the castle's outer wall, there was an opportunity for fresh air to pass through, but it seemed none did. The unrelenting stink of the chasm below soaked into his nostrils and his clothes.

For a small piece of silver, however, the guard provided distraction with more chatter than Sir Ortwinus. Day by day, he learned exactly what happened to the Hungarians and to Franciszek. The guard spared no grisly detail and, in fact, seemed to enjoy the obvious torture of words inflicted upon his prisoner.

For the first time he could remember, Krawcyk wept. True, the big, yellow-haired oaf was little more than a hound skilled enough to do his bidding, but he was the only companion he'd ever known. There had been women to satisfy his needs from time to time, but they proved themselves as irritating as the stink of this prison. Whatever he was, Franciszek was faithful to his master. *A good dog was he!*

One other thought pounded his brain. Duke Sokorski oversaw the murders of many dozens of men, even if only Hungarians, but he let Big Franciszek burn with them. His vow for revenge became even more fervent.

Krawcyk could hear the clatter of hard leather boots and light armor approaching on the long, planked gallery floor outside his door. The first thought to occur to him was that the Teutons would be true to their reputation toward the Poles, and he would be executed before the noon hour. He was trembling in the chilly, spring morning air, when

Sir Ortwinus appeared with another man, bearing not an axe with which to sever his head, but a tray of foodstuffs.

"You said you could be of service?" asked the noble, continuing their conversation of a week before as if no time had elapsed at all. He had his man set the tray on the table, and invited Krawcyk to sit with him. "Let us discuss your service over a bit of lunch."

The two men ate and talked about nothing at all for some minutes, when Krawcyk reached under his elegantly sewn tunic—a move giving Ortwinus a moment of fright—and, as if by magic, presented a pair of gold coins imprinted with the image of Louis of Hungary. "This is how I can be of service," he said, and waited.

"Where did they come from?" asked the surprised Ortwinus.

"Ah!" Krawcyk responded, and smirked, "your men searched me for weapons, but not for coins sewn like a shield into my undergarment." Krawcyk lifted his tunic and glinting in the few rays of sunlight finding their way within the apartment was a blanket of gold and silver coins covering his chest. "A clever seamstress in Poland did this for me while I waited one night."

Sir Ortwinus took it all in. "What's to stop me from killing you and taking all you have, my good Squire?"

"I have already paid off your guard, good sir." He nodded at the coins sparkling on the table like golden diamonds. "These are for you. In a moment, I will rise and leave the castle on your best horse, and you'll never see me again."

"Why should I not raise an alarm?"

"Hasn't there been enough dishonorable killing in this castle?"

...

In Giverny, the summer commenced with Chevalle and each of his men laboring their utmost on the designs worked out by the Brezchwas. Chevalle's collaboration proved most important in that he had demonstrated himself a master at the clever concealment of the secret compartments so much in demand.

What spurred them further was the implied promise from the illustrious and powerful Maurice Dampierre of unending orders from those with the means to pay for them. Though the king's taxes would be high, the net result meant the Brezchwas, Chevalle, and his men might look forward to a comfortable winter.

Etienne showed himself a true mimic, successfully and beautifully imitating much of the work Chevalle was able to produce. Phillippe and Marcel worked equally hard assuming duties with the temperamental steam presses.

The most astonishing development Jan and Irina noticed and appreciated was how Chevalle beamed with pride at the transformed abilities of slaves who'd become free. During one day's visit to the shop, in fact, Chevalle and Jan were talking. The former shook his head, and looking in the direction of the three black men hard at their labors, said, "It must so be true."

"What's that, *Monsieur?*"

"That all men are at their best when they're free."

Altogether, their harder and faster work foretold a productive summer. Everyone knew the pieces had to be carved, manufactured, stained, and varnished, with plenty of time to cure before the show date written in charcoal upon the whitewashed wall of Chevalle's shop: "September 21!"

...

Not waiting for Sir Ortwinus to reconsider his silent assent for the fate of his prisoner and his gold, Squire Krawcyk secured the best horse in the castle's nearly empty stable, and rode off into the spring sunshine toward Berlin.

Several days into his journey, as he and his mount floated on the Oder, he learned from his many conversations with the boatmen and at overnight stops along the way about the time and distance in front of him. No obstacle was too great. Revenge became his energy.

His story was simple: He, one Janusz Krawcyk, was a squire from Gniezno, Poland, on his way to meet with his uncle from Poznan, Duke Sokorski, who lay injured in Berlin. Thus, everyone understood his interest in traversing land and water without delay. Based upon reactions and responses to his plight, he guessed he was on the same path the duke and his party had passed the year before. Even better, in most towns where someone of nobility resided, he was put up for the night and fed with sympathy, given the purpose of his travel. He'd even heard how brave he was to make such a journey alone.

At one of these stops, a village past Frankfort, he aroused a bit of curiosity when he asked for someone known for their potions. Nevertheless, he was directed to an old man who, by his appearance and surroundings, seemed to be an outcast—by his own desire.

The squire's first words to the man called Vodo were slow and cautious, but soon, without a single explicit word between them, the plant wizard, as some called him, produced a small clay vial sealed with a carved bit of cork. "This will serve you well, Squire," he spat out through broken teeth and wisps of untended beard, and he held out both hands, one with the vial, and one to receive payment.

The squire's first impulse was to skewer the man on his short sword, just as he did the greedy seamstress, but he thought better of it, and simply laid a coin on the man's palm.

"You will be very satisfied, my friend."

Finally, Krawcyk reached Berlin, situated at the junction of the rivers Spree and Havel. He found an inn looking sufficiently prosperous to board someone of his stature, and spent the next day listening at various alehouses nearest the castle, more a glorified stronghold, just beyond Berlin, at Spandau.

At one, just at dusk, he heard Polish words amidst the noise of men who'd had too many steins of ale, and sidled over to the speakers, a personal servant to Duke Sokorski and his doctor.

"Because the man won't be still, the leg will not heal," the doctor complained.

"And taking care of his personal needs will soon fall to the hands of another, if I have to say anything about it," the well-dressed servant said.

The most important thing he noticed was that neither of the men had been in the duke's retinue back in Poznan, and he wondered how they happened to be there. Better for him, thought Krawcyk, and good luck just the same. So many others around the duke would recognize him in a moment. The more he listened and observed, his plan seemed to form on its own.

Feeling it was safe to do so, he introduced himself and the three enjoyed more steins of beer, all at the newcomer's expense. They conversed in their native tongue, laughing at the Germans and their haughty manner with impunity. Krawcyk told the men he was passing through to Paris, and would be on his way early in the morning.

At the end of the evening, the duke's retainers invited him to stay with them, and when they'd finished their bread and cheeses, washed down with a good pilsner ale, the trio walked to the duke's stronghold. In their rooms, the doctor produced a leather flagon of ale to further quench their thirst.

Once the doctor and servant were deep asleep, Krawcyk slipped out of the room and stepped carefully through the stone-floored hallway. At the duke's chamber, he listened, and hearing nothing, went in without knocking. Only one candle, nearing its end, flickered by the duke's bedside where he rested, sitting up, asleep and snoring softly.

"Sire," Krawcyk whispered, "you must awaken."

"W-what?" He opened his eyes and looked at the bearded man in front of him. "Who are you? Where's my servant?"

"Not to worry, Sire. Your man sleeps well after too much beer," he said lightly.

"Then what do you want?" the duke demanded, now fully awake.

"Your doctor insisted I bring this medicine to you. One of its properties," Krawcyk went on blandly, his eyes on the floor, "is that it helps heal bones much faster, thus allowing you to travel in no time at all."

"That doctor knows nothing, but let's have it, then. You can tell the man you followed your orders."

Krawcyk proffered a small pewter tray on which lay a silver cup engraved with the duke's herald. The duke took the drink and downed it. Exhaling deeply, he leaned back on his pillows.

"You did not say who you were. Squire, is it?"

Krawcyk ignored the question, but waited quietly.

"Why are my legs tingling?" the duke asked, making a face of distaste.

Still, he said nothing.

"My arms. I have no feeling in them. What medicine is this?"

"That's how Wolfsbane works, My Lord," he said, then let his smirk be seen.

Slowly, the duke recognized the man before him. "You!" His voice became hoarse.

"Remember what you had me do to the Jews?" He waited. "Then you condemned me."

"But I have repented," Duke Sokorski said, his unfeeling hand moving toward his throat.

"But I have not," Wodowicz said softly. He waited until the duke's eyes were unblinking, then held the candle to the man's nose to make certain no air moved.

Snuffing out the candle with his fingertips, he retraced his steps, and after leaving the near-empty vial on the candle table by the doctor's bed, fled to his lodging in Berlin where he slept well through the night.

...

"These mounts cannot go fast enough," Jerzy Andrezski called to Eduoard Kwasniewski, who rode alongside him on the road from Poznan to St. Stephen's. Ahead was a small, covered coach, pulled by two fast horses, and inside were little Zuzzie and Sister Agnes Mary, a nun sent along by Sister Luke of the Dominicans.

Andrezski and Sister Luke had debated the issue. "Sister, we must travel to Paris as soon possible. I'm certain Irina Kwasniewska's life is in danger from Tomasz Wodowicz."

Incredulous, Sister Luke asked, "How can you be sure, Jerzy?"

"Because he came to kill little Zuzzie, not his father. His father died only because he tried to protect our little angel."

"But why should Zuzzie embark on such a dangerous journey? She is but six years old, a little girl with you and her big brother. I'm sorry, Jerzy, but that does not seem proper to me."

"Then send one of your young nuns. Didn't you send two nuns with Irina Kwasniewska last in May a year ago with Duke Sokorski and Father Madrosh?"

"Yes," she responded, "and my two nuns are on the way here now, along with Father Madrosh."

"And the duke?"

"Duke Sokorski, I am sad to say, is dead. A messenger delivered the news to Father Shimanski a few days ago, and you were away."

"Dead? How so?"

"They say he was poisoned by his doctor, but no one believes it according to the messenger. The doctor and the duke's servant are in prison and may be executed."

Andrezski stood and began to pace. "That news, Sister Luke, gives us even more reason to make for Paris."

"Why not simply send a messenger by fast horse? He will be there in a month or so and Irina Kwasniewska will be warned."

"This may be the only time to let Zuzzie meet the only sister she has—and unravel the mystery about the woman they call Lady Irina."

"That all sounds very noble, Jerzy, but very impractical."

After much pleading, during which Zuzzie ran in and begged to see her sister, Sister Luke relented. "I hope you'll not regret this, Jerzy Andrezski."

Two days out, they stopped at Wozna. Eduoard made the acquaintance of Josef and Padasz while Jerzy settled in the horses and their female charges for the night. Not an hour into their conversation with the old man did Jerzy and Eduoard hear the same thing: a man in rough clothing had appeared many weeks before and to their surprise presented himself as a squire from the east. More surprising, Josef reported, was that after an absence of several days he appeared once again dressed in much finer clothes. All Josef could remember was that the squire claimed to have family who'd invited him to Krosno. Well into the night, Jerzy thought about what he'd heard.

The next morning, the party prepared to depart when Josef said one other thing. "Even after he grew his beard, he still had that smirk. It made me afraid."

Atop their horses, Andrezski nodded and said, "You were right to be afraid, my friend, and be glad to have seen the back of him. He is a murderer and is on his way to commit another."

They made it to St. Stephen's, where to their pleasant surprise, Madrosh and the duke's party were encamped to rest before their last leg of a long journey home.

"Father Madrosh," Jerzy began, "we have never had occasion to meet, yet I hope you'll be glad to meet two people accompanying me."

Aged and weary, the priest said, "I am glad to meet you, good merchant, and I have heard of your deeds." Looking over Andrezski's shoulder, he asked, "And the two I must meet?"

"Here are Eduoard and Zuzanna Kwasniewski, big brother and little sister to Irina Kwasniewska—whom I'm sure you know?"

Madrosh's mouth dropped open and he seemed about to stagger with shock. "*Pan* Andrezski, you stun me with your words." Bending low, he said, "And you are the little girl your sister so worried about! My, you are your sister's sister, indeed," he said, and laughed merrily. Turning to Eduoard, he said, "I suppose you have questions for me?"

"Yes, Father. Perhaps we can talk after Zuzzie is asleep?"

That evening, Madrosh answered all the men's questions about Lady Irina Kwasniewska over a roast pig with potatoes and carrots. The monks' ale made the meal go down well.

"You mean, Father, that my sister, a peasant, like me and Zuzzie, is now a French Countess?" Not waiting for the answer, he laughed uproariously.

Madrosh chuckled. "Indeed, sir, your sister is not only a *comtesse*, as the French say, she is a very smart woman married to a good man, and oh, I almost forgot. You are an uncle!"

The trio celebrated that news with another cup of ale, but then Andrezski returned to a sober subject. "Father, please tell us everything you know about the duke's death."

"Duke Sokorski had already sent me and a few others on ahead, so I can only report what has been told to me by messenger," Madrosh said, and provided what information he was able. "Why are you so interested, good Jerzy?"

"Because, Father, a man with my experience does not believe in strange coincidences. Miracles, yes. Sudden poisonings by a faithful doctor, no."

"Then what, exactly?"

"Tomasz Wodowicz, Father. Here's what you don't know," Jerzy began, and then provided missing pieces to the priest to consider.

"Then yes, Jerzy, you are likely correct, but the Germans will probably have hung and quartered the doctor and his servant by now."

"Tomorrow, we ride to Krosno, and a German rider can be dispatched from there with a message from you."

"Most certainly, and now I have a bit more authority."

"How's that, Father?" asked Eduoard.

"When I arrived at St. Stephen's, the abbot informed me I am to be consecrated Bishop of Poznan. A prelate from Rome has been sent, and I understand King Louis will send his own representative." He sighed. "And now I am on my way home."

The men stood and bowed to the priest. "Will it be irreverent, then, Bishop Madrosh, to have another cup of ale?"

CHAPTER XIX

1410

When she met the merchant Andrezski back in '79, not long after his encounter with Madrosh, and heard about his elevation to Bishop of Poznan, she could only be thrilled for him. Underpinning many of the startling occurrences in her life was her relationship with Madrosh, the wisest, and surely the bravest, man she'd ever met. What scholar in 1378, or even now in 1410, would have taken so unusual a step as to serve as mentor and tutor to a young pregnant woman of such uncertain origin?

Midway across the Teutonic territories, Irina had confronted Madrosh on the matter. "Madrosh," she began, "why are you taking so much trouble for me?"

"Trouble, My Lady? Why, I've suffered none at all."

"Surely, Father, were you to take the time to tutor such as Squire Brezchwa, no question would ever arise. But a young woman—with child—whom you do not know, and for whom there is no patron?"

"Perceptive of you, my dear, as always, but not fully accurate, if I might add. You'll remember it was the bishop himself who directed me to watch over you on our journey, and Duke Zygmunt seconded that order to me personally. You were correct when you noted raised eyebrows, perhaps, regarding our talks about the philosophers, but you must also remember our sessions occurred outside of the bishop's knowledge. It was on my own judgment which I relied."

"You always choose your words so carefully!"

"Hah!" Madrosh chortled. "You have me there again. The truth of the matter, dear Lady, is that—and here I'm being a bit indiscreet—amongst our traveling companions, there are few minds of sufficient strength, shall we say, to lift the weight of our topics."

"You overwhelm me with praise, Madrosh!"

"I fear not enough, My Lady."

Velka broke her reverie with a gentle reminder that clothing adjustments, as she said, must be made so that Irina looked her best when seeing clients. That weight was slipping from her like ice melting in a thaw was one thing. Nearing her sixth decade of life, she could not be troubled by the change, but the increasing weakness she felt was interfering with her business and her daily life. Without being asked, Velka had arranged for seamstresses to begin the work of re-tailoring Irina's evening clothes. "These gowns will look much better with a bit of needlework, My Lady, and once done, you'll look young again. Who will know?"

"Bah! You foolish woman," Irina said. "Don't make me laugh so hard."

Velka's timing was superb, Irina noticed, as September was upon them. The evenings were rainy and the days colored by leaves beginning to fly. The monied class, nobility and others of wealth, had returned to Paris, and soon, she would be expected to appear at many soirees. She had come to be known as the face of Chevalle & Companie, and was well-regarded for her commercial sense. Who would have thought a purveyor of fine wood pieces—and a woman—could rise to such prominence? *It was not easy.*

Indeed, who would have thought a woman of such mean beginnings should have come to any notice above that of a peasant or, at best, the wife of a tradesman? Over her lifetime, nothing at all had changed regarding a woman's expected place in the scheme of things.

In looking back, she could never have guessed that when she and Velka struck out on their own in 1378, she could have successfully carried her child to birth while escaping from plague and pursuers. She would never have dreamed that a Polish serving girl would find herself in carriages, on barges, and as the guest of royalty. She could not have imagined that she would find herself in Paris in the midst of Europe's kings and queens.

That she would never see her much-loved Berek in this life was a cold fact. That she needed to survive and thrive was another. Most surprisingly, Irina had not expected the good fortune of finding a man who was willing to forego a dominant role in their marriage—and in their business venture. Yet such a man she did find, and never once did she have a regret.

Irina returned to her exchange with Madrosh, words of his that gave her such pleasure and no small amount of pride. She wondered what Madrosh might have thought had he known about Dampierre. Tight with guilt inside, she turned her gaze outward, across the greensward now bespeckled with leaves of yellow and rosy hues. Their rustling in the chilling evening breezes turned her memory toward another day from another time.

One of the most vexing problems they faced that September was how to manage the visits of *le Duc* Maurice Dampierre and Auguste Sainte Tellier on the same day without the two court rivals irritating each other.

They had not intended to have both men appear on the same day. In fact, they had only agreed on the 21st because Dampierre had insisted on that date. Tellier must have heard about it via the usual court gossips, and let it be known to the Brezchwas that he, too, needed to be at the showing on the 21st.

"*C'est la vie!*" Jan had said, exasperated, when their plans for a more peaceful Sunday were dashed.

"No matter, Jan. We'll send word they are most welcome for the 21st, but let's give them different times. That way, each *duette*—Dampierre with me and Tellier with you—can conduct business without the two of them having contact with one another. *N'est-ce pas?*"

Jan laughed. "We've been here long enough to speak, even privately, in French." He leaned over to kiss her. "I hope we never lose our Polish—you would have said '*nie*,' a much softer, sweeter sound coming from your lips."

"We want nothing untoward to occur, my husband, so let's remember to play our parts with these men," she said, and she, too, laughed and returned the kiss.

They had thought themselves clever, she remembered. But not clever enough.

1379

The day came. Jan and Irina attended Mass at daybreak. The choir and the readings were especially suited for a beautiful September morning, but halfway through the service, the skies opened, and rain pounded the slate tiles above them. It was hard enough to hear *Père* Dubois's mumblings of the Latin prayers before the rain started, and the incessant clatter made it impossible. They received Holy Communion as a few drops splattered on the stone floor near the altar, and Irina chastised Jan when he complained about the rain. "It'll be just another reason for the priest to ask us for money!"

They rode the mile home in the downpour but an hour later, in the midst of a delicious breakfast Velka had prepared for them, the rain stopped as if by design. They breathed a sigh of relief, and even Jan mouthed a prayer of thanks.

Either Dampierre or Tellier had to be the key that mastered the lock of sales to middle and upper rank nobility, they reminded each other. There was nothing so snobbish, so condescending as the denizens of King Charles's court thinking as one. If just one of them criticized or mocked their work, they would be laughed at all the way back to Paris, but if just the right one of them bought a piece and extolled the virtues of dealing with *Chevalle & Companie*, success would surely follow.

As expected, Auguste Sainte Tellier arrived one hour after noon. Jan, however, was nowhere to be found. As Tellier and his valet cantered their horses up the long drive, Irina called out to Rosta, "Where is *Comte* Brezchwa?!"

"Ah, you were not informed, My Lady? He was called to the barns, where his favorite mount came into foal. He said he would remain until the birth had proven successful. What shall I do with his visitor, *Madame?*"

"*Mon Dieu!* Have Velka show *Monsieur* Tellier to the library where he may wait, or he can go to the barn himself if interested."

"I suspect he will wish to settle himself and take some tea. Perhaps some little cakes?"

"Indeed. See that he is offered what he wishes, Rosta. We did not plan lunch, I regret to say. I will spend a few minutes with him and make Jan's excuses, but I will need to attend to my own visitor."

"Yes, *Madame*."

"Whatever happens, be sure to keep the door closed between the library and the salon, *s'il vous plaît*."

Breathing easier, but annoyed with Jan for running off without so much as a word, Irina prepared for her own visitor an hour hence. With her broadest smile and more than a bit of charm, she chatted with Tellier for some minutes before excusing herself. To her relief, he appeared content to wait and, perhaps, nap in the early afternoon sun.

Within a quarter hour, however, Velka rushed into the salon and said, "My Lady, your visitor's carriage comes up the drive—early. He is almost at the door!"

Instantly nervous, Irina did her best to compose herself, muttering under her breath as she hastened to extend her personal greeting. *Monsieur le Duc* Maurice Dampierre appeared in all of his finery, dismissed his footman, and presented her with high charm and a most expectant smile. His luxuriantly curled brown hair and fair complexion did little to soften his otherwise conniving countenance.

Becoming even more agitated underneath her welcoming words, Irina blinked her eyes, commanding her best demeanor to return. "Why, *Monsieur le Duc*, it is so good of you to keep our appointment, even on such a day as this. Let us adjourn to the salon, where we have tea and pastries to help warm us."

"Indeed, Lady Brezchwa! Let us retreat to a comfortable setting."

Not twenty minutes into their visit, teacups aside, the duke put a hand on each of Irina's shoulders, pulling her toward him.

"*Monsieur*, I thought we'd agreed to show you some of Chevalle's work."

"Most certainly, *Madame*, but might we not blend our visit with an activity more pleasurable?"

"Oh, *Monsieur*, I could not think of doing so. My husband, *le comte,* is at this moment in the library—right through there—and might at any moment interrupt us," she lied.

"I think not, *Madame*. If he were here, he would have greeted me as a courtier should—as befitting my rank."

"He is engaged, kind sir, and we must see to our arrangement, if you wish to keep our friendship," she dared.

"Hah! Your friendship, dear girl, is of little importance to me. I have sampled every female delicacy at the king's court, even the essence of the king's own mistress, I might add, and I came this afternoon to taste you." More than his polite but insistent words, his tone betrayed an entitlement tinged with lust.

She could see in his eyes the pinpoints of a predator about to pounce. She felt very much the sparrow in thrall of a cat toying with its prey. "You mistake me, sir," she said as lightly as she could manage. "Let us be at our business or you should find your way out."

Ignoring her words, Dampierre grabbed Irina, spun her around, and bent her forward over one of Chevalle's beautifully wrought walnut tables. As he lifted her gown, he spat out his words with a smirk she could not see as much as feel. "You will enjoy this, *Madame*, damn you!" Dampierre's voice summoned a memory of Tomasz Wodowicz.

While Dampierre busied himself with his buttons, Irina reached for a carved wooden crucifix, the Christ upon it staring at her fixedly, and twisting herself with all the force she could muster, swung the cross, striking Dampierre on the side of the head, a blow so sudden and surprising to him that he backed away, stunned, his instantly flaccid maleness dangling from his velvet pantaloons. He sat himself on the floor with a thump, his silk-clad legs splayed. With his right hand at the side of his head feeling for blood, Dampierre was dazed.

The blow made more noise than damage as it was the flat part of the cross that struck him, and while a mighty bruise might appear under his dressed tresses, there was no blood—only humiliation.

He shook his head, as if to throw off the sting, and stumbled to his feet. When he found his balance, and along with it a snarl, he said, drool forming at the corners of his mouth, "You bitch! Your miserable cunt! I will see to it you are driven from France before the Christmas bells toll the nativity! You are nothing. You and your idiot of a husband would be well to flee France—and soon!" When he realized how ridiculous he looked, he buttoned himself, turned, and marched from the salon.

Irina stood, shaking, her breath coming hard, but even as she set her jaw in anger, she reached for the nearest chair and sat down heavily. As soon as she felt in control of her balance, she put her hands to her face and, with heaving sobs, let the emotional pressure of the encounter find its way out.

She had no idea how long she wept. For the briefest moment, her tears were for the venture lost because of her own moral standard. *Everybody at court seems to think that a man forcing himself on a woman was a perfectly normal thing to do. But why do men think we are theirs for pleasure? Worse, why do women accept it as a condition of their existence? What is wrong with me that I couldn't go along?* Then, after another moment, she wiped her eyes, blinked, and sat up straight. *There is nothing wrong with me, and whether Jan and I stay here or flee France, I will not be a* putain *for some pig's pleasure!*

Velka came running in. "Irina, I came as soon as I could. *Monsieur* Tellier called me to the library. He was very agitated and departed shortly after *Monsieur le Duc.*"

Irina sat looking at Velka as she spoke but said not a word in return.

"Your eyes are red, Irina. What has happened here?"

"*Monsieur* Dampierre left suddenly," she said, debating whether she should tell Velka what actually occurred. "He will not be coming back," she added, her voice flat.

"Something happened here, Irina. When I went into the library to see if *Monsieur* Tellier was in need of anything, I'm quite certain he was listening at the connecting door to the salon. Whatever he heard had an effect on him, but then he sat for a moment, sipped his tea, and began to smile—like a bird about to pluck a rodent from the grass. Now, tell me. What did this Dampierre do?"

Irina looked sideways at her servant, her friend. "I will tell you when I have discussed it with Jan. Meanwhile, you are not to say a word to anyone." She paused, then asked, "Did Jan return from the barns?"

"He did not."

"And so, he did not speak to Tellier?"

"Not unless they met when Tellier ran out."

"But Tellier and Dampierre—did they meet or speak?"

"No, *Madame*."

"I was just curious, my dear Velka," she said, exhaling with some finality. Then she muttered, "I suppose it is better Jan was not in the other room."

"Is there something I can do for you?" Velka asked.

"At this point, dear one, there is nothing anyone can do."

. . .

In the tree line across the road running by the gated entrance to Chateau Fournier, a lone horseman stood watching. He was duly impressed with the grand dress of the two men who'd arrived, each with a retainer riding behind, but he was confused as well. Why, he wondered, would guests of this quality not have arrived at the same time for luncheon? Even more mysterious was the manner in which the men departed. The first to depart rode in anger, whipping his horse to the fastest speed it could go, his retainer unable to keep pace. The second man, only a few minutes behind, rode equally hard, but without injury to the horse, and seemed visibly cheerful.

Mostly, the observer was impressed with Chateau Fournier and what he'd heard about the *Comte* and *Comtesse* Brezchwa. He watched further, and seeing a familiar woman playing with a small boy on the distant greensward, he smiled with great pleasure. He took one last long look and turned his horse back toward the little village of Giverny, where he'd engaged a room.

"I can be patient," Tomasz Wodowicz whispered to his mount, and slowly rode away.

. . .

Rain fell each of the next three days. Most often, the clouds banked and dropped only a drizzle, but on other days, the sky seemed to send unending streams to drench the landscape, making even local travel difficult.

At first, Irina told Jan that Dampierre was unimpressed with Chevalle's work, and he could not represent their work at court. When she next talked about the possibility they might have to leave France, Jan listened patiently. Then he said, ever so gently, "You are so sweet not to burden me as you know I have no head for any of this, but my dear Irina, there is more, much more to your encounter with Dampierre, *nie?*"

"Why do you say such a thing, my husband?"

"Because I watched him with you at court. I saw his look. I heard some of his words when he thought I could not hear. More, I listened to others—friends of Duke Zygmunt—who warned me to be on my guard—for you—when he hovered too close."

Irina merely smiled, and looked downward, suppressing tears. Her hands, clasped in her lap, were cold and ghostly white.

Jan lifted her chin with his hand. "And so you see, my dear one, I never for a moment concerned myself that you would allow a creature like Dampierre to work his will with you."

"Then why," she began, holding back her annoyance, "did you remain away from the house when he was here?"

"Because, my dear, I knew Tellier would not be very far away. I am so sorry."

Irina told him what had happened, and watched his face harden. "But he did not intervene even though from what Velka said, he must have heard."

"For his cowardice, I am saddened, but apologetic—to you."

"As am I, my husband. How could I have thought he wanted only to appraise the furniture? He had no interest in it whatsoever." As she said this, they both laughed at their total innocence. "We have been lambs led nearly to the slaughter pen, have we not?"

"As furniture hawkers, we have failed once again," he said and laughed low like a man consigned to the gallows.

"We can laugh," she said, putting her arms around him, "but what do we do now?"

...

A day after the rain subsided and Atlantic winds began to dry the earth, a lone rider came through Chateau Fournier's imposing wrought-iron gates guarding the entrance. He held the horse to a slow, purposeful gait.

Irina, noticing the man by chance, breathed an immediate sigh of relief. Had there been an official of some sort with three or four soldiers, she would have known *le Duc* Dampierre's influence held sway somewhere in King Charles's court. *Yet who can this be?*

From what she could see, the man knew how to handle a horse, and was dressed well. *It can only be a prosperous merchant or someone in the noble classes.*

The rider continued to come toward the house, his eyes apparently fixed on the façade since he looked neither left nor right. How he handled the horse seemed somehow familiar to Irina, but she gave it not a second thought. *It must be someone we know from the business.*

At about thirty feet from the front door, the rider stopped and simply stared at the house.

Irina called, "Velka, someone will be at the door," but there was no answer.

The horseman stared, then broke his countenance with a smile. No, it was not a smile. It was a smirk.

"Velka! Velka!" Irina shouted, but still there was no answer. She held her hand to her chest as her breathing became rapid and intense. "Rosta. Rosta, *hoch tutai!* Hurry!"

The horse stirred, apparently unsure as to his rider's command. The man's sneer was unyielding.

Incredulous, Irina saw who it was, but without thinking the man might hear her, screamed, "Rosta!"

The rider's smirk broke into a smile of pure pleasure. Slowly, he turned his horse and rode away.

Irina watched, unbelieving that Tomasz Wodowicz was alive, much less that he was here. In France. At her chateau. At the gate, the rider turned to look back at the house, then jerked his horse to the left and rode away. Rosta appeared.

"Yes, My Lady," he said, breathing hard.

"Where is Velka?"

"She took little Stashu out for a ride, and to see *Monsieur Chevalle*," he said, attempting a smile.

It took only a few seconds for Irina to divine what might happen. "Get Jan! Get my horse! Then to the shop! It's Tomasz Wodowicz."

Rosta stood speechless for only a moment, then ran as fast as his legs would go.

Irina knew she had little time.

• • •

Rosta ran to the barn where he thought his master would be tending his foal, but *le Comte* Brezchwa was nowhere to be seen. Without thinking twice, he readied a mount for his mistress and rode it himself to the main house, where Irina paced at the entrance door.

"I am so sorry, My Lady. I could not find him."

"I cannot wait!" She bolted off. *Where is he!*

• • •

Chevalle and his men—Etienne, Phillippe, and Marcel—were behind the shop having a lunch of stale bread, cheese, and mugs of red wine. With the doors and windows thrown open to catch the fresh, cooling breezes, their hot, steamy spaces became bearable on a day that had, so far, been easier than most.

As on most days of late, their chatter—uneven owing to the language hurdles—centered on the lack of orders. Chevalle cautioned them. "You men may be freer than you think. If *le comte et la comtesse* do not produce work orders, we will all be free to leave here."

"But with no place to go," said Marcel.

There was a sound in the shop, coming from the entrance. "Chevalle, come see little Stashu," Velka called out.

Chevalle rose, as did the others, and they all went inside, greeted by Velka's broad smile.

"Look, Chevalle, the boy is taking his first steps, and he is coming to you. Catch him!"

The grizzled carpenter had taken no interest in the boy when the Brezchwas first brought him around. Then, he was in arms, a bothersome noise, and he said so. Now, however, he reached out and waited for the little one to fall into his arms. With a toothy smile, he embraced the child in the same way he caressed a beautiful carving. For a giver of gruff words more often than not, he was speechless.

Velka chortled. "He has found his *grandpère, n'est-ce pas?*" she said in her butchered French.

"Aha! I have found you," said the strange voice at the door. "*Monsieur et Madame* Brezchwa have sent me to fetch the boy immediately."

"And who are you?" Chevalle demanded.

"We do not know...you," Velka's voice trailed off. "Or do we, Tomasz Wodowicz?" she said, surprised at the name passing her lips. She reached for an iron bar used for wedging wood. It was three feet long and thick as a javelin. She swung it with both hands, but Wodowicz grabbed it from her with just one of his and swung it toward Chevalle. It struck home. Everyone heard bones snap as Chevalle held his ribs and yelped in pain. He sank to his knees, and before Wodowicz could strike him again, he fell face first to the stone floor.

Wodowicz stepped over him and, ignoring Velka, went for the three black men who were backing away from the arc of the iron bar. Phillippe picked up a hammer and flung it at their assailant, but missed. Marcel ducked behind a work table. Velka took a running step and jumped on his back, her arms around his neck, but Wodowicz slapped her away with ease.

In the meantime, Etienne, too, had gotten behind him and jumped on his back. Wodowicz swung the iron bar back over his head in an attempt to knock out his attacker but, instead, struck the latch holding closed the large copper cover atop the steam press. Steam forced the lid open.

Wodowicz threw Etienne off his back and, with the iron bar in his arm raised aloft, was about to smash him to the ground, but another pair of hands came at him from the side—it was Jan Brezchwa. One hand grasped the arm with the weapon while the other hand grabbed hold of his tunic. Still another pair of hands wrapped themselves around Wodowicz's legs.

They would have succeeded in throwing Wodowicz into the steam press, boots and all, but for his coat buttons catching on the tray onto which boards meant for bending would be fixed. Only Wodowicz's head and shoulders cleared the lip, and Jan Brezchwa used his free hand to pull down the copper cover, pinning his arms, the oiled leather gasket sealing his fate. Despite Wodowicz's flailing legs, Jan and Phillippe use all their force to hold the lid and him in place.

Wodowicz's growl turned into a nightmarish howl as the steam did its work. Within seconds, the eerie sound from within the copper steamer ceased. His body went limp, and the men let it drop to the floor. His head had become like a boiled melon, like an opaque, pink blister atop a human body. Where once a cruel smirk shone, there was but a slit. Where once cold eyes bore down on his victims, there were two black dots, sockets finally empty of hate.

Velka had already snatched Stashu out of harm's way and was running out toward the road, where Irina had ridden up, leaves and dust flying as she reined her horse to a halt. She took Stashu from Velka's arms and went back into the woodshop, where she saw her husband standing over the grisly mess fouling the floor.

Shaking, Irina handed Stashu back to Velka and embraced her husband. Stepping away from him, she looked down at the remains of Tomasz Wodowicz and, still breathing hard, she said, "May God take your soul—straight to hell."

CHAPTER XX

1410

Even after so many years, Irina felt the same satisfaction at the thought of Tomasz's death. Although Madrosh had reminded her more than once it was not her place to sit in judgment of Wodowicz or anyone, she felt certain—hoped and prayed for it, in fact—that the man's soul rotted in hell.

What happened in Chevalle's shop that October day revealed once more that Jan Brezchwa was a giant, belying his image of an unassuming, unpretentious squire. Her thanks to the Almighty were not just for her husband's bravery, but that at last, a debt had been paid for the Joselewiczes—and Berek.

"Oh, Jan, how did you know?" she had said through her tears of joy—joy that her son was safe, joy that his would-be kidnapper was dead. "I thought you were off somewhere, that I would be too late!"

"It is very simple, my dear," he said, smiling humbly as was his nature. "I was out riding—Rosta had just forgotten—and on my way back, I saw Wodowicz leave our front gate and turn down the road toward the shop, a place where almost no one goes. Don't we know that?" He laughed.

"But how did you know it was Tomasz?"

"What I also saw," he answered, shuddering, "for just the flash of a moment, was the look on his face when he made the turn. You forget, I also knew that face from Sokorski Castle. I knew it was him, and of what he was capable." Jan exhaled. "That's why I followed him."

Irina remembered pulling herself into his chest and hearing Jan's heartbeat, ever grateful that it beat for her and Stashu. *For however long I have left, my love for Jan is what I will take with me.*

She sat in front of the fire remembering that moment when Velka came in to tell her people from the village were talking about another revolt. "Revolts! How many have there been since the one when Wodowicz came—as if he had brought the trouble with him?"

"It is hard to know, dear Velka. To me, it seems that the French people want to live in nearly perpetual battle. It must be their temperament, *nie?*"

Just a year earlier, in fact, the revolt of 1409 had been crushed mercilessly, and, once again, little had been gained, except that for two years running, the cemeteries of France had a steady stream of new residents. The civil war settled nothing and the pain to the nation seemed to have been as great as cancer's pain had become to her.

Throughout all the chaos, she queried every traveler from the east for any news of her Stashu, but her requests were always answered with a simple shake of the head. The world seemed preoccupied with death, convulsed as it was with wars and revolutions. Though cocooned in quiet Giverny, she could not escape the feeling she would never see her *Stashu* again. *The time left for that to happen will soon be gone, mon Dieu.*

Monsieur le Docteur Bernard's recent visit had confirmed that for her.

"*Madame* Brezchwa, I wish not to intrude on your day, but I feel that I must ask how you are doing with the pain."

"Why is it you know all about this disease, but can do nothing about it!" It was not a question but a frustrated acceptance of reality.

Bernard bowed in apology. "*Madame,* there is so little we know about so much. As I said when the weather was much warmer, it is not within our means to treat it or cure it. Indeed, I should have recognized this problem sooner, but alas, it would have made no difference, I am most sorry to say."

"Why do you begin and end in apologies, Bernard? Perhaps, this is God-sent for my sins."

"Think what you wish, My Lady, but it is your body that does you harm, and I do not know why God would want to inflict so much pain on one such as you."

"You can do nothing, then?"

"For the disease, no. For the pain, we can do one or two things. At present, I would have Velka gather ice chips in an oil cloth when the pain is at its worst, and place the ice pack directly on your stomach—it will give you some relief."

"Pfffft! Is that all you can do?"

Bernard paused. "My dear Lady, there will come a time, perhaps soon, when the pain will become more intense. When you feel you cannot cope with it, send Rosta for me, and I will come. We have something the monks have used for hundreds of years—a mixture of opium and hemlock—that will dull the worst of it." Once again, he bowed his head in apology, and imparted to her what else she might expect in the following weeks.

When the good doctor had departed, Irina instructed Velka to scrub everything down. She said, "I want everything as clean as possible."

"Oh, and Velka, please gather some ice." As her mind wandered into her gallery of treasured moments when God Himself seemed to be standing at her side, she smiled as she thought of the events that had changed their lives.

1379

The political storm began brewing inside Paris's walls, and the mood of the people, like the Black Death, spread outside its gates, seeping into every city and village in France. As the nobles struggled to restore order, the Brezchwas remained in Giverny and spoke to no one, lest they become swept away, like twigs in a raging river. Nothing had been heard from Dampierre or anyone else at court, for that matter, and everyone in the household wondered why.

Into the maelstrom, a most unlikely savior arrived on a blustery fall day, someone Irina had never before met. As if a sign from heaven, a man calling himself Jerzy Andrezski arrived from Poland, taking Irina and the entire Brezchwa household by surprise when Velka announced his presence. They were even more astonished when out of the well-appointed carriage popped Zuzanna Kwasniewska. Resembling her eldest sister even more closely than before, her auburn hair, full of curls, framed a pretty picture. When Irina took her in from head to toe, she could not help but notice the striking blue eyes and the wide smile.

Irina went to her knees and hugged her little sister fiercely, as if she would never let her go. In the midst of their happy tears together, she looked up from Zuzzie's shoulder and saw her brother, Eduoard, who had stepped from behind the coach with a broad smile. *How prosperous this man and my brother appear!*

Opening his arms, he reached for his sister, and said, with mock seriousness, "*Lady* Irina? Hah! To me, you'll always be my little redhead." They both laughed, and Irina blushed.

"I will confess all later, brother, but first tell me about our family."

Eduoard held her close and said, "Except for Peter—who is running things at St. Michael—and little Zuzzie and me, dear sister, they are all gone from plague. You couldn't have known *Matka i Ojciec* went to look for you the day after you left."

"And I met them in the caravan from the east on its way to Poznan," Jerzy explained. "Most of us caught the plague, I feel certain, but thanks to my little angel here, I somehow survived."

Irina reached for Jan. "I see," she said in a small voice. It did not take her long to wonder if her family would have survived had they not left St. Michael in search of her.

As if reading her mind, Andrezski said softly, "It is wise not to think about what might have been, Lady Irina. What is more important is that you and your family are safe!"

"You mean, about Tomasz?"

"On our way here, the people talked only about two things—the latest revolt and the man at Giverny who escaped the French axe man."

"I'm curious, *Pan*, why did you come just now?"

"Apparently, My Lady, there is much we all have to talk about, but we hurried because Tomasz was on his way to kill you. Of that, I am just as certain as I am that he killed his father who died keeping little Zuzzie from his grasp. Even Duke Sokorski could not escape Tomasz's madness. Ah, there is much we don't know," Andrezski said, "but thank God, you are safe. He'd gotten very clever, that one," Andrezski said. "Thank, God, indeed."

"We do," Jan said, attempting to lighten the moment, "but we could stand here all afternoon, couldn't we?" Graciously, he invited them all in.

Eduoard said, "We rode hard hoping to arrive here before him. The coach slowed us, but how could we not bring little Zuzzie?"

...

Irina could not have been more pleased to see her brother and sister. To know they were alive and well was such wonderful news. That the rest of her family was gone forever rekindled feelings she'd rather have forgotten. *Perhaps it is the guilt I'd rather forget.*

The emotional whirl was complete only with the revelation that her brothers were managing a large portion of Andrezski's glass business. Then another thought occurred to her. *My brothers! They have become the success we hope to achieve!*

Meeting and listening to a merchant like Andrezski piqued her curiosity even more than how her brother Peter was making glass. It rapidly became clear the wily Pole had a business savvy neither Irina nor Jan understood. Clearly, Andrezski possessed a sense of urgency and was willing to take great risks. *He came all the way to Giverny on a hunch, didn't he?*

The merchant asked many questions about the furniture manufacturing business, noting at one point the many parallels their two enterprises had in common. Through the fall, while the leaves flew and died to dust under their boots, Jerzy learned every important aspect of Chevalle's business, and he, in turn, explained its finer points to Irina and Jan. Jerzy tried to make it simple for them.

All the while they talked, everyone delighted in keeping an eye on little Zuzzie, who played on the tile floor with her nephew. The wooden shapes Chevalle had carved for Stashu kept both children avidly engaged.

"All enterprise is the same," Andrezski said, trying to keep the Brezchwas attention. "There is a good that someone wants and will pay for. The price has to be reasonable to the buyer, but most importantly, the buyer must believe you have a good that he himself has to have. It is the latter part that makes your role, Irina and Jan, the key. You have to convince people you have something they all *must* have. You must pour yourselves into your success. To do less will mean failure."

He went on to discuss the cost of labor and materials, all as it related to pricing and profit. "However, it is you who will make the Parisians want what you have to sell," he emphasized again. "You and Chevalle have to give them something they cannot obtain now, and cannot live without.

"We have tried that, but they say we have what everyone else has," said Irina in frustration.

"You must make bigger plans, then. Bring them here for dinner parties and let them dine on Chevalle's tables! Entertain them."

"Yes," she agreed with more enthusiasm than she felt. His suggestion was a variation of the plan they'd intended to implement. "Of course," Irina said. "What a marvelous idea. Our chateau can be quite charming, *nie?*" She poked Jan in the ribs, laughing some more. "And why didn't you think of that, *Comte* Brezchwa?"

"Ah," Jan said, forlorn, "but dear Andrezski's notions may all be for naught, given what Maurice Dampierre might do to us."

· · ·

One late October day, when the last of the leaves blew across the roads in great swirls, a lone rider came into view on the long carriageway to Chateau Fournier. Irina watched the man's horse gallop closer, and dread overcame her. Tomasz had appeared in just the same way. She stood holding little Stashu, not a year old, wondering how she and her household could make the move to another king's domain. *Would King Wenceslas take us?*

"It is a messenger, My Lady Irina. We will give him some warm bread and soup," Velka said, bowing, not waiting for an answer, and knowing full well her mistress would want the poor rider's needs seen to in the kitchen by the fire.

Ignoring the niceties of nobility, Irina and Jan excused themselves from their guests and, together, went to the kitchen, where nearly everyone, including the rider, showed surprise at seeing them. "Remain seated, good man, and finish your broth."

Two more chairs were brought for Irina and Jan to sit at the rider's level, something unheard of at other estates, but not at Chateau Fournier. Velka stood by, a smile of satisfaction on her face, proud of her mistress and her husband.

"I am sent by *Monsieur* Tellier, *Madame et Monsieur*," he said, nodding to them—his version of a sitting bow—"and he said to give you his apologies for not having returned earlier. The revolt, you know. He will be here in five days' time, along with several ladies and lords from court."

"What are you saying, my man?" Jan said, disbelieving.

"That is all I know, *Monsieur*, but he said your household should prepare for guests."

"Guests?" Irina asked, her turn to be dumbfounded.

The rider laughed, forgetting himself. "Oh, yes, *Madame. Monsieur* Tellier also said something about the other people wanting to see your offerings." Seeing the expressions on the faces of his listeners, he added, "Oh, my, I am so sorry that I forgot to mention that, *Madame,* but your food is so good," he said, grinning and nodding.

Irina and Jan looked at each other, first with relief, then with wonder. "What can all this mean?"

. . .

After much excited discussion, Irina finally came to a decision. "This can only be wonderful news! We have much to do." They enlisted their new friend Jerzy and Irina's brother, Eduoard, to help them refresh the setting at Chateau Fournier. With Andrezski's assistance, fresh foodstuffs were purchased for as fine a dinner as they could manage on short notice. No effort was spared to put a sparkle everywhere.

Most importantly, Chevalle's pieces were arrayed around the chateau's public rooms.

The visitors decided amongst themselves they would best serve their hosts by retreating to their quarters at the appointed time.

Monsieur Tellier's four guests rode in a large, enclosed coach warmed by bricks heated in a fireplace beforehand and situated at the passengers' feet. Glass panels served to further protect those inside from the cold snap, yet allowed them to enjoy the countryside already blanketed in browns and greys. Tellier himself rode ahead on a white horse. Their arrival a few hours past noon allowed time to refresh and join the Brezchwas in the dining room for a repast alongside welcoming fire.

It was clear Tellier's guests were used to more sumptuous spaces with luxuries aplenty, but they were uniformly polite, acting as if they were on a country adventure at a well-kept lodge. Irina and Jan couldn't have been more pleased at the guests Tellier had chosen to bring on a visit, but they remained intensely curious how it had all come about, especially when Dampierre threatened, in effect, to deport them in total humiliation. They agreed it was Jan's task to glean the answers from Tellier, whose apparent attraction to Jan they both found interesting.

The opportunity for a private consultation arose when the guests returned to their chambers for some rest before an evening of entertainment and dinner. Tellier surprised Jan by asking that Irina be present.

Jan spoke first. "*Monsieur* Tellier, *Comtesse* Brezchwa and I cannot begin to thank you for making these arrangements, but we remain in shock, shall we say, that those accompanying you weren't royal guards come to clap us in prison for offending *Monsieur le Duc* Dampierre."

Tellier put his fingers across his lips and began to laugh quietly, then out loud. Finally, he all but guffawed like a street peddler at a dirty joke. Then, embarrassed with himself, he said, "Oh, you don't know, do you?"

"Know what, kind sir?" Irina asked, unable to remain silent.

"That's right, isn't it? You have had no news from Paris because of all the uproar, *n'est-ce pas?*"

"Yes, that's true. We've heard nothing, and in fact, it was somewhat difficult to prepare for your wonderful visit inasmuch as the village of Giverny has had little contact with the outside world as well."

"Well, that explains all, doesn't it?" Tellier looked directly at Irina. "My dear *Comtesse*, I doff my hat to you and your courage. The scoundrel Dampierre galloped all the way to Paris in a frenzy to undo you both. You humiliated him, the poor fellow." Tellier began to laugh once more, surprising his listeners once again.

"You have to understand, my dears, that Dampierre and I, well, let's just say there was never anything between us," he said vaguely. "I hope you don't mind, dear *Comtesse*, but I, uh, just happened to mention to my father what I'd heard Dampierre gloat to you."

"And that was?" Irina asked, but wasn't sure to which insult Tellier referred.

"Please do not be offended, my dear, that Dampierre's horrible remarks to you were of no matter to those at court. It was what he said about Lady Delphine."

"Lady Delphine?" Jan wanted to know.

"Ah, you poor innocents. You should spend more time at court, but no," he said with emphasis, "you're better off." He cleared his throat dramatically. "Lady Delphine is the king's mistress. Ah, I should say, his former mistress."

"Former, you say?" The soft auburn hairs on the back of Irina's neck stood on edge.

"It seems that about two days after Dampierre's return to Paris, and on a day when King Charles left *le Louvre* to inspect construction at *la Bastille*, Dampierre arranged a *tête à tête* with Lady Delphine atop the parapet of a tower adjoining the royal residence."

"And?" Irina swallowed hard. She noticed Jan leaning back in his chair, not ready to believe what he was about to hear.

"It was all so horrible," Tellier went on. "Instead of some sort of tryst, guards reported hearing them quarrel. Dampierre reached for Lady Delphine, who took an unfortunate step backward. It seems that somehow, she slipped and fell over the edge. Dampierre, it was said, made a feeble attempt to grab for her, but he himself lost his footing and went over. Just awful!"

Irina and Jan remained speechless.

"Nothing could be done," Tellier exclaimed, his voice rising. "Nothing! They fell into some debris in the Seine, and although guards along the river's edge attempted to reach them, well, you know how strong the current can be. Apparently, they were swept under where no one could get them. Poor things!" He shrugged, as if discussing drowning rats. "God only knows where they wound up." Tellier sat back, ready to turn the conversation in another direction.

Irina and Jan were stunned. Then Jan spoke. "And everyone is certain it was an accident?" he asked, knowing full well what Irina was thinking.

"Well…I don't know what to say," Tellier responded. "Accidents do happen, you know." He paused. "In any event, the whole affair, shall we say, saved the king trials for treason."

"Treason?" Jan asked.

"Seducing the king's principal mistress, then bragging about it…" he said, eyeing Irina and clearing his throat but not finishing his sentence. "The king would have considered the whole affair an act against the state. Perhaps," he said, exhaling fully, "their demise was the nicest way—for them—to leave this world."

. . .

Irina and Jan continued to struggle with their finances, despite the interest in Chevalle's work shown by the Duke and Duchess of Montpelier. Their order for several pieces carried *Chevalle & Companie* through the end of the year. The Montpeliers had said his work was perfect for their country estate some miles distant. Despite the many *livres* brought to the company coffers, the nobles were ordering furniture for an estate very few others would see. Few orders followed. The other couple had no use for Chevalle's work, saying there was nothing new about what had been presented to them.

Tellier apologized for their bluntness but promised he would seek more clients like the Montpeliers, people who knew fine quality for just the right place and price. More fortunate for the Brezchwas, Tellier lost interest in Jan as a partner of sorts, but it was clear from his many warm words, Irina and Jan had become favorites of his.

One such favor materialized at just the right time. With further unrest across France, Tellier's father, the minister of finance, sought to dispose of what he considered marginal properties in the king's portfolio, and despite improvements made by the Brezchwas, Chateau Fournier was seen as a costly liability to the king. As a consequence, the main house, all the outbuildings, and some two hundred acres were signed over to them.

It cost the Brezchwas a custom chest, intricately carved and made of fine woods, large enough to hold a noblewoman's court gowns, to be delivered to Lady Tellier, the most pleased wife of the minister. Jan suspected the whole transfer of property may have been the king's way to thank the Brezchwas for surfacing treachery within his household. That the deaths of Dampierre and Lady Delphine may not have been accidental, after all, no one ever mentioned.

All the while, Jerzy Andrezski and Eduoard Kwasniewski assisted the Brezchwas in every way they could. The former supplied needed *livres*—"recompense for our lodging these months, My Lady," he insisted—and the latter put himself to work in Chevalle's shop.

1380

When he arrived from Poland, Edouard made two comments that stayed with Irina. She couldn't believe he'd meant anything by them, but they rasped across her conscience like a piece of Chevalle's sandpaper on a soft wood's surface.

The second one, she knew, would stay with her the rest of her life. He told her their parents and little siblings left St. Michael to look for her, and she couldn't get out of her mind the idea that had they stayed where they were, they'd all be alive today. *Did I cause their death? Oh, Madrosh, where are you?* Then, *They must have loved me still.*

The first comment, however, struck home in an entirely different way. She had lived the part of Lady Kwasniewska for so long, she'd all but forgotten that Jan would not know much—the truth—about who she really was. She had looked in Jan's direction to see what he was thinking, but could not read his face.

Making the excuse that she and Jan had a business matter to which they needed to attend, Irina led Jan to their bedchamber and closed the door. He looked puzzled. She stood facing him, her hands flat on his chest as she looked up at him. "My husband," she began in a hoarse whisper, "I'm afraid I have not been truthful to you. Our m-marriage is a f-fraud against the church if you believe you married Lady Kwasniewska from Gniezno."

For the briefest moment, Jan said nothing, then smiled broadly. With some drama, he placed his hands on her shoulders. "I've known from the very beginning, *Comtesse*," he said, deliberately using her title.

"How could you possibly have known?" she demanded, shocked. "Did Father Madrosh betray me?"

"Not at all," he hastened to say. "You have no reason to remember," he added, ever so gently, "my dearest, dearest wife, but on the very night of your great loss in Poznan, you ran around a corner and almost knocked me down."

Irina revisited her memory of that horrible night, and after a moment, her recollection cleared. "Yes!" she said, "but why would you remember me?"

"Irina, my love, I knew nothing about you, of course, but I loved you from that very moment, and hoped that the pretty farm girl in the blue woolen cape would someday run into me again. So, you see, Madrosh needn't have told me a thing, but I decided to go along because being with you was exactly what I wanted. I just couldn't bring myself to do anything about it until I was sure you were ready."

Tears welled up in Irina's eyes, flowed freely down her cheeks, and ran across her lips as she stood on her toes and kissed him hard and long.

...

Despite everyone's efforts, there was little movement for the fledgling furniture business. Chevalle and his men were getting restless, impatient. Worse for all of them was that money was running out.

Early in the year, their visitors began talking about returning to Poland. There had been some brief talk about Zuzzie staying on with Jan and Irina—and her little playmate, Stashu—but in the end, it was decided she should be in her homeland.

One unusually warm day in early February, when preparations for departure were nearly complete, they lunched on the flagstone terrace. After plates of cold chicken, buttered bread, and sliced apples—the last from their fruit cellar—Eduoard asked Irina to solve the mystery for him.

"And what is that, *cher ami?*"

"May I ask?" he said, clearly uncomfortable with his words, but determined nonetheless. "How did you become Lady Kwasniewska?"

Irina looked at Jan, then said, "Let us sit awhile longer." To her brother, she said, "You have been both kind and patient." She then told her brother and Andrezski about the Joselewiczes and what happened to them, but in relating much about the aftermath and their journey to France, she decided to omit any hint about Stashu's parentage. She thought about the lie for days afterward. *Was it not better these men think Jan Brezchwa is the father of my child? Or was it better they think Velka and I had no right to take the Joselewicz silver and gold? Madrosh would have called it my conundrum, but my answer is simple. Jan Brezchwa has become Stashu's father, and I will not change what the world sees.*

Finally, the day came. Zuzzie and the nun who'd escorted her—who had worked at *Père* Dubois's parish during her stay—made themselves comfortable in their small carriage. Just before they left, Andrezski said, "I have not forgotten about *Chevalle & Companie*." Looking at his hosts, he said, "I have two simple questions for you. Are there other types of woods the nobles might want to have? Can you fashion such woods in ways that are different from what they can have now?"

After Andrezski left, Velka came running to them with a leather pouch and a note, which said, "We have been expensive guests, I'm afraid. Zuzzie and I hope this will repay your many kindnesses." Inside, there were enough gold sovereigns to last them another year.

...

Spring dragged into summer and into some of the hottest months the French had known. With little rain, crops dried and died. Workers were idle, and the English, as always, threatened to take Normandy and Calais.

Jan and Irina had hoped to present little Stashu at court in September, when he was just under two years of age. The Telliers, *père et fils*, offered to sponsor them and a September date

was set. The younger Tellier, in particular, encouraged them in thinking their small splash at court might attract a modicum of attention to them and their business venture.

Fortune frowned upon their plan, however, when Charles died unexpectedly, and in an instant, the court was in an uproar. The heir to the throne in the House of Valois was the eleven-year-old *dauphin*, and a regency of nobles immediately asserted itself to manage France's affairs. Restlessness reigned amongst the people, however, and beset by seemingly unending strife, scarce foodstuffs, and an oppressive rule, the people had enough, apparently, and outbursts by one mob after another made Paris a frightening place. Few were in a mood to buy what *Chevalle & Companie* had to sell.

CHAPTER XXI

1410

Irina lay on the chaise and draped herself with a goosedown coverlet to fortify her against the frigid swifts of November air slicing their way through the tall windows. So relentless were they, each candle required a glass globe to keep a struggling flame from wafting away. Under the coverlet, what remained of the large blue woolen square softened the edges of her pain.

Though she had been in France a little over thirty-two years, she had never forgotten the customs of her native land, and neither had Velka and Rosta. The two of them had been at her for days to prepare for *Dzien Swietego Mikolaja,* or, as they had learned it in their adoptive land, *Sainte Nicolas* Day.

She gave them permission to bake the special cookies they would enjoy and serve to guests who came on December 5 for dinner or throughout the day on December 6. Her body was rejecting most foods, and it was painful to partake of even her favorites, but she would make an exception for the thin confection, cut out from raw dough in the shape of a star or heart, baked, then iced in white. With just a little effort, she imagined a bite of *piernicki,* the sugar icing hanging on her lips for her tongue to lick fully away.

In St. Michael, her mother made sure the children had nuts and cookies in the white stockings they hung for *Swietego Mikolaja* to fill. At Giverny, she and Jan supervised the giving of cookies and sweets to the town children, and she knew Velka and Rosta would continue to fulfill the Christmas dreams of the young ones.

At the same time, there was still the business. It was to their workshops that Irina forced herself to go when need demanded it. In the afternoons she would see Chevalle, and she would spend the evenings with the wealthy clientele she cultivated. For this and her son, the other of her life's obsessions, she wondered how much more time she would have.

Like Irina, Antoine Chevalle had survived to the senior years of his lifespan, but unlike her, he remained robust and strong, untroubled by the ravages of age. Irina had come to rely on him for nearly everything connected to daily operations, while she promoted an interest amongst the very wealthy for what *Chevalle & Companie* had to offer. What came of the three former slaves—Phillippe, Marcel, and Etienne—proved the greatest surprise. Though Irina and her family had spent nearly thirty years building their business, the French name was indispensable for success in the right circles.

As a good cook, she knew that an enterprise, like a stewpot, would be ruined with too little or too much tending. In the last few months, Irina's daily prayer sought a solution to the only real commercial problem left in life, and that had to do with her share of the business after she was gone. She knew not where her son had decided to make his life, and she was beginning to understand she might not ever see him again. He had been her great hope. *What am I to do?*—second only to the question, *Where is my son?*—occupied her daily thoughts. "And how are we feeling this fine day, *Madame?*" Chevalle's eyes twinkled with sentiment, while his large moustache arched upward in a kindly smile.

"That is the question everyone asks, *Monsieur.* I am as well as I am ever going to be." She smiled in return, accepting his inquiry in the manner it had been made. "Now tell me, *s'Il vous plaît*, about production. Soon, I will be seeing *Vicomte et Madame* Martine and they will be asking about their piece."

Chevalle recalled for her how much time would be needed for the varnish to dry and cure.

Irina was about to comment further when a sharp, excruciating pain crossed her abdomen. She grasped the material under which the devil himself seemed to pain her, and squeezed hard, as if her fingers might still the pain. She grimaced, her eyes shut to the room.

"*Madame*, what can I do?" asked Chevalle, walking toward her.

"*Nien*, Chevalle. I am sorry that our business must be concluded for the day."

In the carriage ride back to the chateau, she remembered the months she carried her son. The stirring in her belly, then, was different. It was a joyous discomfort, reminding her of a life lost and a life to give. To her bed she went with memories both sweet and sour.

"My Lady," Velka said in Polish a few days later as she entered and found her mistress in a fitful state. "I see you are chilled—and we need to prepare you for company."

Irina looked up, inquiringly.

"Once again, *le Docteur* Bernard is here to see you," she said with a mischievous grin. "Surprisingly, it is a warm day for November"—she cleared her throat—"warm enough to announce the man's presence." She waved a hand back and forth under her nose. The servant and her mistress shared a moment of merriment.

With a resigned nod from her mistress, Velka went to usher in the visitor.

Bernard leaned toward his patient, "Mistress of Fournier, how busy you have been!"

"I must tend to business, good man," she said. "You must have spies in every drawing room, *Monsieur le Docteur*."

"*Madame*, tell me," he said, sitting at her side. "Is everything the same?"

"I do not wish to discuss it with you."

"Come, come, *Madame*, I am your doctor."

"And so much you have done for me!" she rejoindered with gleeful sarcasm.

He said nothing and waited.

Finally, she said, "Blood. I am passing it from both ends, and I feel weak—more so than when you were here last. The ice does little good now."

Bernard sat quietly for some moments. Then he leaned forward and, in the softest voice, pronounced her sentence. "My dear Lady and gentle adversary, it is with heavy heart that I tell you your illness will not pass. It is, I feel certain, a cancer of the stomach, and I fear there is, indeed, little I can do for you." His last words, an admission of impotence, were barely audible.

"Since you know so much," Irina said, unfazed and unable to resist a gentle taunt to her odoriferous friend, "perhaps you can tell me the date of my death."

"You, *Madame,* make things so difficult," he retorted with a twinkle. "I am not so good a fortune teller, but," he said, lowering his eyes, "seeing as how this is already November, I would not let anyone buy you things for Christmas."

Irina said not a word. She had not expected so finite an ending. And at the feast of the Nativity! She worked through his words again and nodded, smiling bravely.

"Remember what I said about the pain." The doctor touched her hand every so lightly and stood, his twinkle replaced by a misty gleam. Without further word, he left the sitting chamber as quickly as he had entered.

1381

Answering Andrezski's questions was what placed Jan and Irina on a path to wealth and respect. The years following were good as they learned and mastered their roles in commerce, and they never forgot the man who surprised them with his visit—and his questions—and, later, another man who surprised them with the answers.

In so many ways, they often said to one another, Andrezski turned out to be their angel. "Yes," Irina mused, "a man without learning, culture, or the power of nobility, Andrezski was Madrosh's example of a man growing into his natural good."

And had my parents not left St. Michael in search of me, little Zuzzie wouldn't have been at the convent church to hear Jerzy Andrezski's cry for a cup of water.

Freeing Chevalle's slaves had done nothing to improve their

financial or business standing, but the very act bore fruit neither Jan nor Irina could ever have expected. To her, releasing the three Africans from bondage was merely an application of God's natural law, and as such, its own reward. It seemed, then, that what happened was godsent. *What else could it be?*

Originally, Chevalle's specialty was wood veneering—a process developed by the ancient Egyptians—but with an abundance of hardwoods across Europe, the art had fallen out of favor. As a consequence, *Chevalle & Companie* sold mostly solid wood cabinets and side pieces.

For other work, the veneering process utilized by the ancients remained the same. Chevalle used a fine wood many times over by sawing it with crude blades to the thickness of a quarter inch or less—a piece called a flitch. A number of flitches could be teased from one piece of lumber, and Etienne grew into a master of this process once his hand fully healed.

One of the other freedmen, Phillippe or Marcel, planed the bottom side until it was relatively smooth, but retaining a uniform thickness. Once a good flitch was prepared, glues made from boiled animal hides were brushed on the bottom side and on the top of the base wood, usually of lesser quality.

Next, Chevalle used a metal blade to "hammer" it down by drawing it across the top surface, especially if the flitch was very thin. The men used wood blocks drawn tight against the top of the veneer by leather thongs. Done well, a cabinet could be made with less expensive, rougher woods as an underlayment while what one saw was a fine piece of wood sanded and varnished to a flawless finish.

As Irene and Jan pondered the flaw in their approach to the French market, Jerzy Andrezski's questions kept nagging at Irina and Jan, but answers eluded them.

That is, no answers presented themselves until one day, when visiting the shop, Phillippe, the former slave, addressed both Chevalle and his partners. "In Africa, where we come from, there are many fine woods, very unlike those we use here. They can be sawed very thin, and fine, and unusual inlays can be made," he said, making many gestures with his fingers.

Irina and Jan listened closely, asking careful questions about the woods Phillippe described, and their origins. *Would it not be better to bring wood from his country than slaves?*

It took still more weeks of inquiry and nearly the last *livres* of what Jerzy Andrezski had bequeathed them, but finally, the right arrangements had been made. A few months later, the first shipments of Etimoe and Ebony Gabon arrived from Cote d'Ivoire. Etimoe was reddish-brown to grey-brown in color with black veining. It proved to be easily cut and finished, just as Phillippe had promised. Its perfect companion was Ebony Gabon, which the Brezchwas later called Coromandel, and finely detailed inlays and veneers could be fashioned from it. Its rich black color could be contrasted with the Etimoe for beautiful cabinet doors and table tops.

After experimenting with the new woods, they found that Chevalle and his men could inlay family crests, court seals, and personal initials, all at a reasonable cost. The results were stunning and, in France, unheard of. For another month, Chevalle and his men prepared beautiful sample pieces.

Soon, everyone's role became clear. Chevalle would manage the manufacturing processes, with Etienne and Marcel, the other two freed men, having much to say about the "how" of things. Irina and Jan would rekindle their tie with *Monsieur* Tellier to generate interest amongst the nobility. Phillippe's role would be unique. Chateau Fournier would once again serve as a backdrop for their work, but this time, the pieces would be unlike any seen before.

. . .

The plan worked better than their dreams, as demand grew for the beautiful new inlaid cabinetry. *Chevalle & Companie*, it appeared, had no equal, no competition.

Inviting small groups of Tellier's friends to evening soirees had proven the plan's worth. They arranged caravans of carriages with stops for cold lunches with wine. The guests often changed their seating along the way and used the time to gossip and play games of chance. Nearly always, they arrived with a grand disposition, perfect for making purchases.

Once a *comte* bought his wife one of their pieces, there was keen competition amongst the monied class to have something made by Chevalle. It was Phillippe, dressed and schooled for his part, who made the transaction interesting. When someone expressed a curiosity about a piece or design, Jan and Phillippe offered to visit them with samples and suggestions. Men and women both were intrigued and captivated by the tall African who spoke French with an entrancing accent. Much to his liking, Jan had to say little except write the order slips and at the right time, collect the *livres*.

What gave Irina and Jan the greatest pleasure was their ability to pay Phillippe and Etienne their worth as contributors to their enterprise. In little time, Marcel used his monies to claim his freedom in the world, and off he went, not to be heard from again.

Successful as their business was, Irina was puzzled by the whole notion of veneer. Somehow, the Brezchwas had convinced an entire class of nobles that a cabinet with a thin covering of varnished wood was superior to one made of solid wood through and through.

The more she thought about it, the more Irina came to understand that the human race, like fine cabinetry, was all about veneer. *What is it about us that we let our judgments of a thing or a person be made by its surface and not what lies underneath?* Later, another thought struck her. *Could I have become the person I am in 1381 were it not for the veneer of fine clothes, manners, and the title I gave myself?*

CHAPTER XXII

1410

Le Docteur Bernard's pronouncement of her fate served to spark a defiant energy in her failing body. She made every effort to rise with the dawn and go about her thriving business, something she knew the two men who loved her in life would have wanted for her. When strength failed, she knew Phillippe could now do what she could not. *He has learned much!* On those days, it was less exhausting to remember her conversations with Madrosh.

All those talks about natural law, divine law, good and evil, and about God. Her wrestling match with these ideas became all the more ferocious as she recalled the crimes by Tomasz the Terrible, the moral challenge posed by Antoine Chevalle, and what the *Duc de* Dampierre attempted in order to assure his patronage amongst French nobility.

As to Tomasz, his very existence seemed to prove one of Madrosh's tenets about man's infinitely mixed portions of good and evil. Either he was born with a greater share of evil than good, or was evil itself.

She gripped her mid-section as the eternal question of good and evil seemed to stir whatever was growing within her. To her, evil thrived in men who used religion, family, and people as their levers for greed and power. *Whatever we are born with, life is always about choice, nie?*

• • •

Swietego Mikolaja had come and gone, and the only ones there to enjoy Irina's recipe for *piernicki* were Velka and Rosta and the families of those who worked on the grounds of the chateau. It had been a tiring day, and though Irina enjoyed the bit of merriment, most of her time was spend on the chaise. That one piece of furniture had become her prison, and while she was glad for a few hours' parole, it was one place where the packs of ice recommended by *le docteur*—more of it more often now—did their best work, if they worked at all.

December's days continued at a slow pace. *That is just fine with me.* Despite the pain, she refused to call *le Docteur* Bernard for the help he promised. Struggling to rise one morning, she called Velka to assist her in her morning washdown, as she called it, and dressed only so she could wander around the chateau to make sure her house was ready for Advent and the Nativity season that followed.

There will be much to do and one never knows, we may have visitors. She knew there was little likelihood of anyone coming, what with the wind blowing snow into every crevice, but that didn't matter. There would be much to do in the coming few weeks and if they were all she had left, Irina intended to make the most of them.

. . .

"Conscience is a terrible thing, *nie?*" *Is the question also the answer, as Madrosh might have said?* She smiled through her pain as she lay on the chaise that had been pulled away from the window and closer to the fireplace for the winter.

"Did you say something, Irina?" Velka sat close by, knitting and concentrating on her stitches.

"Did I? In my dream, I was talking to Jan, or, perhaps, to God, and my questions went unanswered."

"Talking to men can be like that," Velka said, beginning to laugh.

So unused to humor from her servant, Irina broke into a long chuckle, holding her belly all the while.

"In seriousness, Velka, I've sometimes wondered if God—being a man as Scripture suggests—bothers listening to women."

"Do you really feel that way? To my own way of thinking, Almighty God has been very good to us."

"You didn't feel that way when we left Poznan, did you?" Irina asked.

"No, and as I recall, you felt much the same."

"I must admit, then, that it seems the great God of us all has been at our side our entire lives, hasn't He?"

Velka nodded. "I shouldn't have laughed at my own joke, My Lady."

"Nonsense. It was funny, and did me well to laugh."

"Then are you content? Should I send for *le Docteur* Bernard?"

"It is not necessary to trouble him in such weather," said Irina, turning to look directly at her friend and servant, "especially when he can do nothing for me."

"Then what troubles you?"

"Perhaps I am confused. This past year, I have been reliving all that had happened to us since that May in Poznan, and now it is December. More than thirty years ago, Velka! For me, there is little time left, and so much is still to happen."

Velka's needles stopped, and she put a hand over Irina's. "Yes, my dear one," she said softly, "it is already December 1410, and Advent is nearly upon us, but you are thinking of…?"

"Bernard is very likely correct, damn him!" She caught her breath. "My thoughts, my remembrances must become like a fast-flowing river, and given what Bernard has said, I will have to enjoy the rest of what happened in my life in a much speedier fashion." Irina leaned her head back, laughing at her own little joke.

After a further moment of reflection and listening to Velka's needles do their work, she went on. "Perhaps I ask too much, but I miss the men I've known. My father disappointed me but him, I could never forget, and then, Madrosh came along and helped me understand about good and evil. May God bless him. Then Jan and my Stashu." Irina looked away.

"Berek, My Lady?"

Irina looked back in Velka's direction, and said, amidst tears, "Yes, my first love." For a minute or two, she stared into the fire as icy rain pounded on the window glass. "Yes," she said, her voice thick with emotion and memory, "conscience is a terrible thing."

. . .

Irina dozed. When she opened her eyes, Velka was gone. As she brought her focus back to the present, she smiled, feeling good about so much of her life, first with Berek, then with Jan. Yet, if their circumstances had been somehow different, Stashu would be at her side. *Where is he?* Despite her beseechments of every traveler to or from the east, none carried news of her beloved son. The silence was maddening.

And so, sadness was the mantle she wore about her when Velka appeared with a steaming bowl of tea and a plate of crisp crackers. "Perhaps you will keep these down, Irina. Let's see if they will do you some good."

She sipped the tea and nibbled a bit, but within moments, she knew her stomach would reject them, one way or the other. Velka left as quickly as she had come, but thoughts of her remained. *What a wonderful companion she has been!* All at once, she realized how much she had taken Velka for granted. In 1378, they were poor girls fortunate to work in the Joselewicz household. And fortunate they were in leaving Poznan in a very different way than they had come to it. Otherwise, death from plague or a life of only God knew what would have awaited them.

Like a thief, guilt crept into the cold, lonely hours before dawn. Into her conscience stole the reality that her lie and the bag of Jewish gold and silver made her an overlord, a mistress, a member of the wealthy and ruling class, while Velka had remained just what she was, a servant to others. *Oh, how easy it was to forget where I came from with gold in my pocket!*

She continued to remain still, hoping the nausea would fade away. As she lay bundled against the cold, her memories warmed her. She thought of all the years she and Velka had had together, and even now, she had but one regret as guilt stalked her conscience. The years with Stashu went so quickly. *Why did I let him go?*

...

Christmas itself was almost upon them, which meant Velka and Rosta, along with others in Chateau Fournier's household, had already been charged with scrubbing every room within the four walls. From years past, they all knew *Madame* insisted on cleanliness, especially at the Feast of Christ's Nativity. "We must be prepared for whatever the season might bring," she always said, and given that these might well be the last weeks of her life, Irina was not disappointed.

In the third week of December, when the winds whipped up heavy snows and all around them was stillness in sparkling white, a rider appeared at the main door of the chateau to announce that *Madame* Zuzanna Tokasz and her party were less than a day away.

At first, Irina wasn't sure it could be she. *It can't be. It's been so long!* Having Zuzzie for the holiday was the best news she could have. *Well, perhaps not the very best news, but having someone from my family will be wonderful.* Absent her own son, Zuzzie's appearance was a very special gift. She lifted her eyes and whispered, "*Mon Dieu*, it seems you have always been with me."

With the pain becoming more intense, the ice packs so dutifully brought by Velka throughout each day brought small relief. Irina vowed to herself she would not call for *le Docteur* Bernard until the last moment, afraid as she was to let her last days on earth pass in a fog of the unreal.

She called to Velka and made sure that everything was in order for the visitors. Rooms, foodstuffs, and wines had to be procured and prepared quickly, no matter the weather. Irina was ever so grateful for her attachment to a clean house—in that regard, at least, everything had already been done.

Late the next afternoon, just as dusk pulled down the remaining streaks of sunlight, Zuzzie and her party rolled up in a large carriage and a separate baggage cart. Irina put her pain aside and in spite of the cold, went out to greet her sister in the torchlight.

"How wonderful you are here, little Zuzzie! *Wesolych Swiat Bozego Narodzenia*—a Happy Christmas to you! Has it been nearly thirty years?"

"Little, I am no longer, Irina," she said, laughing away the tension of a long journey. "*Duzo dzrowia*—And good health to you!" Zuzzie hesitated a moment, looking closely at her sister, then turned away and continued, "And this lovely man is my Edmund with our little Marta."

Irina opened her eyes wide to hug the little girl who carried on her visage the ghost of her mother taken by plague. For just a moment, Irina winced, both with pain and the memory of her last words with her mother and father.

She recovered quickly when Zuzzie grasped Irina by the arm and said, as she stepped aside, "This is my dear friend and companion, Deena Sklowdowska, and her infant son. I hope you don't mind them joining us."

The petite, dark-haired woman bowed and said quietly, "A pleasure, *Madame*. Thank you for your welcome to us."

"Not at all," Irina said, her voice filled with a generous spirit. Her greeting to the young mother was kindly and open, but unsure. She would ask Zuzzie about her at another time. She tried to peek at the woman's baby but could not, as it was well swaddled in blankets and furs against the winter cold.

"And we have brought the Polish winter with us, you see," Zuzzie said, breaking into Irina's thoughts.

"Stop!" Irina shouted with glee. "We will freeze out here." She hugged her sister once more and led them all inside.

When they were near the fire and in a good light, Irina could see her sister eyeing her carefully. "Yes, I know I am thin and pale, Zuzzie! I am older now, and my eyesight is also not the best." She laughed. "About all of that, we can talk more later."

When *Panie* Sklowdowska asked to be excused, Irina instructed Velka to see to their every need as she led the guest to an upstairs bedchamber. Zuzzie immediately indicated she would like to follow, as it had been a very long journey. Their host informed them a hot supper would be ready for them later that evening, right after first sleep.

Irina forced her broadest smile to cover the pain she was feeling. She longed only for a warm blanket and a pack of ice. Alone, she fell, exhausted, onto the chaise, and watched the fire dance before her.

Zuzzie's welcome arrival made her think of family, but unwelcome were the memories of men having left her alone. First Berek, then Madrosh. And then...

1394

Once *Chevalle & Companie* became established, Irina and Jan found more time for each other, and for Stashu as he grew into a lad and then a young man.

At their estate in Giverny, Jan ensured instruction for his son in horsemanship, fencing, and court etiquette. A quick study, young Stanislaus mastered every skill expected of him and, in addition, insisted on learning Polish and German, as well as Latin. Eventually, Jan arranged to present him at court, where he was well received just after Charles VI attained his majority—and the crown—in 1389. As court seasons rolled over again and again, Stanislaus's sturdy build, along with his patrician face surrounded by rich chestnut curls, made him catch the eye of every young woman who hid her face behind a fan.

Irina had perceived Jan and Stashu to be as close as a father to a son, but she missed the growing difference between them. Perhaps it was just that Stashu was no longer a boy, and as the young always do, he looked at things differently. *How well I know that!*

More frightening to her than any divide in her family was the ordinance issued in the name of Charles VI in September 1394. He decreed, irrevocably, that no Jew should live within any domain of France. Not immediately enforced, the law allowed a time limit for Jews to sell their goods and properties—at great loss—before the king's provost escorted them to the frontier.

What was happening brought a chill to Irina's heart as she recalled a night in Poznan. *Will they consider my son a Jew—and burn him?*

Stanislaus was old enough to understand injustice, and his passionate feelings were no secret within the family. Jan held similar views, Irina knew, but most often, chose to honor the court by his silence. For that and other reasons, the chasm between father and son grew wider, deeper. *Stashu does not know about his heritage, and neither does Jan. What do I tell them?*

One day, Stanislaus asked his mother the right question. Irina did not know what had prompted him, but in the quiet of her mind, she had always prepared herself for such a day.

"Stashu," she said after a moment's hesitation, "why do you ask about your father?

"It is, indeed, about my father that I ask, Mother. I love him, but I have come to sense that I am not truly his son. While we share so much, we are so vastly different. I do not resemble him or you!"

For a very long moment, Irina looked at her son, studying his features with gentle eyes. She stroked his hair and let her hand rest lightly on his shoulder. "You shall sit and listen carefully. Whatever you might say to me in return, it must be said quietly and left forever in this room. Do you understand?"

He nodded. For the next few minutes, Irina told her son how he came to be, and how *Comte* Brezchwa came to raise him as his son. "So, you see? You truly have two fathers, but of the one, we must always take care in what we say."

"If one of my fathers was a Jew, does this mean I have no legal standing in France?"

"Not everyone would say so, but why ever ask the question? You should be proud of your heritage, but it doesn't mean you should climb Chateau Fournier's great chimney and shout it out to the countryside."

"So I am a Jew, then?"

"Traditional Jews, you know, would not take you as one of them because you were not born of a Jewish mother."

"Is that true?"

"Whether it is or not, there is reason to take care in what you proclaim about yourself."

Irina was pleasantly surprised at how well her son embraced the news of his Jewish lineage. Afterward, the bigger surprise was that his relationship with Jan grew warmer, more understanding.

Guilt sat heavy on her shoulders because of her decision not to tell Jan what their son knew. It seemed to have made little difference. They spent more time together, and as the years passed, the men learned to respect their differences.

1397

Jan felt good about nearly everything in the lives of the Brezchwas. He and Stashu spent their days furthering the interests of *Chevalle & Companie*, and in the evenings, they kept Irina happy with evening walks or long chats in front of a good fire.

The Christmas holiday just ended had allowed them to host a number of clients from Paris, and that's where both father and son knew the real genius of the business lie. Irina dominated their soirees from beginning to end with no detail left to chance. Phillippe's growing role proved an immense asset. Because Giverny was a bit of a journey from Paris, Irina and Jan were careful to choose their guests. Some had been invited more than once, and most often they accepted with pleasure.

"See how your mother so casually positions herself in front of the inlaid Coromandel sideboards, and with her sweeping gestures, draws attention to the beautiful detail."

"You are so *correcte*, father. The renderings of Antoine, Phillippe, and Etienne would lie dusty in the barn were *Madame* Irina Kwasniewska Brezchwa not there to let them shine to the world."

Seeing her in action, Jan thought as he put another layer of clothing over himself, made day trips to other chateaux on days like this worth the while. Rosta had seen to it his favorite horse Kaspar was saddled and ready for the winter ride.

"Be wary, *Comte* Brezchwa," Rosta warned. "There may be no highwaymen about on a day like this, but there's the weather to beset you."

"Ah! Never you mind, old friend. That's why Phillippe comes with me—not just to show his pretty smile to the ladies we will visit, but to woo orders from them even on a day like this—and for us to watch out for one another."

"Lady Irina will feel better about this, then. *Au revoir*, good sir."

It was a two-hour ride to the first chateau—a moated castle, in truth—and if all went well, he and Phillippe would be back in Giverny by nightfall. In fact, between the two of them, they garnered three profitable orders at another nearby country estate of a duke reputedly an intimate of the king.

The return trip, on the other hand, proved not to their liking from the moment they rode across the duke's drawbridge and into the turning weather. Cold rain had become snow, and by the time they were halfway back to *Chateau Fournier,* it seemed as if ice fell from the black sky.

"*Monsieur le Comte,*" Phillippe shouted into the wind, "should we find shelter?"

"Would that we could, but this land seems empty of such a place. In any case, we are but four or five miles from our rest. Let us go!"

"As you say, *Monsieur.*"

Jan gave the horse its head and let it get to a fast trot.

"*Monsieur! Monsieur!* The roads have ice in the ruts," Phillippe shouted.

Jan kept up his brisk pace, pushing ahead against the icy blasts. All went well until one of his horse's hooves found an ice patch deep in the cut of the road. He could feel the horse pull back, as if in surprise, as the right front hoof slid for a few feet before coming to a dead stop against the hard earth. The horse's shank collapsed, propelling Jan forward, but he held tight to the pommel.

In a flash, Jan realized he should have let go. Instead, with his other hand, he instinctively grabbed the horse's mane and as the horse crashed to earth, it was he who softened the horse's fall. For only a moment did the pain sear his legs and chest before he felt only a numbing peace as he looked heavenward, snowflakes dancing toward him.

. . .

Irina was sitting by the fire, looking out the tall window every few minutes hoping the storm would abate. Since mid-afternoon, her sense of foreboding seemed to rise each quarter-hour, and at one point, she called for Velka to sit with her and talk while she busied her hands with needlework.

"Calm yourself, My Lady. Last year was a good one for this household, and 1397 will be no different."

"*Bardzo dobrze!* You are always right, Velka."

Within another quarter hour, everything changed, however, when the faithful Rosta came running, tears in his eyes. "Mistress," he could hardly get the word out. "Mistress, there's been an accident. *Le Comte's* horse...on the ice. Not a mile from here..."

. . .

Phillippe, tall and muscular that he was, walked in with Jan in his arms. Slowly, carefully, he laid Count Brezchwa on the chaise, the snow on them both melting in the fire's heat and puddling on the floor. The drip, drip was the only sound.

Irina did not move. Then, deliberately, each step a torment, she knelt beside her husband, who lay as if in repose waiting for her to awaken him. She let her head fall on his chest and sobbed for all the years she had loved him, yet for all the years she let part of her heart belong to another. *You are in heaven now, my love, and now you know what Stashu came to know.*

After several minutes, during which no one spoke, Irina lifted her head and looked directly at Phillippe, silently asking what had happened.

A deep sadness overcame her when Phillippe described how Jan had died.

"The horse rolled on him, My Lady. He had no chance. He was gone in an instant."

"*Merci,* Phillippe. I am so grateful you were with him, and that he did not have to lay there—alone."

For many days, perhaps weeks, Irina wandered the rooms of *Chateau Fournier* searching for the man who loved her so well during their nearly two decades of marriage. Though they produced no children, it had not been for lack of desire and persistence, she knew. Their love for one another other and for Stashu had become enough for them.

1406

For nearly ten years, Stashu stood in his father's place as the business continued to prosper, but year by year, Irina could see he was not meant for that kind of life. She knew it galled him to serve those at court who would easily take everything he owned if they knew of his Jewish father. He told her it gave him great satisfaction to free them of their money.

One winter day, while wandering about the chateau, she found herself in the salon where Stanislaus played as a boy, where he and his father sparred in Latin, where he often came when he was troubled. She stared through the icy windowpanes at the unmarked snow layering the lawns and hugging the spindly trees. She saw little life there. With Jan gone, she had kept herself busy with Chevalle and Phillippe, but it wasn't the same. Stashu was all she had. As she thought about those things dear to her, she failed to hear her son enter the room.

"Mother, we must talk." His voice was low, quavering.

"Yes, I know. You have been unhappy with the world in which you live."

"As are you, Mother." He sat next to her. "What I have to say will not make any of this easier, but…"

"But you must do something different?"

"Yes, and what I do must be elsewhere." He looked into her eyes.

"Eh? How can you consider leaving your home?"

"Father has been gone many years now, and I feel I must find my other home."

"Son, this is your home, and you will always be welcome here. You were born here," she added, hoping sentiment would triumph over fleeting desire. Seeing his determined look, she said, "Where will you go? Paris?"

"No, Mother. I have come to loathe these people and this country, and so I am leaving it."

"Stashu! Why would you feel so! This country has been good to us."

"But Mother," he said with both tears and anger in his eyes, "you do not count yourself a Jew."

Irina was stung. She hadn't realized how deeply her son had come to feel about his heritage. Swallowing her emotion, she said, finally, "You are now a man of nearly twenty-eight years. Because of your father, you are well schooled for two courses in life: commerce or war. Prepared you are, my son. Where will you go?"

"To Poland."

"To Poland?" She cringed. "Poland is the country of my birth where my family perished, where your father was murdered. Because he was a Jew, Stashu."

"That was then. From what I have heard at university and at court, there is no worse place for Jews than France. And Poland? It is not a perfect place, but they have always welcomed us. I am going."

Irina and her son spoke little in the few days they had together before he made good on his declaration. It was with pain of a different kind that she held and kissed her son as he bid farewell. "This you must take with you," she said, presenting him with the diamond cross. "When you were an infant, the Emperor Charles himself gave it to you."

"I consider myself a Jew. I do not think I should take this."

"Stashu, my son. You consider yourself a Jew by birth, but you have been a Christian your whole life. This, too, is part of your heritage."

Taking the cross, he kissed Irina on her forehead and held her for a long time.

CHAPTER XXIII

1410

Irina collected her thoughts as she saw the sunrise peeking above the distant horizon, like candleglow without a flame. Pain had jostled her memories all through the night. As the morning light washed her, she closed her eyes, wishing she had kept the secret about Stashu's father to herself.

Stanislaus—her Stashu always—left Giverny and France in 1406, and since then, she'd heard nothing of him. No visitor to the French court had ever heard his name. Along with the conflicts in France, she knew of other military adventures all across the continent—even in Poland. Irina smiled ruefully to herself as she remembered traveling with Duke Zygmunt and Madrosh across Poland and Germany, when the duke and King Wenceslas swore allegiance to each other. What had she heard recently? Factions of the two countries were at war. She hoped, desperately, that Stashu had not involved himself in battles not his own.

Once again, she fought her own anger. *What kind of son did I raise who would abandon his mother?*

She awoke with a start, the pain in her abdomen having become unrelenting. Irina made herself rise and, as she steadied herself, called for Velka to help her. The old servant came quickly, and helped guide her to the bathing room.

"It is too cold for you to do this, My Lady. Perhaps we wait until later in the day when it is a bit more comfortable for you, *nie?*"

"Nonsense, my dear old friend. You and I have kept up a pretty pretense for how many years now? If I ever had a living sister so close, it would be you, *nie*?" Irina's ritual washing was a slower process of late, but still important to her sense of well-being. Next came her hair, which Velka washed, dried, and fashioned into something presentable.

"I know you are in pain, Irina. Yet your words to me are so kind." Irina's luxurious auburn hair was a radiant sight in any light, she had told her once, but now it was awash in grays and whites, making her look older than her age. "There, are you happier now?" Velka teased. "You have a real sister here with you again. I am certain she is already awake, waiting to see you. She was always your favorite, and it is God's gift she has come to see you this special Christmas, *nie*?

"What you say is true, Velka, and you make me even happier when you say it."

Velka knew she could leave, but remained, silent.

"What is it?" Irina waited. "Ah, Velka, I am so deeply sorry we never had the talk I promised. Something of importance still bothers you—sit here with me. Tell me."

Velka's face reddened as she sat. "It is only important to me, dear Irina. It will be of no consequence to you."

Not at all unkindly, she asked, "What is it, dear friend?"

"Your name was Irina Kwasniewska. Had Berek lived, you would have become Joselewicza, but then you became Brezchwa."

"Yes?"

"Do you see? I have always been nothing. The Joselewiczes took me in as an infant, but I never knew I had another name and they never told me. I've always been just 'Velka.'"

Tears formed in Irina's eyes. "I see. What would you have me do, dear one?"

"Would you think of me as Velka Joselewicza? Would you tell Zuzzie so? Someday, perhaps soon," she paused, apparently realizing she was about to say something she didn't intend, "perhaps, soon," she repeated, then stopped.

"Yes, Velka Joselewicza it will be, and soon, I'm afraid. Yes, a surname—new thing that it is for people—will be of help to you."

"Then," Velka said, crying herself, "you are not offended? It is alright to choose Joselewicz?"

"It is *correcte*, dear one. It is important for us to know who and what we are."

As my own son demanded. Perhaps he is being who he must be.

. . .

Over the few days before Christmas, Zuzzie and Irina spent many happy hours together. At one point, they called Velka in to discuss arrangements for *Wigilia*—the Vigil—a ritual unpracticed by *les nouveau Français* as often as it should have been by true Poles. Indeed, as Zuzzie playfully chastised them, the Christmas Eve vigil had to be preserved. "No matter what," Zuzzie insisted, and they all laughed. At once they delved into the ancient recipes of fish, cheese and cabbage *pierogis*, accompanied by an abundance of *kluski*—the soup—and fried noodles with butter.

"After all, how can Christ be born again amongst us if Poles do not have their *haluski!*"

They laughed again and Velka rose, promising they would enjoy a vigil to remember. She cast a long glance at her mistress as she did so, and Zuzzie did not miss the exchange—or its meaning. She turned—with care—to the pieces of news she possessed, the fate of Madrosh being first amongst them.

"You may remember Father Madrosh was made Bishop of Poznan upon his return from Paris."

"Yes, of course. Did *Pan* Andrezski tell me that when he was here back in '80 or '81? How hard it is to remember. Father Madrosh was such a wise man, and I'm sure the people loved him."

"Indeed, they did."

"Yes?"

Zuzzie lowered her eyes. She hated to be the bearer of such tidings, but before she could say more, Irina spoke.

"You know, Zuzzie, Madrosh was old when I knew him. Surely, he has been gone for many years," Irina said, her voice wavering.

Zuzzie looked up. "Yes, of course. I don't remember when he—in his sleep, I think, it was around 1386. People came from all over *Wielko*

Polska to pray for him, and soon the duke erected a great stone to mark his resting place in the cathedral courtyard." She watched Irina, gauging just how well she could deal with talk of dying.

Irina nodded, whispering a quiet prayer to herself. "What about your protector, *Pan* Andrezski? What a wonderful man he was for both of us. Without him," Irina stated flatly, "our business would have foundered, and even more, you and I would never have found each other again."

They sat close to one another. It was Zuzzie's turn to be reflective. "*Pan* Jerzy, as I always called him, was a special man. He said I was his angel, but it was he who watched over me, the Dominican Sisters at the convent, and all the men in his business, including our brothers, and my husband's own father, Pawel Tokasz."

"What happened to him?" She put her hand over Zuzzie's and held it gently.

"He was dining with his friend, Bishop Shimanski—you wouldn't remember him, but he was from St. Michael—a cousin of ours—and afterward, walking through the city, he fell, stricken with pain in his chest. With someone's help, he made it to the door of the convent where the Sisters had taken him in during the plague time. I was there when he died. He asked me for water." Zuzzie's eyes were moist as she relayed her gratitude that he died at the convent. It had been ten years or more, but to Zuzzie, it was yesterday. "I feel he is with me always, watching over our family."

"You haven't said anything about my Stashu, little sister. What do you know of him?"

Zuzzie smiled weakly. "I'll tell you what I can," she began with as much cheer as she could muster.

"Stashu told me you were not happy about him coming back to Poland when I saw him in Poznan—two years ago, I think. I do not know where he had been before that time, but he seemed very happy. He was on his way to the castle where Duke Mattias—Zygmunt's nephew—was gathering men to fight. The duke took a liking to our Stashu and made him one of his knights."

"He was w-well, then?"

"Yes, dear Irina. I last saw him in the spring—this year—when the duke and his men left the city and headed to the north. Stashu looked his very best leading the duke's detachment of cavalry. I was very proud of him."

Irina's face brightened.

Zuzzie saw how pleased Irina was that Stashu had been the success he wanted to be. The whole truth would have to wait.

. . .

The Christmas feast had been a bright and joyous one, as *Père* Dubois worked what magic he could with the otherwise cold and dour little church of St. Francis. The clipped evergreens surrounding the *crèche* left everyone with a scent they associated with the Lord's birth, and when mixed with the dozens of candles ablaze that morning, a special glow seemed to pervade the church.

That Irina made it to Mass at all with her family, guests, and members of her household was in itself a small miracle. Rosta had hitched the horses to two sleighs, and all made the short ride into the village without mishap. While most others stood, Irina was allowed a chair to ease her discomfort. She repeated the Latin prayers and sang the old French hymns praising the Christ, all of which warmed her spirits.

Over the week following, everyone enjoyed the special foods and treats Velka, Rosta, and the staff had baked aplenty. Dried fruits, vegetables from the cellar, roast pork and potatoes, sweetmeats, pot pies, and pastries topped every table and filled every belly. Irina did not eat or drink much, and through it all, she sought distractions for the pain.

CHAPTER XXIV

1411

On New Year's Day, Irina faced the morning, feeling clear-headed and full of energy. For the first few hours, she enjoyed breathing the cold, thin, winter air as if she were young Irina Kwasniewska again.

As she contemplated her own end, Jan Brezchwa came to mind. There'd been no way for her to bid him *adieu. Will I be able to embrace him in the next world? And what about Stashu?*

Her memories seeming to refresh her, she found strength as the morning wore on. It was just before the noon hour that she remembered what the good *Docteur* Bernard had described to her as cancer's relentless march toward the end. *Ah! But I have lived longer than the buzzard thought!*

Was it true, she wondered, or has the disease reversed itself? Then, with the resolution for which she was known throughout her life, she forced a blink, and with that one easy motion, put the whole question out of her mind.

She noticed that as she went about the rooms, her own disposition seemed to infect all others. Despite the hard chill having seeped into every room of the stone chateau, the atmosphere was warm, due only in part to the blazing fires in every hearth.

Irina found Zuzzie and Marta in the room where Stashu had spent his youth, the same room where Stashu had given her his decision to leave. Marta discovered many things with which to play in what had once been a boy's domain, and the two were enjoying their time there.

"I hope you do not mind us being here," Zuzzie said when she was surprised by Irina's presence. Her eyes opened wide. "You look so fresh and well, Irina!"

Irina blushed with pleasure. "Yes," she said, but decided not to tell her why that might be so. "Of course you should be here! It reminds me that this room yet has a life to live. Stashu will be pleased to learn his little cousin was here." As she said the words, she watched Zuzzie carefully.

The use of the future tense seemed to sting her little sister. *Is there more for her to tell?*

. . .

In the afternoon, the sun gave forth its dry winter light, and inside the chateau's tall windows, out of the wind, there was just the hint of warmth. Irina chose to bask in the salon, but this time, in the pleasure of seeming good health.

Zuzzie knocked gently on the door and came in alone. "Irina, we are all so delighted about how you are feeling today!"

Irina merely nodded. "Come in, little one, and join me in a bit of God's sunshine." Zuzzie laughed, no doubt because of Irina's continued use of "little one." It was an endearment both seemed to enjoy.

Irina decided to indulge her curiosity about something. "Zuzzie," she began, "it is about your friend, Deena Sklowdowska. You told me she was your traveling companion, I know, but still, there seems to be something more than that, *nie*?"

"How do you mean, Irina?"

"When I think back over the time you have been here, I have hardly seen or spoken to her. She keeps very much to herself. There is something different about her."

Zuzzie raised an eyebrow, as if puzzled by Irina's choice of words.

"Had you come at another time of the year, I might never have noticed that this woman is not Catholic. But you came at Christmas. And yes, *Panie* Sklowdowska attended Mass with us, but she did not seem to know what to do, especially when it came to Holy Communion."

Zuzzie put her hands in her lap, adjusting the folds of her long woolen dress. At first, she said nothing. Her mouth formed itself into a half-smile, but her lips remained together, as if she was afraid a wrong word might escape.

Irina waited, her silence an expectation.

Zuzzie's face remained frozen, but soon, lines of sorrow etched their pattern across her brow. Tears formed and hung for a moment before running freely down her cheeks.

Irina sat herself to face her sister, their knees touching. She placed her hands on her sister's. They eyed each other as only those tied by the deepest bonds can do. "What is it you must tell me, little Zuzzie?" Irina expected to hear something untoward about Sklowdowska.

Zuzzie formed her words carefully. "When we arrived here and discovered that you were very ill, I chose not to tell you something. About Stashu."

Irina swallowed hard. Since midsummer, she'd felt certain something terrible had occurred, but chose to ignore her feelings.

"When he rode north with Duke Mattias and his men, it was to prevent the Teutonic Knights from conquering Poland. At first, there was a long truce, but when it ended, fighting broke out. It came to a head at Grunwald last July. Our Stashu was a great hero and led the cavalry charge which routed the Germans that day. His bravery was celebrated all over Poland." There she stopped.

Irina held her breath, knowing there was more. As if to herself, she muttered, "Will Poles never learn? The Germans have always coveted our farmlands, our people! God bless Stashu, *nie?* Where is my hero?"

After taking a moment, Zuzzie continued, "Stashu did not survive the battle, Irina." She held her sister's hands tight. "It was said by those who were there that as victory was about to be had, Stashu reared his horse, and while he was holding aloft the banner of *Wielko Polska*, a German arrow pierced his heart." Zuzzie could not stop her tears. "Oh, Irina, I am so sorry I could not tell you. Not when you were so ill, not just before the feast of Christmas."

Irina leaned forward and held Zuzzie close as her own tears flowed quietly where Zuzzie could not see them.

As she absorbed the death of her Stashu, her only son, she thought, *This isn't the first time I've lost him, and I can bear no more.* She remembered the first time, the day of his birth. For nine months she had borne him, enveloped him within her, cherished every kick, every movement. *Is the beat of his heart in time with mine?* Then came the first contraction as she knelt with Madrosh. When a day or two before she began feeling the pressure to urinate quite often, Kalmus smiled and told her the baby would come soon. "It is settling itself, getting ready to be free from your womb, My Lady." She remembered her utter relief at seeing Kalmus at the door to the church. She felt her waters break then, and Kalmus rested her on a litter. *Thank God for Madrosh's foresight.* Jan held her hand until Kalmus and the porters carried her away, the bitter wind billowing her skirts until Kalmus wrapped her in the blue cape of her youth.

The castle was cold, they told her later, but all she could remember was the aching in her back and abdomen as the contractions began. The midwife held her hand and urged her to ride the waves as the pain became ever more intense. After what seemed like an hour, she heard Kalmus's command: "Push!" Kalmus had positioned herself at the front of the bed, and with one last burst of searing pain, the baby slid into the world with a sigh and a mess flooding the bed.

"You have a boy!" Kalmus exclaimed with pleasure, and just then little Stashu bleated his first cry of freedom as he lay on her breast. From that moment, Irina knew he was truly hers no longer.

Irina let her tears flow as she remembered that day and took in the news of this one.

I have lost all of my men. Why is it, men are the strong ones, yet I am left? Why have I lived so long? She held Zuzzie tight. Anywhere on earth, Zuzzie was all that was left of her family, and she didn't want to let go.

"Oh, Zuzzie!" she said, her voice hoarse from unstilled emotion. "You know, I didn't want Stashu to go back to Poland, but I'm so proud of him. He became who he needed to be."

Zuzzie nodded.

"And I have not been truthful with myself, little one. Although I have been happy here in France, happy to get away from my last memory of Poznan, in my heart I am a true Pole, and I have missed the country of my birth and its people more than you can know."

After a few minutes, Zuzzie separated herself, and said in a whisper, "There is more."

Irina did not speak, but looked at her sister as if to say, *I cannot take another arrow to my heart.* Zuzzie gave her a reassuring look. Her words rushed out, but gently. "I had not planned to tell you this way, but there is someone you must meet."

Irina looked at her questioningly, but Zuzzie rose and left the room. She returned in a moment with the young woman and her infant.

Pronouncing each word slowly, she said, "This is Deena Sklowdowska Joselewicza."

Irina had rarely heard the name spoken aloud for over three decades. It was Velka who had mentioned it earlier, but now Zuzzie had spoken it aloud once more. "I do not understand, little one. What does this mean?" Irina stood to face whatever was to come.

"What I also could not tell you was that when I saw Stashu in Poznan, he and Deena were already married by their Rabbi, in the old customs."

Irina looked from one to the other, uncomprehending.

"When my nephew returned to Poznan, dear sister, he took his father's name. To the duke, he was Stanislaus Brezchwa Joselewicz. No one there was alive to remember the Joselewiczes of *ulica Zydowska.* Deena herself is Jewish, and their little boy was born a few months a-after...Grunwald."

Irina stepped closer to Deena, and without a sound hugged her closely, the infant nestled between the two mothers. "Now I will look at this little boy in a different way," she said most tenderly. "What is his name?"

Ever so softly, Deena Joselewicz said, "His name is Berek. Berek Joselewicz."

Irina's heart pounded to a stop. *This is why!*

...

For Zuzzie and Deena, the purpose of their long journey had been achieved, Irina understood. A family was reunited in both sorrow and joy. For Irina, the answer to her greatest question had arrived, and in a most profound way. She was saddened by her loss, but overjoyed that Stashu lived on in his son. She held little Berek—and said his name—as often as she could.

Near the Feast of Epiphany, when the Three Kings paid homage to the King of all Kings, Irina sent Rosta to fetch *le Docteur* Bernard.

"It is time, *Monsieur le Docteur*. Do you best work, *s'il vous plaît*. You will not have to bother with me much longer."

"Hah! *Madame*, you are so…" he ended, not finding his word.

"*Correcte?*"

"*Oui, Madame*," he said, and bowed deeply. "I shall remain close by for you."

"No need, *Monsieur*. There must be others for you to torture."

Bernard could not help himself. He chuckled, and departed quietly, waiting only a moment for the opium and hemlock to have their desired effect.

...

The weakness and pain had returned fourfold, it seemed. Irina was glad she had called in *le docteur* before her remaining hours became excruciating. With the opiates, she found relief, but her world was becoming a gauze through which she could see but dimly.

It comforted her that Velka never left her side. Irina wanted for nothing Velka could provide, and after so many years, the air around her was not the same if Velka was not nearby.

In the moments when lucidity returned, she used every opportunity to visit with Zuzzie and Marta, and, most especially, with Deena and little Berek. To hold the little one took her back to another time. Only now, it wasn't a distant memory that held her attention. The infant in her arms was real, as real as Stashu and Berek. Another comfort was the blue cape she asked to blanket her. It had protected her near the beginning of her life's adventure, and she was glad to have it now.

When she sighed deeply, her bedside companions thought she was in pain. It was not pain at all, she hastened to tell them. It was the deep satisfaction that all she had ever wanted or hoped for in life had not been for naught. With the powerful effect of the opium, she wasn't sure if they heard her words at all, or if she had even formed them.

In her mind, however, everything was clear. She understood well when *Père* Dubois came to administer the Last Rites. The balm of oil with which he made the sign of the cross on her forehead, lips, and heart had a most soothing effect on her. Indeed, at that moment, opiates were unnecessary. She lay in peace, sprinkled with holy water, as she had been in Baptism. Irina was ready to be born to an eternal life, where greed and hate were no more. *Père* Dubois blessed her a final time, and left her to the wishes of Almighty God.

It was after the priest departed, and when she had said all that needed to be said in farewell to the ever loyal Velka and Rosta, and when she and her family, old and new, exchanged words of love, that she found herself alone again with her thoughts. What came to her were Madrosh's words about a divine plan that might play itself out over hundreds of years, even hundreds of lifetimes. She felt blessed to have but a glimpse of one small part.

The next day, Deena came alone to visit. She sat close by Irina's bed and, wordlessly, reached into her pocket. In her hand was the gold cross emblazoned with diamonds. She attempted to place it in Irina's hand, but Irina's fingers grasped the cross and Deena's fingers, and held them tight.

"This cross should stay with you, my child."

"I do not know why Stashu kept it—it came from a king of people who look down on Poles and hate Jews," Deena said, pleading.

"I, too, have had those thoughts, but I am mindful that the emperor was paying a debt—it was a Pole who saved his Wenceslas."

"But we are not of the same faith, Mother Irina," Deena whispered.

"Yet we are of the same God, Deena, and this cross is a reminder that our same God has never stopped loving all of us. It is right that this be passed down from my son to his son, and all who come after."

. . .

As Irina went in and out of consciousness, her thoughts wandered. She saw clearly how the work of *Chevalle & Companie* explained much about what Madrosh had told her. Veneers were everywhere in life, often deceiving one's eye about what lay underneath. Veneer prised from a fine cabinet reveals scarred, less valuable woods, just as garments hide the body's blemishes. *All most see of us is veneer. What's more important is the nourishment of one's soul, which is, perhaps, seen only by God's eyes. It is what we do with what we are given that matters.*

Irina also remembered Madrosh speaking about what he thought was the most important thing for Christians: It wasn't that Christ's life was an example for us all—though it was. It wasn't that he sacrificed his life for us—though he did. No, it wasn't what happened on Good Friday. It was what happened on Easter morning—he showed us eternal life could be ours. It was his everlasting gift to us. *Even to me.*

Irina breathed deeply and thanked God for her life, hard at times though it had been, and for the lives of so many others. *Will I see those who have gone before me?*

In the time remaining, Irina thought of her love for Berek and their son, and of a kind and deeper love she shared with Jan. She thought of Madrosh, a wise old priest who taught her that Almighty God held his arms open for everyone. *Even me.*

She wondered, at last, how she might fare at the instant of accounting.

As she closed her eyes, she saw faces familiar to her, all seeming to come from a bright, beckoning light.

AUTHOR'S AFTERWORD

"It is not important what is done; it only matters who does it and who is the victim."
Jerzy Rawicz. *KL Auschwitz Seen by the SS*. Oswiecim, Poland,
The Auschwitz-Birkenau State Museum, 1998, p. 24.

Irina lived during another pandemic, one that lasted many decades. How life is depicted during her lifetime when the plague pillaged the population of Europe is as accurately portrayed as I have understood it. If there are errors of any kind, I take full responsibility for them.

The setting and characters of *Irina* are to some degree fictional, but the historical backdrop is, for the most part, factual. The Church of the Heart of Jesus in Poznan, for example, built in 966 and rebuilt 300 years later, one hundred years before Irina's time, stands today along with the city's Cathedral of Sts. Peter and Paul. There is no Sokorski Castle, however, and neither is there a St. Michael village or, in Silesia, a monastery devoted to St. Stephen the Martyr.

On the other hand, the plague, or one of its many forms, visited European cities every five or six years from 1348 onward, until for some reason, it died out many decades later. A conclave of nobles was, indeed, convened in the Christmas season by King Charles in Paris in 1378, with the circumstance of two popes no doubt dominating their deliberations. The name Joselewicz was chosen because it honors a Polish Jew famed in Poland's military history, although in a different time and place than depicted in *Irina*.

Inspiring me to write this book were a few interesting parallels between Irina Kwasniewska, in 1378, and my own mother nearly 600 years later. Irina was born into a peasant's existence, but through luck and pluck, made something of her life that surprised even herself. In a world where every act—except childbirth—was dominated by men, Irina triumphed, and this is why *Irina* is dedicated to a real woman of her time, Irene Kosniewska Gasiewicz, 1914–2003.

The character Madrosh—his interpretations of the philosophies of Plato, Aristotle, Augustine, and Aquinas, and his understanding of church precepts—may challenge some readers. It should be noted that while Madrosh appears as a Catholic priest in *Irina*, some of his opinions may be inconsistent with traditional Christian teaching. This story is not intended to serve as a Christian apologetic, but it is, in part, witness to one man's struggle to make sense of the teachings of his church and the experiences of his life. There is also discussion about the church's view of abortion in the 14th century, and as it is in so many situations, where one stands on the matter depends upon one's heartfelt beliefs and the sources one has chosen to consult. In this regard, no apologies are necessary.

This book is *not* about the Catholic Church, its prelates, or the meanness of the times in which the church struggled to exist. *Irina* and her characters tell the story of the constancy of greed and oppression in the parade of history. The story's focus is on the Jews in Europe and, to a lesser degree, Black slavery, but both history and current circumstances offer many other, disconcerting examples. The point? *Irina* takes us from our high place of pretension and arrogance, and reminds us that we are not as far removed from our biological antecedents as we think. Have we become more civilized since Irina's time? Even a casual survey of contemporary events offers proof of the answer.

History tells us that peoples generally propel themselves forward when they have a firm grasp upon their limitations in the present. Only when we understand and own exactly who and what we are can we say with conviction: We can be better than we are!

What propelled me to write this book was my simple observation that as a human race, we do not yet have it right. Edward R. Murrow has been quoted as saying, "The obscure takes time to see, but the obvious takes longer." Religiously, politically, culturally, we haven't found the right fit for ourselves and our times.

I would be remiss in not thanking my first readers, Mary Gene Kling and Michele Perelman, when Irina's journey began some years ago, and, more recently, Holly Johnson and Judy Sainato, each of whom gave their own valuable input, without which Irina's journey might not have ended well. Then there's Brooks Becker to thank for careful copyediting, Stewart Williams for thoughtful interior design, and Evocative for the book's cover design.

To prepare myself for *Irina,* I consulted the sources listed below, much of the research having been conducted between 2008-2012. How one lists the myriad books and experiences brought to bear in any writing exercise such as this is a question only Madrosh may answer. I hope readers will assume much else has been brought to this effort than the few listings here.

BIBLIOGRAPHY

Caro, Ina. *The Parisian Jewel for the Jerusalem Crown.* New York: The Wall Street Journal, June 25–26, 2011, p. C13.

Dellapenna, Joseph W. *Dispelling the Myths of Abortion History.* Durham, North Carolina: Carolina Academic Press, 2006.

Forsythe, Clarke D. *Politics for the Greatest Good.* Downers Grove, Illinois: Intervarsity Press, 2009.

Gies, Frances & Joseph. *Cathedral, Forge, and Waterwheel.* New York: Harper Collins, 1994.

The Internet was consulted from 2008 to 2011 on various topics in relative historical order:
- European Maps, *mapofeurope.com*, 8/8/10, *mapsofworld.com*, 8/8/10, *worldatlas.com.*, 12/4/10, *en.wikimedia.org*, 3/26/10, 12/5/10.
- Timeline of Polish History, *rootsweb.ancestry.co.*, 3/26/10.
- The Mongol Invasion, *en.wikipedia.org*, 9/11/10.
- History of Poznan, *en.wikipedia.org*, 3/26/10.
- Casimir III the Great, *en.wikipedia.org*, 3/26/10.
- Poland—The Later Piasts, *historymedren.about.com*, 3/26/10.
- Bubonic Plague Symptoms, *plague.emedtv.com*, 4/11/10.
- Black Death, *enotes.com*, 3/15/09.
- Black Death, *sheppardsoftware.com*, 3/27/10.
- The Black Death, *history-world.org*, 3/27/10.
- Black Death Recurrence & Migration, *en.wikipedia.org*, 3/27/10.

- History of Jews in Poland, *en.wikipedia.org,* 3/26/10.
- Jews and the Black Death, *jewishencyclopedia.com,* 3/15/09.
- The Black Death and the Jews 1348-1349 CE, *fordham.edu,* 3/15/09.
- The Jews of Poland, *dangoor.com,* 3/15/09.
- Statute of Kalisz, *en.wikipedia.org,* 3/26/10.
- Jewish Genealogy—Origin of Jewish Surnames in Poland, *nancy. polishsite.us,* 3/26/10.
- List of Common Surnames, *en.wikipedia.com,* 3/26/10.
- People from Poznan, *en.wikipedia.org,* 3/26/10.
- GABIN List of Jewish Surnames, *zchor.org,* 3/26/10.
- Philosophy and Proof of God's Existence, *philosopher.org,* 5/31/10.
- A Practical Man's Proof of God, *doesgodexist.org,* 5/31/10.
- History of Natural Law, West's Encyclopedia of American Law, *answers.com,* 4/26/09.
- The Making of Medieval Glass, *awesomestories.com,* 10/21/10.
- Making Glass, *publicbookshelf.com,* 10/18/10.
- Medieval Warm Period, *en.wikipedia.org,* 9/8/11.
- Little Ice Age, 1250-1870, *en.wikipedia.org,* 9/8/11.
- Louis I of Hungary, *wikipedia.org,* 9/11/10.
- Jagiellonian Dynasty, *wikipedia.org,* 9/11/10.
- Wenceslaus, *en.wikipedia.org,* 1/10/11.
- Charles IV, Holy Roman Emperor, *en.wikipedia.org,* 8/8/10.
- Charles IV, *en.wikipedia.org,* 1/10/11.
- Charles V of France, *en.wikipedia.org,* 1/10/11.
- The Catholic Encyclopedia for a history of the Papacy, *newadvent. org,* 6/27/11.
- Krosno Odrzanskie, *en.wikipedia.org,* 8/9/10.
- Tangermunde, *en.wikipedia.org,* 12/14/11.
- The Saale, *en.wikipedia.org,* 12/5/10.
- Pre-Tridentine Mass, *en.wikipedia.org,* 7/31/10.
- The Code of Hammurabi, *Wikipedia.org,* 3/25/10.
- Life of Moses, *wikipedia.org,* 3/25/10.
- The Burning of Rome, *eyewitnesshistory.com,* 11/26/10.
- Early Mechanical Clocks, *en.wikipedia.org,* 9/11/10.
- French Names, *en.wikipedia.org,* 8/17/11.

- History of Paris, *en.wikipedia.org*, 1/17/11.
- Louvre Palace, *en.wikipedia.org*, 1/17/11.
- History of the Jews in France, *en.wikipedia.org*, 6/14/11.
- African-American History for information on slavery in Europe and pre-Revolutionary America, *afroamhistory.about.com*, 3/15/09.
- Abortion and Catholic Thought, *faculty.cua.edu*, 4/10/09.
- Why Can't We Love Them Both, *abortionfacts.com*, 4/10/09.
- Milestones of Early Life, *abortionfacts.com*, 4/10/09.
- Early Church Fathers on Abortion, *priestsforlife.org*, 4/9/09.
- History of Abortion, *infoplease.com*, 4/6/09.
- Abortion in the Ancient and Premodern World, *womenshistory.about.com*, 4/6/09.
- The Vatican on Veritatis Splendor, *catholic.com*, 3/31/09.
- Wood Veneer, *en.wikipedia.org*, 12/14/11.
- Ebony Gaboon, *woodfinder.com*, 12/14/11.
- Etimoe, *formwood.com*, 12/14/11.
- Polish-Lithuanian-Teutonic War, *en.wikipedia.org*, 8/6/11.
- Berek Joselewicz, *en.wikipedia.org*, 12/15/11.

Kretzmann, Norman, and Stump, Eleonore. *The Cambridge Companion to Aquinas.* New York: Cambridge University Press, 1993.

Maguire, Daniel C. *Sacred Choices.* Minneapolis, Minnesota: Fortress Press, 2001.

Manchester, William. *A World Lit Only by Fire.* New York: Little Brown and Company, 1992.

McGill, Frank N., Editor. *Masterpieces of World Philosophy.* New York: Harper Collins Publishers, 1990. See Sections on Aristotle's Metaphysics, Ethica Nicomachea, Augustine's City of God, and Thomas Aquinas's Summa Theologica.

McGreal, Ian P., Editor. *Great Thinkers of the Western World.* New York: Harper Collins, 1992. See Sections on Plato, Aristotle, Augustine, and Aquinas.

ABOUT THE AUTHOR

PHILIP WARREN is a retired national security executive who reads extensively in historical, espionage, and crime fiction and various non-fiction genres, but prefers writing historical fiction as well as political and crime thrillers. He lives with his wife in western Pennsylvania's Amish country.

Email: philipwarrenwriter@gmail.com
Website: www.philipwarrenwriter.com

As John P. Warren, the author invites you to enjoy *Turnover* and its sequel, *TurnAround,* political thrillers published in 2013 and 2014, respectively. What was true then about political ambition and the lengths to which someone may go to achieve the presidency remains true today. Stories like these never get old.

Made in the USA
Middletown, DE
02 June 2021